The
BULLY
of
ORDER

Also by Brian Hart

✕

Then Came the Evening

The
BULLY
of
ORDER

A Novel

BRIAN HART

HARPER

An Imprint of HarperCollins*Publishers*
www.harpercollins.com

FIRST EDITION

Designed by Leah Carlson-Stanisic

Library of Congress Cataloging-in-Publication Data

Hart, Brian (Brian Woodson)
 The bully of order : a novel / Brian Hart.—First Edition.
 ISBN 978-0-06-229774-7
 1. Families—History—Fiction. 2. Families—Washington (State)—Social life and customs—Fiction. 3. Logging—Washington (State)—History—20th century—Fiction. 4. Washington (State)—History—20th century—Fiction. 5. Domestic fiction. I. Title.
PS3608.A78396B85 2014
813'.6—dc23

                                                                2013048447

      14 15 16 17 18   OV/RRD   10 9 8 7 6 5 4 3 2 1

For my wife.

The
BULLY
of
ORDER

After the incident at the storehouse, *Chief Manager Baranov called the men to the cobblestone beach. The remaining Aleuts were shackled there, kneeling in the rain next to the corpses of those that had been killed trying to escape. Baranov stood over the captives and explained the importance of private and company property and the benefits of drawing a wage. A pointless exercise, being that only a few of those gathered understood our language, and yet they all knew they were no better than slaves, wage or not, we kept them here, away from their villages and their families. At the finish, Baranov pronounced the terms of the enforcement of law, what was owed for thievery, and pointed to the bodies sopped in blood and the survivors nodded that they understood, and because we needed them and because I'd already pled their case, they were pardoned.*

Weeks passed and I was leading a hunt around the point with some of these same Aleuts. On the leeward side of the island I shot a large otter, the first adult we'd seen in months, but when we came abreast we found it still splashing about. I took one of my hunter's harpoons without asking and ran it through. As I was fishing it back, the owner of the harpoon, an old man I'm fond of, said something to the boy seated behind him and they both laughed. I stopped what I was doing and asked what was so amusing and the old man surprised me and replied in English, what he called the Boston tongue, that I needed to beware of the bully of order. Although I speak some English I didn't recognize the phrase and asked him what it meant. The old hunter carried forth in his own language and soon he'd referenced the sea and the land, hunter and prey, husband and wife, father and son, mother and child, even slave and master; but in the end I still didn't see what he was getting at so I asked him who is the bully and what is the order and he said Baranov was and the fort at New Arkhangel was, and that was all. We loaded our kill and departed.

—From the journal of Timofei Osipovich Tarakanov,
New Arkhangel, Russian-American Company, 1808

Book

The whistle tells us to move. Throw off the blanket, light the lantern. Floorboards like block ice, and coal-oil lamps flicker to smoke and muted brilliance to yep it's still all here and not much to see. Short on daylight through winter. Summer could fairly kill you with outdoor work. Animals know enough to choose one or the other mostly. But we aren't animals. We're still searching for the truth of this place, if we knew it or not. From bark to heartwood, work your way in. Dark to dark.

Draw you a map: Imagine the head of a rooster and its bleeding neck is the Pacific, comb points north. At the edge of the beak, fore of the comb, fore of the eye, the first river flows in, call it Hoquiam. Then, just above the beak's break, comes another, call it Wishkah. In the back of the bay, the main nozzle, the Chehalis, flows in a skein of sloughs to the bird's mouth. Follow the Chehalis upriver and soon, from the north, arrives the Wynooche. We're in the shadow of the Olympics here, gods above. Now, to the jaw, wattled, South Bay, we have the Johns and the Newskah Rivers, east to west, respectively. Rough outland country where the Soke settlement hides. Dark territory. Five rivers all told, makes a hell of a puddle. The Harbor proper is at the ridge of the beak, clotted around the Hoquiam and Wishkah Rivers. Flashed from a settlement to a town, kept hundreds, then thousands. There'll come a city, someday.

Directions: Ride the Great Pacific until you catch the perfume of profit and then cross the bar and follow the splinters, mud, and corpses inland. You'll find us among the booms, the mountains of sawdust gone to paste, toiling beneath the seditious cumulus rolling from our stacks.

Constellations, townships, lanterns, cookfires rise. A dream of riches.

The answer is no. The order is quick, no questions. Rain asks no questions. Cows haven't bawled yet and the roosters are stone. Dogs are snoring. Time to move though. The first whistle sounded ten minutes back.

A bent spoon in a jar of bacon grease. Smoke seeps from the cracks in the stove. Turn the screws. Breakfast is a battle won and the darkness relents, a degree, from black to shy of. The wind comes in easy from beneath the sill and makes the lantern smoke. Nail a shirt to it, stop it up. It's a dam with an ocean behind it. Whisper against the dawn.

More whistles say hurry and now it's all right I'm coming.

And outside, more smoke but brined. Neighbors is up. Walk with him. We'll be an army by the time we hit the gates.

"Mornin."

"Mornin."

"Goddamn dog in the path."

"Not mine."

"Not a dog."

"Dead somethin?"

"Nah."

"Drunk somethin?"

"Hear him breathin."

"Should kick him for worryin me."

"Bingham has seven boys, all taller than him."

"My wife's barren."

"She ain't your wife."

"She's sleepin late whoever she is."

"She ain't yours. Someday you'll catch the hook for it."

"She ain't cooked me breakfast for a month."

"I don't know why you think she would."

"She knew what she was doin."

"No one does."

"Go on and kick that fucker and see who it is."

"It's Bingham," I said. "I can tell by the coat."

"*Kick him anyhow. Seven boys and he's drunk in the mud.*"

"*You'd be the same.*"

"*I'd be workin em like dogs and countin my money.*"

"*Step to. Gone be late.*"

"*I'm never late.*"

"*Watch the puddle.*"

"*Goddamn it.*"

"*I gave warning.*"

"*Yesterday,*" Neighbors says, kicking the slop from his boot, "*after the crane cracked and smashed that Chinaman, the* Jenny's *bosun said to me: This is war but bloodier.*"

"*Nah, I seen war and this is darling compared.*"

In the beginning there was a whistle. The beginning was fifty-one minutes ago. Since then they'd been arriving, entering the side doors and disappearing into dark corners. The boilers topped off and fires built, stoked and clamped down. Dirty fingernails tapped at the hidden charms of murky gauges. The lumber pilers teetered in the yard among the bunks with their horses and trucks and tied on leather aprons and gloves, stretched their hands like chicken butchers. No gulls or any other birds yet, just the easy sound of the rain and the rigging of the ships. The mill lights came on in rows and yellowed the ground in the yard, and then the yard lights came up and the pilers dawned universal squints. The dogger, a man named Johnson who replaced a man named Cooper, climbed into the carriage on the headrig. The peanut whistle sounded in the engine room and the headrig rumbled to life, the monster amid the steam. Swink and swimbel. They settled in. Still wet from the walk, the heat of the pipes and the distant boiler are a comfort, for now. Dutifully snapping, the drive belts whipped by and swirled the air. The oiler, Diderot, scampered from beneath the runout table with his gun, off to the edger like a rabid squirrel. Beamis, the planerman, slow starting, still sharpening his knives, one and then the other, finally wrenched them down. He pulled the handle and took a last glance, a last breath. Time to swim deep into it, time to go like hell.

[Dr.] Jacob Ellstrom—Harbor

1886

The story of civilization is written in the mud between the bay water and the plank road, and the tide was on the flood but not there yet. The wind and the spattering rain made arcing, graceful sweeps onto the black water; sagging triangles of foundering sails, seams of current like spilled rigging. And if I opened a window the smell would come wetly into the room and with it all the riotous sounds of the street and the docks. Rotten visitor, dead fish on the boiler, soggy dog. Mine was a king's terrace, bay window overlooking the bay, imagined bretèche. No, not as safe as that. I was a pine marten stranded midriver during the flush.

Across the street, market day on the wharf. Women hauled their children among the vendors, bought fish and new potatoes, sacks of coarse flour, careful always to veer away from the drunken loggers and shore-shocked sailors, crippled beggars and instrumented buskers: ignorant conscripts all. A few boys with serious faces were stick-fishing among the pilings, rigged for sturgeon but undersized to haul one in. Westward, the ships were three deep at the docks, loaded to their scuppers with lumber; brigs and barks, steamships too. Latecomers were anchored outside, drawing slack, twisting and bowing lightly, impatient at their tethers. They'd come from all over the world to be here, followed the stars until the stars disappeared. Safe harbor, our Harbor, not so deep but wide and scrimmed by enough timber to choke every saw in the hemisphere. From the mudflats to the sea blite, from the tidal prairie to the dark woods. The cocoon was finally splitting open on this world: sails of ships, papilio.

A crash suddenly broke through the din, so powerful I felt it in the floorboards of our second-story apartment. Looking down into the street, I saw an oxcart with a broken axle turned on its side, its cargo of milled beams tumbled into the road and onto the walkway, resting against Sheasby's wall. The six oxen were still linked in pairs by chain and oxbow, but they'd left the cart behind and were loafing westward along the wharf toward the docks. I watched as the bullwhacker and his boy tried to bring them under control with a whip and a lead, and they nearly had them when a pack of local strays shot from the alley to give chase and turned the oxen back toward the wreck. The big animals sought shelter on the walkway but they were too heavy and splintered the boards. The dogs leaped onto their haunches, teeth snapping, and drove them again into the street, through a hitching post, trampling the two horses tethered there, one of which did not rise again. Onlookers ducked into doorways, hunkered in the alley, hid behind roof posts. Women on the wharf gathered their children and backed toward the water; others just ran away. Some of the stevedores hurried over from the docks to see if they could help, but there was nothing to be done except stay clear, let the beasts rage, and if they fell in the harbor, shoot them so they didn't suffer.

Then the bullwhacker's boy, ten or twelve years old, caught up to the rampagers and dove beneath their yoke and chains as they came at him, and caught the ring that held them and gave it a yank, and another and another, but they didn't stop. He was trapped there in the middle, as in a raft of logs. And on they went toward the wharf, with the boy hanging from the oxbow by one arm while tugging on the chain with the other. Then one of the dogs caught a hoof in the ribs and another was gored in the neck and flung lifelessly against the wall of Porterfield's Junk Shop. All of a sudden the ferals ceased their attack and the survivors limped back to the trash pile or cat kill or whatever they'd been nosing in the alley before the accident. Seeing that the dogs had fled, the boy yelled something to the bullwhacker and beckoned him in. The man shoved his whip into his back pocket and hurried forward, making loops with the lead as he went. He tossed the rope to the boy, who quickly hitched it to the ring and threw it back to the bullwhacker. Two times around the nearest post and under tension the animals staggered to a halt and heaved in air. The bullwhacker held the rope and craned his neck upward to see how the post was attached to the beam, furrowed his brow, wrapped the rope around his fist, not letting go. With the boy calming them, the animals dropped their heads and sniffed the ground for water. Someone in the crowd cheered and then they all did. The bullwhacker nodded to the boy and the boy ducked and stepped free of the animals and stood proudly in the street, held up his hat and took a bow.

Just then, from around the corner, a doubtful flower appeared and graced the muddy collusion. She wore a bright yellow hat and a white dress. *Narcisse des près*, she pointed and said something to the bullwhacker and blew a kiss at the boy, and then walked into the street and around the accident, careful to avoid the broken boards, the leering toughs cowering on the walk. She lifted her feet quickly from every footfall as if she was fit to dance or come August enter a show at the fair. White here is brave and temporary, steam in the windows, ice in the pan.

All at once I recognized this woman as someone who not long ago had come to my office to have a boil on her tailbone lanced. She knew what she needed because she'd had it done before. The infection had returned and was bothering her awfully. She said she couldn't sit down and had to sleep on her side. When she'd undressed and presented herself for the procedure I saw that she had whip scars on her legs and buttocks. The incision I made was three inches long. I paralleled the scar from the previous surgeon. It had to be incredibly painful, but she didn't make a sound and squirmed only for the briefest moment. The drain from the boil wafted upward in that sulfuric way they do, and after I'd wicked most of the pus and blood out of the wound I removed a cyst the size of a guinea egg. The relief she felt was immediate. Seeing her now as she was, completely changed, I imagined her to be a new woman, de facto citizen, a person formerly but never again employed in what was most likely whorish business. I couldn't help but think that I'd drained the poison from her very life. Such is the vanity of physicians.

The bullwhacker's boy was wiping the oxen down with a burlap sack while the bullwhacker patiently dabbed at their wounds and talked to them. Down the street, men were standing around the trampled horse; the other one was already gone. The beams and the cart remained, blocking the street from all but foot traffic.

The new sheriff, Chacartegui, would need to be summoned, and if an agreement couldn't be made, Judge Lombard too. Who pays for the street? For the walk and Sheasby's wall? The injured horse? Like mother and child, property damage holds the hand of compensation. I wanted to know the reason they weren't on Satsop Avenue like they were supposed to be. It'd be all anyone talked about tomorrow. Somebody might even earn a fine, according to our new and rickety version of the Twelve Tables. Laws are the ax blade, and the enforcement of those laws is the handle.

A work gang arrived with peavey and chain and moved a few beams to the side, and then dragged the ruined cart, the whole crushed mess, to the edge of the wharf, and with a backward glance at the bullwhacker, an acquiescent nod, they shoved it in. It wasn't his, after all; it came from the new mill, name burned on the rail: Boyerton.

While in my corner perch, my bank of windows, I'd learned that the business of things was at the edge, the shadow, the worn corner. The water's edge, the road's edge, youth's. This place we lived was the pool of honing oil on the blade. Say this happens: Due to the wrecked cart a ship is left waiting at the docks for its cargo. The crew gets drunk in the lull and a deckhand lips off to a first mate and somebody is sent walking or worse, thrown overboard in a tussle, and when he hits he breaks his neck against a stray timber. All because the oxcart failed to arrive. And where did the neck-breaking timber come from? Who can say? Perhaps from the busted oxcart. Who built the ship, forged the blade? What drives the boom? Accidents? Providence? Destiny? It was a bull force that moved it, but delicate too. A wife's gentle nagging and a steam engine's crushing yard. What could be better than a frenzy? Find a place at the edge and make a fortune, that was the key. Stay well above the waterline, keep some perspective, always. Feeling brave? Raise a family. Berated? Raise some hell. Step on some necks. Sophisticators arrived by the dozen, sometimes hundreds, every day, and they were, more than anything, of all sorts: ecliptic, slicked by rain, gaunt at the rail, silent faces on silent ships passing through the fog and mist as if they were underwater. Lily hats in the stream. Jawbones in the mud, femurs in tar pits. Half the bones in your body are in your hands and feet. If nothing else, that should tell a person to stand and hang on. And sometimes, just so, I'd catch the profundity as it passed over their faces, like the mud sparrows flying from under the wharf and blocking the sky, when they'd just hit the breaking point, the point of realizing exactly what they'd gotten themselves into: I have no protection. I could die here, today. Now.

When the women of the Line were little girls they'd never thought they could be waking up in sticky beds, scratched by sawdust, listening to the rain pelt the shingles along the shores of this dark harbor, or looking over their shoulder at a grunting logger with a belt in his fist, or perhaps more fearful, a charlatan physician, lancet raised: worried meet worried. The truth of it is that most of us are more like the oxen than the bullwhackers, and it's a rare day when we don't get turned, dogs be damned.

The woman in the hat, the top button of her dress was undone. She must've felt the cold breath of the wind because she grasped her throat as if she meant to choke herself. I knew that I'd remember the white dress and the yellow hat for much longer than I'd remember the oxcart. Who remembers oxcarts? Bullwhackers, that's who. Unfortunate that I could still conjure the scent of the boil and the dead rigidity of her hip as I held her.

The first time I saw my wife, Nell, we were at a church in Cincinnati. She wore a blue dress with a white ribbon. I'll never forget that. Ox and cart. Mud and puddle. Husband and wife.

I looked up when I heard the shot and saw a man standing over the injured horse with a smoking pistol. The wreck had been cleared and loose planks spread over the holes in the street and the walkway. Sheasby was on his knees in front of his broken wall, picking at the damage with his doughy fingers, swinging his fat jowls around to whine, but no one was listening. I'd like to buy him out someday, chase him and his hardware store out of here, just to watch him go. He beats his children and I don't like him.

The oxen were brought over and the boy set chains to the dead horse and they dragged it away, most likely to Fortneau's to be butchered, or, depending on the owner's sentiment, it could be going up the hill to be buried, tombstone and flowers, not likely.

Soon men again filled the streets. Look at them, all of them, beasty little slints. They landed here: torn, dirty, and scared; starving mostly, flashing their frantic grins and yellowpine teeth. Do your best, gents, and welcome to the Big Show. Watch the puddles. That one swallowed an oxcart. That other swallowed a town. Welcome to the white man's burden, the slaughter of war ponies, the poisoning of the well. We're doing it here, and we'll take more if you got them.

Maybe I should still be afraid but I'm not. I learned long ago that it's easier to fail of your own volition than to be defeated, and truly weakness is only a triviality here, like bad teeth when the meat is tough. If you're hungry, you'll find a way to get it down.

On cue, the rain whipped against the windows. The punky wood of the southern sill was swollen. My thumbnail scratch from last night, made to test the rottenness of the wood, was there and beady wet. I beheld a watery reflection in the imperfect glass and lo it was me. Thy ugly self a-blinking.

A face doesn't change anything, but hundreds do, because then they're faceless.

You say San Francisco is a rough town? New York? Shanghai? Our washerwomen are tougher than their meanest ax-murdering thugs. Our smallest, puniest orphan can beat Jim Corbett at arm wrestling. Our shortest Chinaman is six-four if he's an inch.

A body is a mob, a convulsion, an orgasm of destitute rabble. Listen to it breathe. Feed it. Keep it appeased, always. It's written on the wall: THE HARBOR WELCOMES YOU.

Down the street, at the docks, a new crowd was forming, inveterate roil. Among the black sea of hats was the pale flesh of a shaved head and the amber wood of a club. The hats parted and scattered and the bald head lurched after them. It was that mad German, Bellhouse, the barking dog that kept the Harbor up nights. He'd taken the strong and lawless ground and become a structurist (the Coast Sailor's Union labor fight) and harrier (mill owners) and ultimately the king of the rampallions; a company of thieves, pimps, and murderers that served as the tendons and muscle to Bellhouse's brain.

I followed the pale head, a thumbnail among so many blackened hands, through the crowd and up the gangplank of a schooner christened *Feather*. Three men followed close behind him. No mistaking the biggest of the three, Tartan, a head above the tallest in the crowd, a shimmering green greatcoat and a black bowler. His big hands swung around and swatted two men onto their asses to study their feet, behold ye upended boots. On deck Bellhouse was passed a hatchet and he held it up and howled at the rain. Then a shotgun blast rang out from somewhere on deck and the crowd pulsed and shifted back and then forward like tidewater plants. Tartan had fallen. The two other men with him brought out their pistols and fired two shots apiece at the wheelhouse. There was no more shooting after that. A man was dragged from the cabin with a rope around his neck and tied to the rail like a finger in a square knot. Tartan was lifted to his feet and helped toward the wheelhouse. He'd been shot in the leg. My heart thudded against my ribs because I knew they'd be coming to find me. But not yet. The German yelled something at his men and then chopped the stern line. He forced his way forward and did the same thing to the bow. At first the ship didn't move, and then ever so slowly it parted from the dock like ice from the floe and the gangplank slid and dropped into the water. With Tartan injured, Bellhouse and the two others had a tough time chasing the remaining stevedores from the deck into the water. If they wouldn't jump, they were thrown. Hats were lost, tobacco surely ruined. A lone deckhand stood at the rail, nervously looking over his shoulder to make sure Bellhouse approved, and waved the tug into position. The tugman's boy pitched him a line and he tied it off. The swimmers were fished out of the black water and hauled onto dry land. This was a Thursday in May, a day of no occasion.

Bellhouse stood over the man tied by the neck, the ship's captain most likely, pressed the man's face against the stern rail, and waved good-bye to the crowd with the ax. People mostly cheered, save a few brave souls who booed. I never saw the shotgun. I had everything ready downstairs if they came back and needed buckshot removed. I'd sleep lightly tonight, expecting them.

There were reasons for everything, even low piracy. Bellhouse and his men would ride back with the tug, and the next ship that didn't pay the German's tithe would get the same treatment or worse. Pay somebody or make them pay you, those were the choices. He'd abandoned ship's crews on sandbars at low tide and was known to shoot them and stab them too, beat them unconscious and throw them in the water. The floating fleet. Last month he'd made a homemade bomb and blown up a cigar shop on F Street. One story went that he'd eaten human flesh in Whitehorse. All sorts, and Bellhouse was only one. He led his pack, but there were others that could pay to have him ripped apart on a whim.

My father used to brag that he was a friend of Rockefeller, implied a business relationship, although as far as I knew the families had never met. He'd been a surgeon during the War, my father, but he put it away when he came home, tried his shaking hands at coal, and then oil. He couldn't bear to see shoes or boots of any kind stacked willy-nilly on the floor or pant legs hiked up either, no matter if it were children or God save us a woman. I don't think we ever even lived in the same state as the Rockefellers, let alone the same town. He bought stock and lost it, along with the rest of the country, but he took it to heart. There wasn't much he didn't. We seemed to be the opposite of the Rockefellers, but he'd tell you we were of a feather, my father would. At first he'd speak the powerful names like a trained bird, not knowing, but later in his life that changed. The blank cheerfulness subsided and he became more of a conjurer, a moribund circus magician, his incantations turned to questions and finally to pleas for mercy. He wasn't a bad man, though, my father. He was a man in a hole looking up. There were many others like him that the

War had left mostly useless, mostly ruined. When I left home I took his books and his bag and all of his tools. I might be worse than Bellhouse or Rockefeller or any of them, simply because I'm not who I say I am.

A group of fishermen oared through Bellhouse's wake in their Columbia River salmon boat. A boy stood in the stern, to his knees in fish, slicing and chucking guts. The two sets of oars went endlessly, like dragonfly wings.

I stood and retrieved my writing tray from on top of the bookshelf and filled the inkwells and sat back down. With great pleasure I rubbed my stocking feet together and cracked my toes. When I was a child, my mother told me that I had beautiful feet, but the other children sometimes followed me and made fun of the way I walked. In the bedroom Nell kept a full-length mirror, and I couldn't pass it without wondering at the body I lived in. Thank Christ I wasn't a woman. Too ugly for the nunnery or the whorehouse. Napoleon said that women are machines for producing children. I believe that capacity and intent are two very different things. Nell had married down, and I was fine with that; she made me feel profoundly chosen.

The sun slid through the clouds and disappeared, and once it was gone I sat in the dark. My plans to pen a letter to my brother Matius went foggy.

"Nell," I said. "Come in here for a moment, could you, please?"

"I'm busy, Jacob. What do you want?"

"Just to talk."

"We'll talk later."

I hesitated. "Sorry to bother you."

She appeared in the doorway. "You're not bothering me. What is it?"

"Sheasby's wall was smashed by an oxcart. Bellhouse stole another ship."

"When?"

"Just now."

"Don't smile about Sheasby's trouble, or the next misfortune will fall on you."

"I'm not smiling."

"You are. You need some light in here."

I shook my head. She went to the table and lit the oil lamp. Her face changed, and I knew what she was about.

"When is your brother to arrive?"

The letter was in my desk, but I didn't need to look at it again. I'd more or less memorized it. "June, I would guess. He sailed from San Francisco the first week of April. How long did it take us to make our way here?"

"We stopped in Portland."

"Matius is doing the same. Jonas is there with his young wife."

"What kind of father follows the son?"

"He's visiting him. He's not following him."

"Bleeding him dry," she said.

"I know that you don't care for my brother, but he'll not cease to be family, not ever."

"I don't understand why he feels compelled to come here at all."

"He only wants to see how we've done for ourselves. For a visit. I haven't seen him for years. It's the longest we've been apart."

"And the years have seen you in your best condition."

"That isn't true." I basked in the compliment.

"You've grown into this place. You've come into your own. I know Matius. He'll come here and try and weasel his way into the cracks. You'd think you were six years the elder instead of him."

"He won't be here long. A brief reunion."

There was a long silence. "You'll take your dinner in here?"

"Yes, thank you."

"It'll be ready soon."

There was something else I wanted to tell her, but I couldn't remember what. No matter. I wanted a drink, but after last time Nell wouldn't allow it, not with Matius on the way. What was allowed when it came to liquor was difficult to gauge. It was irrational for me to think that since she didn't care for my brother, she didn't care for me. She had her reasons. Matius had been awful at our wedding, fighting with Nell's uncle until they were both bloody, but there was more, a secret that she'd never told me. I knew what it was, though; I could guess, and on the nights when I couldn't sleep, there were times when I prayed for the sun to come up because I could just then get at the nature of Matius, and once I'd touched it, I couldn't easily put it down.

The gaslights in the street were lit, and their light smeared wetly on the grid and grime of the planked world. I took up my father's Lord Bury spotting scope and bumped the brass against the glass as I always did and then leaned back and peeped into Sheasby's windows. Curtains drawn wide; they knew they were being watched and behaved.

Pass me the squash, dear.

No coffee for me. I'll be up all night.

Wouldn't want that. We'd die of boredom.

But if I went to the bedroom window and looked toward the Line, I'd see something. At all hours you could see something there. Eight red houses in four blocks, last I heard. Twice as many taverns and trumpery shops to fleece the loggers. Haberdashers that'd sell you a suit of clothes that would fall off you in panels before you could get properly drunk. All the stinking, pitchy masses loaded into rooming houses built tall and teetering like real city tenements. The Line is the liver of this town; it holds all the poison and decides what to pass and what to keep. Ultimately it keeps us alive while promising to someday kill us.

The scope was said to have been at Antietam, but it didn't have a scratch on it. Twenty thousand dead if there was one. My father let me look upon it but never hold it or look through it. In this way too he limited my reach, by hand and by eye. After my wedding I stole the scope and the cedar box it traveled in and added it to the accumulation to be picked up by the freighters. Judgment is left to those with failed lives, and to God. Therefore, get in line.

Duncan was walking now, running too, until he fell. My son, my lineage, the march of time; he kept mostly in the kitchen and in the bedroom with his mother. He was beautiful like her, and that was a blessing. I can't say what he got from me, maybe his eyes—not the color but the actual hard marbles. During the day, in quiet moments, when I was downstairs, I could hear his bare feet banging against the floor above. I would look up and follow the sound and toy with the strange thought that bones grew, lengthened and grew. Trees grow, but lumber doesn't. Towns grow, and graveyards. My son's bones were growing while millions were dead in the ground and in the sea, uncountable. Twenty thousand in one day. Here again was the confirmation: a single face means nothing. And my brother was coming, profiled on deck, rolling waves, seafoam. What did that matter? I wanted to impress him, always had, and he was coming to see me.

I truly enjoyed these moments, my time alone in the evening. Sanctuary was a word that came to mind when I shut the door behind me. Everyone should be so lucky to have a warm, safe place and a family to share it with. Soon I'd be able to spend more time at home. I'd already hired Miss Eakins to assist and clean up. The old woman was about as gloomy as a turkey vulture, but a great help in matters of consequence. You couldn't shake her. In time, as the Harbor grew, I thought I could find a partner and we could share a practice and eventually I wouldn't have to work at all. Because the stress on a charlatan is real. "Trust," my father used to say, "is found in the eyes," and then he'd pause. "And bank accounts. Trust is also found there. Churches too. The eyes, money, and God." No wonder he was broken and penniless. Failure is more often delivered by maxim than by silence.

Matius was arriving by ship but the trains were coming too, railroad grade was being cut, steel promised to every town. And that was the anthem of the Harbor: "The Railroad Is Coming." I imagined myself the Harbor and my brother the railroad.

When we first tied up on the Wishkah, we'd neither of us, Nell or myself, ever seen a place so dark and slick and brooding, treacherous as a wounded animal; and we'd come from Cleveland and then north from San Francisco, meaning we'd seen more than our share already. We'd even, for the sport and excitement and because we'd never make the same journey twice, stumbled in the wet muck of Portland and saw our first real coast Indians there, camped on the banks of the Willamette, and joked that the Harbor can't be much worse than this, but it was; it was much worse. The trees of the coast were big enough, though, thousands of them, more than could be believed, and there was water to grow them till the end of time and on the mudflats coming in there'd been fowl that blocked out the sky when they flew, and farther in, near the mouth of the

Hoquiam and the sorry settlement that polluted it, we came upon Indians paddling quickly with the tide in their sleek canoes. They looked just like the drawings I'd seen in books, as if they were pretending for our benefit. War paint. Deadly savages. I was afraid of them to the very bottom of my balls. Captain Gray must've felt the same when he arrived in 1792, because when the Indians came out to meet his ship he blasted them to pieces with a nine-pounder. Cannons, I suspect, are the true final refuge of cowards.

"There's been an accident," Nell had said. She stood weakly on her sea legs, pale, not ready for this, her first steps on the shoddy wharf, bent nails pounded flat like drowned worms. We'd been traveling for over a month, and we were finally and completely sick of it all and each other.

I nodded, ignored her. I couldn't believe my eyes. The bastards hadn't even finished logging the streets or any of it. I'd never seen such a mess. The trash we'd passed on the Hoquiam was no better or worse. Town versus encampment versus battlefield. In contrast, a gold camp would be the peak of urbanity. It looked like something seen under a microscope tumbling and wet and then suddenly enlarged and not of this world. Welcome the mastodons and pygmy horses.

"Don't believe the pamphleteers," my father had told me.

"I'm not a fool. I can see the sense and the nonsense in them. I read closely, Father, every word."

"They've already set the hook in you." He hooked a finger in the corner of his mouth and gave it a tug and laughed, stopped all at once and grimaced. "Protect your family. I can give no better advice than that."

"I will."

"You've swallowed their poison—it's in your belly even now."

No, I thought. No, it was only the strictest analysis that had led me to the Harbor. And the pretty pictures and promises of wealth unbounded. I believed in the West and the wide openness of a man's future. To me, independence was a man's gift to himself, the only one to be received with honor. I was going, and I was taking Nell with me. Fire the cannons: I was gone. Oh sweet Christ I was on my own.

So there it was: sloppy piles of turned earth, logs jutting, fires smoldering. They couldn't make it worse, but God they were trying. The hovels—they weren't houses—were made of red cedar shakes and lacked proper windows, shutters and no glass, somehow purely Puritan, like we'd caught them mid-exorcism. Where do y'all burn yer witches? The rain wasn't strong but it was persistent, and even when it stopped the dripping kept its spirit alive until it returned. Everywhere I looked they'd cut down trees too large to move or do anything with, as children might do. I wanted to scream and stamp my feet.

"There, Jacob. Do you see?" Nell said.

I still couldn't quite hear her. So much was not there and not happening on the shore. I'd expected infinitely more than this. Other passengers were coming down the wharfage now, and a boy was pushing luggage on a cart, the wheels sounding like drums over the water, faster and faster. I followed Nell's gaze and a mule cart appeared, bouncing over the torn ground, a man's half-shod feet hanging out the back. The driver and another man stopped and unloaded the limp body onto the stoop of a building with a red X painted on the door and then got back on their cart and were off.

"They just left him," Nell said. "You should go help, shouldn't you?"

"Maybe he's not so badly hurt. He could be drunk."

"You don't think he's dead, do you?"

"Of course not. He's sleeping one off, is all." I put my arm awkwardly over her shoulder, but she didn't curl into me like she did yesterday; she pulled back and looked at me with open-faced incredulity.

"I've never seen a place that made me want to get blind drunk. I didn't know they existed."

"We'll be fine," I told her.

"What is this? This isn't it, is it?"

"It's home. We're home."

A lie dovetailed to the truth.

We took a room in the only hotel, the Regal, a place that has since been converted into a billiards hall, but it was nice enough when we were there, all fresh paint and drafty carpentry, splinters and sawdust. At the Regal we could look out over the water, much as we did now. I fell in love with the storms then, grew lusty for wind and tumult. Duncan was conceived and born in the same room, that's how long we stayed at the Regal. I cried tears of joy as I caught him. The first hands to touch him. My son. Nothing is as real or as unreal as that. Matters of life and death. Gulls and rain at the window, the end of the world or the beginning, and in my hands was life that came from me. I don't believe I'd ever cried until then; there was no subset of emotion or intention or guilt. It was like being swamped by a wave, and at that moment I glimpsed the seeds of religion. *And fires eternal in thy temple shine.* Dryden, if only that were true.

From our window the powerful tides were large enough to watch and wonder at, the stumps rising and falling like concatenate and diurnal creatures that subsisted on mud alone. God, was it a big wet mess of a place. Not that it's improved much. Some of the roads are planked now and we have proper buildings, some of them quite nice with ornate woodwork and various styles of shingles due to our ever-expanding selection of mills and carpenters. Our shipyard is growing, too, and that's a real business. A battlefield doesn't have a shipyard. Still, the Harbor remains a mean, ignorant cousin of civilization. I see a passable mind, but cruel; a functional form, but twisted and ugly. What we lack in greatness we make up for in possibility. And what am I but another spark in this great conflagration of business and empire building? What am I but a man indicative of all I see?

Duncan was suddenly loose from the kitchen and coming at me, nearly knocked over my tray, ink sloshed onto the blank page. I caught him by the arm and steadied him, and when he was still, I let him go. A gust of wind. "You'll be running the streets soon," I called after him. "Running the world." He stopped and stared at me, swayed, swayed deeper, and fell over. I felt guilty as if I'd lied to him, because I had. He was angelic, unmistakably Nell's; but at over two years old, and with a growing vocabulary, he still hadn't called me father. There were moments when I'd rather stare into the sun than into my son's eyes. Surely, one was more damaging than the other. Nell came and scooped him up and without a word took him back into the kitchen.

"He could've stayed," I called after her.

"No sense in him driving us both to wickedness."

In my darkest hours I believed myself to be somehow poisonous and that I should never have had children. It pains me to admit that I preferred the window and the rain and the harbor to my son. Nell understood, or seemed to, and she gave me the room I needed. She believed I would come around just as much as I did. I loved deeply the idea of my family, and I promised myself to someday make sure to deliver on that idea. The contract was signed but the goods were in transit, yet to arrive. I was watching the docks. I'd keep watching. And dinner was ready. Dinner was on its way.

Tartan

The Feather *rolled heavily* with the weight of the lumber filling the hold and stacked on deck. The line from the tug slacked and tightened and slapped the surface of the water and rose dripping, a meaty rope thick as a hambone. Nitz and Burheim were on the foredeck with the *Feather*'s crew. Nitz was swinging from the rail of the lifeboat, kicking his feet in the air, while Burheim was angling to get the captain's boy into a corner, but a few of the deckhands had him courteously blocked.

Tartan stood crookedly by himself in the stern and watched the water easily rise up and slip away, the pain in his leg rising and falling with it. The shotgun had been loaded with rock salt. So he should count himself lucky. It was worse than a steam burn, but he was all right. He'd had worse. He'd have that slint of a doctor with the pretty wife clean him up when he got back. It'd make for a long night, waiting for the salt to sweat down. Think of something else, breathe, and think of something else. He'd worked in the now-defunct Meyer mill when he first arrived in the Harbor and the overpowering smell of the lumber on the deck brought back unhappy memories. Nights in the bunkhouse the continuous drone of the mill, of the engines and cutting blades, came through the walls and tricked him into working in his dreams. Not that he liked being out on the water either. He was no sailor. He'd just as soon stay on dry land and keep his water crossings to the bridges. The mud bothered most, but not Tartan. It was easy to catch people if they ran in the mud, and they were ready to give up as soon as they fell. The mud did half the work. Bellhouse said that if Tartan knew how to swim he wouldn't mind the water, but it wasn't the drowning that scared him; it was the swimming darkness that would slide by his legs and nip his fingertips before it swarmed on him and ate him like an apple, one bite at a time.

The tug stood funeral-calm at idle while Bellhouse and the captain were in the wheelhouse. The door was latched, and a golden, somehow nautical light filled the single window, and like the golden light Tartan felt his exclusion fill him absolutely. I should be paid, Tartan thought. I should be able to face the son of a bitch that shot me, even if he did aim low and with rock salt. But no, I'm the second man, never held command. A fox for the traps and lion for the wolves.

When Bellhouse finally opened the door and came out, Tartan expected to see the old man bloody or possibly dead but he was sitting unharmed in his chair with both hands on his desk.

"Not to the ground then?" Tartan said to Bellhouse.

"The bastard's a straight line. We'll let him run. He's sorry as hell for shooting you."

At Bellhouse's signal a deckhand on the tug began to winch them in. When the two vessels closed, Burheim and Nitz dropped to the deck, and they all went over the rail onto the tug one after the other. Tartan went gingerly, the pain making him swoon, and once he'd boarded the tug he clung to the rail and took a moment to gather his courage. Bellhouse went into the wheelhouse, and moments later the engine was shut down. The wind and the roar of the distant breakers were the only sounds. They drifted away from the *Feather* and waited for the merchant ship to drop anchor, and then they did the same. It was well after midnight, judging by the glow of the moon behind the clouds. They'd wait until dawn to navigate the shoals.

Tartan found a place among the line and tackle and settled in to rest. He took off his pistol and his knife and shoved them behind his back. Nitz and Burheim sat on the massive cleat at the rear of the wheelhouse and pulled their knees to their chests and shared a cigarette. Sometime later one of the deckhands brought them blankets. Tartan watched the clouds and waited for the first drop of rain.

People had called him Michael and Joseph and William before, but it had been Mr. Billings at St. Mary's who bestowed the name Tartan on him, and he'd kept it, allowed it, nudged it along. At the orphanage they'd taught him the value of secondary and tertiary lives. Names were lives. The heart is a light and the body a vessel. They taught him the power of lust and violence. What makes a man willing makes a man weak. Or strong, like Bellhouse was strong, and he could be. God knew Tartan could snap bone, but for now, he was done in, weary to his blood. And Nitz and Burheim were still babbling about one or another of their runs on the Line. What makes a man loud makes a man weak. What makes a man blunt stupid makes a man weak. A hog for the mud, a mule for the traces.

"You shoulda seen it," Nitz said. "I picked him up and spun him and right when I was about to let go and send him headfirst into the fireplace he bit me."

"The fuckin badger boy," Burheim said.

"I slammed him down and I had my thumb in his eye to the root, felt his brain slime go under the nail."

"Mama."

"Drippin like I'd had it up a cooze when I finally thwupped it free."

"And he was dead?"

"Twitchin and pissin in his drawers but not dead, no."

"Eyeless?"

"One-eyed in Aberdeen, worse than no-eyed in Gaza." They laughed.

"Shut yer mouths," Tartan said.

"Apologies, sir," replied Burheim.

"We're stone," said Nitz. And save for a little nervous laughter it was finally quiet. The two of them were all of seventeen, and last week Burheim had killed a man at the Alaska Bar and was to stand trial if anyone could be found to come forward as a witness, which was unlikely. Not unless Hank Bellhouse allowed for it to happen. Nitz had been upstairs with his mom and the girls when it happened. Raised by women and carried a preference for boys. Two faces of the same coin. Surely there are children born onto dairies that can't stomach milk. Tartan had been raised by the nuns and Mr. Billings. Mr. Billings had shown him how to do it with women first, and then with men. Asked him which he favored. *The women, Mr. Billings.* His hands in his hair, gripping his skull. *Prefer the women, sir.*

The mill whistle woke him and he stood and put on his pistol and knife. He wrapped the blanket around his shoulders and limped to the bow and pissed. The sky was bluing and the wingflash of birds blinked at the distant shore. He could just make out the shadow of James Rock and the hills beyond. Bellhouse was suddenly beside him, muscling in for a space at the rail.

"Get any sleep?"

"I can sleep anywhere."

"It's a gift. How's the leg?"

"I'll survive. What'd they pay you, the *Feather*?"

Bellhouse turned his back to Tartan. "A fair amount."

"Any left over?"

"For you and the boys, sure."

"I'll be gone for a week or so then. Can you manage by yourself?"

Bellhouse turned and smiled at Tartan, his silver front tooth flashing dimly in the morning light. "Guess I'll just do my best. Try and get by. Where are you off to?"

"Nowhere. Just thinkin with the leg I could use a rest."

Bellhouse didn't reply and his silence made Tartan nervous.

The glow of the sun was clear to see now, and the water had a shine on it. The *Feather*'s crew was pulling anchor, and soon the tug's was doing the same. It was a sweet and victorious ride back to town, but the endless dark forests loomed before them and soon the brackish smells were replaced by the smoke and steam and resinaceous tang of the mills. The roar grew louder and louder and the whistles blew like they knew they were coming.

Matius

I *stayed for the whole* summer and never once did my brother, dull fuck squiddler that he is, let me go upstairs to his apartment if Nell was there. He'd say the child was sleeping or that Nell was sleeping or that they were out, but I could hear her moving around. In my mind I saw her naked, the dimples of her ass. Ball warmth and ball heat, the lantern of man. We spent most of our time in his office, with me being introduced to the sick and bleeding on their way to the examination table. "This is my big brother, Matius. He's here visiting from Ohio." *Nice to meet you. Take care now.* He had an old woman, Miss Eakins, that cleaned and cared for patients before they went home or to the rooming houses. More than once I had to go outside for air, the smells so strong, the screams so loud.

Once a boy was brought to him, eight years old, who had fallen from high in a tree. His body was pulp. His mother and father were there and his older brother. He never opened his eyes and his face was unmarked. They took him home wrapped in bedsheets, and it was only because he was out of blood that he didn't bleed through. Miss Eakins about wore out her mop cleaning up after that. I could see that Jacob was on the penitent road and it was only vanity that kept him there. But he'd always been a soft fool, he'd always wanted people to like him.

With some pushing he let me look over his books. He was making a smart payday off the mills alone, never mind the feverish and the hypochondriacals. I soon planted the seed for him loaning me some money.

"I'd like to set a stake here," I said. "Prove it up. Make a home, as you've done."

Behind his smile he looked worried, but flattered. Middle of June and we had a fire going in his little woodstove and out the window the rain was crushing down with such force as to make people stumble and run for cover.

"I won't tell anyone about your situation as a physician, if that's what you're worried about."

"No, it's not that. I have other plans too. I want to be more than the town doctor."

"Well, then you should be a doctor first."

"You can't joke about that. Nell doesn't even know the extent of it."

"I'm sure she does. By now she does."

"I'm as qualified as any man here."

"You can think what you like, but you're not."

"Four years of university count for nothing to you?"

It was more like three and he told me himself that he'd never gone to class, but I let him believe what he wanted. He had all the books for reference, assemblage and dissemblage. He probably was better than any man here. It was working for him, whatever it was, and I had to admit I admired the swagger it took to be such an open and deplorable fraud.

To teach him I poured whiskey down his throat and kept him away from home. Blabbardly he confessed his dream of buying out his neighbors, his neighbor's neighbor. I told him he could do it. Let's talk to the bank. So we did, beneath smothering hangovers, and soon closed the first of several deals. Not for any kind of bargain—the interest was wicked—but it made him feel big, and while he was high I borrowed a thousand dollars of his newly borrowed money and staked claim six miles east of the populace, near the Wynooche. Most of the good land had been grabbed up years ago but the road was cut, bridge built, going out toward who knew what else if they cut for rails. Tacoma? Seattle? The ferry had a reliable schedule and the necessary draw to manage the slough and sozzle that was the lower Chehalis.

I hired some Finns and they set to building a house and a barn. I got their price down to nothing with a promise that I'd be watching over my brother's affairs and surely there'd be some big doings with all his new properties. They went about strutting, thinking they'd got the best of me, the doltish cocks. I'd put dreams in their heads.

Before I departed I left flowers outside the apartment door for Nell— she would understand why. Jacob's office window was still broken, with boards covering the hole. Most of his patients had turned on him. There'd been whispers of a new doctor who'd come to town. I took my leave, not a moment too soon, and returned once again to Portland to stay with my son and his wife, where I was welcome. I'd got done what I wanted, irons in the fire. Maybe I'd kicked over some tombstones too. Risk makes the muscle of profit. My only regret was that I never saw Nell. I tried the door a few times, but she kept it locked. I could've broken it down, even with Jacob downstairs, but I knew that after what happened before she was most likely waiting in there with a shotgun.

On the journey south I had time to reflect. I concluded that the ones we are closest to in youth, brothers say, we see things differently as the time we spend apart increases. I can't say I know Jacob now. He has softened, and that says a lot because he's never been strong in any case, but his domestic situation and child-rearing responsibilities have left him with a bend in the wrist and joy at the corners of his eyes that honestly I can't stand. I have a boy same as him, but mine is grown. He came to me that way, finding me late, and surprised me half to death when he handed me a letter from his mother. I don't have any romantic ideas about the state of him. He's another man jack in the world, nothing more. I cared for the girl, a woman now, that bore him, but what is he but a flitch. His mother broke my heart. I'll never forgive her for that. Not for anything. With the boy, strange man that he is, staring me in the face I know the extent of her betrayal. Not a problem, honey. All I did was love you and promise you the world, and you stole my heart and all of the good years with the boy. They got names for that, and the devil thought of all of them.

Nell

I *told Jacob that soberness* builds on sobriety. I told him that we needed
him.

The woman's mother, Mrs. Clark, was in the room and she saw his hands
shaking. It was a breach, and things had gone very slowly and then quick-
ened all of a sudden and had gone out of control. Miss Eakins was home in
bed, she'd slipped in the mud the week before and broke her ankle. Jacob
asked me to come with him to assist, and we had to take Duncan, there
was no time. He was in the room for all of it.

Afterward Jacob told Mrs. Clark that he couldn't have done anything
differently for Mrs. Stevens, her daughter. I don't know what he could've
done or not done. Maybe Miss Eakins could've helped. She usually managed the childbirths, more than Jacob. Mrs. Clark called him a butcher,
her skin as mottled as a gull egg and stray hairs on her lip as long as a
man's. She yelled it in the street as she was running us off. When I looked
back, the husband, Mr. Stevens, stood in the doorway, weeping. Duncan's
feet weren't touching the ground, his hands clamped in ours, I worried
we'd injure his shoulders. Mrs. Clark's grandchild might live, but her
daughter was dead.

"How can this pain feel so new again?" Jacob said as we were going up
the stairs to the apartment. "What else has man been doing forever save

dying? We should be used to it." He went inside and grabbed the bottle he'd been keeping on the windowsill and went back out the door, to find his awful brother, I'm sure of it. As if it could be worse. Duncan looked at me as if I'd done something to make his father leave, or at least it seemed that way until he smiled. I had to remind myself that he didn't think like that, no child did.

That night someone threw a burning can of kerosene through the office window downstairs. We could've been killed, but Jacob was down there drinking with Matius when it happened and they amazingly had the sense to throw it back outside before it could catch. I'm afraid to go into the streets.

———————

The low coward, my brother-in-law Matius, has finally departed, but Jacob remains full of nonsense. I pressed him for information because I knew that something had happened, but he just grinned at me in his torporific way and told me nothing. I'd allowed him to be a drunk and distant and come home stinking because I knew it would end, soon as his brother was gone it'd be done. Apparently I was wrong.

He brought Duncan carved wooden toys from Mr. Kozmin, the inebriate, his current fellow, his pal, and somehow got it into his head he could make them too but didn't get very far before I was helping him stitch up his hand after he'd slipped the blade. Not so good when the surgeon cuts himself, particularly after what happened with Mrs. Stevens. He didn't put up any kind of fuss when I threw his sorry figurines into the stove.

Mrs. Sheasby, our neighbor the next door over, let slip the news. He'd bought property, her husband's and others, on Matius's advice of course, and now he was stuck with it until he could sell it. The bastard brother had stayed at Pinter's Hotel all summer long because I wouldn't let him stay with us. By the grace of God I saw him only once, in the street from the window, and my blood went hot to the roots of my hair and I wanted to be sick. Jacob hadn't said a word or attempted to discuss anything with me; he'd just done it. I questioned him on it again and again until he confessed. How the two drunken idiots had accomplished so much was beyond me.

Jacob tried to sell Sheasby's place—the one building I knew he wanted to keep because he disliked Sheasby so much—but nobody wanted it for what he was asking. After that he tried to sell the other two properties but met with much the same result. He was suspicious and he told me that there were men colluding against him. The office and the apartment are all that we need.

The new doctor that moved to town, a man named Haslett, came by to visit. He reminded me of someone. Hadn't skipped any meals. We had coffee in the apartment and then he and Jacob went downstairs to see his office, but something happened, I could hear them yelling. When Jacob returned he wouldn't speak of it.

Jacob left, he said to go check on a man he'd been seeing about an ulcer, and didn't return. He took his extra coat. We said good-bye to each other and he kissed me on the cheek. He picked up Duncan and kissed him too, which wasn't his regular behavior at all. He said he would be home in the evening.

Two days and he still hadn't returned. In a panic I caught Mr. Tartan outside the hotel where he stays. I asked him to please look for my husband at the saloons and public houses because this had unfortunately happened before and I wanted to find him before he got himself into trouble. When Mr. Tartan called for me at home later, I met him on the walk. He had liquor on his breath and no news. He touched my arm and everyone could see, and I let him.

———

I went to see Mr. Hayes at the bank, and he told me that the last Jacob had been in was on Monday.

"How much did he take out when he was here last?"

"I can't tell you that, Mrs. Ellstrom. That's between the bank and your husband."

"Did he take it all? Can you tell me that? It could be three dollars or three thousand, I wouldn't know."

"He owes the bank, ma'am. Not the other way around."

"You're saying you wouldn't give him money if he asked."

"He didn't ask."

"So why was he here?"

"To discuss the extent of his debts." Mr. Hayes opened the drawer of his desk and produced a box of cigars. He took his sweet time trimming and lighting one. He smiled at me through the smoke. "Have you seen the new post office since it's been finished?"

I didn't care about the post office. "What would the response be if I asked for a loan against my husband's holdings?"

Mr. Hayes began to cough and couldn't control it and had to set down his cigar on the ashtray. He opened the top left drawer of his desk and produced a bottle of Dr. D. Jaynes Expectorant and unscrewed the cap and took a drink. In a moment he was back at his cigar. "They're not your holdings, Mrs. Ellstrom, so you can't borrow against them. Is there something I should know? Has Dr. Ellstrom gone somewhere?"

"Of course not. He's at home as we speak. Good day." I took Duncan's hand and fairly dragged him outside.

Going back to the apartment, the drone of Boyerton's mill gave me a headache. The mud gave me a headache. Duncan gave me a headache. When I shut the door behind us I was relieved, but I didn't know what we would do if Jacob stayed away too long.

I stood at the window and watched the masts of the ships pass over the low rooftop of the shingle mill, like portable gallows.

That night I let Duncan sleep in my bed, but I didn't sleep a wink. He kicks like a mule and snores, conditions he inherited from his father, whom I hated and hated and hated the whole night through.

The next day I sat Duncan at the lunch counter at Heath's store and we shared a sandwich. When he brought the check, Mr. Heath passed me a small wooden toy, a carved cat, finely rendered, for Duncan.

"The hermit Kozmin paid for his dinner with this. Thought the boy might like it."

"Look at that," I said, smiling. But I wanted to crush it or burn it or cram it down Jacob's throat. "It's beautiful. Say thank you, Duncan."

"Thank you." He held the toy like it was alive in his hands.

I paid for our lunch and asked if it'd be all right if I had another cup of coffee and sat for a while.

"I'd be thrilled if you did, Mrs. Ellstrom." Mr. Heath is a large man with narrow shoulders and small mouselike ears that stick straight out from his bald head.

When he returned with the coffee, he asked how "the good doctor" was faring.

"Fine. He's fine." He knew about Mrs. Stevens, everyone did. He knew there was little to be trusted about Jacob and that the tide of the town was turning against him.

"He usually comes in to visit on Tuesdays for the pot roast, but he wasn't here so I thought he might be home sick."

"No, he's fine. Just busy, you know."

"I hear he's got big plans." He motioned toward the street.

"I wouldn't know."

"My wife says that too, but she knows more than I do about most things, me included." Mr. Heath made an awkward wave to Duncan and went back to his shelves.

We stayed there until the lunch hour passed and the store emptied. I sipped my coffee until it went cold and then let Heath take it away.

He wiped the counter, and when he leaned in I could smell the pipe smoke in his clothes. "Stay as long as you want, Mrs. Ellstrom. If people walk by and see you in the window, they're sure to come in." He blushed, and I could see the sweat beaded along the edges of his eyebrows and on his upper lip. "I mean to say they won't turn and run like when they see me."

"Thank you, Mr. Heath."

"Yes, ma'am."

I brushed the crumbs from Duncan's jacket and straightened his hair. He knew something was amiss and was behaving. I knew that he was too small to understand, to be worried about me, but he seemed to be aware. I thanked him for being so good. Thank you for being patient. He had the toy, and that contented him.

Mr. Heath was in the back where the kitchen was and I could hear him talking to his wife. The story was that she'd come from Buenos Aires bound for Alaska with her husband, but he'd died at sea a week into their journey and when the ship came into the harbor seeking refuge from a storm she'd come ashore and found Heath alone stocking shelves and with hand gestures discovered he was unmarried. A year later they had a daughter, delivered by Jacob, born blind.

By the time I mustered the courage to leave, Duncan was asleep in his chair, his chin stained green from candy. I felt for a moment like a failed governess and then much worse as a failed mother. I couldn't walk through the streets unattached, unclaimed.

The new doctor, Dr. Haslett, wasn't home, so we waited on the porch. The day was nearly gone. I would've liked to be on my way before nightfall. He had a sign hanging from a post in the yard stating his qualifications. Jacob had no such sign. A rain-soaked bench sat between the trees, a rusted bucket sat atop the bench. The doctor's garden plot was neglected and lumpy and clogged with weeds. The house needed paint. I didn't remember who'd owned it last, but they hadn't done much for upkeep. A mongrel dog came from the neighbor's yard and slinked into the garden and used it for a privy. When Duncan caught sight of the mangy animal he tried to go down the stairs to catch it but I snatched him up and pinched him tight between my knees so he couldn't get away. I told myself ten more minutes and then I'd go. I play games of patience, particularly in moments I find overly miserable. Ten-penny nail and a bucket of wax. Sink into it.

The doctor noticed us on his way up the walk and his face brightened and he hurried like the bowlegged fat man he is up his steps.

"Well, hello, Mrs. Ellstrom. What is it that I can do for you?" He unlocked the door and held it open.

"Duncan, take off your shoes."

"Leave them," the doctor said.

Duncan held my eyes, waiting for my instruction, muddy almost to his knees. "Go on. Off with them."

"He's fine."

"I'm telling you, he'll bring in the whole street with those shoes. You'll be sorry."

"Never." Haslett put his keys away and rubbed his hands together, smiled down at Duncan. "William Pitt professed that necessity is the plea of every infringement of human freedom."

"I'd say children are the infringement he was referring to. Duncan. Shoes."

The doctor smiled at me, and I could see the blue streaks in his teeth, the cracked skin on his lips. "I insist, Mrs. Ellstrom; it's of no consequence. Let's get us all inside. I don't do the cleaning anyhow."

"I won't have you apologizing for me to whoever it is that does." I knelt down and took off his little boots and cleaned my own as best I could on the mat. The doctor gave me his handkerchief for my hands.

I thanked him and ushered Duncan inside, into a mildewed blanket of old cigar smoke.

"It's unavoidable," he said, motioning to my feet, "all this mess. They're trying to clean it up by planking the streets, but we'll never escape it. The patterns of the weather, you know, they're different all over the country. Here we have rain. Sometimes it feels like we have all the rain in the world."

I smiled as best I could and watched the doctor's face change as I filled his thoughts, all of him; I knew this trick. Then I said something to him about necessity being hastened and shaped always by the weather, make hay while the sun shines, and all that nonsense.

He cleared his throat, touched his stomach. "'Necessity is the argument of tyrants, the creed of slaves.'"

I again studied his face, his eyes, looked into them one and then the other, green with flecks of gold, yellow where they should be white. "Which are we, Dr. Haslett?"

"We're both, my dear. Operating on several planes, all of us. Come in and sit down. No more lollygagging." He feigned a kick at Duncan's backside, and my boy ran squealing weirdly down the hall. The running legs of children are a miracle to behold. If he chose, I believe Duncan could kick himself in the nose while he stood.

We passed by a dozen or so framed pictures in the entryway, strange men with dogs, stranger women without, and into the warmth of the living room. The doctor motioned to a chair near the fire. I sat Duncan on the ottoman and sat myself in the chair but he wouldn't stay put so I held him in my lap like a squirming piglet. He had a scratch on his cheek and was making bulldog faces.

"I'll make tea. Stay right here."

When the doctor was gone, Duncan moaned and squirmed and kicked me in the thigh.

"Stop it right now."

"Rot rot rot," he said. "Crummy rot."

"Please, Duncan. Quiet now." There's no shame in this, I was thinking. I don't have anyone else to talk to. Not a soul. I'm not here for—I wasn't sure why I was there and why I wasn't. I'd been betrayed, is why, abandoned. I felt sick, so I came to the doctor. My usual one was indisposed.

Out of his coat and dried off, the smartly dressed, slightly gray and waddling doctor returned with a silver tea service and milk for Duncan.

"Well, here we are," he said.

"Here we are."

"And to what do I owe the pleasure of your company, Mrs. Ellstrom?"

"Just a visit, really, because I'm fine, you know—my husband sees to my health. I'm in good health. And Duncan's well, hale enough to run me ragged. I believe I liked him better when he only crawled."

Dr. Haslett sat patiently with his back an inch or so off his chair. I couldn't bring myself to say what I'd come to say. "Take your time, Mrs. Ellstrom. I have nothing on the schedule that can't be put off until tomorrow." He smiled a close-lipped smile and then took one quick drink from his cup and then another twice as long. I watched his throat work beneath the fatty layers of his prickly neck. The color came into his face and he took a deep breath. He struck me as being two men: a narrow and average man and a fat man that had engulfed the smaller one. *Knuckled* was a word that I thought fit Jacob well, and *ensconced* was a word that fit Dr. Haslett. Just men, as they are.

The doctor was about to say something else, and I quickly gathered my courage and spoke right over the top of him: "It seems my husband has disappeared."

"What's this?"

"On Monday. He left and never returned."

"I'm sure he's fine. He's probably been detained somehow, is all. I wouldn't worry." By the look on his face, I could tell he was pleased at my misfortune but didn't want to show it.

"I had Mr. Tartan look for him in the places I wouldn't go. Where men usually go when they don't want to come home."

"I see. Would you like me to try and find him? I could ask around."

"People trust you, like they once trusted my husband. People are mostly honest with doctors, don't you think?"

"Honestly, I don't think anyone's particularly honest with anyone."

"That's a dark view."

"Perhaps."

I let Duncan down, and he crawled across the room and busied himself pulling on the drapes.

"Duncan."

"He's fine. Leave him."

"The real trouble is"—my voice was barely above a whisper now, and the doctor leaned in to hear—"I spoke with Mr. Hayes, and it seems Jacob, Dr. Ellstrom, is deeply in debt—I don't know what we'll do." I did my best to fight back the tears, but they were there, hot on my cheeks, smeared onto the back of my hand. I hadn't gone there to cry. Duncan was watching me with a look of terror on his face, so I smiled through my tears and he half-smiled back.

Dr. Haslett stood up and came over to me. "He'll turn up. You stay here. Make yourself comfortable. I mean it, pretend that this is your home, sleep in the beds, eat all the food, break the dishes—I don't care one bit. We'll get to the bottom of this, I promise you."

"Thank you, Dr. Haslett. I didn't know who else to talk to."

"You'll be fine. Wait here." He spoke to Duncan. "I believe Miss Falvey, my housekeeper, left some cookies in the cupboard. Better go and see if you're tall enough to reach them."

I thanked him again.

"You'll be fine. I won't be gone more than an hour."

He got his coat and left. Duncan and I stayed in the living room for a few minutes after the door shut, and then we went into the kitchen and I heated him some milk and fed him cookies like you'd feed carrots to an old and well-loved horse.

Dr. Milo Haslett

His coat was still damp. Something about putting on warm and wet clothing bothered him immensely more than cold and wet. It wasn't simply uncomfortable and impractical; it was disgusting. He stood in the entryway for a moment, wondering where to start. He thought: I'm weary of this whole business. No wonder that swindler Ellstrom had disappeared. He understood. Hippocraticly speaking, Dr. Haslett would just as soon first do nothing than do no harm. Not that he believed that; he believed he was doing good, and without that belief he would be lost, nothing, a vessel filled with smoke. A lustful but mostly empty vessel. *Women and God are the two rocks on which man must anchor or be wrecked.* And Mrs. Ellstrom came for my help. This pleased him. Not so old and bloated and worthless as you felt this morning. Not quite.

He'd see the banker first, Hayes, the twerp. Not long ago the little man had slammed his hand in a door and broken his fifth metacarpal, and when he'd straightened the finger to splint it the banker had wept like a child. He'd seemed hard behind his desk, but with the tears he went instantly wainable. There are degrees of toughness, and from the doctor's experience he judged women to be generally about three orders above men. Give them a reason to weep and pat their heads. And isn't life hard. And isn't pain painful. Your wife gave birth to a ten-pounder and didn't so much as whimper. Not that you can compare that to the pain of a man, particularly the pinkie finger of a banker. Tearful slints, their bravery so easily abandoned, as a pocketwatch left upon the dresser.

The inside of his derby was dry, and for this the doctor was thankful; without this he would be wrecked. Women, God, and hats. His wife's umbrella was there behind the door, and every time he noticed it, he wanted to take his scalpel and cut hundreds of tiny slits in it and send it to her in Seattle or wherever she was now, California. He went out the door into the wet with the picture of his wife's face sizzling on his mind. She'd stopped the world for him the first time he saw her, that's how he chose to remember it, but in his heart he felt duped somehow. She'd set him up for this. She'd known that she would do this all along. Then it occurred to him that his children were being raised as Californians; illiterate gold chasers, opium-addicted carpet vendors. Thoughtless little brutes who would someday be arrested and hung for stabbing a store clerk with a penknife. He'd rather they be raised by wolves. But they were, weren't they? Katherine, if nothing else, was a wolfish bitch, wasn't she? He smiled and his blood went hot as if he'd been standing too close to the train tracks when it passed by. She scared him, his wife. She'd weakened all the parts of him that mattered. She was his bad weather, and even when she was hundreds of miles away she beat him down, eroded him like the sandcliffs on the coast.

He went to cross Heron Street but had to wait for a goatherd to push his animals by, more goats lately and more people. The whole Harbor was filling up. He'd heard there was another doctor in town, that made four. But minus Ellstrom, well, still four, three and a half.

He checked the Alaska Bar first, had a shot of bourbon with Persimon the choker setter gone double amputee. No news from him or the bartender, Meigs, but he didn't have to pay for his drink. Not a bad stop. Good day, gents. Velchoff the doorman asked him about a goiter.

"Come see me next week."

"Why not sooner? It really hurts."

"Don't whine, it causes goiters."

Going out the door, he replaced the hat on his head and was thankful again for silk because the silk lining of his hat reassured him and caressed him like a nurse he'd had as a child mending his fever. Sweet memories, silk kerchief. Explains why your wife walks all over you. He understood love to be glacial; it's bigger than anything and it grinds you to bits and leaves a big hole.

Daisy at Ed Dolan's Eagle Dance Hall had seen Dr. Ellstrom three, maybe four days ago, post-leaning drunk, said he was drooling a little.

"You clean him out?"

"Not me, but somebody was gonna if they hadn't already. Why don't you come upstairs and let me rub your feet."

"Another time."

"I didn't really mean your feet, Doc," she whispered.

A raised hand, unspoken promise, and back in the street, three bourbons down. There are limits to what is allowed, the doctor thought. Each man according to his fate, like barefoot height and eye color. You can't push against the great mass of things. Life so often calls for burrowing and sliding and forgetting, and foot rubs. Helplessness is a choice made when you can't stand against the immovable.

Jacob Ellstrom was a lucky man, and like most lucky men he probably disdained to admit his luck, and if he did he loathed it, felt he didn't deserve it, hadn't asked anyway. He didn't seem particularly clever, and he was far from being handsome; he was quite unattractive, really, ugly even. Says the walrus. He'd heard rumors that Ellstrom's father was a wealthy man, but he must've turned off the spigot now. They always give you something, if you can manage not to nod off, or plot patricide, as they ramble, as they go on. Like dogs beg, so do we. Young men so often think pride repairable. How wrong they are. Some debts call for marrow.

Or it could be that Jacob Ellstrom, the fraud, was kind and loving or even a comedian when he and his wife were safely behind walls, a big laugh, a good Heath. No, it was something else. Perhaps he shouldn't be looking at Jacob at all but at Nell. She could've been the one that chose him, but she had to be, didn't she? What kind of woman, not much more than a girl really, settles on such a mess to be unmade? Oh, she was the best kind, the very best. Above all the saints and martyrs, God loves a beautiful woman who of her own choice weds an ugly man.

The liquor in his belly made him feel unsettled, so he skipped the bank. Hayes wouldn't know anything anyway, and no one he asked at the docks had seen Ellstrom around either. He'd left his cigars at home. He went to the Coast Sailor's Union.

Hank Bellhouse was behind his desk working his pugio over a stone, oil glistening on his fingers and on the backs of his hands. The room was large and open, with a spruce slab table and a bank of windows that looked out over the harbor. Leaflets and posters adorned the wall along with random taxidermy; animals and fishes, a flower made of the carapaces of Dungeness crabs. The union seal painted eight feet tall and lopsided. He'd only just opened shop.

"Look at you, physician, all fuss and feathers. Fucking rumpled tissue in a widow's palm." Bellhouse was febrile, sanguinary, every part of him. His eyelids were muscle.

"What do you know of Dr. Ellstrom?"

"I know his degree says it comes from Brown."

"Besides that."

"Didn't you tell me and everyone else at Dolan's that night that they don't turn out doctors at Brown?"

"So I did."

"Strange his degree says it, then."

"Letters aside, he was here before me, and what I hear speaks of a moderate competence."

"You weren't saying that at Dolan's."

"No, I wasn't."

Bellhouse held the knife up to inspect the blade and then dragged it over his thumbnail to test it. Back to the stone, working as he spoke. "You were talking like we should run him out of town."

"Looking back, I think I shouldn't drink so much, but looking forward—you don't have any whiskey, do you? I've got a chill."

Bellhouse smiled and shook his head, his arm moving without break. The stone took its measure from the blade equally, three passes to a side. "I've met my share of physicians, and none of them are any good to drink with. More fun to drink with a dead sailor than a live physician."

"Don't blame the trade, it's the rain that does it to me, the gray gloom."

The blade stopped with the doctor's last syllable, and Bellhouse raised his eyes. "All I can say is, we're all just plain lucky you arrived and saved us from Ellstrom's inadequacies. Who knows what kind of injury he could've visited on us?"

"I've apologized to you enough."

"A stack of nothing is still nothing."

"If you'd give me a drink, I could better suffer your insults."

"What use is it to keep liquor on hand if everyone arrives at my door already drunk?"

"I'm not drunk."

Bellhouse set the knife down, leaned back and reached into his desk drawer. He produced a puny, dented oil can, spurted oil onto the stone, and spread it with the edge of his thumb. He weighted the knife in his palm and then continued sharpening.

"I thought you were going to pull out a bottle."

"I know you did."

"Give me a cigar, then, would you? Mine are at home."

With his chin Bellhouse motioned to the box of cigars and the matches beside it. The blade coughed out one after another of its lonely dying breaths.

Dr. Haslett lit the cigar and dropped the spent match in the ashtray. "I should tell you that whoever you're sharpening that blade for, don't send them to me. I don't have time."

"A farmer complains about the dirt and a sailor the wind."

He liked Bellhouse despite himself. "And a logger the trees."

"A logger the fucking trees, right?" The short-necked German was like a bulldog that had been trained to act like a man, but not stupid. The muscle ended at the mouth, fleshy lips. It would be folly to confuse his strength with simplemindedness, his rigidity with an unwillingness to act or slowness.

"A boy of seven had his hand cut off in Boyerton's mill this morning." Dr. Haslett leaned back and admired his cloud of smoke.

"I heard."

"His mother asked what they paid for a lost hand."

"I think I know this one."

"They don't pay, Hank. Not a dime."

"Half a pair of mittens must cost half as much. He's looking at some savings long-term."

"Is that the compassion we can expect from your union? Which, I should say, I think is bullshit. I don't believe you even have a charter. I think you're running a game against that lot in San Francisco. These are fine little cigars, aren't they?"

"I got cases of them." He opened the box on his desk and with a flicked wrist, a flourish of pageantry, offered them up. "Help yourself." Less an invitation than a dare. His eyes narrowed, and he grinned as if strings were pulling on his lips.

The doctor puffed away and met Bellhouse's eyes through the smoke, had a flash of memory of being caught in a stall behind a mean mule when he was a boy, remembered thinking: If I don't move, I won't be kicked. But he was kicked anyway, broke ribs. Just stood there and waited for it.

"They'd never allow me to flub a charter, Doc. No way. How many ships come up this coast? Don't you think they'd shut me down if I was fraudulent, as you say, or somehow misrepresenting my union brothers to the south? If I were anything save impeccable I'd wager they'd steam north and throw me off the fucking pier."

"I don't want any more bloodshed. Hear me? I don't care who ends up on top."

Bellhouse winked. "The one doing the fucking is usually on top."

The doctor forced a smile and leaned forward, filled his coat pocket with cigars, leaving the box empty.

Bellhouse stabbed the knife into his desktop. "If we're critiquing each other's professions. If that's what we're doing. I don't want to have to get up in the night three times over to piss, but you haven't been able to help me with that, have you?"

"Maybe you should've seen Ellstrom."

"Fuck Ellstrom."

"I did what I could, Hank. You showed up two days after the fact. I think you should be grateful to Chacartegui for sticking you with a clean blade, might've saved your life."

"Promises were made, you understand. Oaths were uttered." He held up his hands; the knife stayed in the table, barely moving. "I'll never sleep through the night."

"Dying will solve it."

"Yours or mine?"

"Don't threaten me."

"You'll know when you're threatened." Bellhouse slapped the knife free and went back to sharpening. "It's never a change of subject with you. Never a 'Did you hear what happened with the Russian dancer and that Tlingit fella they call Jameson?' "

"Fine, why don't you tell me?"

"The way I hear it, they had to tie him down to free the slipper from where she'd crammed it up his asshole."

"News of the Harbor."

"It is fucking news. More than your tin-pail stump speeches."

"Jameson isn't Tlingit. He's Quinault."

"I fucking care." His eyes brightened, knife raised. Haslett didn't want him to stand up; he might need to leave if he stood. "It must take a big heart to pump blood to all that fat."

"It's the same as yours, Hank, about the size of a fist and going all the time."

"I'd like to train mine to turn off while I'm sleeping so it'll last longer."

"If you trained it to listen, you'd never sleep again."

"You are a fucking slint, aren't you?"

"I am something." He sucked his cigar till it wore a ripe orange ember. "Did you hear about the corpses found bobbing in the slough last Tuesday?"

"Dead men?" Bellhouse faked a bout of shivering.

"They were yours. I put them on the slab, and I know it was you."

"No, you don't."

"I'd tell you you can't murder your way into power, but I'd be lying."

"Yes, you would."

"Beware of the starving masses."

"I am the starving masses, Sawbones, fucking mutt-hungry."

"Sure you are, except it's not food you're after."

"Wisdom might be your salvation."

"For all of us, as it should be." The doctor dropped the cigar on the floor and ground it out with his heel. "Send someone over to my place if you see Ellstrom, would you? His wife and child are camped out there for now."

"She's a pretty lady, that one. Haven't I heard Tartan talk about her sometimes? Will that be available? Will the shelves be stocked with the wives of doctors?"

Dr. Haslett couldn't stop the smile that crept onto his face.

"And you're watching over them? Huzza huzza. Lions and lambs."

"Hardly."

"Sly old devil, all wrapped in lard."

"Says Lucifer. Thanks for the cigars."

Back in the rain, the doctor's feet were squishing around in his boots. The light was failing behind the clouds.

He stopped and had another shot with Persimon before he went home.

"My feet itch, Doc. Where'd you put em, so I can go and give em a scratch?"

"Worms ate them by now, Persimon. Sorry."

Persimon, as if he'd spilled a drink in his lap, leaned back and studied the stumps of his legs. "Sometimes I feel like I could get up and walk."

"We all do." And with that the doctor got up and left. He'd had enough, enough watery liquor and dogged bar top. Enough of the hard harbor. He wanted his comfortable home and to see the woman waiting for him there.

As he walked in the rain, his thoughts returned to Hank Bellhouse. Society wasn't uplifted by men like him, but eventually he'd bury his chisels and pry and move the population along just the same. A slow grind.

With killers comes progress, and with progress come new, more insidious killers to replace the rougher and more real ones that preceded them. This wasn't the doctor's first boomtown. The real trouble would set up camp on Bellhouse's grave, but here he was a sailing man who didn't even care that the steamers were coming up behind him. To have blind guts like that must be lovely. To know your throat's slit and keep smiling.

Nell

1889

D*r. Haslett helped me* organize the sale of Jacob's equipment. It was crated and shipped to Seattle, all of it. In order to keep the bank away I held nothing as precious and got rid of everything I could.

I found work in the bakery and it kept us fed, but the hours were difficult. There was no sympathy for me because of what Jacob had done, how he had lied. Women treated me as if I'd stolen their husbands, and most men just laughed in my face. I wasn't anything to them. I had to lock Duncan in the apartment when I went to work because no one would watch him for me.

Eventually Mr. Hayes sent boys over to post notice on the apartment door. I was so angry, with my last dollars I hired men from the livery to freight our few belongings to Matius's claim. I'd tried to sell it before but had no legal right to do so. Moving there, it was the end, where I never wanted to be.

Nearly two hours by wagon, an hour if we took the ferry, and another to walk the mud road from the Wynooche dock to the house. The direction was east, northeast. I found a map with the deed in Jacob's desk. We took the ferry. It was a new ship operated by a husband and wife from Minnesota. We were alone on deck. The freighters had taken the road.

I'd heard people complain about the noise of steam engines, but I've always found them calming. As we chugged upriver on the shoulder of the tide, we passed by the sloughs of various legend; corpse farms, keepers of lost children, sad and desultory mires. At one point I thought I could see the shadow of the arch of a bridge through the trees. No sign of the freighters. They were well ahead. All this circumnavigation, as if anything would ever be easy or nearby. I was told ours was the second to the last stop on the ferry route. The dock was new and well tended, just on the lee side of the unsure mouth of the Wynooche. When we gained the road, the workmen bid us good day and I asked if any freighters had passed and they said yes and pointed at the wagon ruts.

The walk was pleasant and we saw deer through the trees, so I ducked down and held on to Duncan and we watched them until they wandered off. They never saw us, or if they did, they didn't care. In time we came to a road that branched, but the freighter's tracks continued. I led Duncan down the lane. There was a homestead there, but it had been abandoned. The door was nailed shut and the windows boarded over. Some of the chimney stones had fallen and sat jumbled in the tall grass. There was a grave in the trees, with a wooden marker that was soaked through and mossy. Back on the road we could hear men logging in the distance, the thud and ring of an ax, the breaking timbers. Duncan hadn't said a word since we got off the ferry. I touched his cheek and kissed his head and he smiled at me.

"We're kings," he said.

"How do you mean?"

"Who else is here?"

"Nobody, but it doesn't make us kings."

"What would?"

"There are no kings here, and there never will be."

"What about a queen?"

"A queen and a prince maybe, but no kings. The kings are all gone."

"Will you read to me when we get there?"

"Yes. After we eat. Are you hungry?"

"Yes."

We followed the wagon tracks of the freighters through a gap in the trees into a meadow, and there it was. Relief is what I felt, and I said my thanks that it was a new place and apparently well built. Long live the queen. There were seven windows (shuttered) and two doors (bolted from the outside), single story, shake roof and shingle siding. If Jacob had built it, I would have been overjoyed. But he did, didn't he. It was ours. I must never forget that. No one had taken any time with anything but the house and the barn and the privy, and outside of the hand pump in the yard the land was still as raw as the day it was born. No garden, no fence, no clothesline.

The freighters carried our things inside while we sat on the porch. I thought we might be able to sell some of the timber.

"Nobody else lives here?" Duncan said.

"We live here."

"But nobody else. It's lonely."

"Not if we're here." He was right, though. Looking out at the swampy bottomland and the dark forest—it was lonely. If there was ever a place that could make you feel exiled, this was it. We needed to leave this coast, but I didn't know how. Standing at the front door, I thought I could just hear the river whispering through the trees.

———

Duncan got an ear infection from running around in the wet and mud. When I took him to see Dr. Haslett, the doctor took pity on us and offered me a job, and I accepted. I was to buy his groceries and cook his dinners three nights a week, but the other woman, Miss Falvey, would still do the cleaning and keep the house. I also agreed to help him in his work if needed. Jacob had taught me some things regarding nursing.

Dr. Haslett was nearly the same age as my father. The idea of this sometimes lodged in my mind and put an awful chill on me. We were both adults with children, and we should've, a long time ago, resolved ourselves to our roles. It would be a huge mistake, wouldn't it? But Jacob was gone, possibly dead, most likely dead. Dr. Haslett's wife had left him too. She didn't even want money, is what he'd said about her. A judgment on all women. I didn't immediately understand the loathing in his voice, that it'd be better if she did want something from him. To have no use for him at all was the strongest insult she could muster.

Most mornings I felt alone and completely forsaken. The fallen women crowding the balconies of the Line couldn't feel as wretched as I did. At times I felt so small that I would look at Duncan and want to ask him what path I should take. Your father left us, and we don't have any recourse. The strange thing was that the longer he was away, the more I believed that I might not have ever loved him. What was he doing, and where? I began to see what a withering kind of life Jacob and I had shared, small and without purpose. Then I started to dislike him, not for abandoning me but for being who he was—a weak and transitory man who had been spoiled as a child—and my dislike grew into disgust and eventually into hatred. I thought it would all be much easier if he were dead, and more than once I wished he were.

———————

Duncan was old enough to know that Dr. Haslett and I were acting strange, but not nearly old enough to assign guilt. On the nights I cooked dinner, we stayed over. It was too far to walk alone in the dark. Duncan and I shared a room off the kitchen. The room was small and cramped, with a partition and a Dutch stove. Duncan never stirred when I'd get up during the night, and when I returned his breathing was always there for me, steady and deep and in him as if the sound of the ocean could be in him.

Mornings, I woke him in the dark and we began our walk home before the sun came up. Miss Falvey would've started rumors. The ferry didn't run until it was light, so we usually walked. Passing through the empty streets of town, we measured our steps between the gaslights and counted the boards by threes, three-six-nine-twelve, and Duncan would hold out three fingers and bless them like a priest. Sometimes the mills were between shifts when we passed by; the lights were on, but the engines and the blades were quiet. Through the sawdust and steam-glazed windows I could make out the shadows of the workmen inside and hear the saw sharpeners filing away and mechanics tinkering like an orchestra tuning up. And on the days when the rain had yet to start we would take a moment to watch the ships in the harbor, where they rested perfectly at equilibrium, acting by weight alone with no motion. A deep calm filled me when I watched the ships.

At home, the cold bones of the house were hardly welcoming, and sometimes it took all day for it to feel like someplace you'd like to be. After we finished the chores I often read to Duncan, whatever he liked. He had several favorites. The rain beat down on the roof, and we were dry and safe. More than anything I wanted him to grow up and be a man of his own, a better man. I wanted it soon, even though I knew that it wasn't fair. He was only a boy, a child.

Jacob

1890

I*caught a steamship out* of Westport, and when I arrived fresh and for everyone the New Face, I told all that would listen that I'd been crimped, drugged and dragged; shanghaied, comrade. Friendski. Remember me? Rampage of a story. With my cash out, new pals, like hens to scratch, assembled. I relayed how a man named Gibbons got me drunk in Montesano and I woke up passing the mouth of the Columbia. Which was true. Gibbons was no friend. I'd been around but not far—Oregon, California, a month at Cooney's penitentiary not three miles from my front door—but I told them tall tales of how I'd been to Australia and seen brush fires burning from a hundred miles offshore. I had to tell them something, so I told them what I'd heard other people say. Heard about Australia in a redwood camp on the Smith River. Japanese whaling ships I'd heard about in Portland at a mudflat bonfire. Cliffs of Dover in a San Francisco whorehouse. Pygmy cannibals, same whorehouse, different room. Foolishness to think that after years away a person can return to an establishment that he was lastly thrown forcibly out of and be treated with any degree of kindness. Worse for me, though, was that they didn't even remember me or care that I'd returned.

Eli Bernhardt, a former patient, saw me and came over to ask what I'd been thinking, leaving without telling anybody. Called me Doc, like he hadn't heard the news. "I'm not a doctor." He apologized as if it was his fault and said he'd found a new doctor named Haslett, and by the way your wife is working for him. Wink. So there were no hard feelings. He remarked that I was bent lower than when I left and asked what had happened.

"I did something to my back falling off a woodcart."

He looked me up and down like I was lying, but that was the truth.

"Riding a woodcart on a ship?"

"No, before I got on the ship."

"Riding a woodcart when you were shanghaied?"

"Before that. In fact it was on my way to getting shanghaied." I was wearing my broad-brimmed hat, tin pants, and Bergmans with the frilly false tongue, gleaming with bear grease. Everything I owned. A wad of money in my pocket the size of a child's fist. They knew I'd been in the camps because I wasn't dark and scurvious like a sailor returned from Australia, but pale and rope tough like them. Roll over the log and find a logger white as a grub. If a photograph were taken, I would be a creature of the main herd.

At the Pioneer I found myself seated beside a wayward powder monkey who was often ringing the bell, and when we struck up a conversation I admitted to formerly being employed as a physician and he confided, yelled into my face like I was the mouth of a cave, that he had recently been a patient of Dr. Haslett's, and "Whoowee, shoulda seen the nurse."

"That's my wife."

"Yer wife? How is that yer wife if yer you?"

The bartender and everyone down the line were listening, and honestly, I couldn't answer that.

"We took the vows, all of it."

"Hell of a world. She doin workin for that behemoth?"

"I've been away."

"But yer back."

"Yes." I yelled it. "Yes."

The powder monkey climbed up onto the upper rung of his stool and yanked the rope on the bell. Cheers erupted, and the bartender stepped to. My neighbor peeled off bills and let them float to the bar top.

"She assisted in the surgery that removed my appendix. She had to shave my belly. Saw my mighty whitefish."

"I wouldn't worry about it."

"I wouldn't either. Ain't my wife."

"No, she's not."

"Maybe she could be, the way you let her run."

When the bartender poured our drinks, I slid mine away and walked out. The smell of cordite was stuck in my nose.

My empire, gone. Wife, gone. Son, gone. A fine joke was unspooling against me. It was then that I went entirely sentimental for my days as a physician and the respect that came with it. I'd been great. I'd been right there in the cupboard where I was to be found, and then I'd left. Now my place had been taken. I'd come home and presented myself as a fool and a liar and had been treated accordingly. Another among the fallen, and when I got up I didn't rise half as far, and that's why they laughed. Shaking with rage, I headed out; what was expected, what I'd deliver. Another bar, another drink. I could be a man about this and go find her and cut her throat. Truthful now, the last thing I wanted was to hurt her. I'd rather let the smug bastards kill me. Nothing so kind as that, they laughed me out the swinging doors. Still, it took me three days to break free of the Line, my big stories all told, my money half spent.

Up the road, dreary and forlorn. Since I'd left they'd planked most of it, but the work had gotten shoddy as they moved away from the town proper. Half the planks were going to the mud by the footfall, some were missing altogether, slapped onto someone's chicken coop or icehouse wall most likely.

Without a knock or call, I entered Matius's house, my home. Nell was speechless, eyes locked on the upended corpse. I was what had been missing, so I thought, but I was useless to her, plain as that. A broken hinge served more purpose than me. She said she'd heard that I'd returned and she'd packed all of her possessions to take to Dr. Haslett's. She was leaving me. She'd left.

Her speech concluded, she walked by me, dumb stump that I am, and went to the bedroom and gathered the boy in her arms. His dirty socks kicked stains on her dress. He'd grown long and wiry and wore my furtive brow.

I reached in my coat pocket and produced a small, fuzzy-looking bear I'd carved from redwood. "For the young explorer, grown so big while I was away."

"What is it?"

"A bear. What does it look like?"

He took the toy with him to the table and sat down and studied it. "It looks like a pig. Are you sure it's a bear?"

"It's a bear."

"How do you know?"

"Because I made it."

"You did not. You can't make bears."

"I can."

"No, you make pigs." He looked at me and pushed up his nose and snorted.

"Why did you come back?" Nell asked.

"You're my wife still." From the other pocket I brought out my wad of money, what was left from town, and set it on the table. I gently kicked my toe against Nell's steamer trunk, opened the lid, and looked inside at the folded clothes. "You'll stay the night at least. No time to be struttin off into the darkness lookin for a place to sleep. You ask me, you belong under this roof with me, not someone else's."

"I'll not share a bed with you ever again." She gathered the boy and went into the bedroom and shut the door. I pulled out a chair and sat down at the table. She was in there thinking that I'd be coming in after her but I let her stew, let her get worked up with excitement for the fight or whatever she thought I'd bring in there. Imagine her surprise when she came out the next morning and discovered that I was gone.

I came back in the afternoon. She was still packed and still waiting. Duncan was sitting at the table, dressed in a stiff, brown suit.

"Haslett isn't coming for you. I talked to him." This was a lie, I hadn't talked to the man at all. I'd played trumps at the Eagle and won seventeen dollars.

"I'll walk then."

"He doesn't want you."

"Well, I don't want you, so aren't we a pair."

"Stay here with me. It's for the best. We'll forget this whole business."

"You stink of liquor."

"I know."

"Why couldn't you stay away?" She had started to cry. She hated me, but I knew her and knew that she could love me again.

"I missed you."

"Get out."

"Are you stayin?"

"Get out."

The next day when I returned I was churchly sober and glad to see that Nell had unpacked her things. I'd found a job working at Camp 21, but I didn't tell her. It wouldn't mean as much if I told her now. I'd wait until she showed her claws so I could turn her from anger. That was an easier move than turning her from disgust. Duncan was taking a nap in what I saw in the future as being our bed.

"You'll stay then?" I asked my teacup, but talking to her.

"I don't have a choice, do I?"

"It was a low thing that Haslett did. He took advantage of you."

"He did not."

"Well, it seems that way to me. He should be ashamed."

"Is this your new adventure? To pretend you're an ignorant logger from God knows where?"

"It's a new start."

"Jacob, I want to be clear." Then she told me she didn't love me, didn't remember if she ever had. "I married a doctor."

"You married an impostor."

"I don't want to be married to an impostor. I don't want to be married to you at all."

"I understand."

"You understand? You're a fool, a weak idiot fool."

"Duncan's sleeping."

"I know that. I know what he's doing." She turned her back to me. "You stay out of my garden and the henhouse too. That's our food, not yours."

And that's how it went. Nell and Duncan stayed in the bedroom, and I slept on the floor in front of the fireplace like a dog. I didn't have anything to lose, but I wasn't like my father, a man looking up from a hole. I'd climb into this new life like I was climbing onto a springboard, ax in my hand, kerosene bottle hanging from my belt. My partner across from me, waiting with the whip. Day in.

Nell

If there were a headline in the paper, it would read "Wife Surprisingly Un-Forsaken Retraces Bad Road." I thought he was dead, that I'd never see him again. Strange the way that can play on your mind. It was like we'd never met or maybe I'd dreamed him, but then there he was like a stray dog, and one that had rolled in something besides.

I went to see Milo but couldn't bring myself to knock on the door. It was no secret what I'd done, and since Jacob had returned I could see that people were gossiping; their faces changed when they saw me, as if they'd been talking about me or thinking of me. It's no good searching for guilt in other people's faces. I was treated coldly, but I felt that walking around shamefaced asked for it, so it was my burden.

Jacob hired on with a logging outfit and disappeared again. I didn't know him anymore. He said he still worked as a physician if someone needed it, but no longer advertised. He'd never done that anyway, and I could see now that it was part of his plan, not to be noticed or bold, to fit in. The quiet chicken that eats and scratches and roosts but never lays. Before he left, I had him order supplies delivered from Heath's store so I wouldn't have to go to town. Duncan and I worked in the garden, and with the money Jacob brought us, we bought three pigs and four lambs. We had a bit of clear weather, and the sun felt lovely. He writes me letters; they come with the supplies or with whoever's passing by the house.

———————

A family, the Parkers, moved into the abandoned homestead south of us. Edna was around the same age as me, and they had a boy, Zeb, the same age as Duncan. Lewis, the husband, worked at the mill and was gone most of the week, sleeping at the bunkhouse. They raised goats, and you could smell them from a mile off. Edna and I became friends, and Duncan and Zeb did too. We visited often, and soon it was them that brought the mail and any other news deemed valuable.

To my surprise, I began to expect and perhaps need the letters from Jacob, and it felt like maybe I understood him, or at least understood why I'd married him in the first place. I felt that in some ways I knew him for what he'd always been, but in others he presented himself fresh, whole cloth. He told me that he'd once stabbed his brother in the leg when he was a boy because Matius wouldn't stop teasing him. He stabbed him and locked him in the tack room in the barn and wouldn't let him out. He told me that with his back to the wall he felt the boards shake as his brother kicked and screamed to be let out.

"You can only take a thing so far," he'd written.

I didn't know if he was bleeding to death (it sounded like he was dying) and I didn't hate him any longer but I was terrified of what he would do when I let him out, and also what my father would do to me for stabbing my own brother. It was a pocketknife and short-bladed but I stabbed him deep enough to hit bone. He still hasn't forgiven me. Even after the savage beating I received when he finally escaped. There's been occasion when I've caught him looking at me with the same murderous look as when I let him out of the tack room, and like then, it makes me want to run. I guess it takes little to turn a man to fear and worry. Each of us has his own recipe. I wake up most mornings worried that I've failed you, and I know that it is true. I needed honesty after what I'd done, who I'd pretended to be, and the woods welcomed me. There are days when I can't bear the thought of coming home, and I don't know why that hasn't changed. *I can't blame you for your infidelities. I can't blame Haslett either. I write that, and in the same moment that the ink stains the paper I pray that you burn this letter so no one can shame me with what's transpired. But doesn't everyone know? It seems the case. On and on.*

Work in the woods is like you'd expect, toil and sweat. Our task is one of hubris, but it teaches me what a man, a dozen men, can do. There are bears and ghosts in the woods and strange noises that come through the tent walls in the night, louder than the rain, which isn't quiet. Once we found a mass grave from what the Indians call the Big Sick (smallpox), and there were skulls like river rocks piled up, some with the flathead fronts. A man named Bennoit took a skull and kept it stashed in his bundle, but no one wanted it in the camp for the bad luck it would bring, so they made him get rid of it. We don't think he did, though, because the very next day a man named Wilson working on another part of the crew was killed in a mudslide. First time anybody had seen that. It took half a day to dig him out. Bennoit slipped away sometime in the bustle, lucky too because the dead man's cousins were looking for him and might have murdered him. When we freed the body the mud had been packed so deeply into the man's eyes that they'd been pushed inside his skull and we never found them. He had a vein of mud thick as my wrist packed down his throat as far as we could dig with our fingers, and we couldn't get it out without cutting him open. We talked of doing it, and I said I could because I'd done surgery before. A man who has hung up his scalpel to work in the woods is a man that scares people. They started calling me Doc then, and there wasn't an endearing sound to it. We decided against the surgery because what difference would it make and who wanted to see such a thing anyhow.

For this work it's not so much strength that is required as endurance. You cannot quit. Like chain and cable don't quit, like the donkey engine doesn't. Often I feel as if I'm drifting into another life, a prouder one. I could be a strong and sober man someday. I could rise from this field of battle. My father had a war; I have this. I hope you'll wait for me. Who knows, perhaps I'll return and you won't recognize me for the obvious improvements. Your loving husband, Jacob.

The letters stayed tucked under the mattress, and when Jacob returned and we were alone and Duncan was sleeping I would read them back to him. The darkness he forced on me, I mirrored back to him, and I suspect the sting of it was nearly enough to break him. I felt out his weaknesses with my words, probed his very joints like a butcher. But he liked the place at the foot of the bed, under my hand, and seemed to develop a taste for my spite and venom. He begged me for it, and without knowing what he was doing created more reasons for me to lash out.

"If you ever hurt me again, I'll leave and never come back."

"I'll never leave. I'll never hurt you again. Stay with me."

Belief is a fast runner.

Tartan

Four days they'd been locked in the union hall. Knives had been thrown at the taxidermy. Nice shot, the elk nostril. Not bad, the beaver ear. The lovingly designed flower constructed of crab shells by Bellhouse's recently absconded girlfriend had been torn down and trampled. His desk had been used for a sawyers' contest that he'd won. They were waiting on a telegraph. A vote was to be made, and after that an announcement. Bellhouse sent for women and liquor. Said: What the fuck is the bolero? But they'd all danced it now. Where are these women from? Skin like polished oak, but soft. Someone, Nitz maybe, had dragged beds in from next door in the rooming house. Must've evicted someone. He had a gash on his forehead, and he'd lost his sidearm. The beds kept coming, and couches. Bare legs spilled out from hairy backs. It was a wet, fouled slaughterhouse of a room, vomit and blood. If it weren't for the drunkenness, no one could've stood it. There was a tin of whale fat that had traveled from the Arctic and Bellhouse had it smeared all over the front of his pants and his bare chest and lathered on his face. Caligula had nothing on their sinning. There was a dead man in the corner; Bellhouse had shot him for being glum or lying. Either way, he'd need to go for a dip when the tide came up.

Tartan had managed to take a turn with five of the whores, but three remained. He sat on the floor and worked out the math. Someone needed to slow it down or he'd never make it. Bellhouse had finally paid him for the last few months, and what did he say? "Blood is required."

"I don't know what you mean, Hank."

"They don't take paper money in Alaska, and they don't take coin either." He had his hand down the front of his britches, applying more whale fat as he eyed a dark-skinned woman with a man's haircut. She'd taken a smack at some point that had split her lip but she didn't seem to mind. The blood had dried in a nice straight dribble from her mouth to between her tits, disappeared into the dark hair at her crotch.

"They take gold where gold is being taken. I've heard that before," Tartan said.

"Have you? Well, everybody's got a little twist to their spine, and their peckers go the opposite way." He flopped out his prick to show Tartan the proof. "We're all turned. We're all screwed. If a man asks how you dress, he's talking about your cock." Tartan was surprised that Bellhouse was circumcised and not bigger, and also relieved when the pale grease weasel choked by a fist was grabbed by the mannish whore and slipped delicately into her mouth. Tartan watched her and then reached out and slid his hand between her legs and probed her morosely with one finger, and then two.

"My sweetest time," Bellhouse said to the top of the woman's head, "was when I was a boy on the farm, Fritztown. We had cattle and it was butcher day and my cousin ran to me with a still-beating steer heart and we went in the milkshed and both fucked it at the same time. Warm as your mouth."

The whore glanced upward, and Bellhouse caressed her hair. Her split lip was bleeding again and the blood dripped from her chin onto her chest. Tartan stopped his finger fucking for a moment when he saw the blood but then continued, driven to it, wanting to share this moment with Bellhouse. The woman lifted her hips and worked herself against Tartan's hand, slick and open. He fumbled his prick from his pants and slid it over the arch of her foot and she pressed him there with the top of her other foot and he fucked it, closed his eyes, and thought of Bellhouse and the cow heart.

"When I got older," Bellhouse said, "I had the opportunity to do the same to a man's heart. I was a mile from the Liberty Bell when I did that. Evilest thing I ever did if there's ranking, which there is."

The whore kept sucking, but she pressed her hand to her chest to protect her heart, and Bellhouse smiled down at her. "Not yours. Oh no, not yours. None was as good as the steer's, anyhow. My cousin was there, is why. He made it what it was. I believe we come from the devil, or at least he did. I loved him."

Tartan didn't have the energy to enter her so he kept at her feet and increased the depth and force of his fingers. She whimpered and pushed harder against him.

"Sadly," Bellhouse continued, "my cousin lost his eye after he fumbled the rape of Auntie's kitty cat, so they put him in an asylum and he hung himself, or they hung him. However it went, he died an eye short and covered in scars and scabs. Riddled with all the diseases of beast and men. Just as I imagine he would've liked." Bellhouse had his hands in the woman's hair, tracing the edges of her ears with his thumbs. "You're a sweet spot too, sweetie. Sweet as anything. Warm as blood."

Tartan rolled onto his knees and buried his face between her ass cheeks, and then rushed her and pushed himself inside. Bellhouse smiled at the ceiling and Tartan whispered his name. The whore offered her bloody hand to Tartan and he took it and held it tight.

Then the half-wit Willy Toker was suddenly there above him with his Russian .44. Schofield impersonator, coal-field bounty, in his hand.

"There's something amiss with the trigger," Toker said, interrupting but not really. This meal wouldn't end. "See the way it hangs?" Tartan thought of Bellhouse's cock speech, screwed; but mostly there was a gun and he wanted to hold it. He had some familiarity with the model and its workings, but Bellhouse snatched the gun from Toker's hand before he could. Tartan brought his prick out of the girl's slit and then put it back, stayed there inside her, gripped, unmoving.

"You unloaded it, didn't you, Toker?"

"Course I did, Tartan. Course I—"

And they'd never known what surprise was until that unloaded, apparently friendly tsarist pistol blew off part of Bellhouse's skull. The whore spit out his prick, and Tartan saw she'd very nearly bit it off. She screamed, and everyone fell over themselves and watched the blood. The party was ended.

The dead man left with Burheim and the whores. Tartan counted his pay and was glad at what he found. Dr. Haslett arrived, and after stitches and drugging, Bellhouse was deemed among the living. Tucked into one of the many beds, Tartan stayed near his boss, mourned his own drunk, embraced the rising pain behind his eyes. Word was passed on, a boy on the stairs. The vote was in their favor, charter expanded, membership dues forthcoming. All success, all victory. Huzzah.

After the long sleep and the slower waking, Bellhouse's mind seemed to be in the wind. He confided to Tartan from his yeasty sickbed that he wished to sever his own hand because he feared he was going berserk and might kill himself. A killer's hands look comic clutching bedsheets.

But Bellhouse soon erupted from his invalidity and murdered Toker, used his horn-handled knife, slid it up under the jaw and made the simpleton's eye bulge out. Tartan hauled the body out of town on the back of a borrowed mule and sunk it near Preacher's Slough. The Spanish whore with the man's haircut disappeared from town, and Bellhouse wasn't the only one that looked for her.

Not so guiltily Tartan collected his pay twice due to his boss's injury, and as soon as he could he put some room between the two of them. Shows like that, the one at the hall, were enough to fade his soul to nothing, to bile. He'd had questions for himself, questions that he'd been afraid to ask, and now he knew: the black mouth of hell would have him. The price of debauchery was absolute, and absolutely everything would be absorbed by it. It had to be. No one could bear this kind of pain. His being was a rotten tooth, and he wanted it extracted, dropped in the pan, marveled at, and finally chucked or crushed under a boot heel. That is to say, he wanted to die.

Then Dr. Haslett sent him a note that gave him a purpose, and if not that, at least a destination. Tartan's cousin had died—not his actual cousin, but a friend from his Chicago childhood. He had been born Chad Wutherstrom, but people in the Harbor knew him as Oly Knox. Dr. Haslett told Tartan that he'd fallen from his springboard and lodged a splinter deep into his knee. A month later he was dead. Tartan hadn't seen Wutherstrom since Christmas, when they'd gone fishing for bluebacks. He assembled everything he thought he might want and hired the Indian, Cherquel Sha, to ferry him upriver.

At their destination Sha tipped his packs onto the bank, barely clear of the waterline. Tartan stood and wondered how he'd carry everything. Sha's outstretched hand confronted him. Tartan reached in his pocket and dropped the crumpled wad into the canoe. It was three, but they'd agreed on five. Sha stuffed the bills in his jacket pocket.

"Why you need so much shit?" the Indian asked.

"I'm wondering the same thing."

"Plenty of time to wonder while you're sweatin yer ass off playin the mule."

"I'll get you the rest next time I see you."

"No, you won't. Go on yer walk, Dickerson."

"Not my name."

The Indian grinned and pushed off, and with one graceful sweep of his paddle he was in the current and gone. He hadn't said so many words during the whole trip, kept calling him Dickerson. Tartan believed that a man who didn't speak was more than halfway to being a great man, but he didn't like being teased, less when he didn't comprehend the method.

The parcels of food, bedroll, rifle and shotgun; he thought he might be able to lash it all to a couple of decent-sized tree limbs and drag it like he'd seen in the army. Failed career number four. The Indians hauling bodies and babies and everything they owned, skid on, antithetical to the railroad, the whole of their world the same way—one lasts, and one's gone with the first storm.

He made a decision and stashed what he couldn't easily carry and shouldered the difference and went on his way, to return later. No hurry. What were they calling this now, the bosses? Holiday. Some folks were going to the coast beaches and just sitting and eating, as if the world had ended and they were waiting their turn to take the throne.

He came to an abandoned mill, looked to have been that way for a long time. Tartan opened the door and peered into the darkness, whistled. Anyone home? He found a lantern hanging from a nail on the wall and lit it, a splash of fuel remaining. Some of the machinery had been stripped, and none of the saws had blades. He set the lantern down on the bench for the edger and found a crate underneath and filled it with all the hand tools he could find and shouldered it and picked up the lantern and went back outside. A few hundred yards up the trail he found a place in the trees and hid the box and the lantern there. He'd been good as a boy and watched over his brothers and sisters and his parents too, but they were all gone now. He knew that what makes a boy lonesome makes a boy mean. Hide what you can and destroy what you can't hide.

The trail was overgrown in places, and the wet ferns slithered over the backs of his hands and licked his cheek. Hemlock, spruce, cedar, and fir, brush like barricades, tall and thick enough to hide an army. He couldn't be lost here, because it was the beginning. Can't be lost in the womb. Adam gave up a rib over by that stump. Hannibal slaughtered his horse in that draw, and the blood drained into the roots of the ferns, that's why they grow rusted. General Washington washed his feet in the gentle water of that spring, and when he stood on the carpet of the needles and rotten leaves the wind whispered to him like God would and told him to be brave.

The cabin was a windowless hovel with a cracked woodstove and mouse turds all over the floor. Tartan left his gear outside and sat down on the stump in front of the stove. When he'd rested and the sweat had dried, he searched the books on the shelf until he found the one he was looking for. Inside its pages were pressed butterflies, and in the back were the dead man's savings. Somebody must've taken his rifle already, or he'd sold it or given it away or lost it at cards. The Colt was stashed in the rafters, wrapped in oilcloth. Tartan found coffee and made a pot and poured some whiskey from his pack into the tin cup. The sun went down before he knew it, just dropped off and was gone. He built a fire in the dark. There wasn't a lantern or any candles he could find, and if he left the stove door open it didn't draw and the room filled with smoke. Later he heard the rain on the roof and there was nothing to do, so he unpacked his roll and flipped over the pallet bed to the fresh side and went to sleep.

In the morning he swept and cleaned and put his cookpot and cup with the bowl and the fork on a string on the wall hook. The rain quit before too long, and the sun came out. He walked back to the mill and fetched the lantern. After that he stayed inside and read and searched the rafters again for other hiding spots, but he didn't find any. He boiled potatoes for lunch and had more coffee. After he ate, he ventured outside and found Wutherstom's sad garden and a broken-into and bear-ravaged henhouse.

Wutherstrom had been at the orphanage for a year before Tartan arrived. Mr. Billings had him working the train station, and when Tartan was assigned the bunk next to him, Mr. Billings sent them out as a team. Wutherstom was as protective as he was patient. He couldn't be rushed into anything. It would be months before Tartan began carrying a knife. They strolled into the service entrances of the mansions on Prairie Avenue and poked around the kitchens and pantries but rarely ventured into the houses proper. A person could get lost in the upper floors, and it was difficult to find anything small enough or nice enough to take without being told what it was. When you're a boy, it's difficult to steal from the rich and easy to take from the poor, but that changes as you get older. It's like learning the difference between lazy and tired.

Sometimes Wutherstrom would take off his shirt to reveal his scars and beg on the corner in front of St. Michael's, one of the few churches that would survive the Great Fire. Even then, years before the spark, it felt like a place that would stand the test, and that's why they chose it. Tortured Boy, the sign said. Need Help. Please. The pay was good with begging, but the pity wasn't worth it. A day or two of that and they'd be on to something else. Grave robbing was the outside wall, and normal employment was the inside; anything in between was open contest. Mr.

Billings took suggestions and told them over and over that he encouraged independence.

"Be fearless now, while you're boys, and you'll be smart when you're old. The best lessons you'll learn are from making mistakes, not from me teaching you. Wisdom comes from failure, not success. And remember, they might whip you and beat you, but they won't hang you. Not when you're children, they won't."

Wutherstrom would've done anything for Mr. Billings, and if the old man hadn't died, he probably would still be there with him now. Tartan had a clear picture in his mind of Wutherstrom climbing from his bed in his dressing gown and going quietly out of the dormitory. He'd read *Twist* that year, met Fagin, a mirror spanning the sea. Bare feet on cold stone. He was always back from the groundskeeper's house by morning.

Tartan heard the horses long before he saw them and leaned the shovel against the garden fence and put on his gun belt. Behind the trees he heard a man yelling and a whip crack and crack again. It was Bellhouse, leading two packhorses loaded with supplies.

"Found you. I fucking finally did. Christ." He let go of the lead and it dropped to the ground. "Cortez had it easier. And the fucking horses." He scraped up a handful of mud and threw it sidearm at them, and they shied away and moved toward the garden. They were lathered in sweat, and the one in the front had the stob of a treelimb stuck in its shoulder. Bellhouse took off his hat and revealed the pink glistening besmirchment of his scar.

"Why'd you come up here?" Tartan said.

"They hung Nitz and beat Burheim to death."

"Who?"

"The fucking mob. Hired shit heels."

"Who hired em?"

"Couldn't say for sure, but I'm leaning toward Boyerton and his partners. Stevedores pitched in. Got lively with all the fucking baboonery."

"I'd guess most of the Harbor pitched in on those two."

"We'll let it rest, and when we go back we'll stand them down." He brushed the crushed leaves and mud from his pants. "Help me with these fucking animals, would you?"

They unloaded the packs, and Tartan brushed down the horses and watered them and staked them behind the shack. He got bit when he tried to help the injured horse, so he left the stob where it was. The wind began to blow from the east; storms were imminent. Tartan went back to the garden, and Bellhouse pulled up a stump and opened a bottle and watched him.

"If you had another shovel, I might help."

"There ain't no more shovels."

"Then I'll set here and get drunk." Bellhouse looked around to the dark forest. "Hell of a place this is."

"Not much to it."

"How'd you know the man that lived here?"

"Cousin."

"But you're an orphan."

"So I can't have a cousin?"

"Have whatever you want. You're like the Indians with all your cousins. Everybody a cousin. I'm probably your cousin."

"No fuckin relation."

"That hurts." Bottle swash and cringe. "If you'd left it alone for another week or so, these woods would've swallowed all of this. You'd never know it was here."

"There's potatoes in this garden."

"I brought a few pounds of Fortneau's finest stew meat. Puppy steaks. You got a pan?"

"Sure."

The wind brought in the rain, and soon they were indoors with the woodstove. Bellhouse told his story about stabbing his old friend Julius Beddington in the neck with a farrier's file.

"Stuck him with the rat-tail and the blood shot into my open mouth and gagged me and I was puking up everything from the bottom of my fucking boots while Julius bled out."

Tartan obediently bobbed his head, smiled, and waited. "You couldn't a done anything for Nitz and Burheim, then?"

"Nah. Had to let it play. I get in the middle, and I'd be with them. It wasn't like they were fine or smart or worth fucking saving, either one."

"They were boys, is all."

"Hardly. Those two were born full-grown in a downpour and died too stupid to get out of the rain." Bellhouse began nibbling at the loose skin hanging off his thumbs and fingers, as was his habit.

Tartan opened the stove and pitched in another mossy hunk of hemlock. "If it's gonna be a real fight over our hall, I don't see how we'd win. There's not ten of us that work or even really give a shit about who pays what regardless. Do you care about gruntin away for eight versus ten or twelve hours in a day? I think not."

"You might be wrong about that."

"Well, I don't see the upside of starting a war with the mills. Let the labor unions do it, and we'll work the angles off em, just like now."

"We are the labor union."

"The fuck we are. Sailor's union. We're less for labor than the fuckin mills."

"Watch it."

"Between the two of us we haven't worked a wage job for decades."

"You can't just wait for these men to straighten themselves out," Bellhouse said. "We aren't the only ones telling them what to think. They'll need someone to lead them, to set them on a course so they'll get what they deserve."

"That stray bullet must've battered yer senses if you think you'll lead anything but a raid on a fuckin timber scow."

Bellhouse turned to face Tartan, and his eyes settled on him, as dead and unnerving as a doll's. "You have to stir the pot, son, or you'll only get broth."

Tartan didn't know if they were talking about the union fight any longer. His blood was up, and he wanted to test the fence on Bellhouse, see if the injury had shortened his scope, maybe even weakened his knees a little. *We're just dogs in the traces, after all, overtake and trample is the name of the game.*

Tartan sweetened his tenor. "Hank, you ever noticed that I don't tell you stories? Never give you the history of my life, or the big-time adventure I had back then, wherever the fuck I was?"

Bellhouse sucked in a deep breath and then fairly squirmed with anger. "I offer you the recollections, the gathered insights of my days, because you're a big dumb goon and you require education."

"I'd say I'm smart enough not to stab my friend with a file and have to tell the story every five minutes to feel better or not forget. I don't know why you do it. I heard that story a hundred times if I heard it once."

"You're drunk."

"I'm not."

"Then keep talking and I'll take you outside and pummel you."

"You couldn't."

"Oh, we'll see about that."

Tartan stood and went outside, and in the light from the open door and the pouring rain they fought. Bellhouse did as he said and left Tartan bloody and unconscious in the mud, and in the morning that's where he woke. He must've crawled under the eave, or Hank dragged him there. His head was a ripe melon of pain. Bellhouse and his horses were gone. A note carved in the center of the rotting wood panel of the five-piece door: TRUE STORY.

Duncan Ellstrom

Fourth of July, 1895

Mother stood straight and ready, looking out over the water. She smiled when she caught me staring and I smiled leaving her smiling. I slid my feet back and forth on the polished nailheads of the wharf. Long and jagged slivers were waiting if I took off my shoes. I'd already gotten in trouble for that on the walk in but I liked the mud on my toes. The nailheads were the size of dimes.

The ferry was coming special because it was the Fourth of July. Some of the kids from school were there but I stayed apart from them and threw handfuls of sawdust into the water and watched it drift and spiral and sink. Ben and Joseph McCandliss showed up and no one wanted to play with them either. They were orphans now since their father had been sent to the penitentiary in Seattle. I remembered when my father left me and Mother when I was little. He came back but he still wasn't around very often. Mother sometimes called him the boarder. Ben and I were both eleven years old and would be in the same class if Ben went to school. Joseph was fourteen and had already, more than once, spent the night in jail. Miss Travois had taken them in but I'd heard they didn't sleep there, they just did whatever they liked. Wharf boys, we'd all been warned against them.

"We ain't waitin for the boat," Ben said to me, climbing up into the lumber cribs to be with his brother. I was too scared to go up there with them so I went back to the water and threw some more sawdust.

It'd been an hour at least already and everyone had cleared off somewhere to sit among the shingle stock. The mill was shut down for the holiday. I'd never seen it like that, and it was like when I saw the dead horse because I'd never seen that either. The doorway was filled with the smell of my father, grease and kerosene and sawdust. He wouldn't be here today, off working, always. Didn't see him much but I'd got used to that.

My mother called to me but I stopped my ears with my fingers so I couldn't hear her. I took one step forward, waited, and then kept going. The blood was pumping in my ears against my fingertips like I was underwater. The mill floor had been swept and I could see the broom marks and where they piled and scooped up the dust. It was cool and silent inside and crammed with machinery. I'd heard the mill sounds for as long as I could remember. It was strange, it being so quiet. I thought: I'm a little machine and when I go silent I'll be silent and I'll be dead.

A driveshaft connected to the ceiling followed the main roof beam the length of the building. Attached to it were flywheels of various sizes, all six-spoked. I counted them twice. Drive belts a foot wide stretched like taffy to the machines below. The wheels on the pony rig were caked with resin and didn't want to spin when I tried them. I touched a steampipe but it was cold. The boiler was far off, all the way on the other side, visible from the road but not from where I was. Someone was moving around in the back of the building, banging on something. There was the weak light of a lantern climbing up the wall behind the edger. I went forward to hide and put my hand on a flywheel that was taller than me and kind of hugged it and put my feet in the spokes and it felt good in my arms, big and solid, heavy and round and perfect. I scraped my fingernails over the belt and felt so peaceful, so content.

"What're you doin there, boy?"

I jumped down at the sound of the voice and ran for the door, ran right into my mother's legs. She had me by the shoulder and led me back to where her bag was and sat me down on a bolt of shingles. And there we stayed. Bored as I'd ever been.

Each time I looked up there were more people. Most of them were families with fathers carrying the burdens of a picnic, but there were bachelors too. Roamers, mill workers, loggers, they filled in the cracks in the crowd and bunched up in knots around bottles and the few lonesome women with no families. I'd never been on a real steamship before, an oceangoer. I'd heard their birdy whistles and watched them move up and down the river but I'd never even touched one up close. The other children at school hadn't been born in the Harbor so they'd arrived by steamship and knew all about them and how fast they went and how far, to China and everywhere.

My mother was chatting with some of the women she knew from the bakery but I stayed silent and waited and when I saw my chance I snuck back to the water's edge and threw sawdust and splinters into the murky slick, little boats that didn't sink as long as I watched them. When the whistle blew I jumped, but I wasn't the only one, and people laughed. It was just the stupid ferryboat that I'd been on a hundred times. They'd said it would be some other special ship for the Fourth.

Me and my mother were ushered up the gangplank and helped down to the shining deck by the deckhands. They were wearing special white-and-blue uniforms with shiny silver buttons.

"Hello, Mrs. Ellstrom. Welcome aboard, son."

Yer a dopey dimwit and a slint-faced turd. I silently practiced my insults like I'd sharpen a knife.

Mother chose a place at the stern rail and I watched to see who else would board because not everyone would fit. I'd been getting teased at school and it had made me cagey. Donald Church was the worst and he was in line with his family waiting to board but they were too far back and had to wait. A month ago I'd been different or at least unseen. The story of the ugly duckling told me that it was better before knowing, so maybe it would be better later too. But for now I was scared all the time that someone would yell at me, some older boy like Donald would pick on me.

The lines cast off. People were talking and laughing all around. The whistle blew and I could feel the engine in my feet. Once we were away from the shore I slipped down the rail to look around. The boat was full of women and children. All the loners and Donald and the other complete families were watching us leave. I waved and people waved back, even Donald. Deep water off the rail, below, perilously dark.

"Why're we goin?" I asked Mother, just to irk her, to get her talking to me.

"You like the Fourth."

"I guess so."

"Don't get in a mood already, and try to stay close. I don't want to have to spend the whole day looking for you."

"Will it be cold?"

"Not much colder. There will be wind."

"Can we see whales? Zeb said his dad took him fishing and they saw whales."

"Maybe from the beach. We won't be on the water." She adjusted her hat and smiled, three small moles on her left cheekbone, a constellation. "I'm glad you and Zeb are friends."

"Course we're friends. We're best friends. I'm smarter than him."

"Why would you say that?"

"Because I can make him do what I want."

"That's not the way you should think of your friends."

"Why?"

"It's important to care for people. To be kind."

"I'm not mean to him. People are mean to me."

"They're just teasing. Don't let them bother you."

"I don't care."

"Of course you don't."

"But sometimes I care."

"They'll give it up. You'll see. You just need to outlast them. Don't let them get under your skin and don't let them know when they do."

Easy for her to say. She was pretty, everybody said so. Everybody watched her. She had her hand on my shoulder and I leaned against her and felt the boat roll.

We passed log booms and shacks and slash fires, newly built and painted houses and shops, bright and streaky with colors that seemed to run into the air and leach into the mud.

We docked at the mill pier because that's where the ferry always stopped. We got off and went along the plank road to the wharf where the real holiday steamers were assembled to take us to the beach. Ribbons and streamers were everywhere. Sleek, shining ships filled the harbor. People crowded the streets. I could smell the bakery even though it was closed. We used to live here when I was a baby. I don't remember much of that time. Mother was looking off up the hill toward the middle of town where the buildings were biggest. The bakery was too short and low to see with everything else in the way.

There were dozens of children from other schools and I didn't know any of them by name. My mother pushed me toward them but I spun around and hid behind her stiff muslin skirt. Some of the boys had hats and I wanted one. Mother had her hair up and her plaid blouse was ironed and flat. She carried a canvas bag with our lunch and extra coats. Little girls with braids and white dresses held hands and ran in circles on the wharf.

The ship we were to board was decked in blue bunting like the rest. A band was marching in the streets of town, and after boarding, a band set up in the bow and started right in and the band onshore stopped their song and waited, and then joined in with the band on the boat. We stood at the rail in the stern of the steamer and watched the wake. It was loud with the two streams of music and the wind and everybody talking and crowded and I was ready to get off. The ship was just like the ferry, no different. The wake was just the same, only bigger. We weren't going any faster. Steel was colder and somehow just as slimy as wood.

"Stop that," Mother said.

"What?"

"You're moping."

"I'm not."

"You are. There's a rumor that a ship is beached on the coast."

"A shipwreck?"

"Yes."

I thought of pirates and deserted islands, solitary endeavors, days and eventually years surveying an isolated and foreign land, surviving, prospering, escaping heroically, a flash of genius and daring; upon my return a celebration not unlike the Fourth. My mother let me read by the fire before I went to bed and I had the stories in my head always.

Gulls passed through the smoke from the stack. I'd had an apple after breakfast on the way to town earlier but I was hungry again. The mist covered the hills and blocked the openness of the coast. The carts of clamdiggers dotted the shoreline, their shadowy figures working the tide, ebb harvesters. Pelicans and their sagging bags. The grass on Rennie Island was flattened by the wind and the trees all leaned after it, giving needles and leaves, whatever they had. A boy climbed onto the rail and his mother tugged him back down by his pants and gave him a whipping. I wanted to run away but there was nowhere to run.

Mother was speaking to a man in a bowler. It wasn't anyone that I'd seen before. She told me we'd be seeing Dr. Haslett today but it wasn't him—they wore the same hats is all. We hadn't seen Dr. Haslett for a long time and I rarely thought of him anymore. This man had a mustache and a big nose and he was big, much bigger than Father. His gray suit didn't fit him and it was too tight to button over his chest. He smelled strongly of vinegar and his fists hung out of the inadequate sleeves like kneaded dough that had been left on the board to dry out. His mustache was red and black and gray and so was the curly hair sticking out from under his hat. Mother caught me staring and introduced the man as Mr. Tartan, a friend of Mr. Bellhouse's from the Sailor's Union. He took my hand in his and squeezed until it hurt and wouldn't let go. The pressure didn't increase but it didn't let up.

"He's grown tall, hasn't he?"

"He has," my mother said.

"Give me my hand back."

"I'm not holdin you at all, hardly squeezin. Go and take yer own hand."

"It hurts."

"Let him be, Lucas."

The man let me go and I held my hurt hand with my other one.

"I was playin with him, Nell. I wouldn't a hurt him."

"You're scaring him."

"I wasn't scared."

"Ready to piss yer pants, you toughy slint."

"I wasn't."

"It's all right, Duncan," Mother said.

"I'm not scared a him."

He leaned down and spoke: "A folly of youth is what that is."

The ship chugged on and I turned toward the sea and watched the gulls and thought I saw a seal but wasn't sure. There had better be whales and sharks too. My hand hurt. We went by Sentinel City with its dock practically halfway across the harbor. No one was there, not a soul. The whole project had been abandoned. The hills were logged to the waterline and plotted for streets and graded for a railroad but none of it ever came. Father had worked there and had helped build the dock. We'd almost moved because he was offered land instead of pay but Mother wouldn't let him take it. She liked our place and told me Uncle Matius no longer had any claim. I didn't remember my uncle at all. They said I had a cousin too.

Mr. Tartan's big hand reached over my shoulder and patted me on the chest. I turned to see his face but the sun was in my eyes. Something tapped me on my chin and I looked down and there was a silver dollar resting in the folds and calluses of Mr. Tartan's hand. He leaned over and whispered with vinegar breath. "Take it, boy. Hard currency to remind you of our independence." His breath was hot in my ear.

I took the offered coin and quickly tucked it into my vest pocket.

"Good. Keep it safe."

"What'd you give him?" Mother asked.

"Between me and the boy."

"Let me see, Duncan."

"Don't show her. Keep it private. Me and you."

And I didn't show her. I kept it hidden.

Long before we arrived at Westport, Mr. Tartan had disappeared back into the crowd. I followed Mother down the gangplank and onto the pier.

The high clouds and mist were burning off even at the coast and the sun would be out soon. The slow-moving crowd went on like a funeral procession. I couldn't see anything but legs and backs and hands. Mother kept a tight grip on the collar of my coat. We fell in with a group of women and their children and to my wonderment one of them was Zeb Parker. He was supposed to be at home watching his new baby sister but his mother was with him and she had the baby in her arms.

"Thought you'd have it to yourself didn't you?" Zeb said, grinning.

I smiled at him but didn't say a word. I always felt lonely and I regretted what I'd told Mother about being smarter than Zeb. The best thing that'd happened to us was the Parkers moving in down the road.

We went through the trees to the veteran's grounds where tables were set up among the cabins and tents. A band was playing. We found an open place and spread a blanket and had lunch. Me and Zeb finished our chicken legs and then ran off. Everyone was dressed up and smiling. The sun was out now and the cedar grove was golden and warm and the wind couldn't get at us. I ran through the crowd with Zeb behind me and shoved people in the legs to get them to move. Cedar needles covered the ground and we got pitch all over our hands and pants crawling and wrestling and later trying to climb the trees and their yarny trunks. I could smell the salt of the ocean like a cooked meal drawing me in. Mother was yelling for me, Duncan you come back here Duncan. I laughed and smiled at Zeb and we ducked low and used the crowd for cover and snuck into the madrones.

We followed a sand path out of the trees and over the bluff and stopped dead in our shoes when we saw the open water. Bigness required boundaries but this water had none save the shore we stood upon and the end of my eyeball's reach. It looked like the end. There were more people on the beach, all down it to where the shipwreck sat askew, not so big, and so fragile. It was like a gift given to me, that ship. I couldn't be happier if it were my birthday.

As the sand hill sloped away, it lost its grass covering and flattened into low dunes and beach. It went on for as far as I could see. I knew from Mother's books that we weren't anywhere but in a corner of the big world. Like the corner of the corner tackroom in the barn, where the boards met and made a poor joint and in the void was the spider nest, that's where we were. Outside the ocean. I shouldn't have left Mother alone, even though Big Edna Parker was with her, but that man Mr. Tartan, she called him Lucas, he could come back and bother her. He seemed bothersome, like a bear in a trashpit. I touched the coin in my pocket. Zeb was ripping the flowering heads off a handful of sea-watch. When he was done, he smelled his fingers and made a face.

A black dog ran up and jumped and licked me in the face and ran off, so we chased it and played with it until we were at the shipwreck with everyone else. She was a two-masted schooner sunk in the sand like a piece of driftwood. The crew was still on her taking down the rigging and some men from town were on the ground, heckling. Wind blew us and the birds and everything around, gulls hung like twin-bladed arrow punctures in the sky.

"If you'd done that first, you wouldn't be the main attraction here, eh?" The man on the ground took a pull from his bottle, looked at his friend. "Sailors are slint fuckin dumb."

"You won't be thinkin that when I split yer fuckin head with a mar-linspike." The sailor was coiling line, and he was fast, never slowed. He belonged in the mill with the rest of the machines.

"So says the bushy-tailed squacker. Landlocked."

"Most ships," his acquaintance said, "they go in through the harbor mouth."

"You don't say."

"It's true. They seem to perform better when they stay where the water is. Wetness seems to aid the travel of a ship."

"They require great wetness."

The drunks couldn't control their laughter, and one of them fell over. "Fourth a fuckin July, and you—fuck, stop it. You're killin my fuckin insides. Fourth a fuckin July."

"Would you shut up?"

"There're children listening."

"Oh, so there is. Sorry for the language, boys, but let this be a lesson on careers. Don't be a squackin beach-dwellin dipshit of a sailor when you come of age. Be anything but that."

"Ignorant stinking loggers. Every last one of you is bone stupid." The sailor dropped the coil to the beach with the rest of the gear. "And I've seen the world, I know stupid when I see it. You, gentlemen, are world-class. Congratulations."

"Thanks, squacky. Thanks so much." The heckler had given up all hope of control, and he convulsed and kicked his legs, tears streaming down his face, laughing harder than I'd ever seen a man laugh. I was amazed. I went and stood over him, smiling, not believing what a spectacle he'd allowed himself to become. But suddenly he came to his senses and locked his eyes on me and kicked at me and hit me in the stomach and it hurt to breathe.

"The fuck you starin at, you little goon?"

I retreated, and Zeb followed, nervous and quick-footed. A woman called to us to stop and then scolded the drunks and forgot about us, so I turned and headed down the beach, holding my stomach and crying a little; it felt like I needed to go to the bathroom or breathe. It hurt, but running made it better, and the beach it went until Alaska or California or somewhere and there were other dogs to play with up ahead. Zeb caught up with me and we found dungy crabs in a singular rocky crag tidepool and messed with them and stacked them on top of each other and tried to get them to fight. If we guided them, they'd lock their pinchers on one another and we could lift them in a string. I tossed the string at Zeb, but it flew apart in the air.

A boy and a girl close to our age arrived and wordlessly joined in. The boy and his sister—had to be his sister, they looked so alike—ran off for a moment and came back with sticks and beat the crabs and smashed some of them. I took the stick away from the boy, twisted it loose from his hand, and we both fell backward.

"Give it back," the boy said.

"Give him his stick," his sister said.

"Catch me and I'll give it to you." I got to my feet and was off. Me and

Zeb were much faster than them. The boy was fat and ran stiff-legged and slow. Far down the beach I spotted something black and lumpish on the sand and ran to it but it was just kelp. We stomped the bulbs but they were tougher than they looked and caused us to slip. Zeb climbed on top of the pile and bounced up and down.

"Pretend it's a whale."

"Been killed," I said. "By a shark with teeth like this." I held up the stick in my hands to show him the great size of the teeth. And it was then that the boy tackled me and knocked me down and hit me in the shoulder with a hunk of driftwood. I spun around and swacked him in the face with the stick in my hand and the boy fell backward, covering his eye. I stood and dropped the stick and then picked it up again and threw it off toward the surf. I hadn't meant to hurt him, but he was hurt.

"Are you all right?"

"You hit my eye."

"Is it bleeding?"

"Get away from him," his sister said.

I did as I was told. She was pretty and neat, like a toy was neat, even if she did sort of look like her brother. "Sorry," I said.

"C'mon," Zeb said. "Leave em here. Let's go." Then he ran off without waiting for me.

The girl helped her brother to his feet. He wouldn't uncover his eye for her to see it. I'd hurt him and didn't want to get in trouble for it. I dug the silver dollar the man on the ferry had given me out of my pocket and shoved it into the boy's hand and then ran away as quickly as I could. The girl called after me to wait, but I didn't slow down.

When I finally caught up with Zeb, he had a hole going in the sand and had already hit water. Somebody was shooting a pistol down the beach. Dogs barked and barked. There were no whales. The wind made you feel like you'd just fall over if it were to stop. The brother and sister were as tiny as birds way down the beach, walking, shimmering away or toward us, I couldn't tell. It was time to go. The waves were breaking far offshore, and the sound was part of the wind, like the band had been parts of a song. The sun was in the spot that told me I needed to go. I watched Zeb run off and didn't say a word to stop him. People were hanging a swing from the bowsprit of the shipwreck. A man hung from it by one arm and set his loops, and then dropped to the hard sand.

When I returned to the veteran's grounds, Mother gave me a cheese and onion sandwich. My shoes were full of sand, and my eyes were watery from the wind and sand, but it was quiet on this leeward side of the swale. Mother and Edna were sitting on the blanket spread on the ground and sharing a bottle of beer.

"Where's Zeb?" Edna asked.

"He's on the beach."

"Why didn't you stay with him?" Mother asked.

"Didn't feel like it." I turned my back on them and wandered through the trees with my sandwich and watched the crowd. Long tables were set up and the veterans, some in uniform, were getting their food first while everyone else cheered and clapped. I recognized some of these men and it was only today that anybody put up with them or encouraged them in any way. Two dogs were stuck together, and a woman in a green dress was smacking them with a stick to get them apart. People were laughing at her and trying not to look.

I sat down next to my mother on the blanket. I was tired and wanted to lie down. Edna poured me a bit of beer into a jar that had pickles in it before and I took it and drank it. I offered up the empty jar for more.

"That's enough."

I set the jar down and lay back and studied the fuzzy low limbs of the cedars. The band marched by, playing some kind of waltz and the veterans were behind them with their plates full of food. They thought they wanted to go and eat on the beach but they were wrong. Somebody should tell them. But they knew, they all knew what they were doing. The man that had kicked me knew. I smiled thinking of the surprise waiting for all the picnickers when they crested the swale. It would blow the food off their plates. They'd have sand in their teeth, packed into their gums like a dog that'd been eating horse turds.

The sun was lower and there were clouds. Mother was gone, and so was Edna. Everyone was gone. I had a blanket on me, and I didn't know how long I'd been asleep. The tables were no longer set, and the chairs were stacked up under the trees. I hurried to my feet and ran toward the beach. The wind knocked me back, and it took me a moment to realize that there was no one there. The shipwreck was there, but that was all, driftwood and the shipwreck but no people. I stayed on the swale and held my hands out to touch the tall grass and walked north toward the harbor mouth. Maybe the ferryboats had come and Mother forgot me. I thought I should go back, and then far up ahead I saw something on the beach. As I ran, the waves sucked at the sand and the wind blew foam at me, bubbles racing, birds pecking at the sand, fat as turkeys. It was a group of people gathered around something big and gray, not a rock, not stone. I lowered my head and ran as fast as I could down to the hard-packed wet sand, and I could go really fast there and jump the slick waves and foam and the driftwood.

I'd gotten my whale. It was a finback and it was dead, but I'd wanted to see a whale and I did. Mother saw me and came over and put her arm around me.

"It's terrible."

"You left me." I had yet to catch my breath.

"You're old enough to wake up alone and not be scared."

"But I didn't know where everybody went."

"You found us, that's all that matters."

The bugle player from the band started on some mournful song but someone yelled at him to shut it and he stopped. The big man, Mr. Tartan, was there and he didn't look nearly as sad as everyone else. A few of the drunken soldiers looked like they might weep, like the whale had been their friend, like the holiday was for it instead of them. People were touching the whale's hide, petting it. A group of Indians, three boys and two grown women, were on the hill watching us. Mr. Tartan stood apart from the crowd and watched them back, and then he turned and wandered in the direction of Westport.

I found Zeb at the tail with some other boys digging out the sand from beneath it. I found a stick and joined in. The tail would soon be the roof of our fort. My pants and shoes were soaked through from the seeping sand.

The man that had kicked me found me down in the hole with the other boys. "Did you hear me, boy? I said I'm sorry I was rough with you before."

"It's okay."

"I didn't mean to scare you. I didn't hurt you, did I?"

"No. I'm fine."

"All right." The man joined his friends and as a group they returned to the shipwreck. He was walking with some of the sailors.

"Duncan," Mother said. "It's time we get going if we don't want to be left behind."

"Come on out of there," Edna said to Zeb. "I don't want to hear you complaining about being cold on the way home."

"I won't," Zeb said as he climbed out.

I was right behind him. "What'll happen to the whale?" I asked my mother.

"It'll rot, I'd guess. Maybe if there's a storm it'll get carried out to sea. The birds will be after it as soon as we leave, I know that." She looked up at the Indians but didn't say anything else.

The walk back to the wharf was tiresome and cold and the wind was everybody's enemy. The boy I'd fought with earlier was being helped along by two women. His sister pointed me out to them. Mother and Edna stopped to ask if they needed help and the boy told on me.

"Is this true?" Mother asked.

"I didn't mean to hurt him," I said.

"He started it," Zeb said. "He hit Duncan first."

Right then Edna's little baby started to cry so her and Zeb had to keep walking. We'd see them at the wharf. I waved good-bye to him because I was on my own now.

"Don't see how it matters who started it," one of the women said. "His eye's a mess."

"He needs to see the doctor," the other woman said.

"Are one of you his mother?" Mother asked.

"No, ma'am, the Boyertons are in Seattle. We're watching the children for them."

Mother knelt down in front of the boy and pulled his hands away from his face. There was a bruise above his eye, and the eye itself was bloodred and teary. He couldn't hold it open without crying.

"What's your name?"

"Oliver."

"Oliver. And is this your sister?"

"Yes."

"What's her name?"

"Teresa."

"Hello, Teresa."

"Hello."

"Are you going to be all right?" Mother asked the boy.

He shook his head no. "My eye hurts."

"I know it does. I know. Duncan, apologize to Oliver for hurting his eye."

"It was an accident," the little girl said. She was staring at me like she knew me.

I felt the blood go hot into my face. I could tell she wanted to say something else, something mean that would hurt me but she couldn't with my mother there. Oliver had his hands back over his eye and the two women ushered him on.

"Say good-bye," Mother said.

"Bye."

"Bye," the girl said to me.

We heard the whistle and everybody hurried but we were too late. I could see Zeb and his mother at the stern waving to us. Everybody was waving. We waved back because what else was there to do? and watched them until they were gone. The water boiled white and the wake sloshed out in a V and rolled white-edged a few times and then went to waves and then healed completely to blue water. The smoke from the stack caught the wind and was gone, like steam in a warming room. People said it'd be an hour for the next one to come. Mother and I found a good stump out of the wind to sit on and wait. The boy and the girl and their keepers stayed on the other side of the crowd from us. I didn't see them again until we got to town. The clouds rolled in and blocked all of the sun.

While we were filing up the plank the rain started again and everybody grumbled, but when I looked back at my mother, she was smiling. We found our spot and she tucked me in against her side and we were off. I slept and missed seeing everything again.

Father was at the docks when we arrived. He was falling-down drunk and covered in mud. He'd lost his hat. We couldn't do anything with him. He tried to hug me and knocked me over and I had to fight my way out of his arms. Mother pushed him back and was embarrassed, and the women she'd been speaking with when we docked looked away. The girl and the boy, Teresa and Oliver, went by and stared, and my face burned with shame. It was Mr. Tartan that hauled my father to his feet and dragged him up the mole to the Sailor's Union. We waited outside and when Mr. Tartan returned he took Mother aside and spoke to her. He touched her shoulder and bowed slightly and went back inside.

"We're going home."

"What about—"

"He'll stay here. Mr. Tartan has given him a bed for the night."

"The fireworks will start soon."

"We'll be able to see them on our way. From the water. You'll see." She took my hand, and we walked the crowded streets toward the wharf. There were stages set up and music was being played and there were jugglers and a man on a unicycle. I watched a family of Indians walking up the hill into the logged forest until they disappeared into the slash. A man rode by us with his eyes closed and fell off his horse and another horseman ran him over. Mother didn't let me stop, not once, and soon we were back on the ferry that would take us home. The deckhands' uniforms had lost their luster, and they all looked tired. They lit the lights on deck and we headed out in the gloom of the evening. We'd left the celebration behind.

My mother turned to me and held me by the shoulders. "I don't want you to ever feel like you're responsible for your father."

I nodded, but I didn't understand.

"He did that to himself. He doesn't do it to hurt us. He does it because he's no self-respect. That isn't your fault."

"Will he come home tomorrow?"

"I doubt it."

"He peed himself."

She stopped rubbing my shoulders and held me still. "I need you to understand something," she said. "There are choices you'll make that will determine where you end up. Often you'll make bad decisions and regret them. Do you understand me?"

"Yes."

"Don't lie to me. Don't ever lie to me." I could feel her hands shaking, and her eyes were filling with tears.

"I'm not lying." But I was. She wanted me to, she'd cry if I didn't.

"No matter what happens, where you are," she said, "you get to choose how you act. In the end that might be all the choice you'll ever get, but it's a lot. It's more than most people can handle." She hugged me and held me close, and I could feel the ferry's engine all through my feet and into my legs.

The sound was a crack like a gunshot but too open sounding to be a rifle or even a shotgun, and when we turned from each other I saw the spray of red and green fireworks splash against the wet sky.

Nell

Edna Parker came by with Zeb earlier to give us the news of Jacob's camp coming home early. After they left, I made dinner. Duncan killed a rooster, and I baked it with yellow potatoes and onions. I even made a carrot cake for dessert, a celebration. I scrubbed and oiled the floor, and the mazes that came up in the woodgrain were hypnotizing and kept me hostage for I don't know how long. I returned from my ruminations and in the silence of the day concluded that this was our home, and Jacob was my man. Perhaps it was that simple. After everything, maybe that's all it could be, was simple.

Duncan was supposed to be watching for his father on the road, but when I last saw him he was walking away into the forest. He was in love with a girl from school, and you couldn't get the smile off his face with pumice and potash. I guess we were both caught in the throes of a late fall romance, but mine was amazingly and of course not so much so, with my husband.

In each of Jacob's letters were neat little check marks in the margins for all the days of his temperance. Last I counted nearly four hundred before I got tired and lost and quit. I was proud of him. He was delivering on his promise to me. Our vows felt renewed. When I told Edna how I felt, she said: "We're all fallible, dear, but some are more foul than able."

She'd brought some of her homebrew over, and we shared a glass. Zeb and Duncan were outside, throwing knives at the side of the barn, even though Edna and I both had told them to stop. We could hear the blade thumping home and Zeb laughing. Duncan was growing into himself. He was already as tall as Jacob and was darkening and outgrowing Zeb's playfulness, as if my wish for him to become a man was coming true. I regretted begrudging him his childhood. "But Jacob has been making the effort," Edna said. "I'll give him that." And I thought: I'll give him that too. I'll give him a chance. I'll give him my heart. Again.

Later I heard someone on the porch when I was coming from the pantry, and I couldn't help but smile. My body fairly ached for Jacob's return, but the door opened and it was Matius. He stood there blinking, waiting for his eyes to adjust to the darkness. When he saw me he took off his hat and sniffed the air.

"Did you fix me dinner? I smell chicken."

"Why're you here?"

"My house. My homecoming. I don't remember inviting you to stay here, but sometimes I'm forgetful." He shut the door behind him and dropped his pack and sat down at the table.

"Jacob will be home any time."

"Good. We need to settle accounts. I believe you owe me rent."

"We owe you nothing. Get out."

He smiled. "Go on, fix me a plate."

When I looked at the shotgun above the door, his eyes followed mine. "Duncan's just outside," I said.

"No, I saw him through the trees. He looked like he'd been put under a spell, talking to himself and singing. Dim as his father."

I fixed him a plate. I set it on the table.

He looked at the food and then back at me. He had the same long jaw and crooked eyebrows as Jacob, but his eyes were cold. "I've returned with my son, Jonas," he said. "But on account of he's a low, sinning scrub like your husband, he's in town with the whores and drunkards." He held up his hand and rubbed his index finger against his thumb. "We made a fortune in the gold fields of Alaska."

"Go and spend it then. Anywhere but here."

"Speaking of prodigals, how is my brother?"

"Doing just fine without you. We don't want you here. You'll finish what's on your plate and go."

"Once again: my house."

"Jacob gave you the money to build it."

"Still mine." He took up his fork and poked around at the food on the plate and then set it down again without eating anything. "Maybe I'm not hungry. Maybe I need a bath."

"There's no tub. Not for you there's not."

"I don't need a tub. Heat me some water, and we'll do it here at the table." He grabbed himself. "We'll start in the middle where the smell's the strongest and work our way out."

I looked again at the shotgun, and Matius leaped to his feet and he was on me. I fought him back and pushed him over, and he tripped over the chair he'd toppled when he got up. While he was on the ground I hurried by him and fetched the shotgun and cocked it and leveled it at his chest.

"Here I was thinking you'd be glad to see me. Might even thank me for building you a house. Where would you be now if it weren't for me?"

"That's a question I've often asked myself."

He used the chair to get to his feet. "You better shoot me, woman."

"I tried to be kind and give you a meal, but you've refused, so get out."

"If you don't shoot me, I'll come back here and beat you until my hands break." He picked up the chair and hurled it at me and knocked the gun sideways, and then he was on me again and he had the gun and he tossed it away. He had his knee between my legs, working them apart. He pressed his palm to my forehead with his thumb in my eye and held me down to the floor.

"I'll kill you," I said. "Stop. Please."

"I've been waiting for this day. Last time, remember, that was so sweet. I love you, you know that?"

"You don't. Please. Duncan could come in. Don't do this."

"He'd be lucky if he had me for a father. Anybody but Jacob. Calm yourself and let me at you."

"Why do you hate me so much?"

"This isn't hate, darling. This is my love. It can be a bit brusque at times, I'll admit, but for me, oh, I feel rosy. I'm bursting. Be still and love me back."

I was trying to keep my skirt down when my hand brushed the paring knife in my apron pocket, where I'd left it when I came from the pantry. I put it to his throat.

He froze when he felt the blade. "Two chances," he said. "Once with a gun and now with a knife. I repeat, you better kill me if you won't submit, because I'll come back here and take everything from you." His breath caught in his throat. "I love you is why." He smiled, his eyes lunatic. "I'll kill yer boy."

I pushed the blade into the skin, and blood began to trickle out. He took his hands off me and sat back and I followed him, never letting the pressure off the blade. "If you come near him, I'll kill myself."

"Dark talk."

"It's the truth." I walked him toward the door and gave him a shove and picked up the shotgun again with the knife in my palm, flat against the forestock. "Get your bag and go."

"I'll come back."

"Don't."

He hoisted his pack onto his shoulder. "Time for some paint in here," he said. "Yer lucky, I'll let you pick the color."

The door opened, and Duncan was there. He saw something was wrong and stepped back, and his uncle went by him.

"He's tall," Matius said.

"He's better than you in every way."

"Maybe tonight, Nell. Maybe I'll come back tonight."

"Jacob will be home."

"Not if I find him first."

Then he was gone. Duncan shut the door and took the shotgun from me and stood at the window.

"That's my uncle?"

"Yes."

"Did he hurt you?"

"No." I straightened my dress and smoothed my hair. I still had the paring knife in my hand, and there was blood on the blade. I set it down on the table and picked up the plate I'd fixed and covered it and put it above the stove.

"Should I follow him?" Duncan asked.

I sat down at the table. I felt like if I laid my head down I would fall asleep. "Never," I told him. "Never follow that man anywhere."

Jacob

A *sober morning, and without* warrant I arrived. No thunder ushered me in, no lightning, only a quiet and endless rain. This had been coming. The making of a road ends in the end of it, an ocean voyage, the shore. Fall tumbles to winter. The making of a brute completes in a murder. The ruin of a life; I stand waiting. There's no other place, even if I had strayed. And I had, mostly, I had.

My brother Matius remembers things differently than I do. He broke his foot when we were boys, not me. He swears it was the other way. I can see him now clearly in my mind, as clear as the mud on the ground, crying in the lane at the bottom of the hill, the gray horse twisting under a riderless saddle and disappearing into the fog.

Crying too hard to have cake. That was the last thing I remembered him saying when we were on the road, before we went in. *Crying too hard to have fucking cake.*

Approaching the house, a velvet night with smooth, oily rain. No matter, faces up to it; we did not care. Three of us: nephew Jonas, brother Matius, and me, the father and husband. Three separate but shared, call them staggering bloodlines; bottles emptied, slung crooked, gargled. We pulled the road beneath our boots, bent at the waist, arms swinging. Mud splattered. The windows were bright and squarely inviting, like hot sun on calm water, on naked flesh. We could've been robbers with knives and clubs. We could've razed the house and pissed on the ashes. Nell was in there unprotected, with only Duncan to watch over her. I left them this way often. We abandon what we cannot protect.

Before the three of us left town, when we were at the tables, after Matius and Jonas found me at the paymaster's, I remember thinking: She loves me still, somehow, of course she does. With the letters it didn't seem far-fetched. If I thought this again before we started home, I don't recall. Don't recall anything but the fucking cake. Happiness is such a strange and illusory contentment; it was yours, and then it left and hid behind the clouds. What was once fleeting soon became imaginary, the ghost of a memory that was itself a ghost, mirrors looking at mirrors: that was joy. Bottled smoke. I couldn't hide from her disappointment, my own failures, the strict privation in her eyes. We sometimes touched, not in greetings or good-byes, but in the night or when Duncan was away at the Parkers'. Upon my return from the camps, it was as if we were feeding our sad memories one by one, like so many misshapen pieces of coke, into the firebox until we were tired and emptied out, but warm.

Matius said he wanted to charge us rent. We were living on his claim in a house I'd paid for, not much to argue over, but argue we did. I gave in. I told him that we'd leave. He said we could stay, we just needed to pay him what he was due.

The light in the windows. I didn't remember anything after, not really. Pieces, imagined scenes: Nell bleeding. I wasn't sure what had happened until after, and Matius told me. She'd not look at me and would not let me help her.

That night at the Lone Jack one of the girls had made her way onto the bar and while dancing for coins she'd kicked over some drinks. She wasn't pretty or graceful, and it made everyone nervous that she was up there making a spectacle of herself. The room was angry and embarrassed for her. Then a man's fist hit the bar top, and worry-faced, she stopped dancing and crawled down, ass out like an alpinist, short thick legs with upturned toe, dolly shoes searching for purchase. She was soused herself. Her little feet kicking, kicking, reaching, and then she kicked over a spittoon and dropped to the ground, unsure of her footing, and discovered the wet and slimy pool she stood in. It was better to watch than the dancing because it had an end; it was over. The man stood over the little woman. She wasn't avoiding anything. His arm came up slowly and dropped fast. Her hands stayed at her sides. The sound was like a leather belt folded over on itself and shucked. It made my teeth ache a little to hear it. She lifted her face, grinning, said: "Hit me again, daddy." And I laughed, I couldn't help it. I laughed alone and loudly. It was a moment in time, an ugly and sharp little moment, a mean steel sliver, the jag. Then we all laughed, even the men with their drinks on the floor. I laughed until my eyes watered. Later in the night I stood to go outside to piss, and the greasy spit from the spilled spittoon had spread across the floor and was all on my boots. The gelatinous pool made me very angry, but I couldn't say why. I guess it made me feel small, like the woman was small; and it's not like my boots could be harmed or filthier, but I stood there feeling corrupted just the same.

In my drunken dream Nell wouldn't speak, wouldn't say a word. She watched the floorboards, the corners of the room, doorways, watched, it seemed, the places I'd been or the places where I would soon go but not where I was. I'd fallen down there. I'd slept there. I'd eaten there and entered there and opened those cupboards. Mine. And Duncan too, he was awake now, tight-lipped and kaolin pale, a gorgeous, only barely male half piece of his mother.

I wondered if memory could change a person's future.

Matius and I had a dog, Hammer, when we were boys. He was kept in the side yard, picketed to a locust post. He wore a mule-run around it and barked endlessly, each time as if it were the first and he was surprised at the sound coming from his mouth. He drove our father mad. Our mother never said anything about him. The stableman's boy fed him. He'd been named after Thor's hammer. He was to be our hunting dog, and he'd been expensive. Maybe he was chasing something, it's impossible to know, but he tore the post out of the ground, dragged it a fair way, and went onto the porch. From there he wrapped the rope around the table and chairs and finally broke through a loose section of porch rail and hung himself. I'd come home from school to find Matius crouched in front of the hanging dog; its tail was touching the ground and the skirting on the porch was clawed down to raw wood. Nobody had heard anything, not our mother or Matius or anybody that had been at the house working. People were always at the house; it was a busy place. I asked Matius where he'd been when it happened, and he just smiled. He'd finished school the year before and was usually to be found at home during the day. I didn't understand how no one had heard anything. It'd taken some time. I was crying when I hugged Hammer and lifted him up and cut him down with my pocket-knife and he fell on me, pinned me to the ground, and I had to wait for Matius to pull him off. Sometimes I imagined Matius watching Hammer die without lifting a finger and wondered what kind of mark that would leave on his soul.

The eve dripped and formed the veil of my arrival, or my departure. We've all done horrible things, but I've done the worst. I'd gone beyond forgiveness and entered a foreign and evil land. It's not that only the strong survive or that the meek shall inherit the earth; it's that there's a middling and lowering in all things. The strong too will die and get sick and weaken, and the strongest of the meek will dominate the weaker. When we cleared the forest the scrub came back first—the alders, ash, willows, vine maple, cascara—and uniformly took over. It choked on itself and never amounted to anything of value but it kept us out didn't it? It kept us away, like a bandage protecting a wound. The giants we fell were gods. What we left behind was mortal. What we left behind was us, but wait a thousand years and you'd see the difference. God would return. We were just trashpickers, beetles and crows, and to the destitute nothing is useless.

Nell, honey, can you see why I failed?

My blood, my family, save Matius, was on the other side of the world from here, the lighted side of the moon as it compared to the Harbor. I thought: They can't know what's happened with me, but could their memory of me lead them here? If they study it closely enough, can they find me? Does a man's history transmit forward depending on how the rope is pulled or slacked, or is it all just a tangle of telegraph wires with most of them out there unattended? What if there is only one wire or route, and that's where you're going? How do you know when you'll find yourself standing shoulder to shoulder with the hangman? Will it be the wires you left untended that hang you? The worst place, this solitary juncture; it came at the end of my arm, the end of my reach. I'd never struck someone, besides Matius, out of anger in my whole life.

Looking out at the rain, I stood ready to be counted, preferring to be wretched than nothing at all. They might come for me to put me in jail. I figured let them and be quick about it. Be bold in your surrender, if not in battle.

The rain drilled trenches in the ground. My boots were soaked through, and the backs of my hands were spotted with dirt and cedar needles that made designs like frost on glass. Sobriety is like a rope too, three days swinging from the yardarm. Three days Nell had been getting worse, and I knew my discomfort was paltry beside hers. Gray skies like the inside of my skin. Today I could become a murderer, a woman killer. She lived her whole life, and it ended with me.

The rain was moving out to sea, a lighted column of transfusion, a light in the bow of the ship of the storm.

All the days and seasons tumbling by and we were like the slaves waiting at the stoneworks for our masters, unchained and unguided, chattering and scared. Nobody bothered with where I came from. I felt like a king, with my father's books and tools, my fine suits, my beautiful wife. You are who you tell them you are. They are who you tell them they are. Then they came with the shackles, and I offered up my wrists and my ankles and my neck. I bent my back to their weight and at first felt straighter for it, but they fed me a porridge of sawdust and whiskey that stunk of the embalmed. My disillusionment was a lighted column. My moral failure a transfusion of salt water.

It was the year after we were married. The sound of falling trees used to wake her in the night. Nell dreamed it. I touched her hair and talked her back to sleep. We had a child. If I spoke of him now I'd be speaking of the future, pulling the strings of my past. He was there with me, somewhere. I couldn't think about that. I'd delivered him into the world, terrified of what I would do wrong. I didn't have to do anything except catch him. Steaming rooftops, I remembered that day; boiled sheets, there was a rainbow and the rebuilding of the pier was finally finished.

I unmade myself here, the Harbor unmade me. I should've never believed the probabilities, stillborn motives. I wanted to be equal but honestly superior. I wanted to be better, but I don't have it in me. I have death in me. Dear Christ, all men are my enemy because I am my enemy. I knew myself to be capable of horrors, and now I'm sure. But she would forgive me. She always has, because I wasn't this way. I was someone else. She went to the dance with one man and spent the whole night with another, a brute. She'll go home in a coffin. She can't. What should I write to her family? Her brother, her poor brother Zachary. What will I tell Zachary? We arrived strong and sober, with plans and energy and adequate resources. I opened an office (never mind the pretense) that prospered. We had a child. The end came hurling toward us like a spring river and washed over us, pushed us absolutely down. I could send Duncan as an explanation, as proof. But he's a child of the Harbor; he belongs here. I can't send him anywhere. Is that pride? He's from me. Is that hatred?

I have a prayer: The woods take me. Bury me beneath your branches, crush me down. Drown me in sap.

Nell was inside the doctor's house. I could touch the door, but I couldn't go in. Not yet.

I chose the woods because it wasn't easy, because I truly did have something to prove. I swung the ax. I pulled the whip. We all saw the future, fortune-tellers, fortune fellers.

A cart passed by on the road, captained by children. The stevedores were yelling somewhere far off, always yelling, always loading. I found the bottom of the world, behind the waterfall. Cudahey's tug was out there, moving like a spirit. That's a man close to God, parquet, near the music, sure. Divine. He knew the way in and the way out, knew all the shifting sandbars and currents; shoal avoider, deepwater seeker, never highgrounded. No matter what happens, Cudahey knows. Who's better than that?

We didn't make it through, Nell, and I'm sorry. We came here, and I thought it was liberation. A fogged window, like looking into a block of ice. Is she really in there? Yes, and bleeding from her ears. The end of the world is at the end of my arm. When did she ask for a new table, two years back, three? It was when ours broke, when I broke it falling over myself, and Duncan mended it wrong because he was too small and didn't know what he was doing, or was it me thinking she wanted it, that she wanted new things and I couldn't get them? No man is as mean as a man that has known privilege and then finds poverty.

Father, I've been in the woods working the big cut. I can count seasons, and I can count trees. The logger has seen the world die a thousand times under his ax. He's cut through the scars of lightning strikes from before our independence. I've seen trees drive a man into the ground like a nail driven into a rotten board. But I'm a tourist in any trade in any life. I need a clear—no, not clear—a dull mind. I need what I gave my beloved wife. In this too I'm a charlatan. I feel the pull of responsibility and the weight of regret, but it's somehow not for me. You've got the wrong man, sir. I'm from a good family. She's my Nell, my only chosen family. The one I wanted, not the one I was born to. I'll be known for this from now on, and nothing else. Is my pity for her or for me? This confirms the monstrosity. It's official.

Duncan was on the other side of the house. I snuck up on him just to see him, to know he was there. He was carving something into the back of Haslett's bench with his pocketknife. When he saw me he ran off fast as a rabbit. I wasn't welcome. I considered Haslett's garden, untended and long dead. Reverend Macklin said it, didn't he? First service Nell and I went to at his new church. "We rely on abandonment as much as cultivation." My fallow son won't look me in the eye, and my bedded Nell won't open hers. The name, Teresa, carved in the bench wood.

Dr. Haslett was sunk in his chair by the fire. The fire, only coals, black and red.

"I didn't let you in." His voice was skinnied by his anger, thin and rabid as a ribby dog.

"I know. Can I see her?"

"The lips of a fool consume him."

"I'll be quiet."

"She doesn't need to hear what you have to say, and if in fact it's an apology that you came to offer, it's come too late."

Tears on my cheeks, into my beard and like snakes down my neck. Toward the door, not sure if it was the right one, but it felt right. I could feel her. But the doctor stomped his foot hard on the floor, and I stopped midstride.

"Stay away from her."

"I have to see her."

"Oh, she'll be gone soon, and you can forget all about it."

"Don't say that. I didn't mean to do it. You could do something, couldn't you?"

"You think I haven't tried?"

"There has to be something. Please, you're a better doctor than me."

"I'm a doctor, is all. You're not anything."

"You could help her."

"I could get Chacartegui to hang you." And now we were tangled together in this rusted wire. I walked in kicking at the barbs alone, and the doctor joined me. The beasts and their rolling eyes.

"I didn't mean to hurt her. I didn't."

"What happened?"

"I don't know. I came home."

"You came home?"

"I couldn't have meant to. I'd never—I don't remember what happened."

"She'll die just the same."

I wanted to tell him that I'd been outside wondering the same thing, wondering if my joyless strata, days-months-years, could be peeled apart and evaluated for further hints of destiny or tack. Because I'd concluded that there was no patriarchal explanation. I didn't come from a long line of woman batterers, murderers. There was no other responsible party. There was no other rope but mine, and my neck would fit the noose like a knife fits a wound.

"She was better than you." His anger was in full bloom, a woodstove as the flames warm the metal, still black but not so dusty, shimmering. "She came here in your trust, and you've done nothing but fail her."

"There were troubles. This is no easy place."

"Adversity, you twit."

"Yes, adversity."

"You're a coward."

"I know."

"She's no coward."

"She deserved someone to talk to, I guess, while I was away."

His bulk filled the chair, sad blob, fat fingers gripped the armrest. "I should've kept her here. I should've stolen her away from you. I waited for her to come, but it was no time to wait. I should've acted."

"I told her you didn't want her."

"You what?"

"When I returned, I told her that I'd spoken with you, and you didn't want her."

He stared silently at me.

"I swear I didn't intend to hurt her."

"Every word that comes from your mouth is like a trickle of shit."

"I'd take it back. She should've left me. I wish she would've. I'd rather have that than this."

"You should've stepped off the ship when you arrived and slit her throat."

"No."

"You're not capable of mercy either. Not capable of much, as far as I can tell."

"I changed when I got here. I'm changed now, from this. I'm not always going to be this way. You understand, don't you?"

"Oh, of course. And I'm sure you'll be much improved. Much improved. When you're nailed into a box and buried, you'll be at the true pinnacle of your character. The peak of your goddamn game."

"I'll not hide from death any longer. You can trust me on that."

"I hope it hides from you, though. I hope you suffer under this memory until you're a thousand years old."

"I can't imagine living through another night."

"I pray that God will keep your mind clear, endlessly fixed on what you've done. That you'll have no respite."

"I pray he kills me."

"No, not that easy. You have ten thousand days to serve." The doctor shifted in his chair. "The only question for you now is, what will you do with your boy?"

"How do you mean?"

"How do I mean?" The doctor strained to his feet, and the bottle in his lap was suddenly in his hand and then smashed into the fireplace. The bricks were wet blackened, and the smoke smelled of whiskey. I'd be lying if I said I didn't lust after the spill.

"Should I not come back here? Should I go? My brother says he'll be staying for a while, longer if I leave. He's with his son."

"And the two of them will raise Duncan?"

"No, he should live with the Parkers. He'd be safe there. They'll take care of him." Dr. Haslett seemed to be considering this and finding it not disagreeable. Wretchedness of this color was uncommon, shame of the deepest red; it was a curiosity, even to the carnage of the Harbor; it was enough to stunt rage.

"I want you to leave. Go suffer alone."

I wanted to argue with him. I wanted him to know what my mistake had been, what led to this. I wanted to tell him of the wrath and hatefulness that filled me like black sand. It didn't come from inside; it came from without. Nothing is independent of time, no man or ideas.

I heard the front door open and shut, and Duncan was suddenly standing there, muddy clear up his front, arms hanging practically to his knees. Ropes had more meat on them. He had a dead mouse dangling from his long fingers, and his eyes were red from crying. The doctor kicked at the dying coals with the toe of his boot and then again took to his chair.

"Throw that outside," I told Duncan.

Duncan stood his ground; nothing about him so much as twitched. The doctor turned to see what he had, and my son hurled the carcass at me and it hit me in the chest. I stood above the dead mouse, and looking at it, realized it was not a mouse; it was a rat. I picked it up by the tail and could see the ticks embedded in its body, hair missing along its back, tail like the rings in a drainpipe. Not just a rat but a sick rat, crusted in salt and mud and disease. When I say I saw myself in it, in its rimed drudgery, I speak the truth.

"Take this," I said, but he wouldn't do it. "Take it outside."

"Leave him," Haslett said. To Duncan: "Go and sit with your mother. Talk to her. Your father's leaving now. Say good-bye."

The boy went widely by me without a glance and I hated him for not looking at me, more so than for the chucking of the rat. I hated him like I would a dog that dodges out of the way of my boot, more for the dodge than for the initial wronging.

What else was there? "I'm sorry," I said to Haslett.

"I don't care what you are."

"I guess I'm sorry to them."

"Don't think of coming back here. Go."

I went out the door, dead rodent dangling. My new luggage.

Dr. Haslett

————

Dr. *Haslett stood in* the doorway, looking in. His jacket was undone, and he had a hand inside, searching for his watch chain. When he found it, he pulled the watch free like a frog held aloft by its leg. Ten after four. The boy had moved the lamp to the dresser, and the light fell over his bent back and left his mother's face in shadow. She was as she'd been since she arrived, weakening, pupils unresponsive. If Jacob Ellstrom wasn't gone soon, the Boyertons, the Millers, the Pratches, the Luarks, they'd see him hang for this, and if he escaped them they'd blame the doctor for letting him get away. *Never put your hands to something you can't stand killing*, an oath of disparity, his own; versus *First do no harm*, an oath of despair, warm milk but sour. It is true that men desire to be better, even bad men, but betterment doesn't come easily; great suffering is due the saint as great luxury is due the idolater.

He loved her, but he'd obeyed the law of marriage, both his own and hers. His was done now, officially severed. Bachelor life agreed with him. The anguish of cohabitation could be profound. Prisoners understand, psychotics too.

Although the treason pleases——. If they'd left together, she wouldn't be like this now, or perhaps she would. Odds were favorable that if one way killed you, the other might let you live, but there was no way to test it. Odds were just that, not certifiable.

The child had his head bowed. At the doctor's next step he turned, his mouth parted slightly. It was Nell that was grinding her teeth, not him. She was suffering in there. She was fighting. The boy mumbled something.

"What's that?"

"I said should we get a strop between her teeth."

"She could choke on it, son. Her teeth are the last part of her well-being that I'm worried about."

The boy nodded and crossed his hands in his lap.

The doctor allowed that from most angles Duncan Ellstrom was an awkward child, awkward yet angelic, but truly remarkable because he was Nell's. Her light was in him.

"She's sleeping so she gets better," Duncan said. "Like when I had the fever, I had to sleep. I slept for a week before I was well."

Dr. Haslett motioned the boy over. "Come out here with me for a moment."

The boy rose like a marionette and followed the doctor into the living room. He was wet and shivering from being in the rain. The doctor sat in his chair and waved Duncan in front of the fireplace.

"Where'd he go?"

"He didn't say."

"Is he coming back?"

"I don't think so."

"Do I have to leave?"

"No, you don't have to leave. You'll stay with me until your mother gets well."

"She's not getting well."

"We don't know that for sure."

"I heard what you told him." The boy looked nervously around the room and then sat down on the floor beside the doctor's chair like a dog would. The doctor thought of caressing his wet hair but didn't. When Nell was here, she smelled of lilac. Once she'd taken off her wedding ring as soon she walked in the door, set it on the mantel like the last shell from an unloaded pistol.

"I can't help her."

"I know you would if you could."

"She could wake up." The doctor felt the pressure building in his sinuses. He couldn't cover himself like he used to. With age he'd acquired a bruising sentimentality. "Your mother is a wonderful woman, Duncan. Do you know that?"

The boy didn't seem to be listening, couldn't comprehend what he was confessing. "You think she can hear me?"

"I do."

The doctor led him into the kitchen and poured him a cup of coffee. "What can you tell me about your uncle, what kind of man is he?"

Duncan sniffed at the coffee and then sipped, tried some more. "My mother doesn't like him."

"Why do you say that?"

"She had a shotgun pointed at him."

"When was this?"

"Last week."

"Did he hurt her?"

"She said she was fine."

From the warming closet on the cookstove the doctor retrieved a plate of bear sausage and proceeded to cut it into pieces with a large but dull knife. They sat down at the kitchen table. The boy unfolded his pocketknife and cleaned the blade on his pants and then stabbed a piece of sausage from the plate and ate it. "Him and my father kind of look the same, but his son Jonas doesn't look anything like me."

The doctor ate with his fingers, sucked the grease from his thumb. "Most brothers don't look so much alike, and they share parents."

"Do you have a brother?"

"No, a sister, and she looks nothing like me. She's skinnier than you." Duncan smiled, and there was Nell, and the doctor had to fight back the tears. "Nobody's making you leave here, son."

"I know." Duncan pocketed his knife and took his coffee with him, carried it in both hands like a bird nest.

The doctor heard the cup smash and went after him. Duncan was on his knees, picking up the pieces.

"Leave it."

"I'm sorry."

He lifted the boy by his arm.

"You'll make it through, son."

"Her face changed. She looks different. Is she dead?"

Dr. Haslett put his hand on her throat, around her neck, and felt her pulse, stronger than before. "No, she's not dead. Her color's improved."

"I didn't know her when I walked in. She didn't look like herself."

The doctor reached out to put his hand on Duncan's shoulder, but he dodged away instinctively. Haslett hovered his hand over the boy's head. He wanted to touch him. "I'm going to the market, and then I'll be back. Wait here."

Duncan nodded but didn't speak. His hands trembled at his sides.

Duncan

The doctor left and I sat there and listened to my mother's breathing. I had to cover her eyes with my hand, cover the bruising, so I could look at her. Her lips were dry. Her callused hands, resting on her stomach. The blankets were tucked around her body and her feet pointed skyward. The picture in my mind was one of a carved saint. I lifted my hand from her face and it hurt me to see her. As I was watching, her lips cracked and began to bleed the slightest bit. I wet a washcloth in the water glass on the table and wet her forehead and then her lips, and despite myself I thought of Teresa. I felt bad for thinking of her. I held the damp cloth in my lap and looked away to the steamed window and let my mind wander because anywhere would be better than here.

The new schoolhouse had been built over the summer and when we got there on the first day the floors were still sticky with paint. It was supposed to be the good school compared to the old but it was just the same. That first day the paint burned my eyes and I was targeted for being weepy. Oliver Boyerton had lost his eye and wore a patch. Everyone knew that I'd done it to him and it brought me a little bit of fame. I wasn't getting picked on so much any longer. My pals were wicked through except for Zeb, who was dull but kind, a good friend. Oliver was older so we didn't have class together. The patch made him look angry but I figured that's the way a patch makes you look. He asked me once if I wanted to go fishing sometime but I said I was busy because I felt bad about what I'd done. The McCandlisses were watching us, and Oliver was one they liked to pick on. He walked off and I followed him and aped him and Joseph and Ben both laughed and laughed until Oliver turned around. I felt low when he eyed me.

I was in the same class as his sister, Teresa. We sat in the same aisle, she had the seat behind me and I could feel her eyes staring at the back of my head. Joseph said she loved me. I went to talk to her once but she laughed at me and pinched my nipple through my shirt and called me Double Ugly and laughed some more. She was sticking up for her brother, and that was admirable enough. I didn't try to talk to her again. I avoided her like an anthill but felt driven toward her the same way. Meaning, I suppose, I wanted to poke her with a stick.

Joseph was the first with her out of our group. Then his brother, and then Zeb, of all people. I'm not saying they went for the final stop, just a tour round. A couple older boys from South Harbor were after that. To be sure, these were all rumors. Joseph and Ben were big liars, and Zeb just did what we did, said what we said. But something was happening with her. She burned at the edge of my world.

Walking home one day I met her on the road. She had mud on her hands and her dress was stained at the knees. Oliver was walking a few hundred feet back like she was a flock and everywhere, and he was herding her.

"What're you doing?" she asked.

"Goin home. What're you doin?"

"Running away."

"Where?"

"I don't know."

"Is Oliver going with you?" He'd stopped walking and was watching us.

"No, he's trying to stop me. Do you want to run away with me?"

"Do you know where you're going?"

"No." She turned and looked back at her brother. "He'll follow us, so you have to run fast." And she ran from the road into the forest. Before I could think, I was right behind her. I looked back once and Oliver was there but he wasn't running. It wasn't long before we were all by ourselves.

When we stopped we were looking across a wide and secret field of grass hidden in the trees. I knew somewhere before us there was a creek, but you couldn't tell from where we were. If it weren't for the creek, this would be my way home. I'd gone that way before, figuring that it was better to swim the creek than to walk, but I was wrong. The water was cold, and even though I'd stripped naked my clothes stuck to me afterward and made it not worth it.

Teresa sat down in the grass. I stood ten feet off and waited.

"Do you think he'll find us?" I asked.

"No, he'll go back."

"How do you know?"

"He gets scared in the woods."

"He's older than me, and I don't get scared." I was like the schooner that sank last week in clear sight of the dock where it'd been moored because it'd been overloaded, except I was full of shit, not lumber. She didn't know that. One thing my father told me is that people only know what they're told.

She smiled. "I think I scare you."

"No." I couldn't say anything else, thought of a few things but couldn't slide them out of my mouth.

"Come and sit with me."

When I sat down, she took my hand and held it in both of hers.

I had to swallow hard before I could speak. "I wish we were at the beach."

"Speak quietly. My brother might find us."

"I thought you said he wouldn't."

"It's not like he's a monster. He's not as awful as you."

My blood went hot, and I took back my hand.

She sprang toward me and kissed me and held me there until I kissed her back. She pushed me down and we were lying in the grass and it sheltered us from the wind and from sight. My lips ached fiercely and my pecker was swollen to bursting and embarrassing there in my pants. Then someone was crashing through the woods and into the field. Teresa jumped up because it was Oliver. We could hear him yelling. She pushed me down so I wouldn't stand up. She walked away. I heard her say something to her brother. I waited for them to come back but they never did. When I stood up, they were gone.

After school we'd run from Oliver, and after a couple more times he quit following us. Teresa said that her mother was a lady of the darkened room. Meaning she hid out and didn't bother anyone with the hope of not being bothered. Her father was always working. She didn't have to go home. The housekeepers didn't tell on her. We didn't know or really care what Oliver would do.

"Your family is rich," I said.

"Yes."

"It makes you different."

"Not as different as you."

"Here we go."

"Put your hand there."

I did as I was told. She kissed me and I tried to crawl on top of her, but she pushed me off.

"I didn't say to do that."

"Sorry."

"Show me it."

"Show you what?"

"You know what." She reached down and touched my crotch and then started to undo my belt. I helped her get me unhitched and pulled it out. After a few long seconds of staring, she finally grabbed it. "Don't tell anybody."

"I won't."

"You're all liars. Every last one."

"Not me." I had my hand down the front of her dress to the elbow, and I could hear the stitching begin to tear.

"Stop that and lie back."

It didn't take long and when I was done she left me out and sticky and wiped her hand on the grass, musky as a fox trap. I was taking a chill, so I stood and shoved my slimy pecker into my pants and buckled up.

"Where are you going?"

"There's a creek. I'll wash up."

"Not now. Sit with me."

I sat. After a few minutes of staring at the grass and the clouds that were rolling in, I asked if she liked it.

"Doin that to me."

"It's fine."

"Do you like it when somebody does it to you?"

"If they do it right, and they don't have dirty hands or scratchy nails." She picked up my hand and inspected it. "Not good."

"I'll cut my nails tonight and wash up."

"All right."

The clouds were dull and heavy and the ripe green grass smelled of yesterday's rain. "We used to be rich. Not as rich as you, but my father was a doctor. He owned a whole city block."

"Why isn't he a doctor anymore?"

"I don't know. Some people still call him Doc."

"Oliver told me that your father never went to school to be a doctor. He just told people he was."

"How'd he buy a city block then?"

"He was fooling people."

"Maybe. I don't know. He's a logger now, anyway."

"My dad says loggers are one generation from being wild beasts. He says they prove Mendelian inheritance."

"What's he mean by that?"

"He means two black dogs don't have white puppies."

"Loggers don't marry loggers."

"In a way though, they do."

I was just smart enough to be insulted, which didn't do me any good at all. "I'm goin to wash up. I'll be right back."

"All right. Hurry, though. It's going to rain."

She was my girlfriend. We met every day, but we had to be sneaky or her father would find out. Zeb and the McCandlisses learned to keep their mouths shut about her. To them I think I existed somewhere between pity and wonder. She made me late for supper, but it didn't matter because my father was always gone, and Mother didn't keep me to schedules. Sometimes I'd sneak out to see her and she wouldn't be able to get away to meet me, so I'd just go home, walk miles in the dark, scared of bears and everything else, for nothing. Once I left the lights of town, I was alone. No one there except the ones that'd like to do me harm. Your mind tells you this: darkness keeps danger. You can't listen to your mind. It took everything I had not to break out and run. I would think of her so I would be brave. I would've walked ten times as far in even darker woods to get the chance to see her. I wanted to see her now, but she was in Seattle with her mother and wouldn't be back for another week.

I decided then that my mother would live if I left. I was afraid of what would happen if I stayed. She couldn't die if I wasn't there. I had to leave before the doctor returned.

In the street I looked back at the doctor's house, with its six different styles of shingles. The windows mirrored the gray sky. Painted on the side of the shingle mill at the waterfront, it said: "We Do It All." She was still in there, deep sleeping, as if she'd never lived. They do it all.

The McCandliss brothers, Ben and Joseph, spotted me down the hill and took off their hats and waved and yelled at me across the busy street. They didn't have a mother either and would surely like to compare loss to loss. Ben was trying to grow a mustache and looked like an ugly bearded woman, with his long hair grown past his shoulders. Joseph looked the same as he ever did in his too-tight clothes. His thick hands hung from his cuffs, curled and meaty. I waved and made like I was crossing the street, then cut between Weatherby's horse barn and the empty corral and hit Front Street running. Ben and Joseph's father, August McCandliss, was in the penitentiary for murdering a cattle rancher in Tacoma. And mine should be. We're none of us so different now. Somewhere out of my mixed-up thoughts rose the idea that life wasn't so much of a thing, you couldn't hold it except in your own body, but more of a season and too short, because when it ended everything changed and looked different and smelled different and that's where you were, you couldn't go back to where you'd like to be. You wake up one day and it's winter. You wake up one day and somebody is dead, and it might be you.

I went at a fair pace, with my back bent and my arms swinging. People on the street mostly stepped out of my way. A man dressed in a stiff and burned-smelling suit pushed me, and I smashed into the wall of Fitzgerald's Lodging House and spun and glared at the back of the man's head and his cauliflower ears sticking out from under his derby. I went on, both inwardly more scared and outwardly bolder than before. A black-haired girl blocked my path, plump in a blue dress with blood rising in her cheeks. I charged right at her and she slipped trying to avoid me and fell down in the mud, and I stepped over her legs like she was deadfall. When I looked back, I saw the ghost of my mother there on the ground. A skinny man dressed in black with a long beard came out of the crowd and leaned over her and offered his hand. A parental visage: death reaching.

So I ran. My lungs felt wooden and cracked. I hoped I'd be trampled by a horse, or fall somehow into the harbor and drown. I thought I could go with her, like I'd gone with her to town and to church. All the people had stopped talking and going wherever they'd been going and were watching me now. Birds watched me, horses and dogs. My strides lengthened, and I ran faster until I was at my ultimate, elemental pace, full, brimming; and I kept at it although I could feel it slipping; I ran as if I could run from this life to another. I could run to death, into its open arms, but I didn't want that. Fearfully, no.

At the intersection I stopped and huffed and hawked up stringy phlegm and wiped my eyes. It seemed the options weren't left and right but future and past. I walked up the street breathing and blinking and stretching my jaw, spit a yellow lunger from the very bottom of my lungs and wiped my chin on my jacket sleeve.

Bernice Travois, the old midwife, adopter of the McCandlisses, half-mother to all, was sitting on her porch. Someone had painted her house up to the height of a man but stopped there, no ladder. As I approached, she offered me a piece of bread from the basket on the porch. In the yard were six, maybe seven toddlers, wobbling and crawling in the trampled grass and mud, runny noses and scabby foreheads, pinkeye, jug-eared mud babies. I went into the yard and took the hard bread and bit into it and mumbled a thank-you through my chewing. I looked at the children in disgust. I was little once.

"I'm so sorry for you, Duncan," the old woman said. "I'll say a prayer so that you'll be safe." Bernice used to help teach school, but she didn't any more. Ms. Kletchko was the teacher now. Bernice raised the whores' unwanted children. Raising bastards up like corn, I'd heard said. The McCandlisses slept here.

I couldn't swallow, so I spit the bread at her feet and then scraped the wet crumbs from my mouth with my fingers, tasted my dirty hand. "I don't need nothin from you. Not yer pity or yer bread."

"Heh," the old woman said, sneered, showed missing and black teeth. Ben and Joseph said she was mean as a snake once the door shut you inside.

"Heh, yourself," I said, and went on my way.

Since I missed the ferry, I took the road. I didn't have any money anyhow. I could sneak on, could free-hire a skiff, but I'd be against the tide. There was no stopping me from doing any of the wrong things anymore. The McCandlisses said that Hank Bellhouse told them that in wartime boys my age would be soldiering by now, saluting and marching and killing. "And what is peacetime soldierin if not criminal?" Joseph McCandliss said.

"If there's money that's not blood money," his brother said, parroting Bellhouse, "I ain't seen it."

Crossing the bridge, I spotted someone up ahead and was ashamed of myself, so I left the road and went overland, hiding, and not hurrying either. There was a path but I avoided that too. The rain made no difference to me. I hadn't even taken it into account until I was soaked through. The trees offered shelter and I zigzagged between them, more for the stillness than the dry. I rested for a while and the tears came back. The squirrels chattering in the trees and the lulling rain settled the question of my significance. I wished my father wouldn't have left me too.

Hours later, I came up from the river bottom and stood at the edge of the clearing and looked at the house. There was no smoke coming from the chimney. Our three remaining sheep stood rooted in the corral among the stumps and rotting logs, the standing water, looking in my direction. The milk cow must've heard me because it began to low. I wondered if the cow would miss her; if the birds might, the sheep, the mud, and the garden, the parsnips: the little old men.

The kitchen table and chairs had been pushed aside, and Uncle Matius's and Jonas's things filled the room. Their cases stunk of grease and wood-smoke and there were drag marks in the soft wood floor. Hay from the barn was scattered about and stamped into muddy footprints, but nothing in the bedroom had so much as moved. Father's rucksack, muddy and threadbare, was at the foot of the bed. He hadn't left at all. He'd be in town, lurching from bar to bar, moaning at the streetlights like they were burning him.

Father, get up. Mr. Bennet put you on his crew, remember? Mother promised him you'd be there.

Get away from me. I know when I leave. I know what. I know. I'm the best faller they got. I'm the bull of the woods.

Then get up and show them.

Show you.

Mother's brush and a paring knife, a file for her nails, were on her dresser. Next to the bed was a small wooden box with hairpins and some tin jewelry, her diary. She had two dresses besides the one she had on, and they were both hanging in the closet.

If Father left, he didn't take anything, and if he didn't take his bindle, he wasn't gone. They'd lied to me. He couldn't have gone without that. Now he was going to show up and ask for what? He wouldn't ask for anything. He never did. Relief was what I felt, and it made me sick. Don't be glad if he comes back.

I sat at the table in the corner with the shotgun and watched the door. The sound of the fire in the stove went on and on like there were tiny men working in there. I told myself that I was ready to kill him, and I'd do it too. I'd sit there and wait and when he came in I'd shoot him like he was an animal and I didn't know him and it was nothing. But sitting there I was as scared as I'd ever been.

The sound of the wagon and horses outside woke me. I waited, ready, while the wagon was unhitched and the horses put away. Jonas, the big cousin, came in first, and then Uncle Matius. They were both carrying crates of supplies. Neither of them saw me in the corner, both barrels aimed at the door, my finger on the trigger. The small heat from the fire was quickly sucked out into the night. Jonas saw me first. "Your father isn't with us," he said. "It's just the two of us."

"What in the hell are you doing, boy?" Matius said. "Put the gun up."

"Where is he?"

"Who knows," Matius said. "I said put that away."

I lowered the shotgun and leaned it in the corner behind me. I had to push the table away to get out. "Is he coming back?"

"Sure he is," Matius said, smiling.

"When?"

"I wouldn't care to speculate." My uncle eyed me like I was food.

"He'll be away for a while," Jonas said. Both he and Matius had on Belgian serge coats, like they'd been here all along, real Harbor regulars, but Jonas wore peg-top pants like a shingleweaver. Somebody should've told him.

"He said he was leaving," I said.

"So he did. Help us bring all this stuff inside," Matius said.

Not knowing what else to do, I did as I was told. Into the rain, to the wagon, arms heaped, flour and coffee, the bag leaked and spewed into my eye and burned. Inside, set down on the counter then out again. When we were finished Jonas shut the door, and we stood together in the kitchen.

"I'm sorry about your mother," Jonas said.

"God knows she deserved better than your father," Uncle Matius said, scratching his beard.

"Not now," Jonas said to Uncle Matius. "Are you hungry, cousin?"

"This food has to last," Matius said.

"I'm not hungry."

"Your father left some money for you," Jonas said.

"He left the money for me to watch over," Uncle Matius said.

"You can't hold the boy in your debt for his own money."

"He should know that if I let him in the door, I'm doing what's right by him, and I wasn't married to her." Matius took a bite from his plug of tobacco, worked it into its place with his tongue. "He needs to understand that."

"He understands fine," Jonas said.

"He didn't take any of his stuff," I said. "None of it."

"We saw him at the docks." Matius lifted the lid on the soup pot on the stove and looked into it, then spit and put the lid back. "I'd say he's in open water by now."

"You'll be washing that, you filthy coot," Jonas said.

"What should I do with his things?" I asked.

The two men watched me and then glanced at one another.

"And my mother's things?"

"Watch what you say, goddamn it," Jonas said to his father.

"Watch your own self."

"There's no hurry to decide," Jonas said to me.

My uncle didn't move; he stood and looked down at me, his mouth working at the plug. "There isn't anything to talk about. It's done." He spit through his teeth blasphemously this time onto the floor.

I pressed my tongue to the roof of my mouth, trying to staunch the coming tears.

"You hear me?"

"Yes."

"You sure?"

"He said he heard you," Jonas said.

"Good. That's good advice I just gave."

"No lesson there to be had," Jonas said.

"You could thank me," Matius said to me. "That would be a start."

She'd said, "Duncan, go to your room. I'm fine. Go on to bed." Her eyeball was quickly turning the color of old blood, and there was a dark purple bruise rising at her temple. I went toward her, but she fended me off and pushed me toward my room. Jonas's hand on my back urged me on. I sat on the bed, and I could hear Matius and my father yelling outside, and then the sound of them fighting. Jonas went out and pulled them apart and Father went away yelling in the night, in the rain. Later Jonas came into my room and told me to get some sleep. "She'll be fine in the morning, just a bump on the noggin." I did as I was told. I slept till morning and didn't remember dreaming.

Jonas passed me his kerchief and then squatted down in front of me and asked me again, like I was dim, if I was ready to eat dinner.

"Oh Christ, look at this," Matius said.

"Leave him."

"Crying doesn't help anybody."

"I said, leave him. It's all right, Duncan. You can cry as much as want."

"That's a hell of a lesson. Just a fine way— And I'm stuck with both of you. My worthless brother leaves me with this. I could've gotten my own clean start here, but now— What a mess."

"It isn't your house," I said. "You were supposed to leave. I heard him tell you to leave when you were outside, but you came back. It's my house, not yours."

"You don't know a thing about it," Matius said. "It's all of it, every acre and nail, my house. I hold the paper."

I wiped my nose on the back of my hand. "You can't stay here."

Matius gave me a steady, hate-filled look. "Stop your fucking blubbering, boy, or I'll crack you one."

Jonas stood up hugely between me and his father. "There's all that grain that needs to be put up. Why don't you get to it?"

"Let the crybaby do it," Matius said.

"No, you get out there and put it away, or by Christ I'll whip you in front of the boy."

Matius's face twisted childishly. "You're not going to help me?" The roles of father and son had reversed. I wondered how old I'd have to get to have that happen. If my father would ever shrink, and if I'd ever be as brave as Jonas.

"I've had about as much as I'll take out of you," Jonas said to his father. "You hear me? Go on outside. I'll start dinner."

"And he's crying."

"Yes, he is. And you'll leave him to it. Now get."

"I'm your father."

"Well, act like it."

I was shaking all through my body, but I didn't think they could see it as much as I felt it. I didn't want them looking at me anymore. It wasn't even their house. Without another word I went outside, beat Matius to it.

The rain had stopped, and in between the clouds the stars were out, something secret revealed, gray sky and black trees. Her footsteps were underneath every one of mine. Her shadow was in the trees.

The barn was completely dark except for the faint light of the house-lights coming through the open door. The cow was chewing on the fence. I watched its bottom lip wrap under the slat like a giant hairy slug. They think they can just walk right in here. I wasn't crying anymore. I promised myself that I wouldn't, but when Jonas came to get me for dinner the tears came again.

"It's all right. You go ahead." Jonas put an arm around my shoulder and hugged me and I rested my head against his chest. He was a big milky-smelling thing.

"She was fine before. Nothing was wrong."

"I know."

"I could've stopped him. I should've got up soon as I heard him and done something. I'll kill him if I see him again."

"I'll tell you something you don't want to hear. She wasn't even mad at him, didn't blame him at all."

I pushed his arm from my shoulder. My face was hot all the way to my teeth.

"I'll find him and kill him."

Jonas looked steadily into my eyes. "It's time to eat. I guess if you still feel like it, we can talk more about murder after dinner."

"Don't joke with me."

"I'm not joking."

"You are. You're foolin with me, but I'm not a fool."

"I know you're not. You're a tough case, clear as day." He smiled just slightly, and I could see my own sadness reflected in his face. This was an unrecognizable place from where I'd been before. I didn't know what else to do but follow my cousin inside.

Dr. Haslett

The doctor sat alone and watched the fire burn down. Earlier, he'd set an armload of wood on the hearth to dry, and now there was only the one piece left. The steam was no longer rising from it, so it was ready. The rain always blew in under the eaves and soaked the woodpile. He'd meant to build a shed this year. He could've hired someone. He'd be left behind now. Nell would be gone. People are loved more for dying than for living. We love the image more than the being itself. How's that make God, he wondered. It's likely that the image is a far cry from the being. We pity the poor but loathe the beggar. Love the frontier but cower in the wilderness. Man's imagination is at once the blade that defends and the stone that crushes. He could've married Nell if he weren't married already, if she weren't. If he weren't exactly the man he was. Marrying the wrong woman was the worst kind of mistake. He imagined losing a limb in some drunken accident and having to tell the story for the rest of his life.

He must've fallen asleep. A sound in the rear of the house woke him. At first he thought Duncan had returned—and where did that boy get to anyway?—but that wasn't the sound at all. The doctor was on his feet and waddling, huffing toward Nell, and when he went through the door she was looking at him with one open eye, the other was yellow-black and welded shut with pus.

He had her by the wrist, his watch out, taking her pulse. "You almost made me turn to prayer, you know. Your pulse before, I barely had you, and now, oh, you're back with us. Thank God." He was laughing, and his eyes brimmed with tears.

"Milo, listen to me. Don't say anything."

He nodded obediently, exhausted as a child, tantrum finished.

"I don't want to be here anymore."

"You shouldn't go home. It's not safe. I won't allow it." He held her hand with both of his and bowed his head. "I wish you would stay here with me."

"I didn't say I wanted to go home, Milo. Listen."

"I'm listening, dear." He wouldn't look up.

She pulled her hand free and touched his cheek. "I want to leave this place."

"Fine, I'll go with you. Soon as you're well."

"No, you aren't listening. I'm going alone." She sat up and carefully slid her finger down the bridge of her nose and her cheekbones, feeling out the damage.

"You can't travel. Not yet. You need to rest." He was confused. "You can't leave Duncan here. You can't leave here by yourself."

"I have to ask you a favor."

"I'll do whatever you want. You know that. I'll do anything for you."

"Duncan will stay with the Parkers. Edna will raise him. I trust her. Please, Milo. He can't come with me."

"We'll both come with you."

"You can't. I've already decided. Just help me arrange it. Please. It's more than I should ask, I know, but I don't have anyone else."

He had his lip out, and he was turning his head from side to side like a hunting owl.

"You're a good man, Milo."

"I'm right about it being too soon to travel. You know I am. Let me come with you. I won't stay if you don't want me to."

"That can't happen. Nobody can know." She had his hand now and she raised it to her lips and kissed it, her brutalized face in profile; it broke his heart.

"Are you thirsty? I'll bring you water or coffee. I made coffee earlier."

"That would be nice. Thank you."

But he didn't make a move, and she didn't release his hand. "I have to ask, where would you go?"

"To live with my brother Zachary."

"And if you leave Duncan behind, what will become of him? You'll destroy him."

"The Parkers are a good family. Edna's my friend. Zeb's as good as a brother to Duncan. He'll be better off with them than with me and Jacob."

"No, he still needs you."

"But I can't tell him, can I? Because if he knows, everybody will. He won't be safe if I'm here. I don't want to leave him."

"I don't understand."

She patted his wrist and squeezed his fingers as she let him go. "He's nearly grown. Soon he won't need me anymore. You'll all forget about me soon enough."

"No, he still needs you. I need you."

"I want to be dead, Milo. I don't want anyone looking for me."

"You want me to lie."

"I want a funeral. I want my death to be the truth that people remember. This isn't an easy choice for me, but it has to be this way. If I leave, I'll save my life and Duncan's. If I stay—I can't stay. I can't. I've had enough of this place."

"I don't know if I can do it, Nell. I mean, I want to help you, but I simply don't know how. There are other people involved. Records are kept, even here."

"Bring the coffee, and we'll talk through it. There's nothing we can't talk through, is there?"

The doctor acquiesced and went for the coffee. He set the pot back on the stove and waited for it to warm. Standing at the window, palms flat, his belly resting against the counter, he wept, but only for a moment. If she left, for him, it would be that she'd died twice. Not fair. No. He would help her, though. He'd do whatever he could. He'd ask Bellhouse to book her passage. On second thought, he'd ask Tartan. Less talking with that one. Less trouble altogether. He had a vision of Nell hidden belowdecks with a load of lumber, all by herself, neatly composed, gone. Sadness filled him and pity, but this is how it was. This was the promise: I will give no deadly medicine.

Book Two

The whistle tells us to stop. We stand dumb and stiff as turtles until the doors swing open and the tulle settles over us and pulls us toward the darkness. Slackjawed gossip has it that up the peninsula a windstorm killed two hundred elk with falling timber. Two hundred men are waiting, staring at roof beams and sawdust, and another two hundred are outside waiting to come in. This life is a game of chance, but you try anyway. During the War they found the muskets of the dead tamped full with thirteen balls, never fired.

"Sure, I'll have one with you, but then I'll be home."

"Yer wife is waitin."

"That she is. The children too. But the pull from the drink is truly tidal."

"Because you need it, and now I'd say you need a swig more than a child needs a father."

"Sounds frigid when you say it out loud. Let's walk."

No rain tonight. Just a bright lovely place with light in all the windows. Music tinkling out over the water to meet the jangle of the ships. A town rises impossibly. The victors stand clean, covetous, and mean. Opposite, the failures, foreheads scarred by the tumplines, fill their dreams with graveyards and graveyards with dreams. There is a toll, and Jesus says he's got the bill, but we'll see about that.

Even the doorman is laughing. Even the one-legged girl is dancing.

"If I had my pay I'd drink myself to death tonight."

"The union men are here, see em?"

"Bellhouse."

"Right, means a few for free. Adequate bow and scrape, of course."

"Honestly, he scares me."

"Drink enough he won't."

"Posthumously then."

The barman has pinkeye and the mirror's been cracked.

"Didn't there used to be a chandelier?"

"Tore down." Points up to the dangling roots. Points across the room to the piano and the Mucker at the keys. "Freshly tuned instrument," the barman says, "much improved."

"Its guts may be steeved, but the tack of the melody no less dour."

"If you don't like sad songs," the barman says, "you won't like it here."

"We'll like it fine. Let's have it."

Drinks arrive, vessels of shimmering joy, opposite of panic. Coin to the pannier.

"I'm a nothingarian, so to nothingness."

"Adam, with such counsel nothing swayed. —Milton"

Shot glasses nearly gobbled, licked clean.

"Whiskey is second only to nothingness."

"Looks like a footrace tonight."

Bellhouse stands to give a speech, raises a hand. All faces turn to him, waiting for the free drink at the end. The abused piano player continues, lost in the teeth and timbers of the keyboard. Bellhouse hammers a look into the side of his head, yards clear of a glour.

"He should stop that sorry tinkering tune."

And just like that he did. Silence flooded.

In a whisper: "Got a bit of Pekin egg under his eye, Bellhouse does."

"Somebody caught him nappin. Bet he's grumpy when he wakes."

"Quiet, oration crowning."

Says Bellhouse: "When I'm burning in hell it will be that fucking piano I hear."

Laughs all around except from the speaker and the musician. Bellhouse caresses with a busted paw the bruise under his eye, then winks at the pianist. Chicken meet stump, ax will be by shortly. Harbor God continues with a threat aimed at specific rail interests, Northern Pacific, moves on to what nearly turns into a teary-eyed thanks to a high class of working man, follows emotional pucker with a promise of violence for all those that stand against said high classers, falls into verse. "'Before him came a forester of Dean, wet from the woods, with notice of a hart taller than his fellows—' You, gentlemen, are those foresters, and you've seen the stag which is your rights and your deserved rewards. I am your Arthur, and tomorrow we go hunting."

Applause all around, sawdust huffs out of sleeves and rains from the tops of the jug-eared's trophies. If the chandelier hadn't been uprooted, the faces of the fledged would've mooned their hard mother.

"He quotes the Right Honorable, Alfred Lord."

"Poets like politicians kill more than they comfort."

"If there's a human endeavor that at some point doesn't require shoveling, I'll drop dead from surprisement."

"You speak not truth but close."

"Another footrace."

"Does the one-legged girl give a discount? I've three dollars."

"Let her dance. Save yer money. Drink up Bellhouse's leavings, and we'll get. Yer wife and children are waitin."

"For nothin."

"Grist to the mill."

"Dawn comes earlier every day. I'm stayin."

"Then so am I."

There's an engine in the heart of the world, and it's built to kill us.

Duncan

_____

1901

Each footfall was a point of strict quietude, a flicked toenail, a dropping leaf. Far off, after a bit of concentrating, I could just hear the Chehalis, a bag of bones, highwater rattling. Splashdams clogged the creeks all up and down, veins in a leaf, banking water for the flush, a wonder that we don't all dry up and blow away. The clouds glowed in the notch, but the sun was down. Yellow and gray with a seep of red; I call this sky, mother's flower. It'll blush, then go. I held midstride and waited, and what I thought would happen did: she turned gray.

I was close now. The widowmakers were up ahead, the last marker before town. It went: square boulder with mouthcrack, twin stumps (the sisters), broken signpost with a nail in it, and then the widowmakers. Cold cracked the rock, long gone loggers made the stumps, a falling limb broke the signpost, and someone, a not very smart someone, had chopped down the first widowmaker to start the tangle where it fell wrongly and hung up in its neighbor's crown. Other smaller trees were cut to try and knock down the first, but they all leaned one against the other in a kind of spiral around the forked hemlock. It had been there for as long as I had memory, leaning mostly toward town, hanging now from as much moss as limb. When it went, it would go in all directions, like mud from a spinning wheel, somehow familial.

At the crest the quiet was snatched away. The lights were up in town and the timber haulers were moored at the docks, awaiting cargo. The new drawbridge was raised, and wasn't it a triumph, made me think of a book with a broken spine, ripped in half with half the meaning on either side. I'd seen the Harbor grow, old docks failed, new docks came, wharfs and warehouses, mills, junkshow jetties, highbar leavings, pilings like cobbler's nails. Bridges were stitching us together. We got our trains and they're noisy all the time, but it's a good sound, shows we're all a-bustle and not lazy.

The birds were gabbing and hawking to each other, squeaking corks. In my mind I tied strings to them and then tied the strings to the men at the wharf yelling at each other and at slings full of lumber that hovered in the air not so high or safely above and to a man came a gull and a raven, a pelican. Unclaimed I imagined they turned restless and tormenting: either the lone raven was dead-eyeing you from a broken branch or the velvety bitches were waiting till you were hungry and alone and wouldn't mind any company at all, and then they hid. So it went, you wanted both you got none, you wanted none you got both. We're the puppets of the winged slashers, three-toed do-dahs. Maybe some lucky slint would get a bear paired to him, and he'd get bear dreams every night. Others, sailors most likely, they'd get the boneheaded seals with their black eyes that go all the way through their heads. Salmon fishermen must have dreams of bluebacks cobbled like stones across the rivers, and the sturgeon men dream of the bottomless dark and boats that can't be turned over. Drunks dream of ponds of liquor where they drink like deer, proudly and aware, never slipping. Fools dream of being wise and respected and drive hard bargains that will break them before they wake up. I know these things because my mother told me, or I thought she had. My dead mother has been as good a teacher as my living one was. And I couldn't always re-member what she'd said and what I'd made up, so I blended the two and called it my attributable faith, my intestate philosophy. Like the Harbor, all rivers run to me.

Foreground, the biggest show, four blocks long, was Teresa's father's mill, the Boyerton Pacific; leaking steam from the towers and pipes, cracks in the walls, like it was being crushed. Teresa was my girl, further even, my secret fiancée, and when I looked at the mill I'd be lying if I said I didn't see a bright future for myself. Watch what you wish for, you might end up a bootlicker. Cousin Jonas was inside there somewhere, one known man among hundreds of anonymous immigrants. Shoulder to rib with what Uncle Matius laughingly called "proud humanity." Said: "The better man deserves more and the best man most." By his logic the worst man deserves nothing, but that's not what he'll get. The worst man sometimes takes it all. Matius holds up his meager prize, smiles for the photographer. The ripsaws screamed, their pitches rising, octaves crossing and then falling when they met the wood; it was a song, an anthem, a dirge. The endless corrugations of the log booms made it look like they'd planked over all but the shipping lanes. Loggers dream of sharp axes and barren fields, wake screaming with their iron fists clutching at amputated limbs.

Behold the Harbor: trouble and toothaches, a face of mirrors. Here she comes, and I'm going in with my fists up.

I found the McCandlisses in front of the post office. Ben had his foot on the base of the lamppost like he was stretching for a climb up the drainpipe. The oil lamp above stunk and flickered. But would you look at the gleam of Ben's buttons, the sharp fella. I stood beside them, as tall as Joseph but only seventeen to his twenty-one, and waited for them to say hello before I did.

"Another piece of joy," Ben said, snapped his kerchief off his shiny boot.

"Say hello then," Joseph said.

"Fuckin hello then, you filthy slints. Hello."

"Hello yourself, beanpole," Ben said.

I had aversions to these public displays, but Ben and Joseph had given up any hope of normality while mine remained, perhaps stupidly so, intact. Machiavellian is how it made me feel. "Let's hit the water," I said, "embrace the lull before the bustle."

"I'm workin," Ben said.

"At what?" his brother said.

"Preenin," I said.

Ben touched his nose with his index finger and gave me a wink.

"Should we hit the water?" Joseph said, like he'd thought of it.

"Sure. Greener pastures," I said.

"Shit green," Ben said.

"Slint preen," I countered.

"You both listen up." Ben did a quick jig and tugged at his collar. "From hell to the bulgy cock-lap of God himself—I'm revered as fuckin brilliant. Gleamin sweet. I make diamonds cloud and gold tarnish."

Joseph spit and hooked his brother with a finger in his armpit and hauled him along behind us, laughing as they went.

At the wharf we rested our backs against the railing with our legs out before us like we were ten feet tall and watched the shadows of men move down the boardwalk, dancing twigs, from the darkness into the light. The fleas came off the boards and coated our legs like flax seeds. Itching commenced. Cigarette smoking convened. Smoke bloomed to heaven, and heaven turned on the rain blaster. We kindly huddled.

"Have you kept up your studies?" Joseph asked.

"On occasion," I said. "But time gets in the way."

"Too fuckin much of it," Ben said.

I went to class more to see Teresa than for any learning or to please anyone else. Dr. Haslett kept on me about it, so I dawdled to bunch him.

"And your uncle?" Joseph asked.

"A barrier to all things."

"Ten dollars is a barrier that I'll cross tonight." Ben stuck his pinkie into the corner of his eye to dislodge a white glob of sleep and then blinked a few times to clear his vision. He had a permanent condition that left him weepy-eyed, baby deer blinking cute. Small predator, new and sharp teeth.

I searched out and caressed the locket that Teresa had given me, felt it through my shirt. She was with me in the form of smooth metal. Her tinker soul. Love like a hot bath. Who am I to resist? Will you marry me. Yes, I will. Yes. Had it really gone that way? I'm sure it had. Surely.

"What's his angle now?" Joseph asked, tugging at the stitching on his worn cuff.

"Who?"

"Uncle Matius." The elder McCandliss enjoyed hearing about the various schemes of my uncle. He received much of the attention that our split fathers avoided, the loathing as well as the ardor.

"Commandeering Boone's splashdam on account of recklessness."

"Reckless how?" Ben said.

"Public safety and all that. Apparently he killed Done-head Dunne's dog."

"That animal was deaf and crippled."

"I don't think he's arguing the state of the deceased," I said. "He's trying to build a committee to put himself in charge and send Boone to the back of the line."

"One drowning, and a man's called reckless," Ben said. "But if you crush, maim, and slaughter a couple every week in the woods, it's a tragic predicament. No answers, no explanation. Dangerous work, they say. Shame you can't avoid the losses."

"Payday is a soothing balm," Joseph said.

They'd picked up this rhetoric from Hank Bellhouse and liked to throw it back and forth to each other like a stick for a dog.

"I've heard trees are heavy because they're completely composed of wood," I said. "I'm talking pure through, made of lumber. Every inch of em." The weak and mocking laughter died out, and we were soon silent. Waves slipped over the mud and slapped into pilings. Salt and fish guts and lowish tide, brined slop, the boundary of terra firma and the beginning of the end of the world.

"Waiting," said Joseph.

Ben spit and admired his boots. "I pissed for five minutes straight this morning. Felt like I was back in time, like I'd turned into a little boy again, holding my prick like it was something I could pass back to someone when I was done with it. Like I could be swallowed into myself and come out my own whizzer and splatter on the ground."

"More likely that you'd dry up and be nothin save molderin socks and a pair of beautiful fuckin boots," his brother said.

I agreed. "Truly wondrous boots," I said.

"Sure, but just boots on any other le-whicky-whicky but me," Ben said, tongue at the side of his mouth, eyes full of trouble. "Teresa waved to us earlier. She was with Margaret and that other girl with the missing finger."

"Sarah Mulch."

"She waved and smiled," Joseph said.

"She's friendly."

"Not so much. Not to us. Not usually." Ben made the cunny tongue at me, and I worried we might end up slugging it out. "Duncan, it's this," he said flatly. "A woman's got yer balls. Her name is Teresa Boyerton, and she has every bit of you. Admit it."

I wanted to tell them that if the alternative was slinking the alleys with them, yes, it's true, but I didn't. I kept quiet and steadied myself for the next barrage.

"Are you not planning a wedding? We've heard rumors," Joseph said.

I searched their faces but found no clues. "Who told you that?"

"Gettin married, then what?" Ben said. "Babies? Christ, it'll rain frogs. Duncan spawn."

"News to me," I said.

"News to all of us," Joseph said, and patted me on the shoulder, like congrats.

"Well, fuck off about it."

"For now," Ben said.

I watched the crowd and worked on the problem, which was, as I saw it, that Teresa had been snitching on me. On us. But no, but it had to be her. On one hand it was good, because now I'd be onto what I was supposed to be onto, which was getting her father to sign off. He wouldn't, though. I knew it as completely as I'd ever known anything. She knew as well. Might explain the blabbery. Boyerton's daughter would not be pledged to the likes of me. Unless something changed. Unless I changed.

Or he did. But what was she doing, confiding a damn thing in these dirty bastards who were, if anything, my best friends in the whole world, but at the same slint fuck of a moment also ones who'd laid hands on her before? Ben could be making it up, slipping up with fake news to make me slip myself so as to tell them the truth, a truth that wasn't theirs to have. The truth was mine alone. I could've howled, my soul was so bent and confused. The hairs in my nose hurt. Love at its most essential is pain.

A skiff came bobbing in and ran aground beneath the wharf. We all stood and leaned over to see who was playing captain, but it was too dark to tell much except that he was alone.

"Who's there?" Joseph asked.

"The bringer," came the voice from below.

"And what do you bring?" I said.

"Worthless fuckin slint," Ben said. "Telfer," he woo-hooed the name like a little girl crying. "Telfer, the slint."

"Not worthless, Benjamin. I bring nothing worthless." The small man jerked the boat a little ways onto the bank and uncoiled the bowline to tie up, but it wasn't long enough to reach the piling, so he pitched it back into the boat and heaved the boat higher onto shore. "I've got instruments."

"Instruments?" I said. "You're talking sextants, fuckin slide rules and abacus."

"I robbed the band," Telfer replied.

"Evil slint," Ben said. "Evil sneaky fuckin slint."

"No piano?" Joseph said.

"Should I go back for it? I'll need help lifting."

"Get up here," Ben said.

"I should bring the haul up with me, right? So's we all don't get muddy, I can pass it to you from here."

"Leave it, you fuckin unbelievable ass. Can't sell the band's instruments," Ben said. "Can't. Fool. Idiot."

"Why not?" said the ferretous little man, huffing when he reached us.

"If they could play, don't you think they'd be in the band already?" Ben said.

"I didn't take them all."

"You might as well take them back," I said.

Telfer smacked himself in the forehead for the big idea he just had. "I could sell them back to them."

Ben grabbed the man by the collar and shook him. "I should send you over the rail."

Telfer pried himself free and stepped away. Below us, the oily water lapped hollowly at the square stern of the boat. "I did like you said."

"You did nothin like we said." Ben ground his fists into his own eyes, and they came away wet.

"Did you take Pelican's guitar?" I asked.

"I did."

"Take it back to him," Joseph said. "He'll fuckin die without it. He cradles it when he sleeps. He buys strings instead of food."

"God," Ben said.

"What were you thinkin?" I asked, having fun with him.

"I was thinkin I'd sell the stuff to someone else."

"But you didn't think who that would be?" Ben said.

"Leave the boat and all the rest. It'll be found and returned, I'm sure," Joseph said.

"They know it was me, though."

"Slint, fuckin dim slint," Ben said. "I hope they stomp you flat."

"What were you tellin me to do if it wasn't what I done?"

"Nothin. We didn't tell you nothin. Leave it," Joseph said.

"Oughta stomp him ourselves."

"Ben."

"I'll take em back."

"Leave em." Joseph walked away and we, the three of us, followed him. Shortly we entered the street, and the crowd filled in around us. Firelight in the eyes, brass buttons. Watch the knives on the belts and the rare bulge of a pistol. You could be killed, swimming in these dark waters. The opera house was letting out as we approached, so we eased and aimed and went breathlessly through the exiters like oil on ice. I touched a billfold but lost it in the spin. Snagged a cufflink and then a hatpin. Ben snatched two watches and gave one to me and the other to Joseph. Telfer got nothing. In the alley his little fingers popped loose a pipe from his hatband and filled it from an oily sack in his breast pocket, but as soon as he had it lit, Ben snatched it away and smoked it for him.

"I apologized, Benjamin. You can't stay mad at me. I'm not as quick as you fellers. You know I've got the mental problems. Deficits, the doc calls them, since my accident."

"Don't blame injury for your condition," Ben said.

"What else but an apology can I offer?"

"Cut off your head and give it to me."

"Benjamin, please."

"It'll be a good beginning."

"He's still with us, Ben," I said.

"I wasn't there when that was decided."

"You were," said his brother. "Sometimes you like the man, admit it."

"Fuck I will."

"C'mon, Benjamin," Telfer said. "I'll make it up to you."

"Not to me you won't."

"To the band, then. I'll lift a case of the finest stuff I can find, and I'll tie ribbons and bows to it and get on my knees and beg that they forgive me."

"You are a fuckin beggar, slint."

"I am. I'm a humble devotee to the brave musicians of the Harbor." He whistled a little tune and danced as if with a partner, a woman. He wasn't unlikable. "Benjamin, I mean it, I'm sorry. I didn't think."

"Don't make this out to be some little thing, like I'm razzin you."

"I'm not. I swear."

"Say amen."

"Amen."

"He fuckin swears it," Joseph said.

"You stay out of my way tonight, or you'll be floating facedown by morning." There was a pause because he was serious, Ben was deadly serious, and Telfer was scared.

"Like slintin gabby women," I said, and after a moment the tension finally broke and we laughed, even Ben.

Later, in the darkness of the alley, we waited, motionless against the wall. The piano music grew louder as we stayed quiet. The lights of the upstairs windows died high on the wall above us, and I felt small beneath them. Telfer climbed up the drainpipe and watched the windows for naked women, but we knew better; it was the lights of the hallway and nothing ever passed them but shadows. We'd spent enough time in the alley to know. Bellhouse told the McCandlisses that drunks are like wounded animals, they go downhill towards water, and their shame always washes them out the back door.

I didn't have to hit our first customer, but I did, and it sounded ringy, like dry wood hitting dry wood. Down he went. Pockets emptied. Telfer tried to take his shoes, but Ben punted him in the ass and sent him limping off back against the wall. Joseph and I hefted the limber mess and stashed him behind a pile of broken chairs and covered him with a tarp. If he woke up, we'd help him and reassure him that it hadn't been us that'd robbed him but some big hairy bearded fuckers instead. No one wanted to believe they'd been undone by what appeared to be a few boys—only Joseph was man-size—and a tiny half-wit; they just couldn't face it.

The second man fought back briefly, but he ended up on the ground with four sets of boots coming down. Breathing heavy, we dragged him over and stacked him on top of the first, covered him with the tarp. It quit raining for a minute or two and then it cracked and really started to pour. The wind came up. Telfer wanted to leave, so Joseph gave him three dollars and sent him packing. As soon as he left, four men came out at once and Joseph said, Ben, but Ben was already swinging. I joined in and Joseph too and it ended with a broken board beating on bloody heads and two got away but we cleaned out the others and that was enough for the night.

Joseph went and found Bellhouse and paid him his half. Ben bought a bottle from Teddy Ponto out of his wagon and tried to get me to join him, but I was all set, shaky. All done. Moving on to better things. The whistle sounded at the mill, announcing another shift change. Seventeen dollars apiece wasn't bad.

"We'll find you," Joseph said.

"Stay and have one with us at least."

"Next time."

"You've got girly brain." Ben laughed. "I wish you'd get whiskied and spill out the details. You can give us one, can't you?"

"Good night, Duncan."

"Joseph. Good night, Ben."

"Good night. Fuckin good fuckin night."

I left them standing bloody and bruised, the bottle going left and right, up and down, making the H, and walked stiffly up the hill. That was nearly a bad fight. Can't get beat, or Bellhouse will pull us and get new help. Big men, though, and not so drunk at all. I half wondered if maybe Bellhouse had sent them out to test us. It'd gone all right if he had. We'd mostly won. Ben finished it with that busted board, a wet, broken rafter tail, had a bird's mouth cut in it. I'd wrestled with Ben a few times before but never fought him and hoped I never had to. He was working on getting under my skin, but I wouldn't have it. Nope, peaceful man, sweet lover. Me and my salvation. Out of town, my legs carried me. Money in my pocket.

I slept through most of the morning and didn't stir. Matius was off on splashdam errands and Jonas was staying in the bunkhouse, so I had the place to myself. There were chores, but I wasn't doing them. Matius could chuck it, for all I cared. I got up for the relief but was too sore from the fight to be about yet, so I went back to sleep. I'd been waiting all week for this day, though, and by noon I was on the move.

I snuck by Zeb's place as was the usual course. I'd been banished from the Parkers', and for good reason. Big Edna was in the garden, but thankfully she didn't see me. I missed visiting with Edna and Lewis, saying hello. They took me in when Mother died, and for a time Zeb was my best friend and we thought of each other like brothers. But it ended with a busted ax handle stabbed into the rotten heart of a spruce stump, jacked up and down, and Zeb, laughing like his guts were falling out his ass, said: "It's how they reproduce."

On our way home from school we'd relieved a drunken Mox Chuck fisherman of his tackle and the remains of his bottle. We were sprung. Zeb's red hair was bracted to his skull, his hat was in the weeds where it'd fell off when he hurled up a swig. Up and down, with the ax handle, like he was pumping water. His eyes were outpaced by his bobbling head. I called him tree fucker, laughed, called him rapist. "She didn't ask for it. Or he. Is it a he, Zeb?"

Zeb's face froze, mouth open, wet salamander eyes. "Yer own daddy's a dang murderer, and you call me names? I don't care if it's a joke, you don't call me that. I ain't no lowdown bastard, no slinkin Ellstrom."

We'd only spoken of my father once before. Two Christmases back I'd spent the holiday with Jonas and Uncle Matius until Matius took the hide off my back with a twist of wire for leaving the chickens out and letting a fox zero his flock. Zeb found me walking the road afterward and stayed with me even when I tried to run him off because I was embarrassed by my tears. We walked way upriver through the snow, farther than either of us had ever been, and found a narrow canyon and climbed up, and from high on the cliffs we discovered a man below us panning for gold. We snuck easily by him and went another quarter mile upstream and rolled boulders from the canyon walls into the water. The water was muddied and we followed the flowing cloud downstream, and when it got to the gold panner he stopped and looked around, nervous like because he didn't know what had caused the disturbance. We never let him see us and walked home, the last stretch in the dark.

When we got to Matius's we stood in the road, shoulder to shoulder. There were lights burning, but I didn't want to go in. Zeb put his arm around me and told me I should come back and stay with him, where I belonged, but I was getting tired of all that. Didn't like the sweetness, tasted like lies, and I had to face Matius anyway, or he'd know he'd more than whipped me. He'd think he'd won.

"He don't matter," Zeb said that day. "Yer just you, and he's him. He ain't anybody."

"I know that."

"Well, I thought I should tell you anyhow. Yer yer own, and yer uncle is a son of a bitch."

He waited until I made it to the door, and then he owl-hooted and I hooted back. We were pals after all.

But it wasn't long before I forgot about his kindess. I started staying away from the Parker house sometimes, slept in the woods or in Matius's barn, even though he didn't like me around, and if Jonas wasn't there to stop him, he'd run me off. Edna Parker and Dr. Haslett both raised a fit when I went missing, but that faded the more me and Zeb bickered and brawled. I hated how he would clam up if I mentioned Teresa, and if I went to meet her he'd get a sour look on his face, like I'd put a hair in his food. And when I asked Teresa about him, she said she'd never said two words to him in her whole life. So he'd lied like the others, like I knew he had. There he was with parents while me and the McCandlisses got ours ripped. He was safe on the plain while we were wallowing in the bitumen. He had no right to fuss with me.

So I said to him that day: "My father is a killer, Zeb, and it bears to reason that I might be a killer too, if by nothing else but bloodline." I paused to let this settle in. "And if you keep talking like that, we might discover my birthright. I'll bash you and wait three days for you to die." It truly did hurt me more to say this than it did for him to hear it.

"But we're friends, aren't we?" Zeb said.

"I don't know about that."

"I didn't mean nothin."

"Didn't you?"

"I don't like being called names, is all. Yer not mad at me?"

"I am mad."

"Oh, but I didn't mean it. You know that. I was just talkin. I got carried away. I'm sorry, Duncan. I truly am."

We left it at that, but he carried the ax handle with him, wouldn't let it fall, and if I'd gone for him he'd have hit me. Brained me like a rabbit.

We wandered off to one of our fishing holes and used the stolen tackle to rig up a pole. I tied up the rig nice and handed it to Zeb and he thanked me, smiled, and I smiled back, like we were friends again. But when he turned, I lunged at him and buried a rusty fishhook under his jawbone below his ear and then ran him off the bank into the river. It's deep there, and Zeb was gone for a second and I thought I might've drowned him when I meant to hurt him but he bobbed to the surface with one hand clamped on his jaw while the rest of him kicked and swam. I didn't wait for him to make it up the bank. I felt sick for what I'd done. It was a No. 17 Mustad with a barb and would hurt like hell to get free. I'd felt it hit bone when I stuck him. After that I wasn't welcome at the Parkers' and stayed well clear, and following several skirmishes with Matius I moved in permanent with him and Jonas. Dr. Haslett tried a couple times to get me back with the Parkers, but I wouldn't have it, and if I had to guess, neither would they.

Later, Jonas told me that he'd heard Zeb couldn't get the hook out by himself and he'd walked all the way home and had his mother cut it out. He has a scar now. Makes me sad to think about it, but what's a scar without a story.

I kept to the high ground and avoided the river, even though the going would be easier. I liked the ridges and didn't want to bump into anyone at the water. I wanted to hurry, but I made myself go slow because I didn't want to be the first one there. The forest is a cathedral, and when you're alone there you're close to God. Time is a gull heart, trapped in a stupid bird, so it runs, knowing no other way.

At the edge of town the roadmen were cutting away the hillside. A boy brought them water and they stopped and drank. They beat their shovels against rocks and logs to get the mud free and went back to work. I watched them for a while and then walked on.

The rooftops were steaming in the afternoon sun. There'd been lightning earlier. I half remembered the sound of thunder dragging me from sleep. I watched the drawbridge open and a tug slip by. The sun glinted on the steel of the bridge.

Teresa was waiting in the church shed, like we'd planned. Her hair was up, and she had her coat pulled high to her chin because of the chill. She looked lovely with the color in her cheeks, her black eyebrows and hair, scar on her lip like a grasshopper's leg. She smiled, and her little teeth made me smile.

She touched my face. "You're all beat up again."

"Scratches."

I sat down next to her and kissed her cheek.

"You're sure that Reverend Macklin won't find us?"

"He's making his rounds all day. We won't be bothered." I hitched up my pant leg and set to unlacing my boots.

"If we won't be bothered, then we don't need to rush."

"Course not." I finished taking off my boots anyway and was embarrassed at the holes in my socks and the smell, so I stacked the left foot on the right to try and cover it.

"Father caught Oliver sneaking out of the house with one of his pistols, a big silver one he brought back from Wyoming."

"Where was he going?"

"He said out for some air, but Father wanted to know why he took the gun, not where he was off to. He said he needed protection. He'd been bullied. You wouldn't know anything about that, would you?"

"I haven't seen him in months."

"What about your friends?"

"They don't mess with him." I looked at her finger and thought of putting a ring on it.

"I think they do. I think that Ben McCandliss torments him."

"Nah."

"Yes, he does. He does it because of me."

I suddenly wanted my boots back on my feet. "Let's not talk about this."

"Fine."

I touched her hand, caressed a knuckle wrinkle. "I bet it'd be easier to aim with one eye. He's probably a hell of a shot."

She leaned against me and lifted my bruised hand into her lap. "I worry he's getting mean."

"Someone told me he has a girlfriend."

"That's what he told my father, but I don't believe him."

"I heard she's older."

"She'd have to be scheming, don't you think? Have some plan to get something from him by way of my father."

She rested her hand on my crotch, and I felt the absolute stirring of myself, living blood. Had she thought the same of me, that I was after her money?

"Maybe they're in love," I said.

"Don't be silly. It's Oliver. Even if someone was deranged enough to fall in love with him, he's incapable of love himself." Teresa liked talking about love and people's capacity for it. At first I thought she was naive, but as time went on I began to think she had a sensibility that maybe I lacked. I began to listen to her and to trust in her ideas of romance. Fully aware that I had fallen for her completely, splash, like an osprey going for a fish.

As she took off her boots, the last bit of liquid yellow sunlight spilled in the window and across her bare legs. I found the blankets I'd left on the shelf and carefully made a bed on the floor and Teresa slipped out of her underthings and beneath the blankets. The bed was cold. It wasn't what I wanted yet, and Teresa seemed disenchanted too, so I curled around her back and pressed my knees against her smooth cold thighs and kissed her neck.

"Tell me we're in love," she said.

There was only one answer, and I was relieved it wouldn't be a lie.

"Yes."

"Yes. Say it."

"We're in love."

She reached her hand back and pulled me against her. "Closer," she said. "I want you to crush me."

The sound of rain on the metal roof, wind against the windows, not a storm, just weather; it would pass. Slowly the light went out of the room, and in the gloaming the whole world was the shed and the sounds and flickers of light from outside were nothing to me. The truth was, we were together. The truth was, we were in love, and we held each other as tightly as we could so we wouldn't lose what we felt. It seeped into my blood and filled me like a sickness. Somewhere out there was the world and my father, and this love was against them, like one army standing against another.

Tartan

———

They **were to meet** the man from the Northern Pacific in his rooms at the Arctic Hotel. He'd rented the entire third floor for his delegation, mostly hired security, but simple handshakers too. It was only Bellhouse and Tartan that were going upstairs, but six other men were on the street out front.

Bellhouse stopped on the landing to double-check his revolver. "I got married here once." Behind him was a massive painting of a naked woman in a flaked gold frame. The woman in the painting was standing in a stream, with her hair over her breasts. Tartan had studied it before when he lived in the hotel. The woman had a familiar face; she looked like Nell Ellstrom.

"Hear me?"

"You got married here once."

"Divorced too, before I came down in the morning."

"I thought we were comin here to cut a deal for pennies on the ton. What's with the hogleg?"

"I'm not paying anyone for something I can take with a fight."

Tartan followed his boss up the final set of stairs and then stood back when he pounded on the frame of the door with his fist.

"Open up, Gendle. It's Hank Bellhouse."

The door behind them opened, and two men in gray suits came out.

"Is he here?" Bellhouse asked.

"He'll be ready in a moment," one of the men said, the taller of the two.

"What, is he fucking sleeping? It's fucking noon."

"I suggest you join us in our room until he has his coffee."

"We already had our coffee. And our naps."

Bellhouse tapped Tartan on the leg, and they were on them. It wasn't a quiet affair. The first man was sent sprawling down the stairs with a dent in his face from the butt of Bellhouse's pistol. The second screamed when Tartan stabbed him in the armpit and then brayed when the blade went in his neck. Two more doors opened down the hallway, and more men came out. Bellhouse kicked in the railroad man's door, and he was on the other side of it about to open it or making sure it was locked—in any case, the impact of the door sat him down with a split in his forehead. Tartan slid a dresser in front of the door for a battered woman's blockade.

"Morning." Bellhouse lifted Gendle to his feet and threw him on the bed. He hadn't finished dressing, and his pants were hanging off him. Shirtsleeves swam about his scrawny white arms.

"This is unacceptable," Gendle said.

"A bigger lie has never been uttered," Bellhouse said.

The door opened a few inches, even with Tartan bracing himself against the dresser. Bellhouse raised his revolver and whacked Gendle across the face with it.

"Move aside," he said to Tartan. He fired three shots through the door and smiled at the grunts and moans that followed.

"You're coming with us." He reloaded from the loose shells in his pants pocket.

"Why?" Gendle said.

"Need you to send a telegram."

"It's too late for that. We had an agreement. Nothing you can do now will change what you've done."

"We'll see. Move that fucking furniture and watch him."

Tartan did as he was told, and Bellhouse ripped open the door so hard that it hit the wall and bounced back and slammed shut behind him. The shooting started, and it didn't sound like it would stop.

"How many are up here?" Tartan asked.

"Seven. I don't know, eight. Some might be out, but they'll be back."

"Of course they will."

It went quiet for a second and Gendle rolled off the bed to get away, but Tartan dropped to a knee and stabbed him through the webbing of his left hand, pinned him to the floor. Down the hall he heard someone kick in another door, and then there were more shots. Gendle squirmed and whimpered.

"Please."

"Hush hush, pinhead." Tartan eased the blade out of the wound and wiped it on Gendle's shirt. He put the knife away and pulled his pistol and pointed it at the door. He could tell by the footsteps that it was Bellhouse, and he lowered it.

Hank came through the doorway with blood on his face and a hole in his arm. "Kindle me a fire. I'd like to warm my bones." Blood dripped from his hand onto Gendle's legs.

Tartan smashed the lantern in front of the door and struck a match. They threw Gendle off the balcony onto the roof below and then scaled down after him.

"Catch this son of a bitch," Bellhouse said to his men on the street. Smoke was already pouring out the windows above. Tartan tossed the railroad man down and the men below held out their arms, but not with any conviction, and Gendle slapped through them and slammed into the deck and was knocked dumb. Bellhouse jumped down and landed like he'd hopped off a mule cart instead of a second-story roof. Tartan wasn't about to jump, thinking, With my luck I'd break my leg, so he opened a window to an upstairs hallway and took the stairs. He lifted the painting off the wall on his way out. The crowd in the street knew enough to not stare too long.

"Someone ring the bell," Hank said. "We got a fire burning down the Arctic Hotel." He threw Gendle over his shoulder and strode off toward the telegraph office. No one moved.

"Get Chacartegui then, you fuckin idiots," Tartan said. "We can't have the whole town burnin up."

The bell started ringing and filled the streets with panic. And why wouldn't it work out? Tartan thought. At least for a little while. Why wouldn't this pay? The smoke looked brilliant as it blackened the sun. He strode off happily with the painting tilted hugely onto his back.

Duncan

———

I *woke alone in the* shed, with a milky yellow sun pouring in. I'd walked Teresa home some time after midnight and then came back to the shed to sleep, not wanting to walk all the way home or be there when Matius returned. The bells were ringing. There was a fire. I heard footsteps on the gravel path outside and sat up just as Macklin came through the door.

"Duncan?"

"Reverend."

He studied me for a moment and then gestured for me to stand up, to hurry. "And your boots. Get on your boots. You're coming with me." He passed me a shovel and emptied the tools from the wheelbarrow in the corner, and I held the door for him as he wheeled it outside.

At first I thought they'd been burning slash and that maybe it had spread and taken a house or an outbuilding because the smell was wrong for pure timber, but when we rounded the corner of the church I saw the Arctic Hotel engulfed in flames. One building among hundreds, one match burning inside of a box of matches. Macklin went bowlegged and elbow-wide down the road, the empty wheelbarrow banging and clanking, and I followed him with the shovel on my shoulder, knowing that there was nothing to be done about a fire that size until we were looking at rubble. People were out of their shops and houses, and they filled the streets. I abandoned the shovel to help Macklin load people's belongings from the nearest of the rooming houses into the wheelbarrow and haul them into the relative safety of the road.

By ember the fire jumped from the Arctic to Walker's saloon and then crossed the alley to the Olympus. The flames flapped raggedly in the wind and Macklin and I watched while the jail caught fire and the deputies let the prisoners out and put them in the bucket line. Chacartegui arrived in time to see the firehouse catch flame. He was interim fire chief, since Grosso had died in a well collapse. He couldn't find the key to unlock the pump, and his little gang of firemen in their blue coats and red hats were antsy to get to work. The law star on Chacartegui's chest shone uselessly. Ben and Joseph spotted me with the wheelbarrow—Macklin had disappeared, and they had me help them load Bernice Travois into the barrow, still in her rocking chair, and Joseph wheeled her into the street. The old woman had lost the ability to talk. Ribbons of drool slung off her chin. I still remembered her giving me the bread the day my mother died. When we set her down, I leaned in close and whispered into her ear, "I'm sorry that I was ever rude to you, Miss Travois." She smiled up at me and patted my hand. Ben pinched her ear and stuck out his tongue, and the old woman smiled at him too. Mean as a snake.

Joseph was yelling to come on. Chacartegui and the firemen wheeled the hand pumper to the end of Hume and sank it in the river. The sheriff caught us gawking and waved us over.

This was no longer about the Arctic Hotel and the Mack Building or even the whole of Hume Street; it could spread up the hill; it could burn the whole town.

"Look," Chacartegui said. The water tower was burning, going up like a rolled newspaper. He had tears in his eyes. Ben and I stepped forward and took our turn at the pump.

"You better not have had anything to do with this," Chacartegui said to me.

"With what?" Ben said.

"This fire. I've heard Bellhouse's name and Tartan's, which means you two were nearby."

"I was sleeping," I said.

"I'm deathly afraid of fire," Ben said.

"So pump, or I'll feed you little goujeers to the flames like pitch wood." The shield bearer strode off to who knows where. He was a good man, so they said, but a bit of a merganser.

The pump was gushing water all over our boots and pant legs.

"You think it'll stop? That it can be put out?"

"I think she's set to burn us all to cinders," Ben said. A look of mischief crossed his face. "We're combing the hair of a dead man."

Just then there was an explosion and the flames jumped Heron Street and the State Bank was burning. Two firemen came forward to spell us. We scanned the masses for Joseph but couldn't find him. Ben called his name a few times and whistled, but the roar of the crowd and the wind building inside the flames drowned him out, just a wild place to be, and the heat was enough, even where we were standing, two hundred feet away, to warm the buttons on my shirt to the point they felt like they'd burn me. We went to watch the bank burn.

"You think the money's still in there?" Ben said.

"Where else would it be?"

"If it's locked in the vault, it'd be like an oven, wouldn't it? They won't pull any hard currency outa there, just dust."

"Coins'd melt."

"Can you believe this, Duncan? Look at it."

The fire kept going north up G Street and the north side of the river, sending up neat curtains of smoke hemmed with flame. They'd raised the bridge, and ships were lined up like ducklings to leave. Ben and I made our way through the crowd and the mess of furniture and precious items vomited from the now-burning buildings and watched a few of Chacartegui's men dynamite John Young's place so the fire wouldn't make it to the hospital. I don't think anyone was thinking it would work, but it did. It was like nothing I'd ever seen. Ash rained down, and if you stopped to notice and peer through the waves of rolling smoke and tumult, it was sunny out there behind the chaos. A perfect sunny day. If only it would rain.

Joseph found us, and him and Ben started grabbing what they could carry from the piles of belongings in the street. I took a pistol in a holster from a table, but Macklin saw me and pointed, so I put it back. Joseph was wearing four coats and two hats. If we were older or even a bit slower, I believe we would've been shot.

The opera house was on fire, and Ed Hulbert's. Men were drinking bottles of beer and some of the whores had a tit hanging out and looked swagged on something harder than lager. We stopped and watched Central School burn for a while. We'd all gone there at one time or another. Doc Haslett used to walk me to the door and wait for me after so I wouldn't skip, but I'd go out the window first chance I got. The fat doctor couldn't stand cleverness, so that's all I gave him. Double helpings.

We trudged up the hill. The big houses looked unburnable, but the pitchy gems caught the light, dripping from the siding and fascia, a thousand wicks.

Charlie Boyerton and Oliver were in their yard with a dozen others, filling buckets from the yard pump and hauling them up a ladder to wet the roof. Mrs. Boyerton and Teresa were nowhere to be seen.

Oliver spotted me and waved, so I passed through the gate and shook his hand and asked if I could help. Joseph and Ben hadn't followed me and were already gone. Oliver's eye patch had a long brown hair stuck to it. We hadn't spoken for some time, and I'd grown half a foot taller than him. Mr. Boyerton was watching me. He knew who I was from Oliver, and I suspected he might know who I was from Teresa as well. We were different species, and the way he looked at me I felt I was still dwelling in the mud, burping at the moon, while he was strolling the esplanade. Such is the oppression of the young Occidental.

With shame flickering in my heart I joined the bucket brigade to soak the roof shingles and found my place halfway up the ladder. Through the tall windows on the second floor I could see the portraits on the stairway wall. Grandfathers and great-uncles, uncles and cousins, no necked hatchet-asses in black suits with canes and hats and watch chains, posing, all of them dead in the War and otherwise. Teresa told me that Oliver was the end of the line and judging by the paintings that seemed about right.

The wind changed and the smoke rolled over us, and I had to tie my kerchief over my face to keep from choking. The rivers wouldn't save us, and neither would the sea.

Dr. Haslett told me once about the Great Chicago Fire of 1871. He wasn't there, but he'd read all the reports. Black bricks and burned dogs, ash, all that was left. No place to sleep or even rest. He said in the end the city benefited from it, like every now and again a body benefits from a fever or a good sweat.

Teresa passed in front of the window. She was dressed to go outside and carrying a small purple suitcase. Miss Dalgleish, the housekeeper, was with her, carrying two more. I yelled to her, and to my surprise she turned and saw me and after a worried moment she finally smiled and pressed her palm to the window. Miss Dalgleish hauled her away down the stairs toward the back of the house. When I looked down to catch the next bucket, Mr. Boyerton was looking up at me, short, squat, and from my angle all of two feet tall. It was a low, dirty feeling that passed over me, because I wanted the man to like me. I needed him to, or my life would turn away from where I planned it. Away from Teresa. Oliver was watching his father. The buckets kept coming, and the water sloshed all over and soaked my clothes. The uniformed brigade, led by Chacartegui arrived, and we all climbed down from the roof and ladders and helped them drag their big pump to the cistern in the back of the house and unroll the two hundred feet of moldering hose they'd brought with them. The sheriff put two men on the pump and they got to work and sprayed down the porch and the bushes on both sides of the street. They looked ready to face whatever came up the hill after them.

I stood with Oliver in the yard and watched what was left of the town below be swallowed by smoke. We couldn't do anything but wait. Boyerton had left to check on his mill. I wished I had talked to him before he'd left, but Oliver would have to do.

"Where is she now?" I asked.

"Father put her and Mother on a boat."

"Why aren't you with them?"

"I need to stay and make sure the house is safe."

"I heard you got a girlfriend."

Oliver blushed and looked away.

"Who is it?"

"I'm not at liberty to tell."

"She pretty?"

"You could say that."

"Does your father know?"

"It's not his concern."

"Does he know about me and Teresa?"

"No."

"But you do."

"I've known for a long time."

"You wouldn't say anything, would you?"

"It's not my business."

"I'll do right by her. I swear it."

"I plan to do the same by my Mabel." He was squirming with his unique version of glee, and he would tell me who it was if I asked, Mabel who? But I didn't. I didn't care, not that much. I'd find out anyway eventually.

It was that the town was burning, the Harbor was burning, and that I could've chosen a better time to square with Oliver. His father would hear about me and Teresa soon enough, if he hadn't already. It didn't matter. The smoke was rolling out over the water now, like a storm, yellow and gray and black. This was a catastrophe. Hundreds would be homeless to-morrow. We'll never be the same after this, said somebody nearby. I'd thought of Teresa as a fire once, a burning house. It seemed a long time ago when I was scared of her. I couldn't imagine feeling that way now. Ships were all adrift and moving out, an armada in retreat. The Harbor was burning, and when I looked at Oliver, he was smiling, trying to hold it in, but his one eye was clearly shining with what had to be joy.

Jacob and the Hermit Kozmin

'd cobbled together a shanty. Water dripped from the waterlogged shingles like honey from thin-sliced black bread. The land was unclaimed. Wind blew through one wall and slapped loose paper to the other. I didn't poach or rage or trespass and was therefore left alone. The door was open, and the rain dribbled down on the roof and the two sailcloth tarps covering my woodpile. There was an oilcan under the eave, near the wall, and every minute or so a big wet drop would go *plekink* against its side. I counted it as my clock, and time went faster in relation to the storm, which was acceptable, although contrary to my experience. For the drop to form, a capillary draw was required. This of course was aided by the leaks in the roof, which relied on gravity alone, but there under the eaves, the rising and the falling drips met and formed a drop. I thought of this as being symbiotic, as it should be, not as failure, as it was.

Someone was coming out of the forest. I closed the book I had open on my lap and nodded a greeting to the shadowy figure, said: "Evening, Cossack."

"Greetings, Dr. Ellstrom."

Kozmin, covered in clay mud, had three dog salmon strung on a piece of rawhide and looped around his belt. He untied them one-handed and stretched an arm and threw them onto the woodpile, and then removed his hat and showed his wild gray hair, ducked his head and came inside. My furniture was a couple of row seats that I'd hauled off from the burned theater on Heron Street and a table I'd made from a stump and a slab. Kozmin picked up the closed book, sat down, stretched his legs before him, and farted.

"A man who never farts loudly will never live well," he said.

"Then you live well, Kozmin, often."

"I do. You look as awful as ever, Doctor."

"I don't keep a mirror."

"I have a question."

"Ask it."

"Why don't you cut off that filthy sack of shit hangin from your chin?"

"My beard?"

"Filthy sack of dirty shit hangin from your chin. I can smell it from here. Jesus."

"Who created all the heavens and earth."

"So they say. So they say." Kozmin produced a kerchief and rattled and shook the pluggage from his nose. "The city burned."

"I was there."

"I didn't see you. Were you haulin water or lootin?" His eyes darted over the features of my face.

"Neither."

"How's a city to burn if you go and do somethin to stop it?"

"I wouldn't know."

"Fuckin tragedy. Nice of you to stand by."

"We do what we can."

"Little succor that."

"You can little succor this." I grabbed at myself, and the old hermit smiled toothlessly.

"Bellhouse did it, you know. Set off the Arctic to hide his murdering. He's apparently the proud owner of three miles of Northern Pacific track." Kozmin tapped the side of his nose with his index finger.

"That won't last long."

"I wouldn't guess it would take long to squeeze a lifetime's worth of wages out of those rails."

"No, a solid month would do."

The oilcan dinged, and we both looked at it. Kozmin studied the source of the drip, waited for another, then spoke.

"What of the War?"

"Which is that?"

"It's been two years since I seen you last. Your friend Perlovsky told me you up and joined the Oregon Volunteers."

"You saw Perlovsky, when?" The two of us had been sawyers together in the redwoods, but he'd disappeared one day. I pulled on the saw and he didn't pull back, ten feet of tree between us. When he didn't answer to his name I hopped off my springboard and circled, but he was gone. Never returned to the camp.

"In the spring. He was in Willapa Bay with the oystermen."

"I thought he was dead."

"He thought the same might've become of you."

"I unjoined my regiment not long after joining it."

"They let you do that?"

"They do if you volunteer."

"Did you make the trip across the ocean?"

"No, I quit while we were garrisoned in San Francisco. They hadn't even given us rifles yet, or pay."

"They say it wasn't much of a fight. The paper said that."

"Tell that to the Spaniards swimming in the wreckage."

"Someone had to lose," Kozmin said.

"Funny you saying that to me."

"Not that funny."

"I know. I know it's not."

He opened the book and thumbed a few pages. "I saw your boy the other day."

My heart like a fat toad leaped into my throat. "How's he keeping?"

"Honestly, I think he's destined for trouble."

"Is he living with the Parkers?"

He gave me a hard look. "Ain't been stayin there for years. They kicked him out. He's with yer brother as far as I know, gettin pummeled if'n he gets caught."

"If he's breathing, I'd say he's doing fine. He'd like to kill me, you know."

"Maybe it's time you tested his mettle."

"I'd appreciate it if you didn't bring him up again."

"You'd appreciate it? Well, that's nice, isn't it?"

"A courtesy for being in my house."

The hermit laughed like only a mad hermit would. "I know who I am, Jacob. I'm a man that gets drunk and pisses himself a few times a week. I'm not welcome most places. The whores won't even have me. Not interested. Keep your money, they say. You need it more than me."

"Your point is?"

"You're givin us hermit types a bad name. With that goddamned beard and the rest. You've turned into a rotten swamp goat, is what it is. What I see at least. You've gone garbanzo, friend."

"They still want to hang me for what I did."

"Nobody cares no more."

"I do. Duncan does."

"You know what he said to me when I told him to stay clear of Bellhouse and those McCandlisses? Said that old men and wisdom are like two parallel lines. He held up his fingers at me, like so, to show me that they would never meet, never touch."

"He's not stupid."

"No, he's smart enough."

"What's your plan for that mess on my woodpile?"

"You don't like fish?"

"When did I say that?"

He tapped the cover of my book with a mossy knuckle. "Homer would've liked you."

"I'm just killing time."

"Quality work you're doin of it, too, journeyman."

We sat like spectators and stared out the hole in the wall that served as a door, two chicks in a partially hatched egg; a ritual of nothing, an absence of ritual that was built to dispel the previous absence. Ass to the wind.

Eventually Kozmin cut one of his salmon into steaks and pan-fried them over the firepit.

After we'd eaten, the hermit picked at his teeth with a fishbone like a miniature scimitar. "Myth intervenes in all the stories we tell, especially those we tell of ourselves. Speaking on a grand scale."

"Like you'd know another way. Christ."

"Who created all the heavens and earth."

"Amen, Cossack."

"Scavengers are found out in time and pinched for their lowness. Hunters turn to farming for stability."

"Aren't you a prescient mummer."

"God speaks through me." He smiled and leveled the fishbone at me in a not unthreatening manner.

"Your ass."

"What isn't a concern to my bowels? Alvine is my middle name."

"I see you as more spry than wise."

"Eh?"

"I said spry."

"Sure, demon spry, cat spry. I leap anthills just like they were"—he paused for effect—"anthills."

"Your athleticism matches your ample gift for bullshit."

"It does. Of course it does. That said: Do you have time for a tale this evening?"

"If it's worth a damn."

"Oh, it's worthy. It's even true."

"Where'd you hear it?"

"On the mountain."

"Alley betwixt four whorehouses."

"Who gives a damn where I heard it? It's a good story, and long."

"Better be. I'm not a bit tired. Get to it."

"In the long, long ago—"

"If you start it like that, it already sounds like bullshit."

"No bullshit. That's how it starts. It's the beginning."

"Then begin."

"The hero's name is Tarakanov. He was on the *Konstantin* when the Russians made their fort at Katlianski Bay, and while his comrades were busy taking wives and counting their profits, he'd been watchful. The Kiksàdi were angry and on the move. It was the middle of summer, when the sun was restless and there were voices in the gloom of the forest like seals barking and ravens. An attack was coming, any fool could see it, but his comrades drank too much to notice and relied on the sheer numbers of the hired Aleut hunters to protect them, but none of them held any true allegiance to Baranov. Wages in the end are only wages. The battle would be fast and bloody."

I waited for him to go on, but apparently that was all he had to say. He chipped at the now dried mud on his pants and sleeves and then gathered up his pack to go.

"You said the story was long."

"It is. Not tonight, though. I've lost the spirit."

"I guess I should thank you for the fish."

"Guess you should."

The old hermit stood and shouldered his pack and was gone, lost in the seeping closure of night. I listened to his footsteps disappear and then rose from my chair and put another hunk of wood on the fire. I hadn't spoken so many words to a person in years.

Duncan

Looking down from the hill it was a scene of a battle won, sacrosanct yet festive. Those that'd been burned out and hadn't been taken in by church or neighbor were living in tents—delivered to us by the Populist governor himself—along the waterfront and among the unclaimed lots of town proper. The moth-white glow of the canvas checkered the night, and cookfires flickered among the few remaining streetlights. Ships were moored at the wharf and along the docks too, but they looked lost, like they'd misread their charts and arrived in the wrong port.

Along with the steam and smoke, sweet sawdust hung in the air above Boyerton's mill. They'd been running nonstop since the fire. Behind the fence, men walked in and out of the mill lights, carrying scaffoldage and timbers, bracing for the inevitable expansion, ever outward, as if setting bulwarks against the nonmillers. Join us or move. The tent people didn't know it yet, but they'd been relegated to serfage. Someone in the mill yard called out in Swedish and another in German. I could tell the difference, but I couldn't tell you how.

Beyond the mill, the streets swarmed with drunken sailors and loggers home from the camps, along with the usual off-shift mill workers. A hundred cookfires spiced the air. Small children smeared in ash darted among the ruins, eyes flashing and moon-white teeth like cracked night.

I passed the last tavern (half tent, half burned hole in the wall), on the block and a woman's cackling laugh rose high above the jabber. Then I was into the rows of burned foundations and rubble piles and standing charred frames of houses too. No tents here; the owners still held claim. I'd heard guards had been hired to keep the squatters at bay. Happens quickly, I thought, tenant to vagrant, citizen to nuisance.

From one lot to the next, the burn ended and the noise fell off. There was a real barrier here, separate as an eyeball from the socket. The houses grew in size and ornamentation and spread out as I went bent-backed, laboriously up the hill toward the Boyertons'. I felt the part of an interloper, a dog of the lowest breed.

I pitched pebbles at Teresa's window until she appeared. The light of her father's study was on, but the curtains were pulled. She came from the side of the house, from the kitchen entrance, and met me on the street.

Standing there, I saw the curtains move, and a hand I took to be her father's. I pushed Teresa away from the light into the shadows. This was an old routine but still gave me a thrill. There are no mistakes, or there are only mistakes, all half measures are imagined.

As we went along, she whispered into my neck a story of how at dinner that night her mother had thrown a coffee cup and hit her father in the face. She laughed, but it wasn't joyous; it was a frantic sound guiding in her imminent tears.

"He's terribly angry," she said. "He didn't deserve to get hurt, I guess. He was bleeding."

"He should send her off to the madhouse, let them shave her head and dress her in grain sacks."

She stopped and held me by the arm.

"I wasn't serious."

"Yes, you were. All of you are so awful and callous. I can't stand it."

I took her hand and leaned over to kiss her cheek, but she leaned away from me, away, like she was a block plane and I the wood and the blade wasn't set or it was dull and she just slid over me without the satisfying peel. I needed her to take something, to lock in. I was hers.

We went quietly through the darkened streets under a cloud-sneaking half-moon and looked in on the lit windows of the houses. Nebulated scenes through warped glass. The dark sections of the burn below were like clouds too, stilled shadows.

At the waterfront we skirted the tent city and huddled under a leaky bait shed and looked out over the slapped sheen of the water. Small waves sucked at the mud shore, and rigging clanged on the distant masts of the schooners.

"My father asked about you."

"Why?"

"It was the fire, that you were at our house. He knows who you are from Oliver. From your father, what he did to your mother."

"What'd you say?"

"I told him we didn't know each other, that we'd met at school, but he didn't believe me."

"I helped save your house."

"I know, but someone from the mill, a friend of his, was robbed, and Oliver said it was probably you and the McCandlisses that did it. He said it offhand, but it didn't matter."

"Why'd you lie?"

She hesitated, too long, said: "I couldn't imagine telling the truth."

I turned and studied the fine lines, almost like wood grain, at the corner of her eyes. There was something more to this than indignation; she had a plan; she was justifying herself. I could tell by the set of her jaw. Here she was getting a run to leap into cold water. We'd been to this place before. This was betrayal, this was a wind I knew. I wasn't with her every night. She could keep secrets. I wanted to believe that she'd only been with me, that she loved me. She said she did. I'd said the words too, but who knew what that meant. No, I did know. I felt it all the way into my guts, like my ribs had been dipped in copper. I needed her. An ache started in my balls and went in waves into my rectum and pulsed dully up my spine. In my mind I saw a gutted deer.

Then, like I'd willed it, she said it: "I can't see you anymore." Her voice brimmed with emotion. "I wish I could die."

I ignored the latter, what she said—*I wish I could die*—the tail of a horse, stagy bits. All I saw was teeth, white eyes, and hooves: *I can't see you anymore.*

"I don't want to live like this, only at night, on the ground. The other girls, girls my age, my friends, they aren't sneaking out at night or fooling with the Harbor boys. They're planning on getting married to someone nice and raising a family."

Harbor boys, as if I were one of many. No one else was me. To convince yourself of this was to survive. I wasn't falling at her feet, if she thought that was what'd happen.

"I need my father." She paused and nipped at her lower lip. "Lack of commitment doesn't mean freedom, Duncan, and you know, just because you don't have anything to do doesn't mean you shouldn't do something."

"I bet your father sounded pretty fuckin smart when he said that."

She smirked at me and lowered her eyes. "Don't be a dunderhead, it only strengthens the argument."

"Your father can say whatever he wants, but he doesn't know the first thing about me."

"But what do you do? When will you do something?"

"I can get a job anytime I want it. I come by money easy enough."

"By robbing old men?"

"If they could control themselves, they wouldn't get into trouble."

"You're horrible. I can't trust you. At first that was fine."

"At first? What do you mean?"

"We had fun sometimes."

"That's all this was?"

"Of course not."

"You think I've been with someone else?"

"That's not what I'm worried about."

"It's what you said. You can't trust me."

"I'm thinking of what would happen next, is all."

"Why can't you trust me? What have I done? Name one thing."

"Why do you want to marry me?"

"Because I love you." It sounded untrue even to me, and I believed it.

"Don't say that if you don't mean it."

"I'm not."

"You know you're lying. I can see it in your face, it's in your voice. You're standing here lying about—do you even know? Do you even care what you're lying about?"

"I said I'm not."

"Where does that leave me?"

We were on the ice now, above our true intentions, sliding, stumbling into each other, stumbling on. I took a hold of her wrist and squeezed. She tried to pull away, but I tightened my grip.

"You're hurting me."

"Tell me everything they said about me. What did your father say? Your slinty one-eyed brother."

She dug her nails into my thumb, and I could feel them break the skin. She was almost free and I twisted her arm harder and she gasped and began to cry. I let her go, and she clutched her arm against her stomach.

"Did I hurt you?"

"Yes."

"I'm sorry."

"You aren't. You're not sorry at all. You don't care."

"Maybe not."

"You—"

"What did he say?"

Her eyes darkened, and what I saw in them was fierce and angry, a look I'd never seen cross her face. "He said he'd worked too hard to have me marry trash."

"You're all fuckin deranged."

"No, I'm not. I'm not." She was crying.

"You want bad treatment, and it's because I won't give it to you that you're doing this. It's because I won't treat you badly enough, not that your father disapproves of me."

"I don't want to be treated badly."

"You've been screwy all along."

"I still love you, Duncan. God help me."

"But that's the beginning and the end of it, isn't it? We started there, and here we've ended. Look at the water and the lights. This is it. Fuck all and done."

"I'm sorry."

"Not half as sorry as me." Then I was dragging her along by the back of her coat. The fabric was stretched and ripping at the shoulders. Her feet barely touched the ground.

I undid the hasp on the church shed and pushed her inside and slammed the door shut behind us. We stood and faced each other in the dark for a moment, breathing. I stared at the lumpy shadow of her and then produced a match from the pouch in my hat and lit the candle on the windowsill. The light reflected in the dusty blackened glass, and it appeared that I was looking into another room. She'd stopped crying. Which one wakes from the dream first, and which one is left in the dark?

"I can't see you again. I'm sorry," she said softly. "This will be the last time we're together." All I could see in her gray eyes was her father.

"You said you loved me." The pain of the memory made the breath go out of my lungs in a moan. I pushed her into a pew with a cracked back and dropped my hat on the seat beside her.

"I think it was for the money," she said. "You didn't want to marry me. You certainly don't want to spend your whole life with me. You don't even know what that means, your whole life. You go from one thing to another and imagine that no one notices, but they do. People see you for what you are. Everyone knows what you're doing but you."

"They see you too. When all you do is complain about your friends, your family. You make fun of them and talk about them behind their backs. You might as well hate them. They probably hate you anyway. Your father's making you do this just to make you feel pain. I think that's the reason for him, because he likes to hurt the ones he loves. The reason for you is much simpler. You just like to be hurt."

"Maybe I should hate you."

"You're heartless in the way you can just switch directions."

"And you're not as special as you might think. You really aren't anybody. You aren't smart. You don't matter at all."

"I'm lookin right in your eyes, and I don't understand why you're doing this to me."

"You wanted to marry my family, my father's money, not me."

I wanted to smack her one. I wanted to choke her, but I stayed where I was, rocked back on my heels.

"You told the McCandlisses we were getting married."

"I did no such thing."

"Someone did."

"It wasn't me."

"Don't lie."

"I've always told you the truth, even tonight when I didn't want to and it would've been easier to lie. You tried to force me into lying, but I didn't. I'm not lying now. I'm leaving." She went to stand, and I pushed her back down and stood over her with my arm raised to hit her. "Duncan, no."

I lowered my hand and leaned in to her until our faces were only inches apart and we were breathing each other's hot breath. I held her head, my thumbs just touching her eyebrows.

"We'll be together this last time."

"Is that what you want?" She had her fingers inside my shirt, clutching the locket.

"If that's all I get, that's all I want." I knelt down and rested my head on her lap. "This can't be the last time." I moved my hands up from her ankles to her thighs.

"It is." Then, without speaking another word, she helped me undress her bit by bit, piece by piece.

I had her on a pile of old church curtains and held her there by her shoulders and pushed into her roughly. She moaned, and it was a different sound than she'd ever made before, and when I was ready I held her by the back of the neck and released inside her, and in my mind I saw her face looking back at me, then only emptiness, darkness. When I pulled out, she reached down and with her fingers scooped out the mess I'd left inside and wiped it on the curtains.

I picked up her dress from the pew and passed it over. Her eyes were scared, her breathing uneven; I imagined her delicate bellows, tattered. I looked down at my cock, the drying sheen, the pathetic skin, then shoved it back into my pants like something I'd stolen. She held the dress against her body. When she stood, I saw that dirt and small rocks were pressed into the flesh of her legs. Her arm, just above the wrist, was darkening and swollen. She trembled as she straightened her clothes and put her hair up. I wouldn't look at her face but waited patiently for her to finish, not caring how long she took. There was no hurry; it was done. I couldn't and wouldn't take anything back.

We left the shed, and not knowing what else to do, I walked with her back to her house.

At her gate she stopped. "I'd have never hurt you like that."

"You're all I have." I looked at her, the house behind her full of light.

"I don't want you to leave," she said.

"I guess I'll be around." I left her standing there because if I said anything else I didn't know what I'd do, cry or what.

I walked among the tents, all but a few of them dark and quiet. Dogs roamed in packs but paid me no mind. I decided that there were several kinds of sadness and disaster, and like timber it had grades. Death and fire, heartbreak; I didn't know how they stacked up to one another, or if it even mattered—it wasn't a contest. All I did know was that in their wake all that remained was the funereal candle and canvas glow, linked and common in my mind always as the color of change, the hue of hard starts.

I spent the night curled into the heat of the spare boiler at the shingle mill. In the morning I trudged home and Uncle Matius was there.

"You, devil boy," he said when he saw me, and swung his ax down, snap, and the blade went easily through the limb and sliced into the mud.

"What's this?" I asked. He'd usually hire his labor out if he couldn't pin it on me.

"Contracted with Michelson for posts."

"Sounds desperate. What about yer splashdam?"

"Foundered against legalities. I've not enough friends."

The ground was torn and trampled, and finished posts spilled over the wagon edge. The one man Disston rested on the cradle. The horse, Samson, looked on.

"You've no friends at all," I said.

My uncle leaned on his ax and studied me. "I'm starting to think I'd prefer you to stay away, a permanent situation." He was breathing from the work, and his suspenders had crowded his shirt collar up to his ears.

"Where'd this come from?" I asked.

"Been here waiting for you."

"Do I get a reason?"

"Ms. Eunice and I might shack up."

"Who the fuck is Ms. Eunice?"

"My lady friend by way of Olympia."

"Since when?"

"The Indian princess appeared." He pointed proudly to the road, then with his hands made the shape and size of a piece of bread, held it there in front of his crotch, the ax leaning against his thigh. "She made me a gift of these dried-out salal berry cakes. They aren't dessert-like at all, but you eat enough and they put a serious bull in you. You understand what I'm getting at?"

It felt like I should congratulate him, but it struck me as being a bit slint. "Fine, you want me to leave, I'll go."

"She feeds me salmonberry sprouts postcoitus."

"I said I'd go."

"Good, because there's another thing."

"What?"

"Charlie Boyerton sent a few dipshits out here looking for you."

"They say what about?"

"No, didn't say anything about the why. I told them you'd be in town somewhere. Check with those fucking McCandlisses, I said. You've got yourself into some trouble. What'd you do?"

"Maybe I had too many salal berries."

"Scrawny, low-down fucking prick. I hope they do find you. I really do. You're as worthless as your father." And he swung the ax again without taking his eyes off me and it glanced off the log and he buried the blade in his boot. "Oh, oh my," he said, and fell to the ground with his arms out and made a *cuh cuh* sound that repeated and repeated and after twenty times or so transformed into *God God*. The blood came fast around the blade, and when he pulled it out, it came faster. I was unable to move for a moment, but then I perked up and helped him wrap his coat around his boot. All that blood turned my stomach, made me spit and spit again. It looked like he'd split his big toe from the rest nearly to the ankle joint.

"Help me inside."

At the table I cut his boot free with a rusty set of pinking shears and spread the gash and didn't like that at all, either of us. A womanly wound spotted with bone and a velvet core. I fetched water from the pump and poured it over his foot to clean it and then bound it with an old sheet. There was blood everywhere, looked like we'd killed something of size. My uncle's face was the color of pus.

"I'll get the doc."

"I don't want him." The blood on the floor was dark and red and even foamed a little where it had pooled.

"Yer foot fuckin does."

"Get me some more water."

Matius drank, hands shaking, water down his front.

"That ain't gonna heal on its own," I told him. "It's too deep. There's bones and tendons cut too."

"Get out. Leave me be."

"You don't want nothin? Do you want me to stay?" I wanted to help him. As bad as he'd been to me, it didn't matter. What's family but a reason to do right by somebody?

"Leave me alone."

"I'll tell Jonas what you did, and he'll come out here and drag you to town by your ear. You want that?"

"Better than having to look at you."

"Fine, if you want to take the dogwatch as chief invalid, I'll let you have it." I went to my room and packed my father's old bindle with a few things. "I'll leave the cave bear to his fuckin cave," I yelled.

I went through the living room and out the door without looking at him. When I was walking away Matius called after me, of course, changing his mind. "Duncan, you can't leave me out here. Hey. You can't leave me."

I kept walking, feeling more free and more evil with every step. It came down to the fact that for once in this goddamn life I'd wanted him to be nice to me.

Duncan: A Few Days Gone

I studied my hands folded across my chest, pale and pitchy, a thumb-nail bruise like blood dripped on ice, hard candy. I've got bad hands, the devil's hands. I touched the tips of my index fingers to the tips of my thumbs and made two eyes to look back at myself with. Three days since I'd seen Teresa, two since I'd seen Matius. He might be dead by now. The day before yesterday he didn't even see me when I came in and spied on him. Bleary, drooly, avuncular pile. Where's your Miss Eunice now? I wondered if maybe he made her up, knowing that I might argue with being run off by Boyerton but not by being disgusted enough with him breaking the bed to go and leave of my own free will. But he'd told me one and then told me the other. Always one for overkill—he used to get carried away whipping me with his belt, and to get higher or more slint he'd pick up a stick or ax handle or tangle of wire, whatever was in reach, and carry on with that till he was wasted and blown, or he'd just beat me with his fists and then I'd be the first out, and I'd wake up not knowing where I was or what happened. He contained a fanatical anger and apparently he'd beaten it into me, and now it was showing a clean pair of heels.

I'd told Jonas about Matius just like I said I would, waited in the shadow of the bunkhouse for him to arrive, said: "Go and fetch yer father. He's a red mess and won't listen to reason."

"You doin here?" I couldn't answer him then but I could now. *I can't even think her name. Nowhere to go. Jonas, I need help.* But I ran off without saying anything and left him standing.

Through the forest I could hear my home river, the Wynooche, part of a great and final alluvium washing into the Pacific. Once, not long ago, this was land claimed by the fathers of Miss Eunice's grandfathers, and then it slutted around with everyone with a fur hat, rose to a territory, got hacked, settled abreast the river of slaves. The same thing happens in mud puddles, the little rivers pushing dirty water like the heart pushes blood. I once held a still-beating salmon heart in my mouth until it stopped and then I chewed it up and swallowed it. The small things never hid from me for long. They build to make the world. My blood; it's a river too. My soul is that of a slave. My heart beats in the mouth of my chest. Show me a rain cloud and I'll show you my breath.

Beneath the sky, the only one I'd ever known, I was open to the possibility that I was a dream of dirt and everything else was vapor. No family, no trees, no thimbles or aprons or axes, nothing. I invented breathing at dawn and finished the day with a fart.

There once was a cat known for crapping
in the mouths of young lads caught napping.
I wasn't awake and I apparently partaked
and the cat he walked off laughing.

The treetops above cradled the gray, touched it and sucked from it like a wick drawing oil. The wind pushed through the upper branches in gusts, and dead and green needles alike rained down upon me. I was under the spell of the ebb, suctioned to whatever tidewater interlude was occurring beneath my provisional bed. I turned on my side, and I could hear water running, rivulets; a disgusting word.

I let my eyes close and saw it in my mind. Age eight. I'd found the steelhead frozen in the creek ice behind the house. I squatted down above the fish, and the banks of the creek offered shelter. I'd rested in rowboats to the same effect. The day blustered on above me, without me; I woke at the shore. I put my hands flat to the ice and tried to feel for movement but they soon went numb. Can you feel people moving on the other side of a window if you press your hands to the glass? I'd done some peeping and knew that you could feel something, not like you were actually touching them but something. Teresa liked to window-watch. She said she went without me some nights. I'd assumed alone, but now I doubted my assumptions, save: Love is a cudgel.

I used a sharp black rock found tangled in the roots of a blowdown spruce to chip the fish from the ice. They were in water, below the level of the ice, and it seemed that they were alive but when I grabbed one by the tail it was dead. It took a moment for me to be sure because I was slipping my grip and moving it around and my heart was racing, but it was dead. I pitched the fish toward the bank one after the other. They flew like carved pieces of wood. I thought they might have been moving when I was watching them and then just died. They could've died from me watching. The water wasn't flowing; it was as sealed as a glass bowl. But they had to have died at some point. Why not while I was watching? I was eight and it was a time when all sorts of things were freshly discovered and mislabeled and sent to the wrong place. Half of forever was how long it took to cut down a tree, forever was how long it took them to grow. I was the first person to think this. There is no fool like a little fool. I cut a willow branch and ran the fish through the gills and dragged them home to Mother. I told her how I'd come by so many nice fish without a pole or net or money, but I didn't tell her they were already dead. She looked upon me that day as a bright boy, and I savored the memory. The fish hadn't been a part of anything until I went home and Mother saw them. Of course they had their own piscine lives full of departures and returns, oceans and rivers; but the question was this: Had they been delivered to me by way of some biblical or beyond biblical precept? Not likely. No, it seemed that they'd been caught landlocked and froze. That's to say, they'd had some bad luck. Ice is a truncheon. There was no parchment list that said those fish needed to be there at that time and I needed to find them to take to my mother. And if there was no list for the fish, then there was no list at all, no order to any of it. Yet people thought there was. Teresa did. Like things with like things, she thought; but half of me was defined by her and the time we spent together, while the other quarters were all Harbor and ramble, Matius and misery.

The graveyard where Mother had been buried was on the hill above town. From there you could see the edge-of-the-world cloudbank at the coast. I'd been at her grave last week, during that first snow, and the wind was blowing hard enough to knock down the new wooden markers, seven dead in the last month. Here on the hill, here, for the last stop on the mudboat.

The mound of earth atop her had settled; she was resting, had been for years, finally. No sky for her, and no birds. Mother would watch birds for hours if given the chance. She could tell the difference between the unchangeable gulls and gave them names like pets or people. Harold the Mad, Muddy Mesmer, Margaret the One-Posted, Baron du Potet. And the birds liked her too; they'd gather around the house and sing and squawk and leave malicious little shits on the windowsills. Perhaps she'd swum away into the underground lake and escaped. She could be anywhere by now, free in the open ocean. But I didn't think she knew how to swim. When would she have learned? Jonas had taught me, when it should've been my father. Jacob the Teacher. There's a title he earned. Like the mountains earn snow.

On my feet I shook off the chill and gathered my stiffened jacket around my throat. I gauged the day by the hidden sun, as a fish by his shadow, ice by its bubbles, and I could see my breath and thought I might be wrong about the rain. It might snow.

Through the logged mess the path continued to the Ellstrom plot, No. 164, a mire of downed trees and stumps; huge, tangled slash piles walled up like animal dens, all of it waiting for the strike of a match, a solitary month of dry weather. It was hard to believe that we'd done this work on purpose, this voracious enterprise. There is no machine so wolfish as the able man. Jonas had taught me to swing an ax, how to snap it down like it was connected to my very bones by steel tendons. The chips would fly out thick as the Old Testament, then New.

Matius once told me that the day the windows were set in the house, a robin hit the glass and broke its neck. He said the Finns thought it was an omen and that they'd taken time to bury the bird to ward off the curse. Matius thought this to be the top of comedy. Better or worse, I side with the Finns; and when you die, you find your fortune in worms.

The thin afternoon light filtered through the stragglers, ragged striplings we'd spared or simply missed—an opening in the clouds, a sliver of moon low in the sky, the angle of incidence from the heavens to the mud-stamp homestead, weighted with cold, barn-red and murky; the house: promittor—the light of transition, thunderstorm light at the moment the sun goes. Matius was in there behind the walls. It's possible that stubbornness has killed more than it has saved. To have one leg is a world better than having those evil black veins like elk antlers shooting up to your crotch and into your heart. One leg is something to stand on, but Matius says he prefers to be buried with two. Ashes to ashes, dumbshit to dust. Life is so often compulsion. Take your place among the millions.

"God will embrace you, Nell Ellstrom," Reverend Macklin had said. My father was gone, disappeared to the woods or, if Matius hadn't lied, the ocean, with the gyppos or the Norwegians or someone. What was the difference? The murderer had fled. I stood graveside, weeping. On and on.

Macklin still enjoyed giving me news about my father. A few months back he caught me coming from the alley near the corner of Broad and Davis and dragged me onto the sidewalk to blather at me.

"You'll want to hear what I have to say."

"Not likely."

"I received a letter."

"You can cram it up your ass."

"All men can be redeemed, Duncan." Macklin was shorter than me and didn't like it; the proof was in the stretching of his neck, the straightening of his back. Not antsy though, far from it; the body squirmed but the eyes were stone. His patience was his greatest weapon.

"I've seen the eagle nests way up in the trees," I told him in my best impersonation of a preacher. "The sticks and twigs and the grass they're made of, and I've seen eagles in them, white as snow, pure and godly, but I never sat up there. I never looked down from above."

"Because you've not been redeemed." The reverend smiled priggishly, like he'd found his lost keys or managed to disguise the foulest interdiction as meritorious and yay biblically good. Slint, deeply so.

"I been to church plenty," I said. "I know the game."

"You've gone the other way. You've gone away from the Lord."

"I haven't gone anywhere. I been here the whole time."

The reverend nodded. "Sorrow is given us on purpose to cure us of sin."

"Yeah, well, Cicero said that when you are no longer what you were, there is no reason left for being alive."

"I don't agree with that."

"You wouldn't, because you deal in the fleecing of the broken."

"Judgment, boy, is left to the divine."

"'That which has no beginning nor end.'"

He ignored what I'd said, out of a lack of response, I'd say. Then: "You surprise me with your comparison, redemption to an eagle's nest. It's poetic, really. The choosing of a location, the construction, the soul coming home to roost. You're a smart boy. You should come back to us, come see us and sit with us. I'll cite your metaphor, if you like, in a sermon. This Sunday. Will you attend?" His jacket and tie were spotless and without wrinkles. He had a lady that lived with him, a housekeeper, and the rumor went that he was screwing her in the kitchen while his sickly wife wasted away in the upstairs bedroom.

"No, I won't attend, you fuckin bobknobber. You didn't get what I was sayin at all."

His face went from pasty to pink. "Is that right?"

"Those eagle nests that look so majestic from below, nobody's been up there to check, of course, but I'm guessin they smell every bit as wretched as Dolan's jakes. All the rotten fish guts and bird shit. It's romantic to stare up at them and think of an eagle's nest, a picture in your mind, but you don't know the first thing about what it is. You're on the fuckin ground, aren't you? You get my meaning?"

"This is your argument against redemption?"

I spit at his foot but missed by an inch. "There's my fuckin argument."

"You have a truly blasphemous streak, Duncan, but you will always be welcomed into the arms of the Lord, no matter the depravity of your soul. You can be saved."

"If you want to lose your faith, talk to a preacher."

"Don't you understand? I want you to be saved. The Lord wants you."

"You and the Lord can go and get solidly fucked."

That was all Macklin could take, so he took his leave. Admittedly, I felt slightly bad about the rough treatment, but whenever I heard these rare stories of my father's salvation, I hated the words themselves, like rats running the floorboards, because Jacob Ellstrom couldn't be saved. Nobody had the right to forgive him, not Macklin or Jesus or anyone, without my mother's permission they didn't, and that wasn't forthcoming.

Come on, you've had enough. Let's go home. There he is, falling down in the street, the boy beside him pulling at his muddy sleeve. The two of us stumbling homeward like three-legged racers under a harvest moon.

You go ahead and get pinned to the cross, Jacob. Be righteous. I'm going to see what's happening at the very bottom of the ocean, where I can't see or hear anything about your business or be reminded of you at all. I'll sit there like a trained bear and touch my paws together. Mother said she spoke to a bear once, didn't she; said he had an English accent, which surprised her. I could see God doing that, resting at the bottom of the ocean. The fools probably had it all wrong; heaven was down there beneath the clouds of the sea. Jesus felt so alone and was always trying to make new friends because he'd given bad directions. Walk until you hit water, then go due south.

"Where is the sadness in a life lived?" Macklin had said at her funeral. Some preachers should be muzzled. The nerve of that Calvinist snatch saying graveside that she had lived a full life. No one murdered lived a full life. Vanity, Macklin, you squid, is thinking that you lived well, and to go on and fantasize about your good death, placing sweet punctuation on the fiction of your good life. Three days it took her to die, and she cooked meals for her murderer on two of them. A knot on her head like black water dripped and frozen turned risen pool ice, and we ate and ate. And it was the found fish, or it could've been. It could've been we sipped bowls of warm blood. For kindness or evil disdain—liplickers, bonesuckers—what you would change if you could see the morning next. My father cried when he finally took her to Dr. Haslett. He cried carrying her up the steps, blubbered. "I didn't mean to," he said. "I swear it. I didn't mean to hurt her."

It wasn't easy to hate him—he was my father, after all—but I persevered, for Mother's sake. I spent long nights calculating slow death. I'd sharpen blades and load guns, but all of it ended in a dream. I hated how deeply I could sleep when I lay down plotting patricide. Morning arrived with memories of the old man stomping around the kitchen, and it felt like my own blood pouring out of me, aching as it went. I wondered sometimes if it would hurt more or less not to kill him, to let him live, because I feared, ultimately, that I couldn't do it.

I studied the house for movement and, not seeing any, stepped onto the plank path that led from the southern forest. Girdled with canals and mottled with slash piles, the clearing was both expansive and impassable. Limbs stuck out of the mud and danced in the flow of the ditch currents. Stumps like great statues towered, moated. The garden fence strained hopelessly against the swelling of the mud.

I opened the door and tromped inside without even attempting to clean off my boots. Matius was on the floor next to the cold fireplace, facing the wall. He was wrapped in blankets, and beside him there was a piss pot with a tin plate for a lid. The room smelled of excrement and bad meat.

"Who's there?"

"The skookum."

"Skookum. Where the hell have you been?" The bundle moved. A trembling hand clawed at the floor in an attempt to roll over.

"Workin like a dog. I built an ark. It's waiting outside in a mud puddle."

"Yer shit is tiresome." He had a red flannel scarf tied around his head, like he had a toothache. "You haven't seen Miss Eunice around, have you?"

"Nobody's around but me."

"She picked a fine time to skedaddle."

I could commiserate. "Thought I'd check and see if I needed to drag you outside and bury you so you won't taint the place any worse than you already have."

"Where's Jonas? Where's my son?"

"Work. I told him what happened."

"I been out here I don't know how long. Can't get up. I haven't eaten anything except that bread you brought by. When was that? Three days?" He was talking through his teeth.

"Two. Want me to get you some more food?"

"I didn't say I was hungry, did I? Said I hadn't eaten."

"Jonas'll be by."

"Tonight, you think? I need to speak with him."

"I don't know." I went back and shut the door, skirted the sicky, and set to building a fire. He lay there and watched me. "Can you stand?"

"No, I told you. I can't. I'm fucking dying."

"You should let me take you to the doc. It's just your foot. You can spare one."

"My father amputated a thousand Union legs during the war. I'll go into the ground whole."

"If that's yer reason, yer a fool."

"Woefully dying. I'm poisoned. I can feel it in my heart." He awkwardly lifted his crustily bandaged foot from under the blanket, and when his pant leg slid up, I could see that the black veins had gotten worse.

"You want some water? Or another blanket?" The fire was going, and the light showed the grayness of his face, bristly as a singed hog.

"Don't be sweet."

"I'm not."

"Soft boy. I don't want anything from you."

"Want me to shoot you?"

With that, Matius found the energy to roll all the way over. He couldn't turn his head, his neck was locked. Dirt in his hair and on the scarf. "You wouldn't do it if I begged."

"I might."

"Then do it."

"You're saying that's what you want."

"I'm tired of lying here."

Not hesitating one spark, I retrieved the shotgun from behind the door and broke it to see the brass. "You wanna say anything?" Snapped shut, ready, both barrels.

"I wasn't so bad to you."

"No, you weren't so bad." I stood over him and used the gun barrels to slide the greasy scarf from his head and onto the floor.

"Tell Jonas I wished he'd have come and seen me."

"I'll tell him."

He took a deep breath and closed his eyes. "Go ahead."

I cocked one hammer and then the other. My uncle squinted up at me. "Ready?"

"I said do it."

I tapped the barrels against his forehead and then swung them around and blasted a fist-sized hole into the wall, just below the window, to the left of the door. Matius tried to roll upright, but he was too weak. He was near tears, just done in.

"I won't help you like that." I set the gun down on the hearth, well out of his reach. "Shells are on the shelf by the door." I couldn't believe I could be so awful, but I'd be lying if I said it didn't feel good.

"I know where the goddamn shells are," he said.

"You shoulda been better to me."

"I raised you like you were my own."

"Course you did, Uncle. Course you did." With the blanket pulled back, the rotten smell of his wound was unbearable. I opened the door and the flames in the fireplace sucked out and nearly lit him up.

He wormed his way into the center of the room, leaving a wet drag mark behind him.

I leaned against the jamb. "If you would've asked for anything else, I'd a done it. I'd a carried you on my back all the way to town. I'd a cooked you a steak and bathed you and cut yer hair. I'd a built you a casket."

"Load that gun for me."

"I won't."

"Do it, I said." He'd kill me now if he could. I was sure of it.

"If I see Jonas, I'll tell him your condition. Maybe he'll do what you ask."

"He'll do it if I tell him to do it."

"He might not." I checked to make sure there was water in the pitcher and filled a glass for him and set it on the floor. "So long, Uncle."

"Wait, Duncan. I have something to tell you. Something I've been holding back for a long time. A confession." A dark and toothy grin spread over his face. His eyes were shimmering and red, and his brow was covered in milky beads of sweat.

"I was the first one through the door that night." The grin disappeared, and I could see he didn't want to continue. He took several deep breaths and his bravado, backed by fevered eyes, returned. "I'm speaking of the night your mother took the beating. You were old enough to know, weren't you?"

"What're you sayin?" I shut the door and went and stood over him, towered over him.

"She always had a mouth on her. I did like your father should've been doing for years. He'd spoiled her. Did she ever tell you what happened on her wedding day? What I did to her? Did she tell you? No, she wouldn't. I knew she wouldn't, and that's why I did what I did. No recourse. She'd keep her mouth shut when it came to protecting her own shame. I knew that. But she hit her head against that metal woodbox when she fell and next thing I know yer father comes through the door and he's blind drunk so I says to him, What'd you do, Jacob? Then Jonas is there, and I tell him that his uncle Jacob just hauled off and clobbered his wife. Just look at her face."

I tried to say something, and my mouth may have moved, but no words came forth.

With his eyes locked on mine, he continued. "When I was helping her up, I told her that I'd kill her if she told anyone. She wasn't for it at first, I could tell, so I told her I'd kill you if she told. Neither of us thought she'd die, you understand."

"You let him think he did it. You let me think it."

"Makes no difference."

His eyes followed me as I retrieved the shells and again loaded the shotgun. "If you're lyin, you'd better tell me."

"I'm not lyin."

I rested one barrel against his cheek then pulled it back slightly and pressed them both into his temple and slammed his head against the floor. "Tell me the truth." Years, I felt all the years pour down my arm like lead and weight my fingers to the twinned triggers.

"I already did."

"It was you?"

"Did you a favor," he said, eyes open, daring me.

His head caved and went onto my boots and up my legs. Same house as where he'd hit my mother, not six feet from where she fell. So much blood it could've come from a hose. Reckless hardly captured what I'd done. I hadn't made a decision to do this. I'd done it, and it was irrevocable.

After standing there terrified and watching the red blood blacken for I don't know how long, an hour, two minutes, I wrapped his body in the blankets from the floor and dragged it outside to where he'd been cutting posts. There was no hiding what I was doing. At first I didn't feel like I had the strength to bury him, but once I started digging, I wasn't so tired anymore. I hit water a few feet down and rolled him in and covered him up. I stacked his fence posts on top of him and went inside the house and cleaned, sopped up the mess with some rags and then burned them. I wasn't trying to get away with it, I told myself, straightening up is all. Getting rid of his stench, making him disappear.

I made myself a cup of tea and drank it at the table. To my surprise, with Matius gone, the house seemed sorely inviting. A place to live. I'd nearly forgot. My mother. I sat there and watched the fire die and cried until I couldn't stand the weakness of it any longer. I picked up the shotgun and the shells and I left.

At the edge of our lot the limbless trunks stood damaged where the fell trees had scraped them clean, white as baby's teeth. Beyond, the forest was unscarred; true, huge darkness. I turned and looked back at the small house and barn, like toys tumbled onto the rough ground.

I knew it was awful, what I'd done, the worst thing ever. But I could live with it for now, and it would get easier. Sometimes the things I thought to be right ended up being the most wrong, and this, and what I'd done to Teresa, felt terribly wrong, so maybe when it settled it'd end up being right.

To keep it dry I slipped the shotgun under my coat and watched as the rain returned as a mist and almost disappeared and then turned to sleet. Soon the wind picked up and large flakes of snow tumbled toward me. The edges of the seasons were being torn apart, unraveling, and with the snow a deep quiet befell the forest.

I'd follow the river into town; it was quicker than the road, and I wouldn't have to bother sneaking by the Parkers. Last thing I needed was to run into Zeb, but I'd like to talk to him. I had the urge to confess. To apologize. Not so long ago he'd been a good friend. I didn't have many of those left.

The forest dressed in white, wedded to the faller and the mill. They're coming for you, sweetheart. Flakes fell filtering through the reaching limbs of the giant Doug firs and blanketed the ground. I was in Boyerton's lease now, trespassing actually. Add it to the list. His rights bordered mine like my interests bordered his.

The water in the river had swelled with the rain. Ice was beginning to dully glob on everything where the snow couldn't stick. Downstream, the river strained through a logjam and the current made the tree limbs dance. Someone, a logger named Wilkinson, had drowned in the jam a few months before. He'd been trying to attach a cable to it to break it apart when he fell in. At the graveyard I had straightened the man's windblown grave marker. You treat the dead well because they're still here. Mother taught me that. Even when you can't see the moon, the moon is there.

Watching the swirling water, I had an echo in my head as if it were full of tiny metal springs. I was standing just outside the noisy room of all the bad I had done.

Then I saw someone at the water's edge and crept downstream until I could see the leather patchwork coat and red wool hat. I recognized the coat. The hat looked new.

"Kozmin the Cossack," I said, but the old man went about his business unaware. I shouted again, and the iron man Kozmin turned stiffly and held out his bloody hands and in the right was a knife. He swayed drunkenly. Behind him there was something dead and meaty on the rocks, halfway in the river, naked. A dirty drag mark led up the bank. The old hermit looked like he'd done something awful. I went forward and then stopped and hung on to a sapling so I wouldn't slip down the crumbling bank. But it wasn't a man; it was far too large. No, it wasn't human at all, or it was; it didn't have a head. Kozmin had carved it off. He was speaking now, but I couldn't hear him over the water so I held up my hand and made the jawing motion like a duck quacking and Kozmin squinted back at me.

I made my way down the riverbank. The water churned its muddy soup and was so active and boiling it hardly looked cold. As I crossed the snow-cleansed mudflat a somber feeling passed over me. I thought of Matius, felt the shotgun buck in my hands. I still had blood on my boots, trapped against the eyelets. I took off my hat, and the wind blowing off the river turned my part the wrong way.

Kozmin hopped gingerly from foot to foot. His pants were wet to the knee. "You can help me with this, can't you?"

"What'd you do?"

"Near finished." He pointed the knife at the mess. "But if you help me, I'll split it with you. I get the hide. You won't talk me out of it." The old man smiled. "The meat is what I'm offerin, and you look hungry as ever. This'd feed you for a month at least."

The old hermit had truly winked out. He was talking about a dead man and sharing the meat. The hide?

"What'd you do, Kozmin?"

"How'd you mean?"

"What'd you do it for?"

The old man looked at his knife because I was looking at it. "For the hide, like I said."

We were both murderers, by rights horrible men. I went closer and soon realized that the body on the rocks wasn't a man at all but a bear.

"I thought you'd killed somebody."

"Eh?"

"I thought it was a man, and you'd killed him."

A glimmer of recognition passed over Kozmin's face. He shook his head no.

"It looks like a man," I said.

"Cold weather does that, makes everybody seem purely evil or purely good. Look at that forest." Kozmin tipped his blade to the trees.

I looked at the drifting pale.

"Winter makes a person pick sides."

The bear seemed so nearly human, only one incomplete rotation away from my uncle, from my father, from me. I woke under the trees like a bear in the spring, but it's winter now. Why was the bear awake? Why had it found Kozmin? Was it on the same map that led me to the frozen steelhead?

Like he'd heard my thoughts: "I found it here drowned."

"I'm not eatin it or havin any part."

Kozmin's eyes narrowed, and the wrinkles at the edges were deep enough to hide coins on edge. His features softened as he considered this, considered his outstretched arms. His arthritic fingers couldn't be straightened with a vise. "I wanted the hide mostly. I did, and I got that done." He gave me a once-over. "How's your uncle faring?"

"You heard?"

"Course I heard."

"Heard what?"

"Cut his foot in half. What else?"

"He's dead."

"When?"

"This morning."

"Jonas know?"

"You're the first I told."

"From the foot? The cut killed him?"

"I killed him."

Kozmin pursed his old cracked lips. "I never liked the man."

"Me neither."

Kozmin smiled, and a sneaky look settled onto his face. "Hey, why do old loggers hate oatmeal?" He thought I was joking about killing Matius, that I was joking about him being dead at all, so I let him.

"I don't know, why?"

"Heartbreak."

"That makes no sense."

"To you, a fool that wanders around getting swell ideas like twisting Teresa Boyerton's arm."

"Who told you that?"

"Don't matter." The old man showed me his gums, what was left of his teeth. "Boyerton is gonna whoop yer ass."

"Good luck findin me."

"You hurt his girl. He'll find you."

"It was an accident."

"Don't matter." Kozmin lifted his arm and wiped his nose high on his sleeve. "You can stew bear meat, and it ain't bad."

"It's turned. See the black."

"That's just the fat. Meat's fine. Freezin out here, if you hadn't noticed. It'd keep till spring if nothing fed on it." The old man leaned over and stuck his knife into the dead bear's hip and set to cleaning the blood from his hands and arms.

I watched him and tried to settle the fear from my blood, Boyerton coming for me, Matius dead. Winter wasn't the only thing that made you pick sides. Up the bank a ways, stretched over a boulder, was the bear hide with the head still attached. The land was filled with snow and the ground seemed to be flying upward toward the sky, against the storm, and upward still against the current of the river: all was moving then, and the water stood still. My feet were not touching the ground.

Teresa has gray eyes that almost seemed green, but they weren't. She won't come back to me, not after what I did. Over my shoulder I could see a five-fingered paw, like a hand with the claws added later, hanging in the water, fanning current. And even from thirty yards away the bear's eyes were dead blue and locked on to mine. Strangely, I felt more pity for the dead bear than I did for my uncle. It seemed to want to move on, that's what its eyes were saying, the head with a cape of fur. Get my body gone. I've seen enough.

"The meat's bad," I said. "You can't eat it."

"So you said, and apparently you believe that yer opinions carry large quantities of water, but I'd argue they might be shit and worthless besides." He smiled and patted his pockets until he found his flask. Unscrewed, drank, screwed, didn't offer, repocketed.

"It'd poison you," I said of the meat.

"I've eaten maggoty meat a hundred times, and I'm still here."

"Are you starvin?"

"I'm always starvin."

"Wastin away."

"Right."

"You got the hide."

"We established that already."

Kozmin easily pulled his knife free and tried to wipe it off on his sleeve, but his coat was so greasy that it just smeared it around. He knelt at the river's edge and rinsed it, looked up, spoke: "Yer father's back."

"You've seen him?"

"How else would I know he's back?"

"Where is he?" I didn't want to look over my shoulder for fear he might be there watching me.

"He's got a place cross harbor, not far from the Soke. Know where that is?"

"Not even a real place. Made up fuckin mythical logger nonsense, just like yer oatmeal and yer heartbreak."

The old man blinked hugely and then grinned. "I guess you chose yer side then."

I could strangle him.

"Hate to see that much meat go wasted," he said under his breath.

"I don't want to look at it anymore. I swear it's starting to stink. I don't care if it's frozen or not. Goddamn stinky dead piece a shit." I sat back on my hands, but I only had the use of one because I was cradling the shotgun and used my legs to shove the corpse off the rocks. The bear rolled in the current and raised an arm or leg, all legs—bears have no arms—and was gone in a boil. I saw it downriver, neck full of bone, headed headlessly toward the logjam.

I stood, and the water lapped over my boots and pooled with the blood. I closed my eyes and had a waking dream that instead of standing like I was, I'd fallen in the river. It seemed very real, and I could feel the bear pulling me toward it like I was a tree that'd been cut through but had yet to fall. At first I was in the shallows and wet, but nothing to worry over. I tried to hold the shotgun up, but it got caught in my coat and then I dropped it and fell on top of it. My face went under. When I went to stand, I slipped again and the current had me. Kozmin was in the water, going for me. I swam for him but made no gain. The old kook staggered to a stop and stood alone, rooted to the snow and churned mud like a scrub pine, all dirty cubes of leather with his pink hands. His bear hide on the bank behind him, hollow as the mouth of a cave. He was calling to me but I couldn't hear him. The cold water plugged my nose and I was coughing and wheezing and when I bumped against the logjam I went under. I felt the current drive me down. The water was like smoke, and I was carried by it like an ember on the wind.

"Hey, Duncan, the hell you doin? You all right?"

"Havin a dream."

"They sallow in the daytime."

"Good-bye, Kozmin. I'm off to the wars. See you when I see you."

"You be careful, Duncan. Maybe hoof it outta here for a while. Go see yer father, go south."

"Like a bird."

"Self-preservation isn't nearly so repugnant as yer ongoing stupidity."

"Strikes me as bein a bit vain. Let come what comes."

I left Kozmin as I'd seen him in my dream, a rooted man. I followed the river until I made the bridge. The mist coming off the water froze into crystals and dusted the settling night. The crossmembers were icy and too slick to climb. I had to crawl up the snowy bank on all fours, flopped onto the roadbed like a birthed troll. The noise and lights of town were still too far off, but I could smell the salt of the sea. If I turned my back on it and went inland I'd pass through the log camps and into the mountains. Indian trails awaited, snowdrifts and caverns crawling with bears and cougar. I imagined a future as a lonesome trapper or a solitary gold miner. I saw myself in a wild and unexplored land, noble fool. Maybe Teresa would come to find me. We'd embrace beneath mountains whose peaks were lost in the clouds, beside rivers that had never been forded. We'd raise a family in a cabin I'd built using Matius's bloody ax. His ghost would follow us. My father too. I'd be with the ghosts, forever. I milled around the bridge, kicking the rails and let the flying water do the talking. I had the shotgun, and seven more shells than I needed to do what I was thinking about doing.

Duncan: Welcome to the Hall

Two *men rounded the* corner, dragging something, so I hopped down the bank to hide.

It was Tartan that spotted me. He whistled, and Bellhouse was suddenly at his shoulder. I stood up and waved hello. I hadn't really been hiding at all.

"Get up this fucking hill and be counted," Bellhouse said.

Tartan stood at the road's edge, bent at the waist with his hands on his knees. Behind him was what looked to be a man's corpse strapped to a door that had been ripped from its jamb, hinges dangling. "Cold for swimmin and yer under-outfitted for fishin. The fuck you doin?" Tartan said.

"Nothin. Walkin."

Bellhouse slid a stub of a cigar out of his hatband and lit it. His teeth clamped to it like a golden vise. "Boyerton's walking too. He's in your footsteps, and you don't even know it."

Tartan caught me looking at the body. "You know a man named Gutowski?"

"No."

"Then quit starin."

"What if I were Chacartegui?" I said. "What if it were him instead of me off the hill by the bridge?"

Bellhouse blew the ash from his cigar. "Listen to the little darling." He turned and pissed from the bridge. Two pistols bulged under his coat, and in the small of his back, if the stories were true, there was an ornate, three-pocketed leather holster used to carry a pair of pliers and two knives, one short and one long. He used the pliers to pull teeth.

"I gave you a dollar coin once," Tartan said.

"I still have it." Of course I didn't, but lying seemed appropriate, more so than having handed the coin over to Oliver Boyerton for taking his eye.

Bellhouse buttoned up and came toward me and crowded me and sniffed at me like a bipedal dog, then gave me a slap and took my shotgun away. "Do you want an adventure?" His slight German accent edged through his words.

I'd felt the same emotion pass over me when Matius was whipping me and I quit struggling and just let him have it, let him take what he wanted.

Tartan sat down on the corpse and rested there awkwardly, exhaled, then stretched his jaw. "You ask me, let him go icicle. Farewell, Ophelia."

"I didn't ask you. He'll come with us."

"We got other business, Hank. Leave him and let's get to it."

"No, I got a notion here," Bellhouse said to the sky. "We'll plant Gutowski, then take the boy out for a show. Boyerton'll have him within the week, anyhow. We'll let him have some excitement and thrilling adventures to send him off. A good for the bad, you see?" Bellhouse scowled in Tartan's direction.

"We'll pay for this act of kindness same as if it were viciousness."

"Like it matters to you, sweet or bitter," Bellhouse said. "String him a line so he can help us with the drag."

Tartan smashed a hole in the door panel with his boot heel and wrapped a length of chain around the frame and handed it to me. Bellhouse slid my shotgun under the tarp with the corpse. They took up their lines and we started off. The chain froze in my palms, but I wouldn't let go for anything. A lone raven appeared in the road and stared us down. Tartan kicked snow at it and it flew away.

The tide was out and the flats were covered with a curtain of mist that glowed in the darkness. The water hardly moved, whispered Olympic.

Tartan and Bellhouse surveyed the barren grounds before them, the tidal void. When they pulled back the tarp, Tartan found the lantern and lit it and let it hang from his fist, the handle squeaking like a mouse.

"Don't look too hard, you'll lose yer dinner." Tartan passed me the lantern.

"Haven't ate dinner," I said.

"We had steaks," Bellhouse said, looking into my eyes.

I watched as Tartan tied the heavy chain around Gutowski's torso, and then his legs. The bloody bedsheet fell away and the battered face looked like it had yet to form, it was so badly beaten, a blossom before the bud. A smashed eyeball hung outside the socket. Tartan yanked his hip waders from under the dead man's legs and unrolled them and spread them flat on the ground. He took off his boots and parked his sockless, greasy feet on the waders. He then stepped from the waders onto his toppled boots and carefully pulled the waders over his pants, and fastened the straps over his shoulders. Seemingly satisfied with his outfit, he snagged Gutowski's wrist and dragged him out into the marsh, moving through the water quietly like a man going bird hunting.

"We walk the wavecrests," Bellhouse said, showing me his teeth, silver and gold, a presentation. "We swim and never get wet. You get my meaning?"

I gave a nod, and it was all that I could do.

He looked away like he'd heard something behind him. "Yes, everyone knows what you did to Boyerton's daughter." Then without warning he turned away and walked back toward the road. There was a light coming toward us.

Tartan was still out in the marsh. I set the lantern on the bloody door, not knowing if I should put it out or not. I squatted and warmed my hands over the glass, thought about picking up my shotgun and making a run for it but didn't. Two more bridges crossed and a left turn, and I might find my father. What good would that be?

A few minutes later Bellhouse returned. Tartan came up the bank, breathing heavy, water streaming down his waders. "Who was on the road?"

"Someone searching for the boy."

"Cut him loose," Tartan said. "He ain't worth the trouble."

"No, they're gone now," Bellhouse said. "He can stay. What about you? Are you done?"

"He's mired to the hilt," Tartan said.

"The boy saw what you did."

"I can get more chain."

Bellhouse laughed like a hiccup. Tartan took off his waders and chucked them in my face and then put on his boots. He darkened the lantern and we took up our lines and hauled the broken door back down the road toward town.

When we could see the lights, Bellhouse tapped the brim of my hat. "Keep your head down until we get inside."

We left the door leaning against the shack it had been stolen from. I thought it must've been Gutowski's place. Tartan had the chain over his shoulder and his waders pinched in one hand, the cold lantern in the other. I had my shotgun mummied inside my coat with my finger on the trigger. Walking with them I felt tough and vicious and mostly included. I decided that I'd ride this boat to the dead end of it. Put the coin on my lips, I'm on my way.

The Coast Sailor's Union was housed in one of the newer buildings, suddenly old because it hadn't burned with the rest at the waterfront. A balcony wrapped around three sides, but there were no stairs leading up. The windows were lit on the second floor, but when we walked through the downstairs doors it was dark.

All I could make out were the shadows of tables and chairs, lockers against the wall. Up the stairs it got warmer with each step, and when we hit the double doors, it felt like we'd found the boilers. Twenty men at least were at the tables on the floor, and another ten or fifteen were at the bar along the wall. Waitresses were carrying trays of drinks, and the bartender was a woman too, Bellhouse's woman, Delilah. She had blond hair that was cut to her shoulders. Her face was smiling and friendly even when her back was turned to the bar and I could see her face in the mirror. She saw us then, in the mirror, and spun around. Someone whistled and a table cleared and Tartan pushed me into a chair. He slammed the chain and his waders on the tabletop and broke a few glasses. Bellhouse drank from the bottle that was left behind.

"How goes the night fishin, Hank?" a man asked.

"With every word you cut bait."

Tartan smiled and took the bottle, drank, and passed it to me. I still had the shotgun under my coat, and to maintain concealment I leaned way back in my chair with my legs spraddled like I was the king returned. I tipped the bottle back, and while it was up, Tartan got his hand under my coat and disarmed me. Chain, waders, shotgun, broken glass on the table. Delilah arrived with a fresh bottle and glasses and sat on Bellhouse's lap.

"Who'd you bring back with you?" she asked.

"Un mari brutal," said Bellhouse.

"He's too young to be married anyhow."

"I'm not married."

"Free, white, and single," Tartan said.

The bottle was uncorked, and glasses poured full. Bellhouse was smoking. Tartan drank and refilled his own glass and drank again. The room had returned to the condition it was before we'd been acknowledged. Delilah's eyes were blue and lovely, and she watched me, waiting for something.

"Have another," she said.

I did and thanked her. On my way to the coffin. Drinking with killers. Bellhouse gave me a cigar and told me to call him Hank. A piano was uncovered, and a man in a tall pointy hat began to play. Men at the bar threw peanuts at the pianist, but it didn't seem to bother him. They called him Rodney, Rodney the Mucker, or Muck. I'd heard him play for years but hadn't seen him except far away in the street. He had a humped back and hands purpled from burn scars—lye was the story I'd heard. Debts unpaid.

I turned to Hank and told him it was a miracle that the man could play at all with his hands the way they were.

"He learned after."

"After what?"

"After I burned his fucking hands, that's what after."

Tartan was watching me. Delilah was watching me, her hand stroking Hank's scarred bald head. I realized I was still wearing my hat and took it off and set it on the table. Faces turned to see me, and some showed signs of recognition, Boyerton's bounty. Hank met their glances, and they looked away. Under the vulture's wing, sharpening the reaper's blade.

Liquor was poured, and I didn't resist. I drank what was given. We ate sausages and mashed potatoes later. The hall slowly emptied, and stragglers joined our table. Bellhouse dragged me outside when I started to throw up. He held me by the back of the neck and shoved my face through the rails on the balcony. When I was finished, I sat on the wet boards and felt the cold. Bellhouse was smoking a cigar by the door. I tried to stand, but the pink womb of sky flipped onto the street and I fell on my face.

I woke in the corner of the hall, covered by a blanket on a dog's bed. Tartan stood over me and gave me another glass of whiskey, and I took it. Not so bad now, I rejoined the table. Muck was back at the piano. The McCandliss brothers were on the stairs, but Tartan told them to hoof it, kick rocks. They saw me and waved, surprised. Tartan had to tell them two more times to leave. I kept drinking and threw up again, this time on the floor. Bellhouse made me clean it up. I had beer after that. Bellhouse told a story about killing a man with a farrier's file. When he was finished, I told them what I'd done to my uncle and for what reason. Tartan began to laugh and laugh and couldn't contain it. Bellhouse flicked his cigar at the big man and then they were on their feet at each other's throats. I got between them and worked them apart and they sat back down. I thought I could be their brother or their son.

"You killed him," Tartan affirmed.

I nodded yes, I did.

"Because he was the one that killed yer mother."

Again, a nod. These were men, killers, and I was one of them. Of course I was.

"Righteous cause," Bellhouse said, cuffed me on the arm. "You did right by her."

"If she were dead," Tartan said.

"She is," I said.

"Not when she left here," Tartan said. "Not when I bought her passage to San Francisco."

"Yer lying," I said. Now I was on my feet.

"Sit, boy," Bellhouse said.

"He's lying."

"He doesn't make a habit of it."

"She ain't dead. She left. I helped her. Doc Haslett and I set it up. I admired her cunning, cold as it was to you."

"She wouldn't."

"She fuckin did."

Bellhouse was laughing, and Tartan soon joined in. I drained my glass and felt sick so I went back to the dog bed. They stayed up and drank till dawn. Muck quit an hour before they did. My mind spun through hellish scenarios where I was fighting Tartan or killing Matius again and again, the wet mash of his face. The problem was that we'd all been fooled. And I was sleeping on a dog's bed, the most comfortable bed I'd ever known. And where was the dog?

I woke to Tartan opening the window and connecting a stovepipe and sending it out so he could start the fire and cook eggs. It took him ten minutes to complete the chore and I watched him the whole time. Wind blew in the open window and I curled into my blanket. Bellhouse appeared from a door I hadn't noticed in the back. Delilah followed him, dressed in a red silk robe. Her bare feet were fascinating. I didn't hear Tartan sneaking up on me. He kicked me in the ass and stole my blanket, then clamped a hand on my neck and dragged me to the table and sat me down.

"Flea bite," Bellhouse said to me when I sat down.

"Poor thing," Delilah said. "How's yer head?" She touched my hand. Before I could answer her, Tartan served me coffee and a plate of steaming eggs with buttered bread.

"He didn't keep any liquor down. Why would he feel bad if he ain't been drinkin?" Tartan said.

"I'm fine," I said. "Thank you for breakfast."

"Fuck off," Tartan said.

Delilah's nipples were raised against the thin fabric of her robe. We ate and the wind howled in the window.

"What'll you do today?" she asked me, without looking up from her plate.

"I don't know. Hadn't thought about it."

"He's coming with us," Bellhouse said.

"Is he?" Tartan said.

"I think he should go home," Delilah said. "You boys play too rough for him."

"This slint plays rough. Ask his uncle."

"Ask Teresa Boyerton."

I took a swig of the coffee and burned my tongue raw.

"Yer mother," Tartan said. "She must not a thought you were worth keeping."

"Tartan, let go that rude uncivil touch," Delilah said.

"Don't quote at me, woman."

Delilah smirked at him and then filled her coffee cup and got up and walked toward the door in the back of the hall. We all watched her go.

Bellhouse was watching me. "Finish your coffee."

I did as he told me. I wouldn't look at Tartan.

"Your shotgun is behind the door. Go get it."

"Send the pup on his way, Hank. I'm tired of him."

"Not as tired as he is of you."

I got up to retrieve the shotgun, thinking I might kill them both, because it felt like the answer was coming from that direction, from a future of death. The hall didn't seem so big when you weren't crossing it. The shotgun was where he said it was, and I checked it to see if it was loaded, but it wasn't.

"Bring it here," Bellhouse yelled.

I walked back, not knowing where to look. It felt like I'd forgotten how to walk. Bellhouse produced a flask from his coat pocket and uncapped the coffeepot and poured. Then he took the gun from my hand and motioned me back to my chair. The safety I'd felt when Delilah was with us was noticeably gone. These were true wolves. I drank the spiked coffee and gagged on the spirit burn.

"He doesn't know what he says," Bellhouse said of Tartan. "He insults people's mothers because he's weak-minded."

"I mean everything I say," Tartan said.

Bellhouse swung the butt of the shotgun so fast I didn't have time to jump. Neither did Tartan. The wood cracked into his temple and sent the big man sprawling on the floor. It didn't look like he'd get up, but then he did. He wasn't bleeding, but there was a knot on his head rising like a poison bite. He took his seat and sipped his coffee, squinted his left eye, looked at me, smiled.

"I'm going to ask you to apologize." The shells were in Bellhouse's hand, and he cracked the shotgun and loaded both barrels.

"This fuckin slint gets me clobbered after I cook us all—cook the slint himself—fuckin breakfast, and you want me to apologize."

Bellhouse pointed the gun at Tartan's chest. "I can like you and kill you just the same, but it'll be harder. See? I don't want to shoot my friend. Because we are friends. I want you to try to make it as difficult as you can for me."

"Don't shoot him," I said.

"Stay out of it, slint."

"Give me the gun."

"You wanna shoot him?" Bellhouse seemed pleased.

"I'll do it."

"No, he'll apologize."

"Hank." Tartan rested his giant fists on the table.

"Do it," Bellhouse said.

"I'm sorry, slint."

"That's not nice. Try again."

"I'm sorry I said what I said. Sorry."

"Give me my gun."

"It was an apology." Bellhouse broke the shotgun and put the shells back in his pocket. "The scales are once again balanced."

"Not for him," Tartan said.

"I still don't believe you."

"Ask fuckin Haslett then." He spit on the floor and left me and Bell-house sitting there alone.

Bellhouse *ting*ed his fingernail against his flask. "Family, what makes cowards brave and brave men crumble." He drank but didn't offer any, and I was grateful for that.

"Why doesn't he kill you?" I asked.

"Because he can't."

"He wants to."

"Sure, but I'm the drover of that son of a bitch. Sheep can't kill the drover."

I didn't know what he meant, but then again, I did.

"It might be that you have to tell yourself a few thousand times how you want it to be before it works," Bellhouse said.

"What if I killed Charlie Boyerton?"

"No, he's a drover bigger than me. You're too low to even measure into his flock. Romantic of you to think it."

I poured myself more coffee. "He's the one, though, isn't he? If I could do it, he'd be the one."

"Experience has taught me that there is never in fact only one. The fuckers come paired and clustered, apples on a bent branch. You cut one loose, two more will drop on your head."

"Him gone, though. It'd be me that was making the decisions."

"About what? His mill?"

"No, his daughter."

"Maybe. How would you do it?"

"Shoot him like I shot my uncle."

"Well, all I can say is, kill cleanly if you're gonna kill at all." He was up with his coffee and out onto the deck. Me and the tables and chairs, the piano. Faintly I could hear Delilah singing.

A woman and her two small children came in and swept. The woman wiped down the bar top while the children straightened the chairs. They as a group ignored me and everything they saw. When they were finished, the woman went to the door in the back and Delilah opened it and handed her some money and they left. Delilah was dressed now, and she followed them to the stairs and switched off the overhead lights and came and sat with me. The rainy morning corpse color filled the east side of the hall with a dirty gray light and left the other side, our side, nearly dark.

"Where's Hank?"

I nodded toward the door. She had perfume on, and her nails were freshly painted.

"He jumps down from the rail to the street instead of taking the stairs. One day he'll break his leg and we'll all be sorry. The toughest ones whine the loudest." She touched the coffeepot, but it had gone cold. She puckered her lips and blew air to see how cold it was, saw her breath. "Somebody should start that fire again."

"Why bother?"

"That's one way. The other would be to go and do it without me having to ask."

"I'll be leaving shortly."

"Hank told me you hurt that rich girl's arm."

"It was an accident."

"I've had those accidents before, and it always felt purposeful to me."

"She wouldn't listen."

"Impatient puppies, they nip and snarl."

"We were goin to get married. I thought it was settled."

"Well, covet that heap of disappointment. You could be miserable for years before you had to enjoy a single day. If you play it right, you could waste your whole life for free. What a deal."

"Yer shacked up with Bellhouse and tellin me what to do?"

"We don't count for much out here in the rip. Neither of us. You'd do well not to forget that."

"Delilah?"

"You should call me Mabel."

"Why's that?"

"Because you're just that special, aren't you?"

"Mabel, can I kiss you?"

"No, you may not." She smiled, and I took it for a maybe. I reached for her hand, but she was fast and I was slightly drunk, too slow, tipped the coffeepot. My chair fell over when I stood up.

She held up her hand so I wouldn't come closer. "Get out."

"Yer beautiful."

"And you're nothin but a boy and you smell worse than a dead mule."

"I swear to Christ I know what to do with a woman."

"Like he'd know." She pushed herself back from the table and stood up. There were footsteps on the stairs. I picked up my chair and slid it into its place. Tartan entered the room and crossed it in seconds.

"The squid remains," he said.

"He's on his way out," Delilah said.

"I'll show him the door."

"He can go on his own."

Tartan righted the coffeepot and touched a finger to the spill. He smiled at Delilah and then punched me in the throat and folded me over his shoulder. I kicked and fought him, but he cracked my head against the doorjamb on the way out and I went dark. Delilah was waving good-bye, last thing I saw.

Tartan

He *lugged Duncan across* Front Street, through the morning bustle, and flopped him down in the mud. Rain had melted the snow overnight. The farrier's boy, Libby, hitched a horse and wagon for him and Tartan tossed Duncan aboard and rode out of town. Busy shit of a day, two camps on leave and seventeen ships at last count. Drawbridge stuck open for the ships coming from the new Wishkah docks, loaded from breech to bore. Never used to be a problem till we got a bridge that moved. "Fuckin lower it, Paoletta," Tartan bellowed.

The scrawny pipe-hat tender waved to Tartan from his perch, tin roof and a double-hung window. One, two ships passed, and he finally lowered the bridge.

Paoletta, hanging out his window with his hat in his hand. "Sorry for the wait."

"I don't like that you can control where I get to."

"I don't control anything, Mr. Tartan. I just make the bridge go up and down."

He wasn't getting into semantics with Paoletta. Bridges should be goddamn fixed. End of story. Used to haul the lumber through the streets and everyone was happier. Maybe not everyone.

I could sell the little grunion. Market was up for impressment but it goes against our union goals. Boyerton was an option as well. Nope, time for class, lesson one: Don't aggravate my stomach because it aches.

An hour later, with a sore ass and a horse that wanted to quit, he was at the bridge where they'd found Duncan the night before. Tartan pinched the boy's balls to wake him, and when he opened his eyes, he lifted him over the rail with one hand and threw him in. He thought the boy'd say something smart and make it worth it, but he was just scared and confused, and as soon as he was falling into the fast cold water Tartan felt remorse and wanted to take it back. He wasn't a bad kid. Got me clobbered. Aw, Christ, fetch him back.

"Swim, boy. Swim for shore." But he was underwater and gone. *Drowned a child. Fuck me.* Then he broke the surface and was swimming like a terrified animal, all whites and rolling in the eye sockets. Arms like chicken necks, water for blood. "Giver snoose, fuckin swim," Tartan yelled. But it was too late; he was already around the bend.

Tartan had trouble getting the cart turned, and by the time he did, the boy was long gone and setting to get caught in one of the minor logjams or random cataracts or, below that, get swallowed by the slough.

He finally tied up the horse and walked the river, but Duncan wasn't there.

It was afternoon by the time he got back to town. He had Libby spread word that Duncan Ellstrom had fallen in the river and was most likely drowned. Neither him nor the slow-witted farrier were dim enough to mention the fact that Duncan had last been seen draped over Tartan's shoulder, nor would they unless they wanted to join him.

Tartan walked into the middle of the Sailor's Union meeting and whispered in Hank's ear what had happened. Hank shrugged. "Shame. Delilah'll be heartbroken."

"Sure."

"We should send out a search."

"I already looked. He's gone."

"For appearances we should." He turned to the crowd. "I need your help, men. A boy has fallen in the river, and he might be drowned. We need to find him, save him if we can, bury him if we can't."

Men scratched their heads and looked at their drinks. Hats were pushed around tabletops. It was cold, wet, and soon to be dark outside.

"Little late, ain't it, Hank?" a man with a pinched face in a pea coat said. "We still need to talk about those Willamette sons a bitches crowdin us on the grain shipments."

"That can wait. Down your drinks and grab your hats. We're forming a picket line at the river mouth and going to the bridge. If we don't find anything, drinks on me tonight. If we do, drinks still on me. Let's get."

Damp men put on damp coats and hats and gave up on being dry or getting drunk at a decent hour.

"Be hell to find him."

"Hope it ain't me."

"Who the fuck is it, anyway?"

"Duncan Ellstrom," Tartan said.

"That little devil?"

"Shoulda drowned him and the McCandlisses at birth."

"Ain't Boyerton lookin for him?"

"Enemy of my enemy," Hank said.

"Slinkin slint."

"Quit fuckin moanin," Tartan said.

"Someone fetch a ferry pilot, we'll boat up to the Wynooche and then hoof it," Hank said, cherishing the looks of disgust that a night of slough tromping brought to everyone's faces.

As a mob they went out the door, and when they hit the street, the townspeople thought riot and closed the shutters and locked their doors. Hank climbed onto the back of a trash wagon and addressed the street.

"A boy has fallen in the river, and the proud members of the Sailor's Union are going to search for him. Damn the rain and the imminent darkness. Come join us if you've any decency or community pride."

The doors and windows remained closed. The hermit Kozmin stumbled from the alley, hauling his pack onto his back. "Wait for me."

"Guess we're all alone then," Tartan said.

"I said I'm joinin," Kozmin said.

"All by ourselves."

"You wait."

"Fuckin dead liver crone."

The hermit hustled by Tartan, said: "I got something we can use."

Tartan followed him to the waterfront and helped him haul his coracle up the ladder. The big man put it on his back like a turtle and they walked together to the ferry.

Thirty-five men debarked at the Wynooche pier.

"Can't walk out there." Bellhouse motioned to the slough that was the Wynooche and the Chehalis all at once. "We'll take the road to the bridge and then work back. No luck, we'll call it a night."

The mass of the searchers followed Bellhouse upstream. Some stayed with the ferry, feigning sleep. Kozmin and Tartan slipped into Kozmin's tiny bathtub of a boat and entered the slough. A freezing rain came through the trees in fans of white and spattered the murky slough water three feet into the air. Dismal conditions for any kind of outing. Tartan had the paddle while Kozmin held a lantern and leaned precariously over the side and called the boy's name again and again. They bounced through the channels and mires and scooted over the shallows. Surely they were lost as well. Even if they could find the main channel in the dark, the little boat would capsize at the first hint of the Chehalis's powerful currents.

"Think he made it out of the water?" Kozmin said. "Or are we corpsin? Have to be near dead now from the cold."

"We'll find him," Tartan said. Maybe just so I can kill him twice, he thought. Kozmin called Duncan's name and whistled, and then they heard a sound and Tartan hit the water with the blade like he hated it. There was an island among a dozen other islands, and on it knelt the boy, his hand up, waving them in.

Jonas Ellstrom

The second whistle sounded, and he pulled the lever that stopped the belt and sat down on the bunk of lumber beside him. Light came through the windows, cut into ropes and blobs by the cracked glass, wormy shapes shifting on the rise and fall. Disembodied heads floated by above the machinery, arms shot out to turn valves. Men lived in this beast like mice in an abandoned house.

Dawn was a marker, the only natural one that the mill allowed, and that only dimly. Night was heralded by the illumination of the electric lights overhead, the progressive spark of modernity, from firelight to bulb. Jonas rarely if ever caught the actual moment when the darkness arrived; it came slowly and then completely, and somewhere in the middle, the lights came up.

There were birds roosting in the rafters; small and gray and soundless, they flew in tight nonmetrical patterns. Their chalky shit streaked the beams. Sometimes he saw dead birds on the floor and was surprised how large they were. They weren't much different from dust motes when they were alive, except they shit everywhere and were capable of dying. If the windows weren't broken, they couldn't get in. If the doors weren't open.

The next shift began to file in and take up the spots of the departing, but Jonas would be staying. Double shifts were what he'd asked for and what he'd been given.

He rolled a cigarette with shaking hands. Every one of the boards he sat on had been handled by him, moved and carried by his hands. Sometimes he looked out at the forest and the stumps and imagined he'd slid his fingers over the inside of half the trees in Washington. As if he were a preacher laying on hands. Blessed be. He felt the blood settle in his muscles, a cooling kettle. *Water that's been boiled tastes flat compared to fresh water, and my blood's been boiled.* He was all right today, but last week he'd collapsed and had to be carried outside for fresh air and a drink of water. Dawson, the foreman, had given him a shot of whiskey from the flask he kept secreted in his vest pocket. Dawson wasn't nearly so bad as they said. He'd let Jonas rest for ten minutes or so, and together they'd watched as three men in an oceangoing canoe fought and boated a ten-foot sturgeon. They were yelling but not panicked. The man that had hooked the fish pulled it close and it splashed and swept its tail, and then one of the fishermen stood and quick as a shot got a gaff into the fish's jaw and the canoe rolled and almost went over before another man raised his arm, holding a club, held high before it fell and rose again, like it was on a camshaft, pummeling. The fish finally stopped thrashing, and they set two more gaffs and fell back and the fish slid over the gunwale and landed in their laps. The canoe settled noticeably deeper into the water and the men cheered and smacked each other on the back and shoulders.

Dawson's singular gesture had crushed months of mistrust and dislike. The mind drove the body like the boiler drove the belt, the fisherman's club.

Double shifts meant fewer days total lost. If each shift meant one day gone, two in a day was smarter. He was scraping his time from the margins; pulling stitches. This was temporary, and it wasn't the weight of the lumber but the splinters that drove you mad.

He ground out the cigarette under his boot and produced a piece of venison from his pocket. Dawson was on the catwalk. Charlie Boyerton came out to join him. Boyerton was a smallish man with a stubby neck and a round stomach. His watch chain flashed in the gloom. Jonas had a childish urge to please him, to work hard for him and do a good job. He'd always respected starched little bastards like Boyerton, couldn't say why. He watched as the two men spoke but couldn't make out a word of it. Boyerton made a chopping motion with his hand and stomped off. Dawson reached up and with the one remaining finger on his right hand yanked the chain and sounded the whistle again. Jonas got stiffly to his feet and righted the lever to his machine. Steam burst from the release valve with a half-plugged hiss, and the lumber came trundling on the hooks and chain at him.

The mill was alive, the long house at the harbor's edge, blackened boards and running with water, always alive, always going. Belts took the dust and shavings, scrap too, fed the fire. No peace. It almost made him miss mining, the solitude at least. A bulb burst and rained hot glass down on the conveyor, the smell of burned wood and sulfur. "Watch the dust," Jonas called to the boy setting stickers for him. His name was Amos Rills. "Watch for fire." Amos assessed the ground, nervously wiped the sweat from his face with his shirt. A few minutes later, high above them, a boy dressed in white coveralls climbed out onto the beam to replace the broken bulb; he didn't appear human, scurrying around up there. His little fingers clawed into the bird shit as he pulled himself along. He didn't look scared, but he had to be. Jonas couldn't help but watch him and worry, and the distraction earned him a nice fat sliver in his palm.

Some time later a man came stumbling into Jonas and knocked him down. Amos Rills picked up the plank he'd dropped with great effort and stacked it while Jonas helped the bloody man to his feet. He'd been cut deeply in the forearm, and the blood pulsed through his fingers as he ran for the door. Jonas caught the next plank and the one after, and Amos went back to his rounds.

The hermit, Kozmin, appeared and tried to talk to Jonas, but Dawson ran him off. The old man looked worried and yelled something, but Jonas couldn't hear a word of it, likely it was something to do with his father. Amos brought him a tin cup of water. All the hair was burned from the boy's hands and arms, and his eyelashes and eyebrows were stunted and spotty. His mouth was rimmed with black grime. The water was hot, and Jonas spit it out.

Dawson and two other men came by, hauling a broken driveshaft, and twenty minutes later the mill got louder as another saw came to life. Jonas hadn't noticed that the sound had dropped off. Muleskinners came and hitched their team to Jonas's full truck and towed it out to the dock.

The sun was up now, and the dust-coated windows let in enough of the dawn so that half of the electric lights overhead could be shut down. The whistle sounded again, and Jonas dropped onto the partial bunk he'd been stacking and caught his breath. He opened his eyes when the new man arrived, nudged him in the shoulder to make him move.

Jonas smiled because he was done. He roughed the sawdust from his hair, tasted it mixed with salt when it rained down. He stood and staggered to the post and took his coat down from the hook. He signed out and marked the shift locations in the log, held the pencil in his hand like he was holding a chisel and someone else was bringing down the hammer. The clerk initialed his entry and made it official.

The gray square of daylight on the east side of the building was his landmark, his north star.

Dawson called to him and caught him at the door. He had a drunkard's pitted nose, and when he spoke, he kept his good hand in his pocket and gesticulated with the nub and finger. "A man came to see you. He said your cousin fell in the river. They found him, but he's in bad shape."

The whistle sounded for the last time, and the roar heightened and seemed to blow past them out the door like a hot wind. Dawson ushered him out the door and around the side of the building. The harbor was flat and full of bark and debris, held by its icy edge. The clouds were low, as they often were at dawn; at dusk they rose and sometimes offered a glimpse of the sunset. What did Dawson say? What about Duncan?

"That's some mean water right now," Dawson said, offering his flask. Jonas took it and unscrewed the cap with his clubby, nearly useless fingers and drank, passed it back. Dawson checked over his shoulder and had a nip and then slipped the flask back into his pocket. "There's another thing, and I hate to do it, but Mr. Boyerton come by himself."

"I saw you and him talking."

"There's been some harm done to his family by yours. The same one that fell in the river, your cousin, Boyerton said he hurt his daughter's arm."

Jonas yawned again, tried not to.

"I'm to run you off. It's not my decision. Your pay will be here on Friday as usual. Come find me, and I'll make sure you get it."

"All right."

"I'm sorry."

"Not your fault."

All the trees stood on the hills, frozen white in the gray morning. The scrub brush rising in the clearings was sparse and ratty, and birds skittered about like fleas. Jonas thought of a woman. He'd known her, where'd she go? When did she leave? His mouth went slack, and he couldn't stop the yawn that came.

Jonas didn't think that Duncan would be one to drown. He had a crooked way of avoiding injury, like cats can fly tangled through the air and catch the ground, like a dragonfly catches its mate.

He passed through the mill gates, and the sawdust ended and the mud began. The smell of the ebb tide was heavy in the air. The water's edge was all the way out, beyond the channel even, lower than it had been for months. Ships would be thick on the flood, and the shoals would shift. Put your feet before you and walk. Better than having to whip an animal is to have it know its job.

The drunks around the barrel fire sat bent and rooted to their tree-round seats like idiot fishermen. Jonas lifted a blanket next to a log, and under it was the hermit, mouth open, snoring.

"He ain't dead," one of the men on the stumps muttered. "I just checked."

"There was a boy," Jonas said, "nearly drowned, where'd they take him?"

"Oh, yer him," one of the men said, standing up, deciding against it, sitting back down. "Yer his cousin."

"Where is he? Did they take him home?"

"He's at the doc's," a man said to his muddy boots. "At Haslett's." He looked up, tilted back his hat, and revealed bloodshot eyes and his eyebrows gone, like a skull with a beard. It took Jonas a moment to figure what was missing. "We went searchin, then Hank was buyin. Fuckin Hank, he kicked us out the union hall for bein too drunk. But he's the one that did it to us." Laughter, mostly his own. "He's the one that caused it, then fuck you into the street cuz we got sloppy. Who's to blame?"

Without a word Jonas went back and covered Kozmin and walked away. There was sun on the road before him, but it started to rain anyway, straight and thinly fast. He liked the light in the confused storm and felt uplifted. He held his face up to the cold rain and let the contradictory nature of the divine wash over him. The complexity of a wet and cold sun reassured him. He thought he should pray, but he was too tired, too fed up to bother. Go on and read my mind if you want. I'll tell you, thanks for that. Thanks for saving him.

Duncan

————

There were no shadows, and only the weakest seep of outside light coming under the door. I could hear the distant sound of voices and kindling being chopped and rattled apart. Rain on the roof, a different roof, not any roof that I knew, soothing and monotonous, water. There was nothing to be afraid of; I was in a tomb, and my body had gone away. Nothing to fear. *I've been killed, and my feet have been stolen.* My mouth was dry as talc. *I no longer require liquids. Bellhouse slit my throat.* I touched my neck to feel the wound, and there was nothing except a general soreness, an ache that started at the skin and went to my neck bones and down my back into my arms and legs. *So Tartan strangled me. And now I'm dead.* I closed my eyes and took several deep breaths, ready to fall into oblivion, decidedly on to the next life. There was an odor in the room, though, one that I knew, a dying smell. Someone was breathing, and it wasn't me. I held my breath and heard the breathing. No, I was alone. I was sure of that. All alone. I suddenly remembered that I'd killed Matius. My own blood. My heart raced and raced until it slowed, and I felt my body ease away, drift off. Into the woods.

When I woke again, the room was full of light. It was a room I recognized. I'd been here before. There was a sheet hung down the middle, a clean white sheet. It was the doctor's house. The walls were painted yellow, and the floor was polished. There was a pot next to the bed, but it'd been emptied. I must've thrown up; I could taste the river in my mouth, mud and moss. Had I been attacked by a bear? I felt myself out for wounds but found nothing more substantial than scratches. My toes were blistered and frostbitten, and I thought I could feel it on my ears too. They felt the same as my toes. But I was intact. I studied the shadows on the hanging sheet, like wet sand, shades shifting, and tried to figure what to do next.

"Hello." My voice was a stick dragged over a dry rock. I repeated myself, slightly louder this time. Nobody answered, and I was glad. I wasn't saying another word. I'd tested what needed testing and now I was done. I was alone and could relax. I knew where I was, and it was day-time, but I was not day awake or night awake. When I closed my eyes, I envisioned myself doing horrible things. Bellhouse and Tartan were there with me. Tartan handed me a bloody knife butt first, Kozmin's knife. I stuck it in the bear's side and the two men laughed, but I felt awful for what I'd done. We were in the forest, hiding outside of the timber boss's shack. I'd been there with my father before. There was no smoke from the chimney, but the boss was in there with the cruiser. Bellhouse stood up, and then Tartan. I tried to free the knife from the bear, but it was frozen; ice was running up the blade and onto the handle, onto my wrist. I couldn't stand unless I let it go. I released my grip, and when I stood Bellhouse was gone and so was Tartan, the shack too. A husky dog was there, no rope on its neck. Here, boy. Here, pup. It ran, and I went after it.

Mother was in the bushes, the dog at her side. She waved me over, and we petted the dog. She looked tired. Snow fell directionless and without hurry, melted against the hot skin of my face. I looked back, and she was gone. I followed her tracks and the dog tracks to the mouth of a cave, a place I knew. I stepped into the dark and touched my hand to the dry stone.

Voices in the room played peanut gallery to my dreams. *My old boots will fit him. He's not worth the wearing of them. They're worn out already, no worth to be called for. He doesn't look like the sort to do what he did to Miss Boyerton. His blood is of the sort. I'll testify to that. Poor skinny boy. Pity the child always, but fear the man.*

Then Matius made an appearance. The cave ended, or was gone. I was outside again, wet forest, wet ground. Blood dripped from my uncle's right hand, and around his wrist he wore a bracelet of Mother's hair. We were on the deck of a schooner, being guided into the harbor by the Cudahey tug. Matius went barefoot and bare-chested, with a dingy beard hanging to his flat, starving belly. Something of the skinned animal about him, a cow's knee joint. The hills were bare of trees, and the log decks at the shore were stacked up higher than the roof of the mill. There were mountains of logs.

"We've finally worked ourselves out of this place," Matius said. "We'll soon have the fields of Ohio."

"There's more trees over the hill," I said. "We'll find more trees and cut them too."

"Will we now?" My uncle swung at me without warning, and I dodged the blow but lost my footing and went over the rail. More water. Not anything new, just more. I didn't care. Drown me once, shame on you. Drown me twice— I took a deep breath, and it didn't even catch, not so much as a hiccup. After a few breaths, I no longer sent bubbles rising but instead shot a cold jet of water like a clam, felt it against the backs of my teeth. There was no fear of death. I tromped around in the mud at the bottom of the harbor, and I could see all right. I climbed over a shoal marked by keel and rudder alike and on the other side came upon one of Bellhouse's graveyards. Men were chained around the chest like Gutowski had been chained, sprouting from the floor of the harbor like giant mushrooms. They were mostly sitting upright, with dead open eyes, but some had tipped over, and their eyes were shut. Silt would soon cover them. The crabs were feeding and shredded clothing; a bootlace and after it a laceless boot drifted by on the easy, ocean-bound current. I uncoiled the chain from a bony, naked corpse and freed it; and it floated to the surface like a kite taking off. I hefted the chain and liked the weight, so I wrapped it like a scarf around my shoulders and it felt good, like my coat had felt good before it tried to drown me. I walked on and saw dozens of salmon as big as my leg and told myself to remember where I'd seen them so I could come back later and catch them. I stood there and looked them in the eye, slid my fingers down their bellies and over their tails. Fish look at you like anything does, like people do. Locations seemed important. Later, climbing over a jumble of sunken logs, I came upon fishermen's lines in the water, herring threaded onto rusted hooks. I could see the bottom of their boat overhead. I tugged on their lines and stole their bait and watched the boat rock as they farmed the empty water. I laughed soundlessly. I was unkillable, walking on the harbor bottom, exulted.

Doc Haslett and his new wife were in and out of the room. Behind the sheet there were shadows and there was blood. I could smell it. Nurse and doctor passed like birds from shadow to sun. Someone was moaning, and I told myself to quiet down because it had to be me, but it wasn't, it wasn't me at all.

Suddenly I was awake, blinked at the door, blinked at the wall. The room was quiet. Then there was breathing, shallow, rasping. I was sure of it now: I wasn't alone. There was someone behind the sheet. It didn't matter. The sheet was there; it would keep us apart. Let them be over there, and I'll be over here.

Through the high window I could see that the rain and snow had stopped and it was daylight. I lugged myself out of the cot and stood and looked down at the strange nightshirt I was wearing and my mysteriously damaged feet. My mother might or might not have died in this house. I tucked the blankets under the pillow. The floor was scrubbed clean, and the grain and knots were risen and lumpy. I pulled back the curtain. Zeb Parker was sitting on a cot, barefooted, dressed in rags, looking back at me with dull eyes. He looked dead, and then he blinked.

"What're you doin here?" I asked.

"I've come to kill you." He lifted his hand, and I saw he had a piece of the broken ax handle resting in his lap.

"No, yer not."

"Someday I will." The scar on his jaw was as fat and pink as an earthworm.

"Did it hurt when she did it?" I asked.

"Did what?"

"Cut that hook from yer face."

"You are like yer father. I'll put you down like a dog."

"I said I was sorry."

"Not to me, you didn't. You never said nothin."

"I don't hate you, Zeb. I was scared, is all." I turned and pulled the curtain closed behind me, stood there thinking: It isn't real. He isn't real. "Did you hear me, Zeb? I said I was scared." I waited for him to answer, and when he didn't, I pulled back the curtain and he was gone, hadn't ever been there at all.

I opened my eyes when I heard someone come through the door. Tartan dropped my hat on the bed and then slipped off his coat and hung it on the back of the chair. He sat down and smoothed his mustache with his palm as he stared at me.

"You did this," I said to him.

"I certainly did. Saved yer life."

"Likened to kill me. Kozmin saved me."

"Feelin well enough to argue then. Good."

"Just saw a ghost, or maybe not. Can someone that isn't dead be a ghost?"

"I don't have opinions on spiritual matters."

"How do I know if yer real, if I just saw someone who wasn't?"

He blew his nose into his hand and wiped it on my bare arm. "How's that for real?"

I used the blanket to clean myself up. "What d'you want from me?"

"Sorry I pitched you in the river, is all. That's what I came here for." He stood and put on his coat. "Come by the hall when yer healed. Hank and the boys want to see you."

"Wait."

"What is it?"

"Get that fat doctor in here, and let's talk out what happened to my mother."

"He ain't here."

"Where is he?"

"How should I know? House calls occur in other people's houses." He turned and went out the door, shoulders wide enough to fill the frame. Bald spot on the back of his head was a scar, not a normal baldy spot at all. I studied the crust on my wrist. Real enough. I rested my hat on my face and fell asleep pleased with myself, like I'd passed some sort of test.

"The miracle man," Jonas whispered. "Rise up and greet us."

Eyes open, yet too bleary to see, words in my mind: Blessed are those whose way is blameless. I slid from under the blankets, blinked my past into my present. "Go find me some clothes, would you?"

Jonas left for a moment and then came back with my things folded in his arms, strange boots hanging from his fist. He waited while I dressed, didn't watch me. He kept his eyes on the sheet. My feet hurt awfully going into the boots.

The doctor's new wife was in the hall.

"Is he here?" I asked her.

She scowled at me, pretty, pretty quick to go ugly. "You'll get back in that bed if you know what's good for you."

"Answer my question," I told her.

"No, he's out. Let him rest here," she said to Jonas, "until the doctor gets back."

"When's that?" I said.

"Tonight, could be late. He wanted to speak with you."

"There'll be time for that later. Tell him I'll come find him." I dragged Jonas by his shirt to the door so we wouldn't have to talk to her anymore. I felt like I'd start screaming if I made a peep about my mother. Tartan and I would come back later and get it straight. A hundred times Haslett could've told me the truth. Selfish is what that is, or loyal. To what and who? She's my mother, isn't anything to him. Down the stairs, and we turned left on Water Street toward Beacon. Work crews were cutting tree roots at the roadside with axes, making a path for more new walkways. With all the buildings burned down, they were making adjustments to the streets, squaring and leveling what before had been mostly vineal and random.

Jonas gave me a sidelong look. "Boyerton fired me because of you."

"I didn't do it on purpose."

"I wouldn't like to think that you did."

The bridge was down and the tender's shack was empty. I stopped for a moment in the middle, straddling the gap in the two pieces of bridge, and eyed upriver, sighting the pilings and the masts of ships, reliably plumb. Jonas nudged my shoulder, and we moved on. We climbed into the low hills, and the rain turned to snow.

When we got to the Wynooche there were tracks on the road and down to the riverbank. People had been out in the storm, and after it too. I wondered if they'd been looking for me. Been to Cape Flattery? I hear it's nice.

We walked in step. I was scared. There was no life or uplift, no planks to walk on. We went in the streets and in the wilderness, in the mud. *Let us go into the fortified cities and perish there.* Poor Jonas, I thought. He's stuck with me now. And aren't we all standing in a cloud of gnats, and each one black and buzzing, a little death. I couldn't tell him what I'd done to his father, and I didn't know what lie I would invent when we got home. I labored under the heat in my head and in my arms, Jonas beside me moving like he was made of pig iron and lead, and the sun dropped away and we were soon in the dark. The lights were on at the Parkers', but we didn't linger.

When we arrived at the house, the door was wide open and snow had blown in like a clamshell onto the floor. Jonas lit the lantern in the kitchen. I could still see the bloodstain on the floor, but I doubted if Jonas would notice.

"Where is he?"

"Don't know."

He checked behind the door. "You take the shotgun?"

"Yes."

"Where is it?"

"Lost it somewhere."

Jonas shook his head. "Couldn't a got far with that foot a his."

"No, probably not."

"Would he have gone to the Parkers'?"

"No, he wouldn't be any more welcome there than I would." I remembered the ghost and Zeb's threat. I should write him a letter, I thought. Apologize for what I did.

Jonas was bent over looking at the jagged shotgun hole in the wall. "What's this?" he said.

"It went off."

"What'd you do?"

"We can patch it."

"Sure, but I'm wonderin why, that's all I'm askin."

"I was messin around and it went off."

"Where is he?"

I shook my head. "I don't know. I don't know what happened." I was picking through the discarded food on the plates and the counter and what was left in the pantry, and I found enough to make soup. By the time it boiled, the house was warm and orderly and clean enough. We sat at the table to eat, and it felt official, like we were getting down to business. I expected him to ask about Matius but he didn't.

"How'd you fall in the river?"

"I was more thrown than fell."

"By who?"

"Doesn't matter."

"You could've been killed."

"He didn't mean to kill me, I don't think."

"Tell me who it was."

"Some other time."

"No, you'll tell me now."

"Tartan, Bellhouse's man."

"I won't ask why, then."

"The why don't matter."

"I thought you liked Teresa Boyerton."

I wanted to tell him that betrayal felt the same as a fever, that murder and frostbite are only differentiated by the layers of damage, the perception of the wound. My blackened and yellowing toes weren't any different than what I felt was my rubiginous heart.

"It was almost an accident."

"Almost."

"I hadn't planned it."

"All the things you coulda done."

"I'm not proud."

"If you were, I'd beat you bloody."

"I said I'm not."

"Yer havin lots of accidents of late."

"Feels that way."

"Yeah, well, we better get some sleep."

Jonas stoked the fire and undressed to his union suit and then climbed into bed. I shut down the lantern and climbed in beside him. One of us could've stayed in Matius's bed, but we didn't. The blankets were damp and cold against my aching feet and smelled of mildew. Dark as tar; nothing moved or seemed capable of ever moving again.

"I told you before he wouldn't have you marrying his only daughter."

"I know."

"You had ambitions."

"Yes."

Jonas was silent for a minute or more. I imagined his mouth moving with thought. "The wanting of a thing doesn't make it different. It's still the thing it was before you wanted it."

Talking in the dark was like listening to someone else think. "I don't deserve more than this?"

"Who am I to say what you deserve? I'm nobody. I don't even have a job."

I didn't say anything more. I stayed awake and waited to hear Jonas's breathing change, and when it did I rolled over and slept.

By the time I woke up, Jonas had already left. I climbed stiffly from bed onto my wrecked feet and drank almost the whole pail of water and stoked the fire. I heated the dregs of the soup and ate it from the pan. Looking out the window, I saw that the barn doors were open and the cow was gone. I couldn't remember the last time I'd seen a chicken.

I wrapped myself in a blanket and sat down in front of the fire and picked at the skin on my feet, marveling at the colors. Cold sweats left me clammy, and my thighs stuck together. I caught myself staring vacantly at a dead spider; I didn't know how long I'd been doing it. I imagined a road paved with dead spiders. I stared at Matius's bloodstain until I'd mapped the shape and burned it into my mind, a country of itself, fluid borders of a land unexplored, not straight-edged or surveyed but river stamped, a territory.

I carefully made the bed and then climbed in. I curled up on my side and shivered uncontrollably. The bedroom door was open, and I could see dust in the light coming in the front window and stamping four dim diamonds on the floor.

When I woke, I forced my feet into boots and went outside. The snow had settled on the slash piles and the stumps, and the ground was white and smooth. You couldn't tell I'd dug around the posts or even moved them there recently. I hoped it snowed enough to bury the world. I followed my own shadowy path to the river. The sun was behind the clouds, and a cold wind had come up and was blowing through the trees and making them yaw.

Kozmin's bear hide was still there on the boulder, frozen stiff in the shade, white with frost. Didn't make any sense that he'd left it. A bird or something had hollowed the eyes from the sockets, left it pink and black-lidded, no blood to be seen. No life remained, no pretense of life, not sensible at least. The permanence of death settled like a wet leaf on my mind.

The water had come down, and the bank was shiny and slick with ice. I kept to the margin between water and the ground too steep to traverse and walked downriver. When I came to the bridge, I climbed down and studied the undersides of the timbers and planks, watched the yawning pocket of water where I'd been thrown. I made my way slowly downstream and found my coat, like a rag, hanging from a limb in the middle of the river, Kalypso's cloak. I squatted down on my haunches under the gray sky, thinking: If the water drops a little more, I'll be able to wade out and grab it. But I might fall in again. A chill ran through my blood, black as pollywogs, and quickly ended my breezy pontification. I wasn't going out there.

The sweat was cold on my skin as I walked back to the barn. The fever made my mouth taste awful, and I kept spitting and eating snow. I chewed some fir needles, and that helped.

I used the doorframe in the barn to snap a tine off the pitchfork and then used the bench vise to bend it into a hook. Rust flaked off in my hands like dried blood. I lashed fifty feet of neckweed rope to the hook and wound it around my elbow and shoulder and returned to the river.

From the bank it was an easy toss to my coat, and I hit it the first time, but it was sheathed in a thick layer of ice and I spent fifteen or twenty minutes on every throw, hauling the hook through the mess of snags again and again. I went up and down the bank like a pacing animal. *You've winked out. Get yourself to bed.* My bones hurt, and my muscles were stiff all the way up my back and into my neck.

My coat looked stupidly back at me. The chill was taking me now, and the world looked watery through my delirium. Absolution didn't go by valley or ridge; it wasn't even bound to the land. Forgiveness, for my father, meant all kinds of surrender. I wasn't ready for that. They'd throw me in jail if they caught me digging up Mother's grave. Never think such a thing. You can't. They'll throw you in jail anyway. I picked up my thoughts and threw them to the other side of the fence.

Through nothing but obstinance I managed to snag the coat, but when I was bringing it back, it fell free and landed in the river and, after a brief swirl, washed quickly away. I left the rope and hook and went after it. There's people that'd never do such stupid things as this. People that can afford not to act so repugnant, wasting half a day trying to foul-hook a shitty old coat. The rocks tripped me up, and I slipped and bashed my shin. I kept going, but slower, used my hands so I didn't slip as I traversed the cold boulders. My coat was up ahead in a pocket of slow water, and without hesitating I waded in and hauled it out.

The walk home to the fire and warmth was, like the near drowning, elongated by the cold. I'd be drying out for the rest of the day. Things were never as bad when you knew they would end. Unfamiliar boot tracks crossed my way three times, like I'd been flanked and flanked again. Someone was spying on me. I stopped and whistled, owl-hooted, thinking it had to be Zeb. With my arms out I waited for him, offered myself to whatever vengeance he wanted to take. A minute went by, then two; nothing moved. I covered my ears with my hands and went on, everything sounding underwater and in the wind. I imagined him running up behind me and clobbering me with that ax handle, but the blow never came. It took everything I had not to look back.

Stretched out naked in front of the fireplace, I rubbed the stiff hair on top of my head, played absently with my testicles, thought of Delilah and jerked my prick a few times but gave up for the feelings of guilt it brought to my mind, tainted by all that I'd done. On top of it all, I still loved Teresa.

My boots steamed, one on either side of the fireplace, and my jacket did the same from the hook on the hearth. I hadn't bothered lighting the lantern, and the only light was from the fire. The bloodstain on the floor seemed to have faded. The hole in the wall stared back at me.

After it got dark I heated some water for coffee and used the last of the sugar. The front door had been open for days. In my mind I saw the door swinging in the wind. A memory like that might stay forever. Some memories are sapphires and others are just dirt, full of bugs.

The brass handle on the trapdoor that led into the attic was wet and beaded with water droplets. The roof wasn't leaking; it was just the handle that glistened. My mother's books were in the attic, all with her name in them. The ones from Dr. Haslett read, "Nell Anne." The older ones and her diary: "Nell Anne Lansing." The books that had been given as gifts by a grandmother I'd never met had "Genelle" written in them. I quietly moved a chair from the table and opened the door; only darkness. Of course there was nobody up there, or I would've heard them by now. I pulled myself up and crawled around and scraped my knees and was stabbed in the palm by a shined nail. The small pine box, the one from her dresser, I reached for it, and it was gone. Maybe I'd moved it and forgotten. I probably had. I'd have to think about this. I wasn't right in my mind just then. I'd need to focus. The crates of books were still there, and when I climbed down, I brought one with me. I knelt on the floor and lifted one book and then another to the firelight to read the title until I found the one I wanted. I feared that my father had come back. There was no reason to think this; I was being foolish. He wouldn't dare. The box belonged to Mother. My father didn't even know I had it.

The book's spine cracked like a pullet's breastbone when I opened it. There was no inscription, only a date. This book was mine, given to me by my mother. I started at the beginning but still remembered it word for word, so I skipped ahead and started where the terrain seemed new. Nestor told the story. Telémakhos listened and urged him on with kind questions. I had the idea that I lived in the night of this story, the darkest corner, as if the story existed only in the day. Because who had ever spoken kindly of Jacob Ellstrom? Who wanted to find him except those that he'd done harm? The sun went down in the story as Nestor spoke, and the sun went down in the dark woods too. I moved closer to the fire and read until my eyes grew too weary, and then I curled up and slept on the floor.

I woke with a start, but I'd closed the door, and it was still shut when I rolled over to check. I smelled the full pulpy heaviness of the open book on the floor beside me. I watched the door for a long time, and the dance of the dying firelight on the knob and plate. All the rooms of the world are the same once the door is shut.

The Hermit

He heard the deer moving, the gentle pawing sound, even through the rhythmic dripping of the water from the trees. He corked the bottle and set it aside and crawled drunkenly to his pack. Frustrated inebriate, his hands confused by straps and buckles. He soon quit the struggle and lay back and faced the sky. The trees turned above him. When he closed his eyes, he felt sick. He moaned a little and spied the dancing giants through one reddened slit as if he was taking aim.

"There is no singular David that could level you all, but He could with no effort, all or one at a time. And does, you know. He does it already." Kozmin talked to the trees when he was sober too. The old man reached for the bottle but didn't find it. No more for now. No more. If he found his pistol, he might shoot himself and it wouldn't be an accident. "Might be." Clumsy sot that he'd become, helpless really. Baby with a pistol. With regularity he waged these little wars on himself, no matter if someone had drowned or come close or not gotten wet at all. Search party celebration. Bellhouse is buying. Bellhouse has never given a thing away in his life. You take a drink from him, you're signing a contract. Not that anyone pays me any attention, but if a man keeps nothing he should keep his pride: a piece of down in my hand. As a young man he'd found work plucking chickens, and a child on the farm knocked over the boiler pot while chasing a dog. Feathers stuck to the blistering skin on his feet and legs and someone picked him up from the dirt and took him inside the house, screaming, covered in feathers. Kozmin couldn't remember what had happened after that. Saying it was a lifetime ago wasn't a lie. Depending on the life, he could've lived fifty of them. He didn't want to sit up to drink anyway, didn't want to sit up at all, and he couldn't do anything lying down, not without making a mess of it. *I'll feel like a baby with a bottle if I lie down, might as well put my feet in the air and coo and burp.* Something in drunkenness was like going back to the womb or being just born—safety; if not that, then definitely helplessness. *How can a person do this to himself? I could be murdered by a blind, crippled midget armed with a blade of grass. No defense.* He tried to roll up and stand but failed, lay back down. He was staying, surrendered, recollecting, guilty swimmer, muddy water.

He'd worked with a man on the Salmon River who ate lying on his side, propped up on one elbow, like he thought he was some kind of Persian prince or a dying gladiator. A benefit to digestion, he said.

Above, the ridiculous spinning trees. "I hope they take you all." He smiled, but it was a fragile thing, and he was naked beneath them. Water dripped directly onto his face, but he didn't so much as twitch. "Grand firs, I'll make a pronouncement. We will all be sorry when you are gone." This was one of those occasions when he was truly afraid of sobering up, but he needed to move, get to some shelter and warmth. Soon, he decided, closed his eyes. Aldacot had a bed for him at the still. Since it'd blown, no one would bother him there. *You have a dozen places you can go. You can go to hell. Or try sober. Take hell. Might as well be drunk while I'm burning.*

He'd built the Salmon River mill himself, alone for over a year, and thought that someday it would bring him a fortune. Easy to love the poor, but hard to respect them. He and the future Mrs. Kozmin would raise their children in a grand house with windows in every room, windows above windows. Doors tall enough to ride horses through. Some mornings were so quiet it felt like the world had yet to form, like maybe something had broken during the night. The idea of oceans and whales, anything endless and endlessly moving, the liquid and the living; it seemed completely irrational when the river was frozen and sucked down to the rocks and there was not a sound, not even the wind. Not when the mill had been stopped.

Kozmin had purchased the Case steam tractor from the Salter Mine upriver where it had been wrecked and abandoned. He floated it down in pieces by himself, his first time on the sweep. River current can be the most wonderful thing in the world to the solitary man; it can ease all but the heaviest of burdens. Nothing would've been done without the river. Say this is true for all of history. Piece by piece Kozmin began assembling the engine, but some of the fittings had been pilfered, and the governor and the gauges had been destroyed in whatever catastrophe had led to the tractor's abandonment. He put in an order at the mine for the missing brass and a governor and governor belt along with a complete cylinder and a crankpin, and while he waited, he set to falling and skidding and setting a boom. Three mules and chain. A capstan would be like a god, but even without, there was more than enough to do. He built a smokehouse and a springhouse but didn't do much to improve the cabin. The mine foreman and a few of the crew brought in his shipment and helped him get it put together and bolted to a frame. They were there when he built his first fire and turned the wheel. Glory be thy name. The fury of the thing pleased him to no end, and he and the miners got blind drunk in celebration. A week later, when he set the blade to his first test piece and through it went, faster than any ten men could do it, he nearly wept.

A stranger that had been camped over the hill and heard the sound came to see about the racket. Soon after that, Kozmin and Mr. Harold Burns were working together to get a flume built. Partnerships, like all things, sometimes simply accrete. Harold was building a cabin on his gold claim and worked in exchange for lumber. They got along mostly. Kozmin did the majority of the talking. Harold was quiet and nervous; when he spoke, his hands came up. He'd come from Maine six years prior, and since he'd left home he'd been on the move. He went by foot always, had no love for horses or even mules, feared fast-moving water the way a cat might. Harold could walk forty miles in a day with a hundred pounds on his back. This impressed Kozmin almost as much as Harold's fear of water amused him. They built a diversion at Short Creek and finished the flume in August. When the aspens dropped their leaves, Harold walked out to have a last go among the civilized before the snow came and locked them in. Kozmin worked furiously through every minute of daylight. The snow came late, and by the time it did, he'd managed to mill and sell enough lumber to the new miners downriver to leave his place safely until spring. He would winter in Lewiston and return when the pass opened and finish the house.

The deer was nearby now. He opened an eye, and it was nearly on top of him, sniffing at his pack, licking the salt dried on the leather. Or blood. You trap a deer by leaving a pool of blood in the snare. He shot out a hand to catch its leg but missed, and when the small buck kicked and went to run, it stepped on his forearm and its sharp hoof left a scrape that bled. Nobody will believe this, he thought. And so don't tell them.

Late spring and Kozmin and his new wife, Molly, along with Harold, were headed overland by way of Indian trail to Kozmin's mill. They had seven rented mules and three they owned. The weather was fine, and they were enjoying their days. Molly had formerly been a schoolteacher, and one of the mules carried books and books alone.

"Won't even keep you warm long if you build a fire with em," said Harold.

"I don't need a fire to keep me warm," Molly said and made both men blush. She was a large and lustful woman, and on occasion Kozmin had caught her eyeing him like he was a mule she planned to work into the ground. They'd been married by the captain of a steamship on New Year's Eve, both of them so drunk at the time that they required explanations in the morning. Over the following weeks they gratefully discovered that they got along all right, and Kozmin bought her a ring that cost more than his mill, so he was sticking with his investment. Figured out of all the stupid things he'd done while drunk, he'd finally gotten lucky and done something good.

Last fall, when Kozmin first arrived in town, he'd heard rumors of Harold going on the rampage, and that he'd been locked in jail for weeks at a time. He'd been engaged to a woman—Kozmin never got her name, but she left with a photographer from New York and never returned.

They didn't speak of it, and by the time they were ready to leave, Harold wasn't drinking anymore, so it didn't matter.

The bolts he'd drilled into the rocks on the shore had held. A weight of worry dropped from his shoulders. From the bank it appeared that the winter hadn't done any damage, and the mill was mostly unchanged save for some new rust and the beginning of a robin's nest atop the main beam. He had to reset the irons, since they'd been removed and had spent the winter, along with his two saw blades and all the bolts and assorted parts, wrapped in oily burlap in a dirt-walled hole in the floor of his smokehouse. The flume had not been so lucky. A mudslide had washed away the last hundred yards to the river, but the surge of the flush with all of the runoff was such that if they hurried they could still use it. Maybe they'd dig out the bank while the water was pulling at it, but it was one or the other: log or dig. They worried that the ground on the ridge would be too soft for the mules. The snow had yet to completely clear off the peaks. Harold had laughed when he'd bought the rope from the company store at the Salter Mine to tether the mill platform to the bolts. "If the river comes up that high, no damn piece of rope will save it," he said. And when Harold left in the fall it was a slack and easy piece of river, but Kozmin had seen it in the spring and knew what to expect. The rope and the bolts had held, and what else could he have done? Built on higher ground, or closer to Short Creek, was the answer. But the slope was too steep there, and the creek had petered out by the end of July last year. Where would he be if he'd built there? Might've lost the whole operation to one of those damn mudslides. He didn't like being second-guessed, but he wasn't one to gloat either. The rope had held; it might not have been the best way, but it'd worked. What else mattered?

"You can build your mill wherever you choose," Kozmin joked, as he stripped naked and swam out to his mill with a cable and clevis. He yelled to the shore: "You can build your mill at the top"—he pointed to the ridge—"so you can haul all your trees straight up."

Harold waved him off and told him to hurry up; nobody wanted to see him naked anyhow.

"Speak for yourself," Molly said.

Kozmin laughed and swam the tag back to shore, and he and Harold used a block and tackle to haul it in. The sun-warmed grass on the banks was thick and cool under Kozmin's bare feet. Molly had her skirt hitched up to her knees, and the sun shone on her fat, creased legs. She looked like an overgrown baby and smelled strangely of milk.

"We're in business now," Harold had said, and Kozmin had agreed. But later those words would somehow tell the future and interrupt the rest of Kozmin's good moods, like a pebble in his shoe that only rolled out under his heel when he felt ready to walk for miles and on for the rest of his life. Because what was business, if not violence? No man can profit without another getting poorer, and trees don't grow fast enough either.

The bottle had more in it than he remembered. Maybe he'd pack up and make his way across the harbor. He didn't even know what he was doing here. He'd gotten drunk at Lott's and might've been thrown out. The whole goddamn Harbor is unfit, he thought. He'd come across the bottle on the mole, a sailor drunker than him, plucked it from his hand, laughing. Now you're a thief too. You've always been a thief; moral shortcomings are blameless. Blame God; he likes it.

The cabin that Kozmin had started the year before was passable, although it was small and windowless, with a sloppily laid wood floor. Daylight came through cracks in the mud chinking. He didn't have a proper bed, and he and Molly slept on a grass-tick mattress laid out on a hastily fashioned frame. She built herself a bookshelf out of stone, and it made the cabin seem instantly substantial. It got Kozmin working, and he built out the kitchen with log and then milled lumber for cabinets and even built a real table and three chairs. He was sure Molly would get pregnant soon, as much as they went at it. She'd pull up her skirt and lock her arms against the door jamb, a tree, the wall of the mill, anything in reach, and Kozmin would mount her, squirming into it, digging in his heels not unlike a rooster to a hen. Just loved it. Steam blasting, walls and floorboards creaking. She kept her wedding ring in a check in a log above their bed so she wouldn't lose it.

There was strange summertime frost on the ground when the log came free of the flume and crushed Kozmin's hand and broke his ankle. Harold came with a peavey and rolled it free.

"Shouldn't have tried to stop it," Kozmin said, holding up his bloody and fast-swelling hand. He was in bed for a week, with Molly nursing him and getting obviously bored of it by the minute. Then he was on the bank, one-handed and one-legged with a spud bar, prying the earth away from itself. He would've had to abandon the place if it weren't for Harold. His partner had stopped work on his own residence long ago, but Kozmin didn't know it yet. Heat of the summer, things started to change between them. Molly stayed away longer and longer during the days, helping Harold at the mill, and didn't come back to check on him. They ripped through his meager boom in a matter of weeks, and men came from Salter with a raft and loaded up lumber and hauled it back upstream with ropes and polemen. His hand was healing badly, and he could no longer make a fist. For several nights in a row he made his own dinner and ate it by himself, and when Molly finally arrived with Harold in tow, Kozmin told him: "We ain't got enough fer you, go home."

"I'll be leaving tomorrow anyhow."

"Givin up?"

"Course not, friend. Me and Molly are goin for supplies."

"I'll be healed soon," he said to his wife. "We'll go then."

"I want to go, though," Harold said. "I feel that I owe you."

"You don't owe me nothin, but if you want to go by yerself, yer welcome to."

"Don't worry, I'll bring her back here to nurse you up right."

"She ain't going with you."

"How do you know?" Harold asked, but Kozmin could tell he knew the answer already.

"I'd like to see town again," Molly said. "There's some things I need."

"I'll be up and at em in no time. Let Harold scoot, and we'll be right behind."

"We already decided," Molly said.

"Listen," Kozmin said to Harold. "I want you to leave. I don't want you hangin around here anymore."

Harold stood there scratching his head. Molly looked from one man to the other and then started packing her things. At first he thought she took the ring, but when he was getting ready to burn the cabin down, he found it on the floor under the bed. Years later, he would lose it in a card game, betting on a hand that he knew wouldn't win.

He'd made a mess of his lashings. He stashed the bottle in his pack and cinched it all down and hefted the load onto his shoulders. The prayer he muttered as he made his way through the damp woods was not a prayer of light and hope, of redemption; it was a prayer of guilt and solicitude. Amen. Nobody hardly ever gets what he wants, and that isn't a bad thing. Praise be.

Jacob

I *was hidden in the* trees watching for the sound when Kozmin passed by on the trail. I almost let him go by but I whistled and the old man turned.

"I'm lookin for you." I closed the pine box and shoved it under a fern. We shook hands on the trail.

"He's not drowned," I said.

"I know it. I was there when we found him."

"Been in a bottle?"

"War is what it is. What day is it?"

"Does it matter?"

"No. Guess not."

The wind was gusty in the trees and the sky was gray. I brought out the pistol from my coat to show Kozmin.

"Those make holes in people," he said.

"Traded it for a Disston I found stuck in a tree above Helmick's."

"Found, you say?"

"It was rusted to hell, and it took me all day to chop it out and another to clean it up."

"Hard to imagine walking off and leavin a saw."

"A limb must have come off and brained one of them. That's the only sense I can make of it. They had wedges in."

"I think that saw might've been more useful to you than the gun."

"Tough to fit a misery whip in your pocket." The old man touched his temple tenderly, as if it were a wound. "You'll see how light it is if'n you shoot somebody with it."

"I was going to see Duncan," I said.

Kozmin's face bloomed into a smile. "That's why you brought the pistol."

"No, that's not it at all."

"Yer gonna spy on him."

"That's right. He won't know I was there."

"I'm comin with you."

"Fine."

"Put that thing up before you put a hole in my leg."

"I'm not shooting anyone."

"Should a kept the damn saw."

"Maybe. Hold up."

Kozmin stopped.

"Wait here. I left something." I ran back up the road and got the box and ran back. Kozmin was sitting cross-legged in the mud when I returned.

"I need a drink," he said.

"You need a bath."

"I need redemption, a priest. I need to confess my sins."

"You need a lady. A bit of snuggle would do you good."

"No, not that. Salvation, nothing else will do."

"And another bath."

Kozmin was laughing, but he had tears in his eyes. I almost told him, Kozmin, you're my good friend. But I couldn't bring myself to say the words. Empires collapse from lesser omissions.

I sent Kozmin to peep in the window, and he waved me over because Duncan was sprawled on the floor, looking dead. Inside, we each took an arm and got him into the bedroom and stripped him down. He was a man now. I'd missed everything. Hope may spring eternal, but so does failure.

I soaked his shirt in cold water and draped it over his bare chest to try and drop the fever. We expected to see Jonas or Matius but they never came. With nothing else to be done, Kozmin and I sat at the table and played cards, and he continued with the story of Timofei Tarakanov.

Tarakanov thought that it could be the Americans that were scraping together an army to usurp the outpost. They'd traded pelts for weapons when it was forbidden. He told Medvednikov, but his leader wouldn't listen, said he wasn't scared. Tarakanov let him be not scared and stupid as an animal awaiting slaughter and sent his hunters, his friends, and their families south, round the island in their canoes for an extended hunt, and then took his pack and went inland. Nothing hurried or reckless, for they were being watched.

He constructed crude quarters near the place where his friend Kuskov had been killed by the deadfall. He stood in the spot and craned his neck to see where the limb had snapped. Kuskov was unlucky, or depending, since he felt no pain and was killed instantly, very lucky. On the hillside, in a gaping pit left by a downed tree, he thatched together a lean-to from the root ball downhill and dug a drainage of sorts, but it was watertight enough the way it was, and after he covered the ground with cedar bark, it was quite luxurious. No stinking farting promyshlenniki, no wet dogs or woodstoves that wouldn't draw. He had room to stretch out and have a fire, and he relaxed in his pit, thinking of what could be done about the raiders when they came. It would be best to move off and wait for them to steal inside the barracks and the storerooms and then lock them inside and set it all on fire, but no one would see the sense in ruining so much hard work, even if the storerooms were emptied. The promyshlenniki would wake to the dream of having their skulls cleaved open. To his keepers, the tsar and Medvednikov, the peoples of this coast were a flame that needed to be extinguished. But like a song that ended too soon, they would be missed; at least, by him they would.

Waiting out the rain, he mended his boots and made a small kit for future repairs if he found himself isolated and fit it inside his jacket between the wool and the leather. He rubbed beeswax into the seams of his clothing and scraped his knife over the whalebone club he carried called a khootz, which he'd taken off a Kiksàdi warrior who had tried to tip over his baidairka in a running battle up the coast almost three months ago now. He knew what it was to stand and fight with these Koliuzhi, and he was no coward. He was no drunken fool, expecting an Aleut slave to save him.

"He should've walked from that outpost and found his own way, put down his servitude."

"That would've been impossible," Kozmin said.

"Why?"

"He was a man of honor."

"He was afraid of going it alone."

"It's not dishonorable to feel fear in the face of loneliness."

"Honorable men can be the worst kind."

"This story is part of the first story and part of the last, but we haven't gotten there yet, so be patient."

"I'm patient."

Kozmin continued:

As I said, Tarakanov first arrived in the year 1799, sailing on the Kon-stantin. Chief Manager Baranov was building a fort after a false purchase of rights from the Tlingits. Tarakanov helped build the barracks and storehouses, and later he was at New Arkhangel after the battle was won or lost, depending on how you see these things, but before all that, he was among the twenty-five of his countrymen led by Medvednikov who stayed when Baranov returned to Three Saints. For the years that followed, until the first battle, he guided the Aleut hunters, upward of two hundred in number, on relentless otter and seal expeditions. He alone extended the Russian grounds for miles in every direction, and I should say, making no friends among the Kiksàdi, and the storehouses filled to the rafters and pelts had to be packed into the stockade and in the bunk-houses too.

So it was in the spring of 1802 that Tarakanov saw the smoke above the trees and picked up his rifle and his pack and ran toward the shore. He could've stayed in his shelter under the roots of the great tree and never been bothered. He was a young man and taller than most, and he flew through the woods like a wolf. Behind him was a gutted and skinned black bear, hanging limp from the spikes he'd driven into a fir tree for the purpose.

He prayed then for his friends, for their safety, for the very timbers of the fort to protect them and not to be burning. Surely it was something else that was aflame, a smoke of nothing, a celebration: ocean fires; he prayed for this to be true, but when he finally broke from the forest he was faced with great walls of fire and smoke pouring into the gray sky, and on the ground among the buildings he saw his comrades dead and dying and some headless, and alongside them many of the Aleuts in similar condition, and nearer the water there were dozens more. It was over, nine at night or three in the afternoon; the fight had been done for some time. The blood was black, and the gulls and ravens and eagles with pink and bloody crowns were feasting. The raiders were mostly Kiksàdi, but there were others; he could tell by the war canoes, some hooked, some sweeping. They came out of the smoke hauling the Russians' pelts and the unburned supplies by the armload, some of their heads still covered by large wooden animal masks that made them teeter like giants when they bent down to relinquish their burdens and stood again. Some were dressed in clemmons armor fashioned from leather and wood. Chinese coins flashed on their chests and arms even in the misting rain, and the quillwork of others gave the appearance of raw bone warriors. They had rifles slung across their backs with rawhide, and some had daggers and hammers fastened to their legs and torsos.

Tarakanov retreated a few paces and settled himself behind a stone wall they'd left unfinished the year before. If they were overrun, they were to retreat to the wall and stand them there. But they had no chance to flee. The ship they'd been building was on fire, the steambox as well. Baranov's house was burning. Anchored in the harbor were an American and a British ship that had been there since before Tarakanov left. He'd long suspected that they'd have something to do with this if it happened, and he spotted two American sailors gathering weapons from the dead. He nearly rose up and fired on them. His heart broke, thinking of his *friends and that he was alone now, when before that's all he'd wanted. Grief filled him like wax in a mold.*

He never saw the club that came down behind his ear and knocked him unconscious. The Kiksàdi carried him to the beach and threw him in a canoe with a few surviving Aleuts and rowed them, along with the Aleut's women and children to their village. If it weren't for Captain Barber anchored in the bay, he would've stayed there and might have died there, a servant to his enemy. At the time he thought this to be the worst possible end.

"He was right," I said.

Kozmin smiled and continued. *So it was Barber that lured Shkàwulyéil's raiding party onto the deck of his ship* Unicorn *with a promise of an execution. The condemned man was an Aleut, an elder who had angered the Kiksàdi years before—a thief and a murderer, they said. As soon as the raiding party was on board, Barber's crew surrounded them, placed them in irons, and threw them in the brig. It was these men who were traded for Tarakanov and eighteen other Aleuts, along with the bales upon bales of otter pelts that were taken from the storehouses before they were set on fire. Barber ransomed Tarakanov back to Baranov for ten thousand rubles at Kodiak. Despite himself, Tarakanov had grown to like Barber, and if he had the choice he'd have stayed on board with him instead of where he was now—*

"What do you mean, where he is now?" I said.

"We've moved on in the story."

"Well, go on and tell it then. Stay on the scent, if you can manage."

Kozmin smiled. "No, that's all for tonight. It's late. We'll finish it another time."

"Go on and tell it. I'm not a bit tired."

"Well, I am."

The hermit gathered his pack and went out the door. I went to the window and watched him go into the barn. A few moments later I followed him. I couldn't be there alone if Duncan woke up.

Duncan

———

There *was something breathing* in the darkest corner of the room. I watched and waited for what seemed like hours, could've been days, my stomach full of fear. Eye shimmer, big wet eyes, then a blink. Eye shimmer. It squatted there, the beast, and watched me back.

I could hear the murmur of voices on the other side of the door. I'd been moved here at some point—this was my room—but from where, I wasn't sure. There'd been a winter swim, and I'd nearly drowned. Nearly been murdered, was what it was. Rescued by the same that tried to kill me. After that, going for my coat. Sick again. Stay off the ground if you don't want to be mistaken for carrion. Jonas was out there with Kozmin. My father. They'd found me on the floor, him and Kozmin, much like I'd left Matius. That's who moved me, I remembered now. I wanted to throw something at whatever it was that was watching me, but I couldn't bring myself to move. Over the course of hours, what felt like hours, I made myself accept what it was. I couldn't be afraid. I made myself take the unthinkable into my heart. I had to believe it was there, and that it didn't mean me any harm.

The voices were quiet when I climbed out of bed and dressed and pulled on my boots. I opened the window and pointed so the bear would go out. *You can't stay in here. No old death indoors. Get out.* The bear ambled from the dark corner where it had been crouching and climbed through the window. I could see its spine and its beehive of muscles, the white lines of its ribs rimmed pink and black; an amphibious looking tail and wet, bloody haunches. I closed the window quietly behind it and went out the door.

The living room was lit by the fireplace and smelled of tobacco and fried beef. My father wasn't there. I checked all the cracks and corners, but he was gone. Jonas was asleep on his bedroll in front of the fireplace. His face was open and unguarded, a bead of drool on his cheek. He appeared much older than when he was awake. Men wear out like leather wears, in the end useless. I knelt down and pulled the blanket up onto his body and tucked him in with the care and tenderness he deserved.

I found paper and a pencil and wrote a letter to Jonas, telling him what I'd done and where his father was buried. I told him why. I went back to the bedroom and put the note on the pillow. He would hate me now too. Everyone would. I made the bed and went back to the kitchen.

My legs felt too long and too skinny beneath me. I picked at some scraps on the counter. When she got cold, my mother used to say she felt the worry of death in her bones, and that worry had been in my hand and I'd snapped it and the worry went to Teresa, the pain, just for a moment, then it was back in me. I brimmed with it. And her father, he'll be coming, even though it was an accident. She said she wasn't mad. She was sorry it had to end, and confused as to why I'd hurt her. If I were in her place, I could never react that way, and didn't really understand how she had, wounded without malice, without blame. I knew love like I knew folly; I wanted to go back. I wanted to find her and I wanted to hide.

I found a box of groceries on the back step. Jonas must've brought them. I picked up an apple and looked at it but couldn't bring myself to eat it. Back inside, I pocketed a beef bone from the pot to give to the bear because he was of course outside, waiting for me, and then tossed it back onto the stove because that was crazy. It was then that I found the pistol wrapped in a scarf in the cupboard, loaded and ready. The weight of a single jack. Beautiful and smooth. "Nightwalker," I whispered, "let's go for a stroll."

Mother smiled when she saw me walking toward her on the road. Then she saw the gun in my hand, and her face changed. "No," she said. "You can't do anything about it. You'll make things worse. Go back home."

The idea of killing Charlie Boyerton coalesced in my mind. I hadn't planned it, not really, not until now, until Mother said something, warned me not to, like she had the right to warn me about anything. She tried to hug me, but I held her at arm's length and went on. Behind me I heard the latch on the door close, and I was relieved that she'd gone inside and gotten out of the cold. She'd be there when I returned. I thought this and then remembered, could never forget.

The last of the light from the moon was gone from the path and had drifted high onto the trees. But before I reached the road, the door opened again and Mother came out into the snow and ran to me in her bare feet and gave me a scarf and my hat and gloves and Father's old oilskin coat. I took what I was given and—Mama, go on, go on back inside—ushered her once again indoors. I set the pistol on the dwindling woodpile and put on the extra clothes. The coat was fur-lined and stiffly molded to my father's shape; it smelled of him. I thought I'd burned it, but here it was, short in the sleeves.

The bear came out of the shadows, and without any ideas on what else to do, I followed it down the road.

"What am I going to say to her?" I asked myself aloud. "If she'll even speak to me. She might not."

"She won't go with you no matter what you say," the bear said. He had an old man's voice, like Doc Haslett, and not foreign at all.

Ridiculous, I wasn't talking to the ghost of a dead bear or the spirit of the doc or whatever it was. The vision of my mother had already started to fade, and I fit it into the back of my mind.

"I wasn't asking for opinions."

"Well, I'm the only one here. Who else would you be asking?"

"You aren't here." Dreaming something out here, wandering, seeing my terribly gone and most likely dead mother. If I knew one true thing, I wouldn't be so worried, but not even the gun in my hand could tell me the truth. I thought I'd take a piss, and if I didn't wake up in bed like I always used to with the pissy blanket, then I was awake, and if I was awake, I was on my way to see Teresa.

"Maybe I'm dreaming, and you aren't here," the bear said.

I stopped and looked into the darkness, not seeing but knowing that I'd somehow strayed from the road. I thought it was nice of the bear to break trail because, outside the horse and wagon tracks, the snow was quite deep. Then I caught myself and caught myself again, truly shaken, standing in the dark, lost. Dreams can scare a person into a real death, is what they said.

"We've lost the road."

"Nah. It's before us, just so."

A few steps forward, and there it was. Deal me in. "So it is. Say, how'd you find your head? Last I saw of it, it was attached to your hide, stretched over a rock." I remembered that Kozmin said he'd retrieved the dead bear from the flooding river, and it suddenly made sense that the bear had returned to the spot and found his head there, or wherever Kozmin had stashed it, and simply put it on like I'd put on my father's coat.

The bear ignored my question.

"I want Teresa back."

"It's best you brought a gun."

"What will I do if she won't talk to me?"

"Couldn't say. My question is this: What will you do when you have her? Will you try and explain how your very blood holds claim on your behavior?"

"Shut up with that."

"She's scared of you now. You, small brute, damaged her slender and delicate arm."

"I'll tell her how sorry I am, and that I'll take care of her no matter what."

"Her father is going to kill you. You, my friend, are stuck. Stuck as a thing can be."

"Do you think she's told him what I've done?"

"She didn't have to tell him. He knows. He fired Jonas, didn't he?"

"He did. That's right."

"He's coming for you. He's her father. He doesn't have much of a choice in the matter."

"Jonas could've done something and got himself fired."

"You know that isn't true."

"Then I'll kill the bastard first before he comes to kill me." Weapon in hand, feet under way. The fear I felt was equal, dying to murder, the light of the sunrise against the light of sunset, simply directional, not diminished. I pointed down the road so the bear would get going. "She still loves me."

"Oh, but she might forget you anyway, might deny you out of love. She might already be gone."

I stopped, and the bear turned its head to look back, torn skin hanging from its jaw. "You're just a dead bear, and I'm being slint enough to talk to you."

"I'm not as dead as you might think."

"With your knife-hacked meat and lack of hide."

"How sure are you that you got out of that river?"

The memory was fresh and terrifying, icy hands pulling me down to a place somehow warmer, deeper and warmer, like forgiveness.

We trudged on in silence, and I watched the bear, stepped in its tracks. Like forgiveness, like cold water; it went easier after a while. Then there was someone on the road ahead of us. I stopped, and the bear stopped. We were near the Parkers', but I couldn't make out any house lights through the trees.

"Zeb?" I said.

Whoever it was kept coming and didn't speak.

"Zeb, I'm sorry for what I did. I swear. Please, Zeb. Talk to me."

I still couldn't make out if it was him, but whoever it was, they weren't stopping. I lifted the pistol, and they jumped off the road and silently disappeared into the trees. When I got to where they'd been, there weren't any tracks that I could find. The bear was sitting on its haunches. A thin layer of ice had formed on its body.

"You want my coat?" I said, embracing whatever I could, whatever face of the world was before me. Without a roof you find a tree, without a blanket you pile up the leaves.

"I'm a dead bear. Why would I need a coat?"

"Cuz Kozmin stole yours." I shrugged off my father's long coat and draped it over the bear's back. It wasn't going to stay on. I tried to force the bear's paw into the sleeve but couldn't manage. The thing smelled awful, and the ice was bloody in the palm of my hand. I needed to use both hands. "Hold this." I passed over the pistol, and it dropped into the snow and was swallowed up. I reached for it and knocked my head against a tree trunk and fell back into the snow. The road was somewhere behind me. A strange coat, maybe Jonas's, was draped lengthwise over a low limb. I got up and snatched back the coat and put it on, then dug the gun out of the snow and wiped it down with my bare hands.

Back on the road the snow was gummy with mud and felt like clay beneath my boots. Wagon ruts deep enough to show the axle dragging sectioned out the path.

The lights of town were glowing above the last hill. The widowmaker's tangle, the Janko tepee. I'd lost my gloves, or maybe I never had any. I couldn't be sure. The gun was an icicle in my hand.

Men were busy in the mill yard, walking the bunks and loading carts to go to the docks. The lights lit the steam and made the largeness of the place seem even greater. There was yelling and the hollow sound of chains snapping to against big timber. The screams of the giant saw blades in the mill were dampened only slightly by the walls and the log bunks that surrounded them. Lantern-lit flat-bottomed boats steered by pole men were on the water, straightening out the booming grounds and bringing in strays.

Down harbor the big ships were anchored in the channel, waiting for the flood-tide dawn and the bridge to open so Cudahey could guide them in. I passed a few houses, all dark. Someone had forgot to put their chickens up, feathers in the mud, three or four birds' worth in neat clusters, like they'd spurted up from the ground. Farther on, a dog tied to a porch rail barked at me, and I barked back. Shaggy, one-eared guardian, his chickens would be alive still. If he had any. I climbed from the snow and mud and onto the shoveled and swept planks.

The Sailor's Union was locked up and dark. I went around back, but that was locked too. I'd been hoping for a warm reception. Young hero, come home.

The lights at Dr. Haslett's were on. I went up the stairs and banged on the door. I heard footsteps and then there he was, looking right at me, bloated as a dead cow.

"Is my mother dead?

His eyes narrowed, and he stepped back and motioned me inside.

"I don't want to come in."

"I never wanted to lie to you. I tried to talk her out of it."

"Where'd she go?" I took the pistol from my belt.

"Put that away and come inside."

I didn't put up the gun, but I followed him down the hall into the living room. The fireplace was roaring, and the doctor had to pick up an open book from his chair so he could sit down. I hunkered next to the fire and held the gun to the flames. "You knew what it meant, doin that to me, helpin her leave."

"I had to do what she asked. I didn't have a choice. I loved her. I couldn't say no."

Haslett's new wife was up now, standing in the hallway behind him. She'd heard what he said, and I could tell he'd be getting a ration when I left. He turned and motioned for her to go back to bed. "Wait here," he said to me, and followed her down the hall.

When he came back, he handed me a bundle of letters tied with string. I knew what they were. I slipped the gun back in my belt. "She wrote you and not me."

"I'm sorry, Duncan. I'm truly sorry. I made her a promise, and I didn't keep it. You aren't my son, and it hurt me to see you because you remind me of her."

"What was the promise?"

"You were supposed to live with the Parkers."

I looked down at my hands, shaking in my lap.

"I was supposed to keep you safe," Haslett said.

"This is safe, is it?"

"Men have to be accountable for their lives."

I couldn't speak. I shoved the letters inside my coat and took a box of matches from the table and a cigar, and I left.

I stood outside the tent city and watched the shadows and then went and checked the alleys for the McCandlisses. No one was about. No Bell-house. No Tartan. All was quiet. A safe night, and no one knew it.

I wandered up the hill and left the burn, and the noise began to fade. I climbed a low fence into a vacant lot and waded out among the debris of what used to be the Slade Hotel. The back wall was still standing, and behind it a section of stairway led up to a kind of observation deck built between two massive fir trees, both dead and twisted and charred.

From the veranda I could see all the way to Boyerton's mill and survey the comings and goings of the men on the Line. They reeled in and out of the streetlights like they were attached to cables, tiny donkey engines dragging them along. Women and men and men and men went arm-in-arm down the muddy and planked streets, pressing shoulders together to keep from falling.

The water in the harbor held the lights of the town like a slow river holds stones. I was filled with a deep untethered feeling, wild in all my muscles and veins. Maybe I didn't want to do anything, but I had to. I had no choice.

I climbed into one of the trees to have a better look around. The snow fell away, and wet ash blackened my hands. Below me the town was a jumble of watery lights and crooked shadows. Tegumental snow, the body's protector. Smoke poured from chimneys and hung low in the air. The mud in the side streets was shiny and dimpled-looking. The wind came off the harbor, and I climbed higher and perched on a limb like an owl.

A procession of wagons and men on horseback and on foot was coming down the hill. They passed directly below, and I could see Charlie Boy-erton riding at the front on his fine black horse. Out on some nocturnal business at the mill. The ships in the harbor told the story. There were only three independent mills left, and soon Boyerton would own all of them. I watched as the procession went on and toured right through the heart of town to the mill. The gates were opened, and the lights burning overhead illuminated each man as they passed.

I dropped from my perch and got out of the wind beside the tree and struck a match and puffed the cigar to life and let the acrid smoke trickle from my nose and mouth. I opened the first letter, dated December 15; it began: "Dear Milo, I've made it safely to New York." The match burned my finger, and I dropped it. I lit another and read on.

> *I have found work in the Bath Veteran's Home and am supporting myself. My brother Zachary knows that I am here, but no one else in my family has any idea. You can write to me at this address. Please send news of Duncan as soon as you can.*

I crumpled the letter and threw it as far as I could, and the wind caught it and it landed in the street. I struck another match.

> *Dear Milo, Thank you for keeping an eye on Duncan. I want him to go to school and leave the Harbor as soon as he's old enough. I've enclosed money for him so you can start a fund. Will you do this for me? I am humbled daily by what I see at the hospital. What I ran from, they would kill for, and most of them have. Please write soon.*

Wadded up and thrown into the street, another match.

> *Dear Milo, I'm sorry to hear that the money I sent was stolen from the envelope. I don't know what else to do. Has Jacob returned yet? You said you see Duncan in the streets, doing what? Why isn't he in school? What about the Parkers? Aren't they watching him still? I'm not accusing you of neglect. I just need to know.*

Torn and wadded and thrown. She needed to know. My thumb was blistered, and I only had two more matches. I couldn't read any more. There was something so evil and cold about her leaving me, but all I wanted was to see her. I ground the cigar out beneath my boot heel. The wind blew out the next match, and the one after. I sat in the moonless dark and waited for daylight and imagined my mother bathing invalid soldiers in a place called Bath, and why wouldn't it be.

Not much later, the mill gates opened, and Boyerton came out alone and rode up the hill. I waited, not even breathing, terrified. I hoped he'd stop somewhere or turn off and not pass by but he always appeared again, rounding corners, drawn to me. Then he was there, and under a streetlamp I could see his face, weary and pale. He kept riding, and when he saw the letters in the mud he pulled up his horse and dismounted. He flattened one against the flank of his horse and then struck a light and read it. I thought his night business at the mill could've been about me. He could've been getting men together to bring me in. I had the pistol out, and I stood up and walked toward him.

"That's mine," I said.

He turned stiffly and dropped the lit match in the street. "Who's up there?"

"That's my letter."

"It's you. Get down here and let me see your face."

I went slowly down the stairs. I cocked the pistol and slipped it into my coat pocket. A dog barked in the distance, and a breeze picked up. I took off my hat.

"You're coming with me," Boyerton said.

"No, I'm not."

He held up the letter. "From your mother?"

I nodded, replaced my hat.

"You come with me, and I'll see you're not harmed."

"Where are we goin?"

"To see the judge. You need to be punished for what you've done to my daughter."

"I've already been punished. Been punished my whole life."

"I don't like excuses, never have." He handed me the muddy letter. "Follow me." He turned his horse around and mounted up. "Don't run away. Be a man about this, and it won't be half as bad. Come on."

"I'm not running."

I waited until his back was facing me; it was an easy shot, less than ten yards. Not meaning to but doing it anyway, I took aim and unbelievably squeezed the trigger and the richest man in the Harbor pitched forward in his saddle. The horse ran forward and then bolted away from the gaslight, and Boyerton fell into the mud. I checked the street and the windows for movement and then went and gave Boyerton a nudge with my boot. His throat gaped where the bullet had exited, and there was blood and bone and sinew. He was dead. I squatted there, looking into his face. The gaslight gleamed watery in his dead eyes. There was no mistaking what life was, and where it hid. Wonderful death filled his gaze, utterly nothing. I set the gun down on his chest so it wouldn't get muddy and touched my fingers to the warm blood of the death wound. I was amazed at myself and what I'd made. His horse stood broadside up the block, looking back at me. I had to leave. I had to run.

Book THREE

*D*id you see him?"

"*Course I did. The son of a bitch. Let's follow him.*"

Up the hill the two bedragglers tail the lone horseman.

"*Crap, my lungs.*"

"*I'm blown. That horse can step.*"

"*Fuck, c'mon. We'll catch up unless we quit.*"

"*I thought we were quit already.*"

"*We'll rest.*"

"*Why're we followin him anyway?*"

"*Cuz I've put in seven years, and he didn't even tip his hat.*"

"*He paid you for yer years.*"

"*Course he paid me.*"

"*Is he to be yer friend?*"

"*I'd like to kick him in the ass, is what I'd like. C'mon, let's catch up and swack him with rock-filled snowballs.*"

Running now. Running up the hill for all of fifty yards, then stopped again.

"*My legs are broke.*"

"*Let's sit for a moment.*"

"*Time you think it is?*"

"*No idea.*"

"*If we sleep now, we'll never wake in time to beat the whistle.*"

"*Who's sleepin?*"

"*Yer not tired? Look at you, yer done.*"

"*C'mon.*" *Snow scooped from the walk, and rocks added from the gutter.* "*I'm ready.*"

They're under way when they hear the shot. And stop. And look around.

"*Hear that?*"

The snowball drops, tunk, *on the walk.*

"*Course I heard it.*"

"*Let's go back.*"

"Fuck you. C'mon."

Far up the road the black horse passes under the streetlight. It's being led up the hill, and they walk after, still thinking they'll catch him and give him a good swack, until they see the man in the road, nearly trip over him.

"It's him. Christ it's him."

"He's deader'n shit."

"The killer took his horse. That was the killer."

"Did you see his face?"

"I barely made out the horse. What're you doin?"

"Seven years."

"From a dead man. Don't keep the billfold. Don't keep nothin but the green."

"Closest I ever been to him."

"Me too."

"We can't tell a soul, or we'll be shackled and hung in five minutes flat."

"Let's go home. Don't take the watch."

"Why would I not take the watch?"

"Because. I shouldn't have to explain that."

"I'm takin it."

"You can't keep it."

"It would pain me to leave it."

The gold pocketwatch ticks lovingly in his palm.

"The pain of keepin it could be worse."

"Yer right. Yes, good-bye."

The watch, tucked back into the coat and patted tenderly. "With all this." *Bills wag in the night. "I'm buyin one of the Dolbeer donkeys and gettin in the woods. I'll be a king."*

"Hire someone to work it and stay home."

"Even better."

They stand with crumpled faces and appraise the settled death.

"It's awful, I know, but I still feel that I should give him a kick."

"You robbed him already. Let's go. Downhill'll be faster. You'll see. Go on and run. I'll give you a head start."

"Hell, I can pay someone to race you now."

Another wag of the bills, a bird flies low overhead.

"Put that shit away. I'll meet you at the bottom."

"Short-legged fucker. I'm faster than you at full tilt, and I'm steamin along at a mosey."

Boots on the boards. The night concedes.

Teresa Boyerton

She sat up in the dark and let the blankets slip from her shoulders. Light from the street threw ragged but familiar iodine-edged shadows across the ceiling. She knew the weeping willow by shape, sound, and even, if the winds were strong enough, smell. But it was a noise that had woken her. Something was wrong, besides the poultice on her arm, like an oddly wrapped gift, like a Chinese finger trap she'd seen in the junk shop with Duncan, a memory of connections before she'd made the connections themselves. One finger slid inside the woven sleeve, waiting for another. All her days with Duncan now seemed to be a warning.

And it was him; he was the sound. He was yelling for her, and his voice was a shock to her system, a bee sting without the pain. They'd come to an agreement. They were no longer together. She'd promised her father. She didn't know what time it was, but it was late, and all she could think was, Thank God my mother is in Seattle. Then, My father. He must be gone. He wouldn't allow this sort of thing to go on outside his front door.

Teresa lit the lamp, and Duncan finally went silent, but when she heaved open the window, he started yelling again. He stood under their yardlight in the trampled snow like a man on a stage. He had the reins of a black horse in one hand and a pistol in the other. Snow covered the porch roof below her window, and the husks of the sunflower seeds that Miss Dalgleish had tossed out were intermingled with the tracks of birds.

"Teresa, please."

"Go away."

"You have to come down."

She held up her arm so he could see what he had done to her. "No, I don't. Go away." He turned his back to her and faced the black expanse of the harbor. He kicked at the ground like he was kicking an invisible ball. He dropped the reins and swung the pistol like a bat, raging. He was talking to himself.

She closed the window, and he yelled her name again and again. The tinny repetitive sound itched in her mind like her bandaged arm itched. To herself: "Shhh, Duncan. I'm coming."

She went downstairs, filled with apprehension, quiet as cotton in her bare feet and nightgown. If he asked to marry her, she had to say no, but she didn't want to. She didn't want any trouble. A fine way to live, without fuss. Pets do that. But she understood the facts as her father had explained them to her: She was young, and Duncan wasn't the man to stand beside her and carry her for the rest of her life. He had just been the one for when she was young. In another world he could be her husband. In this, the answer was no. Angry now, she wondered why with Duncan it always came down to getting away with something. It would be nice to be in the right for once, to be proud. Why couldn't he be someone she could be proud of?

She quietly unlocked and opened the door, and Duncan picked up the reins and carefully looped them to the fence rail and passed through the gate. He still had the pistol in his hand, and when he saw her looking at it, he slid it into his belt. She recognized the horse but it didn't make sense that he had it. He mounted the stairs and looked at her arm.

"He's not coming back."

"Who? Who isn't coming back?"

His eyes were wild and his skin was white. He looked like a ghoul. The porch boards creaked as he came closer to take her hand. She pulled away.

"I shot him."

Then she knew what he'd done. "Where is he?"

"In the street where I left him." His eyes were fixed on her arm. "I'm sorry."

"He's dead?"

"We'll be to San Francisco before anyone can catch us. We need money."

"I'm not leaving." She didn't want to believe him, but there was her father's horse, and there was blood on his hand, his sleeve. "My brother is awake."

"If he wants to stand in our way, tell him to come down here. I'll kill him too."

She pushed him in the chest, and he stumbled back off the porch onto the stairs. "I'm going to scream if you don't leave."

"Please, Teresa." He was crying.

She looked into the face she no longer knew or could understand and screamed; she screamed as loudly as she was able, and didn't stop until he was gone. He didn't take the horse. He ran, and when he passed under the streetlight she could see the bottom of his boots caked in mud, his coat flapping, and the glint of the pistol as he took it out of his belt. Then he rounded the corner and was gone. The neighbors came out, old Mr. Jessup and his wife, Audrey, and after Teresa told them what she believed had happened to her father, they sent for the sheriff. Oliver's door was locked, and he wouldn't open it. Even after they'd found the body, and the sheriff and two deputies were downstairs and Miss Dalgleish had made coffee and heated biscuits, he wouldn't get up. Teresa stood in his doorway, begging him. "Oliver, please. Something's happened to Father. Please open the door. Please."

Oliver Boyerton

Some things I've learned:
—Once slowly is better than hurried through twice for carelessness.

—No errand is so trivial as to be done shoddily (if I could only live by this rule, I would be a man illimitable).

—Practice things in your mind to prepare your body, things as simple as walking in mud and on muddy planks.

—Forget dreams upon waking, they're not for the daylight page.

—Anoint thy skin to avoid chapping and chafing.

—Change your skivvies every day, and most importantly: never turn down trim, no matter how rough it may be. It all gets bejewelled in the mind.

Lacking a true scholarly streak, I make lists. Take notes as needed. Addenda adagio.

Presented: A face expertly shaved. A face patted dry and grinning. My teeth, my best feature. If only the rest of me could be my teeth.

Toiletries scattered around the washbasin. Disorder breeds disorder. Breeding is disorder, breeding breeds disorder. Nothing orderly about it except that most fundamental notch and peg of it. Gophers and gopher holes. The thought of rodent sex, then human sex. A childish smile bub-

bled up from my neck as I straightened out the lotions and balm and oint-
ment for my pocked and pitted skin on one side, along with the colognes
I never used but liked to smell, and the brushes and combs and razor on
the other. When finished I cyclopsed my visage in the mirror and was
confronted with the fact that my father dies only once, and today is the
day that we bury him. Take stock and prepare: the presentation shall be
grief mainly, with a fair portion of bravado. I'll have to be the man of the
house, the half a man. One eye crying half a tear.

To me it seemed that my father could disallow the weather and keep the
sunlight away out of spite.

Today we remember a stubborn man, a man (cough) illimitable. I am a
vessel that has been filled with his knowledge, and screwed tightly down
with his lonely mistrust. Separate as cream from milk. Some see independence—he did build one of the most profitable mills on the West Coast
outside of San Francisco—and he owns half the town, and you, friends,
owe him your dark sorry lives. Thank him. Lick his oily boots. But I have
to ask, how did you see him? What was he to you? One can never tell. I
used to believe that people with red hair saw the world in red, and people
with black hair saw it black, and blond and so on. I saw it half black,
which is gray, and that seemed my particular method. Black hair and half
an eye set. Maybe he was a great man. Did you know he liked to throw
knives in his study when he went on a drunk? Teresa and I would listen
at the door, jump at the sound of the blade going home. I spied him once
stumbling upstairs in his skivvies with a bottle. He stopped suddenly and
leaned against the wall—his head unknowingly placed perfectly between
two portraits, one of my great-uncle, the other of my grandfather—and
scratched his ass and then smelled his fingers. He seemed to take great
pleasure in it. At church he never sang but moved his mouth like he was,
not a unique trait, but for a man so mighty, it seems strange now. What
doesn't seem strange today? I have to find an assassin, or *the* assassin,
rather. A cull for a killer, killer for a cull.

Perhaps the sun will show its face today, and we'll all look up and know
that Charlie Boyerton is dead and that we, meaning me, Oliver Morris
Boyerton III—there is no *we* here—is alive and, if you haven't been

informed yet, has just inherited the post of Most Powerful Man in the Harbor. The Head Slint. King Buggo. I'll keep an eye on you.

Yes, it was fear I felt. And true sadness, and loneliness. I was alone now. I would project these emotions today and part of the day tomorrow, and then carve them off at the joint. I would've liked to be better prepared. Not that I could've practiced. I slithered as far out from the shadow as I dared just working in the mill, supervising the payroll. Maybe I could've learned a song to sing at the graveside, a sad, very sad song, but this coward of a murderer, assassin, ureter of death, had left me no time, no choice. But then again, if I were to shoot someone, I would shoot them in the back as well. Father, did you hear the shot? I don't fault the murderer for the angle. The murdered won't care one way or the other. Father, did you feel the bite? I wouldn't have wanted to see his face. Thinking this, a sick feeling washed over me, warm as piss.

I thought of how I preferred to cover Mabel's eyes with my hand when I was near ejaculation, only to reveal myself to her at the very zenith. Surprise! Give me a million little deaths, at ten dollars a pop. My father is rumbling around in my balls today. No, but of course he's in a casket. Of course he's dead. I'm not saying he's actually in my scrotum, standing like a man between two boulders. No, it's the essence of him, the lingering mist and rage. I'm ready for a ruckus time, a big almighty drunk. Bring cash and plenty of it. Mabel might have some toot to share.

From the dresser I gathered a stack of bills and folded them in half and crammed them into my front pocket. My watch looked up at me from the drawer; Father's was stolen. I lifted it and gasped. The time. Christ, the time. I won't be late, not so late at least. I could hear my sister banging around in the hallway. Like the goddamn harridan she is. It was her fault, anyway. That was the rumor, and like most rumors it would probably be proved true. At least it's not my fault. Father told her when she came home never to see him again. Her winky little arm.

"You're my little bird. My dove." Father's hair was loose and flopped over his brow.

"I told him, Daddy. I told him I couldn't see him again."

"And he did that to your arm?"

"I slipped. It wasn't him. He wouldn't hurt me."

Then Father took her hand gently and studied the bruises spreading like ink and then of course not like ink. There was a thumbprint. I saw it. Father saw it. But no, he wouldn't hurt you. Poked out my fucking eye. And now to truly beat the horse and the band and everything else, he's shot and killed my father. What exactly is a Duncan Ellstrom, and how can it be so destructive? Someone should put him down, and they will. The hunt has already started. I won't have mercy, but I will not press because, quiet now, he's done me a favor. It pokes its ugly head from the muddy pond. Yes, in his way, he's repaid the eye.

I could see beginning to enjoy all of this, from gunshot to grave, manhunt to murder. For a murder, mind you. We murder the murderer, and it's justice. We're not animals. People delight in vengeance like cake. Suck it from their fat fingers. If I ride along with the hunters, the lawmen, people will see me once and for as long as they can bear as an implement of righteousness, a deadly blade singing a very sad song, an old song where everybody knows the words, more of a moan, really.

I absently touched the wad of cash in my pocket.

More of a moan. I could fuck a knothole, and might if the funeral took too long. I squeezed my father-filled balls until they hurt. I had to stop thinking about the dirtiness. I'd been crossing all sorts of lines as of late, filthy deviant. If Father knew, he'd kill me. Sorry, no, won't happen. Is it patricide if it's not the son that kills the father? Well, son, the father is still dead. My father. The mirror was also there, and it told me that my teeth are my best feature. It told me to quit smiling; it's a day of mourning. Stone face. I couldn't manage it, not any of it.

Cover your face with your hands. Wait.

And they'll want to see what's under the eye patch, just like they'll want to see what's in the coffin. It's my decision if I want an open casket. Rain against the window, but I'm hoping for sun. I'll pop the hatch and give him one last look. Give the people a peep. A picture of success. Maybe I'll go patchless. I'd rather go naked. I really would. I'd like to show them all my shriveled twaddle, shake it at them like a dead pink mouse. I pushed myself against the basin stand and the water sloshed and some spilled out onto my razor. Now I've made a mess. I wiped the razor on my shirt against the money, and then instead of putting it back where it belonged, I folded it shut and slipped it into my jacket pocket, like a comb.

At least people had mostly quit talking about my eye. How'd you lose it? Lose it? I didn't lose anything. It was snatched out like an olive on a toothpick. Actually, it wasn't stabbed or snatched, it was whipped. Frankly, it was an accident. You should see my sister, or take a quick glance graveside to my father, dead and cued up for a speedy drop into the big, burny brimstone. Would the old man be naked in hell? Wasn't everybody? Not unless their clothes were unburnable. All things burn. The mathematics of hell didn't add up, but neither did heaven or God either. Steel pants and shirt, copper shoes. Dressed like a faller, tin pants and caulk boots. You make your own hell. I hope he goes to heaven. I'll pray for it. He wasn't all bad. He could fix with money or threats whatever I broke.

The last thing I saw with my gone eye was a stick. First thing, maybe my mother. No, some doctor in Portland. Weird to think of it, all the things the eye sees in between. Doctor Stick. If it could still see now, it would be like I was at two places at once. Maybe Dr. Haslett had it in a jar. I could look around his office, the examining table. Naked patient, two words that went swell together.

Who would be at the funeral? That was the question. New people. Old people. They'd want to see what's under the patch, what's in the cellar. They all want to know who I am and what I'm hiding, and I am hiding; I'm hiding who I am, just like everyone else. Let's have whiskey and get the girls naked and pinch their tits. Lick their toes. Slap and dangle. Mabel, lend me your thumb.

I straightened my tie and shrugged my slumpy, narrow shoulders. The razor didn't bulge at all; it was completely unnoticeable until I touched it. Maybe I'd cut Duncan Ellstrom's throat from ear to ear, hang him up like a pig. Feeling truly diabolical, I thought I'd let Ellstrom marry my sister, be gracious, pay for the wedding, then barge in on their matrimonial rutting and shoot him in the face. I whistled at the evil my mind was capable of, no limit but what you can imagine, and I could imagine anything.

The thin black string of the eyepatch always messed up my hair. I looked like a wet rooster, comb and cowlick. You look like a fool. Don't touch it. You'll make it worse. Then I was touching it, making it worse. I'd spent so much time earlier combing and oiling, thirty minutes at least. It had been perfect. Why can't I have my sister's beauty? Why do I have to be this beasty little turd? No one can imagine what this is like. I flicked myself in the eyepatch and then pulled my own hair wildly and stomped my feet like a child.

Tantrum finished, I went to my hat rack and picked out a smart derby and put it on, snapped the brim and hoped I'd get to do it again later when people were watching. No one can tell me I can't wear a hat in the house anymore; it's my house now. I can do whatever I like. I can crap on the kitchen counter. I can raise puppies in Father's room and kill them in the hall. I can be as wrong as the devil's foreskin.

I'll keep my hat on at the funeral, even if the sun does come out. I'll keep it low and sinister, flash them the eye if they stare. Split as Solomon, at least I know where I stand.

My first big idea came to me, and it was to fire Miss Dalgleish. She could be replaced with some young, delectable little piece. Mabel's sister, Maude, perhaps. I'd be bathed everyday, anointed and tugged. But again, it could take years to straighten them out. Whores are so often damaged and dumb. Didn't the Egyptians keep eunuchs? The mill needed to be my focus. The house would take care of itself. Good generals—keep good generals, and a king can slouch through the day. Two kingdoms are better than one. But what if my father was not David but Solomon? What of my wealth and my wives?

My sister was yelling at me to hurry. We'd be late. And so we would.

Tartan

———

J oseph McCandliss slipped the flask into his pocket and then whistled the dog out of the street. The tabby cat it'd been chasing was safe now, stretching and clawing the porch rail in front of the rebuilt Eagle Dance Hall. Seconds ago it had made a forced charge and slashed the dog's face and fled to the safety of the road. The dog gave chase but without much spirit. A few months back someone had doused the animal in kerosene and lit it on fire. Fifteen, maybe twenty seconds it burned before it ran blindly off the pier. Bernice Travois found it and nursed it back to health. She let the McCandliss brothers take it out sometimes. The animal was scarred and hairless except on its rear legs, which from a distance made it appear that it was wearing trousers and might stand up and walk. It came leaping back to Joseph with three neat beaded slashes on its slick and gooey-looking face, tongue lolling. Joseph caught it by the ear and gave it a caring tug, and the dog tilted over against his legs and then slid down until it was resting happily on his boots.

Tartan squatted down and sniffed at the dog. "What d'you call it?"

"Flapjack."

"He still smells burned."

"I think it's a trick of the mind. He's had about a million baths, but I smell it too. Bernice named him Gristle, and I thought it was the name that produced the smell, but Flapjack has made for little improvement."

"Who did it to him?"

"No tellin. I heard there were several involved. Coulda been Lindo or maybe Slod Williams that tossed the match."

"Slod's dead, drowned drunk in the Wishkah."

"So he did.

"And didn't Lindo's teeth get bashed out?"

Joseph grinned. He had three new silver teeth and one gold, stitches in his lip like a deformity. "It was too wet to get a fire goin."

The dog looked up at them; its eyes were bloodshot and sky blue, murdered and at the same moment somehow enameled, cloisonné.

"He blind?" Tartan asked of the dog.

"Not sure. He seems to find what he's after." Joseph set to rolling a cigarette. "What's the story? You got somethin to say, or we talkin dogs?"

Tartan stood up. The cat continued to watch them, as motionless as a pelt. It was ten in the morning, and the street was filling up with women and children on errands. Drunks were teetering upright and heading for a bottle. Noon at Dolan's they gave you a free shot if you had shoes. The upper windows of the Eagle were still closed. Too cold to advertise the strude.

"The boy apparently done it," Tartan said. "Shot Boyerton down. Hank says he's a hero of the revolution."

"Me and my brother seen him."

"Who?"

"The dead man. We came upon his corpse before Chacartegui got there, say we just missed Duncan. Blood hadn't even skinned yet. Ben's been sackin the Luarks' housekeeper, and she snuck us into the kitchen to cook us a meal, ham steaks big as yer hand. When we were walkin out the door we heard the shot and went to see at the noise."

Tartan leaned toward McCandliss. "I heard rumors Boyerton had a week's payroll with him. How much did you get?"

"No payroll when we got there. His wallet had been picked clean, but what gold we got we rendered unto Caesar."

"Gold, huh? Hank didn't say nothin to me about that, about you bein there."

"Why would he? It's not like we had anything to do with the killin, but if someone seen us there or said they did, we'd have trouble." Joseph lifted the contented dog's head with his boot and sucked his teeth at it, then let it gently down again. "As far as Duncan bein a hero of the revolution goes, I'd say that's a bit of stretch. It wasn't labor that drove him, but love."

Tartan turned his head and spit into the street. No one dared raise their eyes to him. "You've heard that Boyerton's spawn has announced a bounty, and Chacartegui is callin for volunteers?"

Joseph wagged the cigarette at the dog. "What kind of slint doesn't see the crosswise nature of a bounty bein offered and volunteerin?"

"Nobody's doin nothin in the name of civic duty."

"I'm sure some asshole is."

"You interested in huntin him up?"

"I ain't chasin anyone down for fuckin Boyerton, and you know how I feel about Chacartegui."

"It's a thousand dollars."

"Nah."

"Boyerton had it printed in the fuckin paper. I seen it."

"I'd stab a nun in the face for a thousand dollars."

An old woman walking by, carrying a bucket of ashes in one hand and a bucket of cranberries in the other, heard this and dropped her jaw and gasped. Joseph winked at her. The dog growled, and the woman hurried on.

"Yer a sweet little cookie, that's what you are," Tartan said to Joseph.

"Understand that I'm no turncoat, but is it our fault they're offerin the money? No, it is not. I say it might as well be us that gets it."

"Good, cuz Hank sent me out to find you, to see if you wanted in."

"He's goin against Chacartegui?"

"It does look that way, Joseph."

"I ain't stupid. You don't have to give me the dummy nod."

"Apologies. What about your brother? What about Ben?"

"I couldn't say. He's closer to Duncan than I am. They're pals."

"I'd side with the boy too," Tartan said. "I have nothin against him."

"But yer still goin?'

"He'll get grabbed by somebody. He's done."

"Ben might listen to that kind of logic. If he's slint enough to get caught, then he deserves what he gets." Joseph puffed on his cigarette, licked the tobacco from his stitches.

"Chacartegui's no priss," Tartan said. "He probably will catch him."

"Duncan's sly, though."

"Sly doesn't last."

"Shit, people're callin me sly all the time."

"Yep." Tartan wore a smug face.

"They say worse about you."

"Who dares?"

"Hank, for one."

"What's he say?"

Joseph smiled and touched the corner of his eye. "Whatever he likes."

"Hank might not be around forever. Somebody grabs this thousand for Ellstrom, they'd be leveraged. You know what I'm sayin?"

"Balls just speakin that nonsense."

"Just between us, right?"

"Of course, big fella. Just words among friends."

"Good. I'll tell Hank yer in for the hunt."

"I'm in. I guess we'll see about Ben." Joseph whistled, and the dog came to its feet. The animal spotted the cat on the rail and was off, furry-assed and bald-headed, dodging through horses and under a wagon, split a mother from her child and nearly caught a kick for it.

"So he ain't blind at all."

"Nope, got good eyes."

Teresa

The graveyard looked openly on the wharfage and the ships, the mill and the expansive log yard that surrounded it, the booming grounds that seemed to go on for miles, ringed in varying shades of mud. Her father had once remarked on the tidal boundaries, called it pewter and slag. She hadn't known what he meant then, and still didn't. Low clouds had settled on the hilltops and blocked the trees and the logged sections from view. She saw the clouds as a courtesy to her father. A widow's veil. Mourners stood like rotten pilings around the grave. She felt horrible; this was her fault and her fault alone. She couldn't have known what Duncan would do. Nobody had told her that independence could double for lonely, for dislike. Someone had delivered a neatly wrapped package of still-warm horseshit to the house with her name on the card. Inside it read: "The Hungry Families of the Harbor Thank You."

Beside her was her brother in a coal-black suit and a ridiculous derby hat. He'd been itching his nose all morning, and it was shiny and red. The acne on his cheeks and neck was inflamed, and in places it was bleeding and oozing clear liquid. She suspected he was drunk. While Dawson the mill foreman was saying his piece, she shoved her brother to make him stop leaning on her. He turned and glared furiously from under the low-pulled brim. She didn't care if he was angry or what he wanted. The nasty little beast. She wouldn't mind if Duncan had killed him. But that wasn't true. She worried about him and what would become of him now that their father wasn't there to keep him from trouble. Their mother wasn't going to make it back until next week, and even then, she'd only want to leave again. Teresa had the feeling that this would all be over soon, her whole family, this place, the mill and the town. She wanted to go home so she could cry. Aside from the gift of shit, people had come calling: friends and colleagues of her father, conspirators and competitors. She gave them coffee and let them stay as long as they wished. Left them alone and cowered in the kitchen with Miss Dalgleish. She'd been crying, or trying not to, since Duncan ran away from her scream. She'd spent three long nights, crying over her father while at the same time hoping to see Duncan appear from the shadows. At the sound of hoofbeats she'd climb out of bed to see if he was there. She might leave with him.

"They say keep your enemies close," her brother had yelled at her locked door. "So you keep them in your bed. How prudent of you. What sagacity."

When the sheriff, Mr. Chacartegui, finally arrived, he'd informed her that her father was dead, that he'd been shot down in the street, and she first thought that, no, Duncan wouldn't do something like that, even though he'd told her. She'd heard his confession and still didn't believe it. Then Oliver had stumbled in the front door, he hadn't been in his room at all, and told Chacartegui everything, about her arm and what her father had said. He even went as far as to retell the story of how so long ago Duncan had cost him his eye. She still denied that he'd bruised her arm. Denied that he'd been to see her, but she suspected that the small-eyed sheriff didn't believe a word she said. He'd been in her father's study before. They'd been associates, if not friends, and the lawman left the house with a purpose, a promise of a thousand-dollar reward from Oliver.

"I'll see Duncan Ellstrom hang for this if it's the last thing I do," the sheriff said. And when he was gone, Oliver threw off his coat and filled two of the never-used crystal glasses with her father's scotch. He bowed and passed her a glass and then raised his own.

"By week's end he'll have him swinging from the main beam of the mill."

"Don't."

"I'm lying?"

"No, it's that you simply brim with hatred. I don't need any more hatred from you or anyone. We're family, and for me, you and Mother are all that I have."

He smiled. "What did Father used to say? Stand it or sink beneath it. I don't care which. Our father who art in heaven." He laughed.

She didn't remember her father ever saying that, but it sounded like him. "Idolatry has a despicable flavor, particularly when it's ironic."

"Who's being ironic? I worship at the altar."

"We're all alone here until Mother returns. I need you. We need each other."

"To what comes."

She wasn't toasting. She wasn't drinking.

"He'd drink to my death as he'd drink to yours."

"I won't."

"He drank to Mother packing up and heading out, before and with his swollen red face after." Oliver puffed up his cheeks and shook his head, a great exhale, laughing. "He drank to keep his crawly little demons in their cages."

"Why can't you be at least his equal, then? Why can't you measure up to a man you so obviously despised?"

He waved off her questions. "He drank to keep the logs pouring into his mill. He drank to keep the saws turning. He drank to keep you away from the likes of Duncan Ellstrom."

"Stop it."

"If not for our father, at least drink to his demons."

She set down the glass and stood. "He'd be proud, if he walked in right now."

"He's not coming back, and I, for one, am glad." Oliver swallowed what was in his glass and then picked up Teresa's and finished hers.

He flung both glasses with a girlish flick across the room, where they smashed, one after the other, against the hearth. He collapsed in the leather desk chair and burped, put his feet up on the desk. "He would be proud, wouldn't he?"

There was swirling mist streaming from the clouds, tearing away like spun sugar, but it wasn't raining, and didn't seem that it would. A smooth and rolling piece of land—care had been taken to clear the graveyard, the brush and tree roots, and the ground was regularly raked smooth by cripples and old women from the church. Stone paths meandered between the graves, not unlike the mist on the hills, snaking down to the coast to be swallowed by the sea.

The mill hadn't been shut down for the service, and there would be no wake, both terms specified by her father's last will and testament. The workingman portion of the crowd, perhaps fifty men, was rangy and impatient before they passed through the gate, but they settled down as they came closer. All of the Boyertons' neighbors showed up, even the Williamses and the Groves. The newspaperman, Smith, came to serve the public record. Hank Bellhouse and Tartan stood outside the fence, talking quietly to one another, their hats in their hands. Bellhouse was feeding a stray cat with scraps from his coat pocket. Teresa couldn't help but stare, and he caught her eye and smiled, an unnervingly kind and sincere gesture. She went red in the face and began to cry. No reason to do it now, she'd held it this long, why not longer?

Reverend Macklin finally stepped forward and opened his Bible. He began with his usual preamble, not unlike his wedding service, which everyone had also heard before: We are gathered here today. If they'd thought to bring chairs, she could sit, or if her brother wasn't such a monster, he would hold her up. Her feet were sinking into the soft earth.

"He was a man with vision, a man who brought to the Harbor what he'd dreamed in his mind."

Her brother chuckled a little and then coughed to cover it up.

"He brought prosperity to himself and so many others."

"He brought death on himself and so many others," Oliver whispered.

Teresa glanced at her brother and he was licking his lips like he was afflicted. The neighbors were watching him. Couldn't they hurry this up? Her father didn't want the time wasted. Just get me in the ground. Had he said that, or was she thinking of herself, for herself?

"He was a proud man, but not prideful."

Miss Dalgleish was suddenly at her side. She slipped an arm beneath Teresa's and held her up. Macklin went on and told the story of Charlie Boyerton arriving in the Harbor like it was the story of a saint or a king, a knight on crusade.

"Stay calm," Miss Dalgleish whispered in Teresa's ear. "It's almost done." Then it was over, actually over, and they lowered her father into the ground. Oliver threw in the first handful of dirt. Teresa took off her glove and threw the next one. The crowd filed past and offered condolences. But he wasn't a monster, Teresa thought. She and Miss Dalgleish were the last ones there, save the undertaker and his two employees. Her brother had gone with the first wave.

"Not a soul said a nice word about him save for the reverend," Teresa said.

"That's not true."

"It is. They just said what he'd done, what he'd built."

"Even so, that doesn't settle anything. We'll be judged by the Lord, and by that measure your father was a decent man."

"I fear the Lord might judge him even more harshly than his enemies."

"I need you to listen to me, dear. What you'll come to face over the next days and weeks, months and years even, will not be easy for you, and I need you to forget, please, most of all, forget about what can only be called public opinion, but which is in fact evil jealousy and scheming by lesser men. Say what they want about your father, he was better than every one of those dullard sons of bitches."

Teresa had never heard the old woman swear. "I don't know what Oliver will do. I don't know if he'll keep the house."

"Don't worry about that either, not now."

The undertaker motioned for his men to follow him, and they went down the hill and out the gate.

"Oliver won't change anything he doesn't have to," Miss Dalgleish said. "He'll simply float along until someone forces his hand. If the union decides to push—and this will be the time for that—your brother will have to decide if he wants a fight or if he wants to sell. I think you know which he'll choose."

"My mother might have an opinion on that."

"Indeed, but it'll be the same as your brother's, just more firmly put."

Teresa took a step toward the open grave. She and Miss Dalgleish were alone in the graveyard now. The wind was picking up, and their dresses were pushed against their legs. "Are they going to bury him before it rains? Should we get them to come back? It's going to rain at any moment."

"They know how to do their jobs, trust me."

Teresa asked Miss Dalgleish if it would make her a bad person if she left the Harbor and never came back.

"Of course not. I think you should go as soon as you can. They'll hunt Mr. Ellstrom down, and you don't need to go through that. Your mother will be here soon. She won't want to stay long, either. Of that I'm sure."

"What about you? You'll be alone with Oliver in the house."

"Come on now. You're right about the weather; it's changing for the worse. Say your good-byes."

"I already have."

"Then let's go home."

The two women walked arm-in-arm to the stone path and then slowly drifted apart. They walked the rest of the way like that, like they weren't bound together at all, almost like they were strangers.

Duncan

————

I *left my hiding place* to emerge near the water's edge on my hands and knees. I'd been under the pier—timbers black and slimy above, bats like folded paper—abusing time, attempting to kill it, but it would not die. I'd carved a poem on the underside of the deck planks:

I found a quick wit with his throat cut.
Nameless harbor whispered hey mud slop.
Chain link feathers like chains
simply keeping me dry and water tight.
Any time of day good time to quit.

I had to use my hands to claw my way up the mud bank. I squatted down in the tall grass, the strong smell of piss all about me like I was standing in it, and surely I was. No one was about. The only lights were across town at the Line, but it was quiet from where I stood. Staying off the road, I threaded my way through the bunks to the mill docks. All birds of prey except me, a crow.

I untied the first skiff I came to, pushed it from the bank, got in, and oared away. It was good to be moving out. I was done, couldn't last another minute in town. Three days I hid under the shingle mill, stuffed into a warm spot near an outburst of steam pipes. I'd read all my mother's letters to Haslett and arrived at the conclusion that I'd never known her at all. She died when she left.

I broke into Heath's store day before yesterday and stole a haversack and filled it with bread and apples. Dug cat holes with my bare hands and slept sitting up with the pistol in my lap. It was as good as a prison. What a good soldier I would be if I lived to see a war.

I came around to the back of the mill, water slapping at the bow, and sat there bobbing and waiting for the day to take shape. Gray skies above and no wind, gulls M-ing seaward. Strikers appeared on the street, crowding the gates of the mill, all boots and bluster. Boyerton just buried, and they were striking. Oliver would have a tough go of it. Someone was standing on a log bunk, yelling down at the crowd, but I couldn't hear what he was saying. Jonas was probably there, and I couldn't help but think that I'd made it up to him getting fired. Surely he'd prefer a job, union or no, but big wages were agreeable to anyone. These were changes to be chalked up on the beneficial side for the workingman. Even I knew enough to see that with all the rules we already had—don't murder, steal, rape, or burn out your neighbor—it only made sense to order out the life of the regular man so as he wouldn't be incrementally or all at once shat upon. It's better to have a plan, keeps people from getting hurt. Thought: If I hadn't just killed Boyerton, I could've run for office and redeemed myself publicly and for all time, but the Truth of it is, I killed the high hog because he wouldn't allow me to continue on godlessly with his only daughter. How's that for revolution? How's that for an eight-hour workday and a lick on the prick? Picket, my balls.

Nobody was paying any attention to the watery edge of the day, but I hunched down regardless as I oared so my profile wouldn't be as easily seen above the booms. The water was black and ripe with the smell of dead fish and kerosene. There was ice in the bottom of the boat, and I slid my boots around on it and then decided to kick at it until it broke loose, and once it had, I scooped up the chunks and threw them out. It felt like I'd done some necessary housekeeping, and I was satisfied with my work, but with the ice gone, water began to leak in. I scooted back and spread my legs to keep my feet dry. I pushed against the oars and looked for a lane that would take me up-harbor and south. I worried that I might have to get out of the skiff and haul it over the border logs that kept the booms together and then realized that of course I would because what kind of corral would be open to escape? I might have to abandon all hope and get out and swim if I didn't plug the hole. I followed the lane I was in and didn't take any that branched off; it didn't matter which one I took because they all came to an end. I'd make my own gate, and there was truth in that too.

Spotting my target, I let go of the oars, and the skiff drifted forward and the bow tonked against the outermost log. Chains held them together, spiked to the butts and linked endlessly. As the skiff drifted sidelong, I reached down and tried to unhitch the chain, but there was nothing doing; it had been pounded shut with a sledge and needed to be pried open with a bar. I pulled myself along by hand to an intersection so I could stand on two logs at once. When I was standing there, they weren't as tricky as I'd imagined. I bounced a little and the giant logs dipped but didn't roll. The chains held them upright.

Once I had the bow pulled up and resting evenly on the log, all the water rushed to the stern and made it doubly hard to pull. I heaved and the logs sank and I was standing up to my knees in water, but still on the logs, and the smooth bottom of the boat came easily over the barkless logs, and when it was centered like a teetering totter I tipped it up and held it there and let the water drain from the hole. The cold water had soaked my boots and begun to climb my legs. I took an apple from my jacket pocket and ate it into a shape that would plug the largest hole and pounded it in with the heel of my hand. I gave the boat a push, and it splashed down and I caught the stern and climbed back in. The boat went effortlessly through the flat water. I felt like I could row around the world. Cross-harbor would be adequate. The wind was in my favor and in my face by turns and angles. There is true joy in rowing a boat, a bit of good work that a man can only get better at.

The bow pierced the frozen reeds, and I shipped the oars. The skiff ground to a halt against the unseen bottom.

Kozmin was suddenly in the reeds at the bank, his hat tipped back to open his face like a stanhope, no hiding under the roof. "Come ashore."

As we met eyes, I felt my stomach tighten.

"Yer in trouble," Kozmin said.

"How'd you know I'd be here?"

"I been watchin for you." He pointed to the bluff. "I figured you'd come this way, so I waited. You notice if you been followed?"

"No."

"Well, I'm sure they're back there somewhere."

"You hear anything?"

"I heard some."

"Like what?"

"Boyerton's dead."

"That's true."

"And you killed him."

"I'll never see the eagle's nest. Never see the heights."

"What the hell does that mean?"

"Somethin I said to Macklin once, talkin redemption."

"They're gonna hang you for this. Won't be any talk of redemption or anything else, I promise you that. They catch you—"

"If they catch me." I pulled the boat higher onto the shore and shouldered my bag. Kozmin was already walking away by the time I'd gained solid ground. "You waited for me, and now yer leavin?"

"I'm not leavin. Yer followin."

"What've you got to eat?"

"Filet mignon and stuffed goose."

"My stomach doesn't take to goose."

"Your stomach's as stupid as the rest of you. I don't have no goose."

Kozmin smelled sharply of liquor and rotting meat, and his eyes followed mine wherever I looked.

"Yer father's waitin for us."

I stopped. Wet boots, numb toes. Apples knocking against my insides to be let out.

"He's a mile on the other side of the hill," Kozmin said.

"I don't want to see him."

"C'mon. Maybe he'll show you yer eagle's nest."

I looked at the skiff, thought: Should I push it out? I was being followed—where would I go? Funny Kozmin saying that about him showing me the nest.

"Just c'mon."

I walked behind Kozmin, into the woods. I wanted to dry my feet is all.

Tartan

———

Tartan *had been walking* for an hour and he could still smell the river through the trees, tangy like rotting berries or the stale sweat of a whore. Bellhouse and the others were inland, making the rounds through the log camps, like they'd find the boy that way. They didn't want to leave the roads; they were afraid. Advance, through the trou de loup. Log camps aren't for anyone but slaves, and you won't find the hunted on the roads. Quarry has a sharp eye for dark shelters, but also for other quarry. They gather like shavings of metal stuck to a greasy magnet.

The Soke, a troggy village populated by the maimed and the mutinous, low-graders, the sickbrained. When you give up, you go to the Soke. Cherquel Sha had told Tartan how to find the trail but wouldn't come with him. There were rumors of leprosy.

Woodsmoke filled the trees, and Tartan held his hand up and passed through like he was walking through the doorway of a circus tent, lifting the flap, and entered the village. Small, tilting shanties were braced to the trees and to stumps to keep the walls from falling down, the roofs from caving in. Centralized among the shacks was a larger U-shaped structure, two stories tall and set on pilings. Colorful curtains covered the windows, and the doors, one red and one blue, were closed to the day. Rows of empty bottles sat neatly on the upper railing, and Tartan thought that when the sun shone on the place, it must be pleasant to see. Bills were posted on the wall, warrants and public notices. If Robin Hood lived, Tartan thought, I'd find him in there fletching an arrow and sniffing at his bags of gold coin. Skiffs and a few canoes were stowed in the trees around the building and underneath. Hand tools were scattered where someone had been digging what appeared to be a root cellar or a grave for a horse. Regardless of its purpose, it was now a pond among many, unique only in its geometry. Where the round pond is common, the square pond is king. Plank walkways went here and there, but they weren't elevated like in town; they were just thrown down, and in places you could see where the old planks had sunk and rotted and others had been thrown down on top. The ground was boggy and cut with fissures where fresh water ran among the moss and ferns.

A man in a calico shirt and tin pants came strutting out of one of the shacks with his boots untied and braces hanging. He stopped when he saw Tartan and looked behind him at the doorway, said something. A woman in a dusty black dress stepped out, and the man waved her back. She ignored him and came out and stood beside him. Tartan lifted his arm, and the man did the same.

"The hell you come from?" the man said. He had a beard and was wearing a broad-brimmed hat with a porcupine-quill band.

Tartan pointed behind him.

"You come from the cave?" the woman said.

"He didn't come from the cave," the man said.

"Where else, then?"

"What cave?"

"He's from town," the man said. "Look at him."

"I followed the river. Found the trail."

"You found the trail. Fuckin road is what it is. Trail. I'll tell you, Dar that filthy Irish son of a bitch Potter and his fuckin parties and bringin folks out here, he'll be the end of us. We want to see you, we'll fuckin invite you. Fuckin send a fuckin card."

"Who's Potter?" Tartan asked.

"Who'n the fuckin slint're you?"

Before Tartan could answer, the woman said, "I'll feed him."

"You'd feed the devil."

The woman smiled. Her teeth were surprisingly white, and too big for her mouth. "Come with me."

Tartan didn't trust her kindness. She didn't seem to be used to offering it.

More men came out of the other shacks, and a few children. The woman in the black dress caught him by the arm and dragged him away from the curious mob and into the darkness of her home.

The table had three chairs around it, and there were dried flowers in a vase against the wall. An oil lantern was burning over the stove. Some kind of meat was stewing in a cast iron pot. The woman pointed to the table, and Tartan sat down. The woman ladled water from a copper cistern next to the stove and poured it over the meat. The man with the untied boots came inside and sat down at the table.

"There's another way to get here, by boat. Why didn't you take a boat?" the man asked.

"How do you know I didn't?"

"I fuckin don't, but you didn't, did you?"

"No, I didn't. I figured the one we're after, he'd be on foot."

"That's what yer doin, eh? What'd he do, this one yer huntin?" the man asked.

"Murdered a man."

"Who?"

"Charlie Boyerton."

"With the mill?"

"The same."

"What're they payin?"

"Quite a lot."

"Interestin figure, that."

The woman took down a tin plate and served Tartan and gave him a fork. He took out his own knife and said thank you. The man watched him intently, like it was his dinner he was eating, and maybe it was.

"You already had yours, Salem," the woman said.

"I didn't say nothin about wantin more."

"You were thinkin it. I can see it in your eyes. Why don't you go do what you were doin before you stopped doin it?"

"I didn't have nothin to do. I was just goin to see if Law had started workin on my boat yet."

"Whose boat?"

"Yours."

"That's right."

"Didn't even have my damn boots lashed on."

Tartan cut off a piece of the gristly meat on his plate and looked at it for a moment before putting it in his mouth. It was bear.

"He's picky," Salem said. "You see that, Dar? He's picky."

"He ain't picky. He ain't sure what it is. I cooked it, and I couldn't tell you where it come from."

"I don't mind bear," Tartan said. "Just been a while."

"That's right," Salem said. "Big damn bear."

"You know a man named Bellhouse?"

"I do."

"I work for him."

"He's out here?" the woman said.

"He is."

"Might be a day to keep indoors," Salem said.

Tartan chewed. He was hungry, but he didn't know if he was hungry enough to eat what was on his plate. He cut it into small pieces and worked at it a little at a time.

The woman slid her chair next to him and sat down, close enough to touch his leg. "You're the one they call Tartan then, aren't you? Bellhouse's big man."

"I am."

"Salem calls me Dar, short for Darlene." She smiled, and her eyes went watery in the lantern light. "My husband passed recently."

Tartan gnawed at the leathery hunk of bear steak and worried that if he didn't spit it out or swallow it, he might throw up. His teeth were coated with grease, and his tongue was sticky.

"Crushed by a widowmaker. Didn't feel a thing, they tell me. He was an angel."

"Sorry to hear that."

"I thank you."

"He got stabbed in the neck by a three-hundred-pound whore for walkin on the bill," Salem said.

Dar pretended to be shocked. "We all need stories to remember our loved ones by."

"Be better to forget," Salem said. "The man was a syphilitic turd."

"Three months to the day," Dar said. "Been lonely here come night-fall." She and Salem sat and watched Tartan finish his food, and then Dar took his plate.

Salem scooted back in his chair and cleared his throat. "Can you write?"

"I can."

"We got paper, Dar?"

"Yes, but I haven't any ink. It all dried up when I wasn't payin at-tention."

"I got a pencil. Fetch the paper for me."

Dar went into a doorway at the rear of the shack. Salem dug around in his jacket and came out with the stob of a carpenter's pencil. "You can write a letter for me, can't you? After Dar fed you and all."

"I suppose." Tartan wiped his knife clean on his pant leg and then sharpened the pencil.

Salem leaned forward and watched him carefully. "Yer good at that."

"You're only as sharp as yer pencil." Tartan smiled but didn't look up from his work. "Who's the letter for?"

"It's to my mother. She knows I don't write em. She's probably too old and blind now to read em at all. Somebody'll have to do it for her."

Dar came back with a sheaf of paper.

Salem snatched a sheet from the top and slapped it down in front of Tartan. "Start with 'Dear Mother.' "

Tartan did what he was told. Salem sat and pondered for a moment and then began.

"Your birthday in 1824 suggests that your life has covered the greater part of our century's history and that your illustrious ancestors were patient factors in shaping its glorious destiny, and call to mind—

"You get all that?"

Tartan ignored him until he'd finished. He had fine handwriting and enjoyed showing it off. If you get one thing from childhood you're proud of and good at, something you enjoy, you're lucky. "Go ahead," he said. "I'm ready."

Salem nodded and went on:

That there was a war in 1812

That your father was in that war

That he wrote some letters to your mother while there

That I am the happy possesser of one of them

That day, there were no steamboats, nor postage stamps

That prior to 1812 the Territory—now Missouri—was controlled by France and Spain

That in that year Missouri became a Territory of the United States

That she became a state in 1821—only three years before your time

That you were born in the grand old state of Virginia

That the name Virginia was from the maiden Queen Elizabeth

That Virginia was one of the original 13 states

That she was the greatest of that memorable constellation

That when a young lady you migrated with the family to Missouri

That even to this day the dearest memories to me are of the old settlement along the banks of Elk Fork in Monroe County

That you are the beloved of eight children now living in several states

That they are all thinking of you today with a love of childhood

That now I am also on the Western slope of life

That I now know what a pleasure it is to be with my children—now scattering—and how I long for word from them when they are away—and I hope you may be remembered by all through card or letter. All sending their love to grandma and wishing her that sweet peace and joy so well merited by a long unselfish life.

Your affectionate son,
Louis

"That it?"

"Yep."

"He don't have any children that he counts," Dar said.

"Lucky, is what that is," Salem said.

"You go by Salem but yer Christian name is Louis?" Tartan said.

"People known me as Salem for as long as people knew me as the other. Not like yer name is really Tartan, either."

"No, I was born under a different flag."

"You're probably a Billy or a Samuel," Dar said. "Or Issac, is it Isaac?"

Tartan ignored her. "Why'd you want to lie to her in the letter?" Tartan asked.

"She's old. She don't know what I'm doin out here, and she don't need to."

Tartan considered this. "She'd likely prefer the truth."

Dar's friendliness evaporated all at once, and she picked at a scab on her hand and glared at him. "You been fed and you been put to work and now you finished that too. How long you plan to stay?"

Tartan had the sense he was seeing her for herself, and all the pieces fit: the dress, the big mouth and teeth, the bear meat. "I'll be goin."

"You say you're part of a posse?"

"No. The sheriff has his own show. We're no part of it."

"What's his name who yer huntin?"

"A boy, Duncan Ellstrom."

"How old?"

"Sixteen or seventeen."

"Old enough to hang?"

"Not for me to say."

"They'll hang him though."

"Most likely they will."

"Aren't you gonna ask us if we've seen him?"

"I don't believe you would've asked me to write a letter if you were hidin somethin."

"If I was a killer like Bellhouse, I would."

"Mind the defamation," Tartan warned.

Salem sank in his chair. "None intended."

"Who pays the bounty?" Dar said.

"Boyerton's son."

"How old's he?"

"I'd say about the same age as Ellstrom."

"Playin men."

Salem looked at Dar and then back at Tartan. "Chacartegui has warrants out for half of us up here."

"Go back the way you came," Dar said. "Don't tell no one you were here."

Tartan pushed his chair back and stood. "Thanks for the meal."

Outside, the sun was high and glowing in the mist in the trees. Through the forest he could see dozens more houses and outbuildings. Women came out of the big house as he went by. They weren't pretty. They all looked about the same as Dar, about to cut your eyes out if you didn't look away or offer to buy them something nice. One was missing a hand. She presented the stump to Tartan and smiled. Children walked behind him on the trail and stepped in his big footprints.

Dogs

Kozmin *emerged from the* dense forest unruffled, as neat and composed as a songbird. Ten feet to his left Duncan stepped over a downed log and stopped, squatted down to survey the small clearing. From where they stood, they couldn't see Jacob on the other side of his camp, only the mud halo and tarps. All around them hemlocks towered and dripped on the ferns and brush and mostly blocked out the sky. Here and there the ground was trampled and grass torn up, low limbs snapped off. Gathered firewood told the story, piled up like drift next to the shack. Oilcloth tarps hung off either pitch to make a pair of drooping lean-tos. It was a sorry piece of work: string, wire, and rope had been employed, bent and rusty nails pounded into trees, and ax-hewn stakes driven into the mud.

When they came around, Jacob was seated on a stump, staring into a small, nearly smokeless cabin-style fire—they hadn't seen smoke or even smelled it—prodding it with a twig. Seeing who it was, he jumped to his feet and nervously flattened his shirt. Kozmin held up his hand to say hello, and Jacob did the same. Finally Duncan showed his palm, low near his hip. They were three versions of the same man, plotted along a line that would stretch from war to war, continental disorder to the first germs of empire.

"Come and sit," Jacob said. "I've been waiting for you."

Duncan put down his pack and sat on it, took out the pistol, and set it on his lap. His beard was like moss on a skinny tree; he was knobby, shaped like a man-size clothespin.

"There's men chasin me," he said.

"I see you're the one that lifted my gun."

"Didn't know it was yours."

Kozmin gave Jacob a knowing look. "They won't find us here," Kozmin said, sat heavily on a stump. "I'd say they'll stay in their boats and hope to get lucky."

"It's good to see you," Jacob said.

"I won't be here long."

The silence stretched to the coast and shot like a snapped cable out to sea.

Kozmin opened his bag and extracted a bottle of liquor, uncorked it. "Me? I'm not goin anywhere. I've got work to do, and neither one of you'll do a dance or cartwheel or a thing to help. I know yer types."

Father and son warily inspected one another. Duncan leaned over and took the bottle, drank deeply, and had to cough to keep it down. His eyes watered. Kozmin snatched back the bottle. "I didn't say I wanted that much help. Jacob, any for you?"

"No."

"Sober man."

Duncan looked over his shoulder at the sound of the wind.

"They won't find you here. They never found me."

"I think by their scales I might rank a bit higher than you."

"I don't like what you're saying."

"I'm not sayin she was less important."

Kozmin kicked his heel into the dirt. "I bet I'm wrong. They probably will be using dogs. They won't stay in their boats. Nothin like a manhunt to get men off their fat asses."

"The only way in is the way you came, so we can watch, stay right here and watch for them."

"Not much for vantage. Won't see em till they step on us." Duncan took off his hat and smacked it against his leg and crawled underneath one of the lean-tos and started taking off his boots.

"Give me those." Kozmin took his boots. "And the socks."

Duncan slid off the wool socks, dripping wet, stained with blood and grease, and Kozmin took them and the boots to the fire and set them down to dry.

Jacob went into his shack, and when he came out tried to hand over some dry socks and a shirt, neatly folded.

"I don't want em. Mine'll dry." Duncan hugged his knees and looked out at the forest. The skin was coming off his feet in slabs as thick as bacon, and there was blood oozing from the cracks. Jacob pushed the clothes into his son's hands and went back to his stump. Kozmin was staring at Duncan's feet.

"What?"

"Put the damn socks on."

"You."

"My feet are dry."

Duncan fought his way into the socks and then held out his hands, behold, to Kozmin.

"Might as well try the shirt."

"Fuck off."

"You'll see."

"I'd say you're right about that."

"They'd have to have dogs to find you here," Jacob said.

"So they'll use dogs." Duncan took off his coat and shoved it onto the woodpile, and then took off his wet shirt and put on the dry one.

Jacob squeezed by and took Duncan's wet shirt and coat and hung them up on nails under the eave of the shack. The smell of the rain-soaked clouds came up from the dirt and leaked from the bark of the trees like sap.

As soon as night came on, they had a real fire and hot food. Kozmin told a story, started in the middle but it didn't matter. Duncan and his father sat and listened like parishioners.

Tarakanov was aboard the brig Nicolai, *commanded by Navigator Bulygin. Six years had passed since he was taken hostage. They were to ren-*

dezvous with another Russian ship, the Kadiak, *a hundred miles down the coast, before they proceeded on. Navigator Bulygin was accompanied by his wife, Anna Petrovna. The crew was promyshlenniki, seal hunters mostly, along with a few Aleuts, including a woman, Maria. The men were chosen for their skill and fortitude, some by Baranov himself. Tarakanov was invited because he was a great hunter and also because over the years he'd proven himself impervious to Indian attacks and captivity. He'd acquired some mysticism among his comrades. He was better than his elders, and envied. The* Nicolai *was outfitted with several four-pound cannons, and the hold was filled with bolts of cloth and beads, fake pearls and brass buttons for trading.*

They sailed from New Arkhangel at the end of September. Nothing was expected in the way of trade. Baranov had instructed them to appease the natives as best they could, not to kill them or cheat them or take any food or accept kindness without adequate payment.

The daylight hours found them close to the coast, and night found them safely offshore. Ten days out, and they took notice of the haystack rocks that marked the point. Storms threatened the horizon but delivered little except thin rain and a westerly wind.

Three days later, the winds began to fail and then they stopped dead. The swell carried them toward shore. Twice they tried to set their anchors, both fore and aft, and both times they failed. Navigator Bulygin's continued attempts to stop their drift succeeded only in breaking their anchor chains. They passed luckily through the rocks and drifted into a small bay and in the gray afternoon and misting rain rolled easily into the pounding surf, and within minutes the Nicolai *was on the beach.*

The crew waited until the wash broke against the ship and watched it slip back, and then jumped down and in this way off-loaded their guns and kegs of powder, shot, and one of the four-pound cannons. They took down the main sails and much of the rigging and used it to make two separate shelters up the beach near the tree line. Some of the Makah people were there to watch, but they didn't come close enough to speak to. The Russians cleaned their rifles and put in fresh charges. When one of the Makah stole a sack of stale bread, they yelled but let him take it.

Bulygin was unsure of what to do, and his uneasiness threatened panic among his men. Tarakanov posted sentries and had them build a huge fire and dry themselves. As he saw it, there were two options: they could either make a more permanent shelter where they were and try to signal a ship if it passed, or travel the sixty miles to meet up with the Kadiak *as planned.*

Their first night was spent huddled under the sails. In the morning, when the tide was out, the navigator took four men to lower the topmast and strip the upper rigging. Tarakanov spiked the cannons and with help dragged them out into the water and let the ocean take them. They broke the locks off the rifles they couldn't carry and gathered up the axes, adzes, saws, anything made of steel or iron, and pitched them as far as they could into the surf. The sails were cut up and used to bind their supplies into packs for the men to carry. Anna Petrovna was soaked through but didn't seem nearly as disheartened as her husband. He'd not considered that this could happen.

"Wait a minute," Jacob said. "You skipped something."

"No, I didn't."

"I know the history, and there was a battle at Sitka with the Russians."

"That's right, in 1802. A great battle. Baranov was almost killed."

"But he wasn't," Jacob said.

"No, he lived."

"Why'd you skip over that part?" Duncan asked.

"Because our man Tarakanov wasn't there. He was at that time in California, and this story doesn't have anything to do with New Arkhangel, California, or even the Kiksàdi any longer."

"Oh, I bet it does," Jacob said.

"We'll see about that. Can I go on?"

"By all means. You finish your dinner, and I'll set water for the washing."

"You're a thoughtful host. Where was I?"

"They were headed south, or about to," Duncan said.

"Right, and it was raining like it was fit to flood the world."

They had yet to break camp when the promyshlenniki had another skirmish with the Makah.

"They're throwing rocks at our men," Anna Petrovna said.

Tarakanov stepped out from the tent that he shared with the Bulygins and was hit in the chest with a spear, thankfully too lightweight to puncture both his thick leather and wool coats. He raised his rifle to fire, and the man who had thrown the spear threw a rock and hit him in the head, but Tarakanov got off a shot anyway, and his attacker fell forward and didn't move. Tarakanov stumbled and fell backward onto the rocky shore and tried not to lose consciousness. He touched his fingers to the gash in his head and the hole in his coat, a little blood, a scratch. His comrades were firing all around him, and the Makah were fleeing. Smoke filled the air, and the sailcloth popped in the wind.

All but a few of the men were wounded in the attack, but none mortally. Bulygin had been hit in the back with a spear, but it didn't penetrate more than an inch. They'd been pummeled by rocks, and they were frightened. None of them had been hit by a rock since he was a boy, and the vision of grown men throwing rocks at them overhand as hard as they could terrified them as much as or even more than if they'd been armed with rifles. Everywhere there were stones perfect for throwing. Their powder could get wet, rifles failed. Three Indians were dead. The Russians collected their spears and coats and even their hats, because really they had nothing and needed to take whatever they could find. They posted sentries and spent another night huddled under their shelters and didn't sleep.

Tarakanov listened to Bulygin try to console his wife but thought she wasn't the one that needed consoling. He wanted to stand up from his miserable bed and tell him, Navigator, we both were stuck with spears, and we're fine. Hit by rocks, but we can stand and travel and still fight. But his head hurt, and his little speech died against the throb. He wasn't getting up until he had to, and if the Makah attacked again he'd fight out of pure anger at being disturbed. He'd kill whoever roused him.

At first light they broke camp and hoisted their packs, each man with two rifles and a pistol. The onshore wind slammed them in the side of the head as they stumbled southward.

The forest was a wall of hemlock, and if they were lucky and found a doorway in, they ran into spruce and cedar, and if they crawled, the ferns smothered them. All felt a kinship to the smallest insect, and perhaps some of them quietly repented for any cruelties they'd previously wrought upon the small and the frail. Not so big in the world, not so bold. So it was down the coast on the rocks and beaches or nowhere.

Anna Petrovna walked in front of her husband and carried a pistol in her right hand. She had a large canvas case slung over her left shoulder and had her hair tied up and one of the dead Indian's hats pulled low over her brow. Half Aleut, she knew how to go forward without complaining. Her husband watched her back and her feet, the mud soiling the bottom of her dress. His eyes betrayed his fear. The promyshlenniki carried mostly powder and cartridges, with very little food. Hunting and trade were their intention and hope, but they weren't above raiding. Come what may, they were moving, and with any luck would catch the Kadiak *at the Harbor, known on British charts by the name* Whidbey. *Called Gray uniformly everywhere else.*

When Tarakanov last looked back at the Nicolai, *it had already begun to be swallowed by the sand.*

They made only a few miles that first day and made camp inside the trees and posted sentries but had no nighttime visitors.

Tarakanov woke rested and went out to the shore and hid among the jumbled and tilting rocks and cleaned his rifle. When he'd finished, he climbed up and watched the waves crumble and flatten on a narrow shelf of sand. He picked out a small round stone, named it Nikolai, *and watched it disappear. The current offshore was barreling northward around the point. Nothing wanted them to go south.*

Jacob was drying their bowls with his shirt and stacked them neatly with the rest of his things. "You like to think you know what he thought, don't you?"

"I do know."

"He's been dead fifty years, if he ever lived at all."

"I know his spirit, so I know what he thought."

"I like this story," Duncan said.

"You should, it's yers."

"Nothin like mine."

"If you think so."

"Go on and tell it," Duncan said.

Tarakanov didn't offer to go ahead by himself. He concluded that the group should stay together, at least until they reached a more hospitable place to make winter quarters, if not until they met the Kadiak.

They followed the cliffs while the tide was out. Single file they climbed over wet boulders and hopped tidepools. The weather was mild, and everyone seemed happier and full of resolve. That night, they again made camp in the trees and had a peaceful rest.

The next morning, silhouettes of men were seen on the bluff. Soon after, a rockslide nearly crushed them, and they knew it had been no accident. The tide had them pushed against the cliff walls, and with every step they were sure boulders would rain down and kill them all. Some tripped and fell because they were straining their necks, watching the sky, instead of looking where they were going. Panic began to infect the party. Bulygin suggested they wade out into the water, into the surf and the barreling current, but Tarakanov wouldn't allow it. He hurried ahead of the group with three promyshlenniki, hoping to find a way onto the cliffs above so they could engage their attackers, but they were trapped. They went on in a scattered line, full of dread. The coast went on forever.

Then fortune smiled on them. Tarakanov found a cave that could be entered by ascending a natural stone staircase, and inside it was dry and calm. Everyone agreed it was far too high to be flooded by any swell, but this was soon tested when a storm rolled in and blowing rain darkened the cavemouth. The waves shook the rocks.

The following day they stayed inside in the fireless hollow, and the waves crashed high enough to wash over the lower ledge, but that was all. In the evening the weather broke, and they could see the unbroken ocean for all its emptiness. In the golden light Tarakanov made everyone clean and oil their weapons, and he reset the seals on the kegs of powder to make certain no moisture would taint them. Some of the men played cards before they went to sleep.

The third day dawned clear, and blue skies welcomed them. When the tide was all the way out they descended the stone stairs to the shore. Not wanting to get trapped against the cliffs, at the first opportunity they went up the bank and ventured inland.

Two men were there waiting at the top. One, the elder, said he was a starshina. The other man was his son. With the help of the Aleuts and Anna Petrovna, they told the Russians that there was a good trail that went safely through the forest, and there'd be slow going following the coast without canoes, and in any case they would probably be drowned. Tarakanov slipped away from the meeting and into the woods to make sure they weren't being surrounded. As he left the din of the ocean, the forest became hauntingly quiet. He found no one, no sign at all, but he did find the trail and he followed it and it seemed the starshina wasn't lying. He hid himself beneath the towering ferns and waited. The two Indians passed first, and Tarakanov could tell they knew he was there or that something was there, but they only glanced in his direction and carried on.

Tarakanov could hear the Navigator's voice before he saw him.

"What should I do, Anna? I don't know if I should trust them."

"We don't have a choice."

"What if they betray us?"

"They probably will."

"What then?"

"We'll have to fight them, Nikolai."

"There could be hundreds of them. We could be killed."

"But they won't have rifles, only stones and arrows."

Tarakanov made a lot of noise so they could hear him coming toward them, and then whistled and raised his hand so he wouldn't be shot.

"Where have you been?" Bulygin asked.

"I wanted to make sure we weren't being trapped."

Bulygin nodded. "Of course."

"What did they say?" Tarakanov asked.

"*That we have safe passage, and they weren't the ones that attacked us.*"

"*Did you believe him?*"

"*No,*" Anna Petrovna said. "*But we need to keep moving while the weather is clear, and there is a trail to follow.*"

"*I agree,*" Tarakanov said. "*Please permit me to scout ahead, Navigator.*"

"*Yes, by all means, Mr. Tarakanov. Take the lead.*"

He hadn't gone very far when he caught up with the starshina. He was alone now; his son had gone.

"*Your friends are far behind you,*" *the old man said, speaking in the Chinook Jargon, which Tarakanov understood.*

"*Yes, they are. Where are your friends?*"

"*My son left me to walk slowly because he is fast and wants to see his wife. She's a pretty woman. I don't blame him.*"

"*Where will you attack us?*"

The old man's eyes lit up. "*Why would we attack you?*"

"*Because we're a party of armed men moving toward your village. How far is it from here?*"

"*Not far.*"

"*You'll attack us there?*"

"*We've given you safe passage.*"

"*You should attack us soon, because if you wait, we'll be ready.*"

The old man smiled and turned and continued walking. Tarakanov let him go, watched him disappear into the reaching arms of the giant coastal forest.

"They attack them, don't they?" Duncan said.

"Yes."

"When?"

"At the river. I wish we had coffee."

"We don't, unless you brought some," Jacob said.

"I didn't," Kozmin said.

"What happened at the river?" Duncan asked.

"The Hoh offered to ferry them across, and in doing so split the party, and when they were far out in the current the men in the larger of the two canoes pulled a plug in the floor and jumped overboard and swam away and left the Russians to drown."

"What about Anna Petrovna?"

"She was in the other canoe, a much smaller one, with a boy, Filip, from the party and the Kodiak woman, Maria, and the old man Pavla. They took them hostage."

"Where was Tarakanov?"

"He was waiting to take the next boat across. The promyshlenniki in the sinking canoe used their rifles as paddles, and one of them took off his boot and covered the holes in the boat with his bare feet. With a lucky turn of the current they made it back to shore."

"And Bulygin?"

"He was in the canoe with the promyshlenniki, and they mutinied on him because he wanted them to follow his wife."

"They'd have been killed if they went after her," Jacob said.

"This is true," Kozmin replied.

"What next?" Duncan had one of his socks off, and he was peeling hunks of skin from his feet like he was peeling an orange.

"The fog cleared—"

"You didn't say there was fog." Jacob laughed, and Duncan lifted his eyes to watch him and then went back to his feet.

There was fog and it cleared and they could see the village across the river and there were two hundred warriors on the banks yelling back at them. Anna Petrovna was gone. Then the Hoh warriors climbed in their canoes and paddled back across the river to finish them off, but the Russians hid behind the dead and silvered trees on the banks and fought for their lives. In the course of the battle several were wounded, and one of them had an arrow stuck in his stomach and wouldn't live. Soon the Hoh retreated to their canoes and paddled out of range and waited because they had all the time in the world.

The Russians carried their injured with them upstream. Bulygin cried and whimpered over the loss of his wife, and the men and even Tarakanov pitied him, but they had to keep going. They dragged the Navigator along by his coat. The man with the arrow in his stomach was called Sobachnikov, and he couldn't travel any farther, and they left him to spend his last moments alone. It was not an easy thing to do, but they would die if they stayed. Arrows snapped through the ferns as they ran, hissed by their ears. They hoped the mountains upstream would offer a better place to stand their attackers than against the walls of the ocean and the river.

Exhausted, under a tree as big as any of them had ever seen, with no food or fire, they huddled.

"This could be where we die," Bulygin said through his tears.

Tarakanov went into the forest and up the hillside. There was no game sign. He climbed as high as he could, but the forest was still too thick for the elevation to offer any kind of vantage. He knew that they wouldn't make it in time to meet the Kadiak.

He returned to his comrades and with Bulygin's tremulous permission led them upstream, and after several miles they found an abandoned lodge. They yelled to make their presence known and then entered the lodge and took the dried salmon they found and fled. In a deep streambed they sat on the ground and ate like animals.

One arrow and then dozens more came down on them, and an Aleut and Ovchinnikov were hit, but not mortally. They made haste up the stream and fired on their attackers, and Tarakanov hit one in the leg, and the rest of the war party picked him up and they were gone.

Farther upstream they found another lodge and at gunpoint robbed the people there of their food. Bulygin wanted to kill them, an old couple and several children, but Tarakanov reminded the Navigator of their orders and they left.

They made camp in a flat spot on the river, and Ovchinnikov, the man with the arrow wound in his back, tried his luck at fishing but had none.

That night two Indians boldly entered their camp. One of them, the old man, had been at the lodge they had robbed; the other was a stranger. They had a sealskin of whale oil to trade, and they asked if they wanted to buy back their woman, Anna. Bulygin was instantly on his feet, and *he had the man by his throat, but Tarakanov pulled him off. The terms were four rifles, and they wouldn't agree. Bulygin begged them, but they could not. He had ceased to be their leader. Tarakanov told him that if they traded one rifle away, he would leave them and surrender to the Hoh.*

"It's winter by now, isn't it?" Jacob said.

"It is. December, the middle of the month."

"They'll freeze to death," said Duncan.

"No, they still have their axes, and they build barracks."

"What about the Indians? The war party?" Jacob asked.

"They don't return to fight them, and the Russians find a different group upriver and trade with them a broken rifle and nankeen cotton."

"For what? What did they gain in trade?" Duncan asked.

"Salmon and a canoe. They could fish for themselves now, but they were no good at it."

"How long did they stay?"

"They left in February and went downstream with intentions of rescuing Anna Petrovna and then making it to the Columbia River country, where they thought the people weren't so ruthless."

Duncan snuck another pull off of Kozmin's bottle, shook his head at the taste. "Do they rescue her?"

"This is the part of the story that I like best." The old man yawned and rubbed his eyes.

"Well?" Jacob said.

"I'll tell you next time," Kozmin said.

"Fuck off and finish it," Duncan said.

"Fuck off and make me. Good night, gents."

The morning arrived blustery and gray, and at first the barking was hidden inside the bending and creaking of the trees, but it grew louder and louder until it escaped and filled the forest. Without a word Duncan hefted his gear and set out, bent at the waist in a flat-gaited run. Jacob had a frying pan in his hand, and he finished wiping it down with a blackened rag and then set it facedown on the rocks of the firepit to dry.

"What about you?" Kozmin asked.

"I'm goin. Give me a minute."

The barking was getting louder, and then it suddenly went silent and a lone brown-and-white hound came crashing through the brush into camp and bayed, circled the sorry trampled mess, and went on. Kozmin whistled for the dog, but it didn't listen. Jacob picked up the pistol from where Duncan had left it and slipped on his pack.

"What're you gonna do?"

"Catch him." And within seconds he'd disappeared into the forest.

Kozmin sat down next to the fire to wait. They'd be here directly. At least Duncan had eaten breakfast and had a good night's rest.

Chacartegui arrived half an hour later with two deputies.

"When was he here?"

"I ain't seen him."

"The dogs tell me a different story."

"Well, I ain't been here long, so maybe he was here before I was."

"He's got two bedrolls, and you can see where another was sleeping," a deputy said.

"What d'you say to that?"

"People come by. I don't keep track."

"You still carving them toys?"

"I quit."

"Why?"

"Goin blind."

"That's too bad. My little girl, she loved em when she was small. Still has a few." Chacartegui packed his pipe from a pouch in his breast pocket and puffed it to life. "Kelly, you head back with Mr. Kozmin here. We'll keep him locked up till we get this settled."

"The hell did I do?"

"You helped a murderer escape, and I'll charge you too if you try and make a stink about it."

"Won't change a damn thing if you put me in jail."

"Which way did he go?"

"The dogs'll tell you that much, won't they? After they told you so much already, about the how and who and when of this particular place, it'd be rude a them to go tight-lipped all of a sudden."

Just then there was a shot, a moment later two more. They'd gotten so used to the sound of the dogs, they were all surprised when it stopped. To a man they knew what it meant.

"Goddamn it, go on, Kelly. Get him out of here. Russel, you're with me." The sheriff and his deputy disappeared into the brush and the mire. Kelly waited for Kozmin to pack up, and then they started the long walk back to the horses.

"How many men are lookin for him?" Kozmin asked.

"I'd say near a hundred. We got people in boats watching the shore, and men at his house. Hank Bellhouse is out here somewhere too."

"He's a boy still."

"Man enough to kill Boyerton, weren't he."

"If you say so."

Oliver Boyerton was waiting with the horses. He had a pocketknife out, and he was squatted down, digging at something buried in a rotten stump. He turned when he heard Kozmin and the deputy approaching.

"I heard shots."

"Yep," Kelly said.

"Whose dogs were they?" Kozmin asked.

"Burright. He'll be fuckin bent if somebody killed em."

"Why ain't he here? Why're you runnin em like they're yers, when they ain't?"

"He wouldn't do it, so the sheriff took his dogs."

"Wouldn't why?"

"Just wouldn't."

"Funny for a man to keep hunting dogs and not want to hunt em." So far they'd mostly ignored Oliver, like a kind of game.

"Who's this?" Oliver asked.

"Mr. Kozmin. We found him in camp. He was with Ellstrom, but he run off when he heard us. We're right on him now, or we were until he shot the dogs."

Oliver came over and offered his hand, and Kozmin took it. "Mr. Kozmin, I'm Oliver Boyerton."

"Pleased to meet you."

"And you. So you know where Duncan's gone?"

"I don't."

"You're taking him to jail?" Oliver asked Kelly.

"Orders."

"That doesn't seem necessary."

"Orders."

"I'll wait here for the sheriff."

"Suit yourself." Kelly took Kozmin's pack and busied himself lashing it to one of the horses.

"I don't ride," Kozmin said.

"Better walk fast, then."

Oliver

The old slag brain followed the deputy down the trail, and I was alone. Chirp go the birds. Roar go the tigers. Mixed up the world; it's happened to me. Last week I wouldn't have shook that man's hand if I were at gunpoint. Nobody said what I should do. Talking out loud. Like it matters. Goddamn this forest. I'll keep that mill turning just so I can change everything into matchsticks and toothpicks, slivers, chips, and dust. A sip from the bottle. Nothing sweet about that whiskey. Nothing smooth. My Mabel will be waiting for me at midnight. I'll stay here until dark. Then I'll have to ride in the dark. I'll have to spend hours alone and in the dark. More than birds chirping. And I know there aren't any tigers, but there are bears and mountain lions, and what the fuck is a lion but a tiger by another name. Twigs snapping? No, shots. Distant shooting. I should go and get in the fight. What if they were killing Duncan? I'd need to be there. I'd need to know. My father's horse, Biltmore, didn't like him, and he despises me. C'mon. Knick knick. That's a neutered cockknocker. Let me up. Let's join the fight. War fucking hoot hoot.

It's better on horseback, the world. Until the limbs start smacking you upside the head. Lost my hat. Off the horse. Stay the fuck put you hoof snorting pig ass turdhammer son of a bitch. Hat applied. Hat adjusted. Bearing set. And. Back. On. The. Goddamn it I said stay fucking still will you I can't get in the fucking crow hop motherfucker. And. Back in the saddle. Rifle in the scabbard and a .44 on my hip. Fuck me, I'm a killer.

No way they could've rode through this deadfall and now, now dismount. Biltmore locks his legs and won't move an inch and looks at me, seen this look before in the eyes of my mother.

I'll leave you.

Like I care, says Biltmore with his eyes. Like I give one twabbling turd what you say.

Across the nose with the reins. Now you care, mean eyes.

The horse turns his head and I stand and wait while he drills a hole through the earth with his one-inch-thick stream of urine. Give me a cock like that, and I'd tell everyone to fuck a half-dead badger if they pleased.

We went together but apart, horse and rider. The tracks were easy to follow, and an hour later we were in Ellstrom's camp. I poked around. Ate some jerky. No liquor I could find. Got my own. Pissed on the firepit with my back to Biltmore so he wouldn't see. He huffled his lips at me, and I couldn't finish. Buttoned up, I sat down on a rock and watched the sky. I didn't want to go any farther. I might stay here. I might go back. I might, the flea declares. The difficult thing about losing my father is that I get the feeling that the storm I have coming is still out to sea. There's a thousand breaking waves coming for me, but far as I can tell the water's flat. Dead calm. Doldrums.

Biltmore watched me and chewed on the roof tarp, tugged it until it fell, and then stood on it.

Yer strange, Biltmore. A real character is what you are. Feel good on the hooves, standing on that tarp? Don't answer that. I'll die of fright if you do. I wish I hadn't pissed, dribbled—compared to you—on the fire, because I'm staying. My outpost, strategist that I am, is behind my enemy's walls.

I had a hell of a time getting the fire to burn, and once I did, it reeked of piss. I was scared and I didn't let it go out until morning.

Jacob

He went much quicker than I was accustomed, and I had to run like I was a young man to catch him, and when I caught up to that hound I didn't want to at all but I shot him and hit him in the shoulder and he fell. I had to look away, and it took two more shots to finish him, but it was quiet after that. I reloaded and took a few deep breaths to ease myself down. I knew there were more dogs but they'd quit barking when the shots were fired. They'd be running toward the sound, so I hid behind a tree and got ready with a piece of rope from my pack. They came out of the trees and found the dead one and sniffed at him and I whistled and stepped out and got the rope on one and after some cajoling the other too. I made a couple of muzzles that looked more like an experiment in knotting than anything else and tied them to a sizable alder. I could hear them whining as I went on.

Duncan was running. I followed the kicked-up dirt of his tracks. He didn't need to run. I distinctly wanted to tell him that. *Don't. Run.*

I found him not far from the river with his back against a tree.

"You don't have to worry about the dogs," I told him, my loudest whisper.

"Was that you shooting?"

"Yeah."

"Where's Kozmin?"

"He stayed behind." I went to him and took off my pack and squatted down. I unhooked my skin and squeezed a cold jet of water into my mouth. I offered some to Duncan, but he declined.

He surprised me then, asked: "Did you take something from the attic?"

"Yes. I had to read her words again. I needed to remember."

"Where is it?"

"It's safe."

"It wasn't yours to take."

"You can have it back."

"Where am I going to keep anything safe?"

I couldn't help but think of Nell when I looked at him. "Why'd you shoot Boyerton? Somebody put you up to it?"

"No."

"What was it then?"

"Teresa, his daughter. He was keeping us apart."

"That's an old story."

We sat there and didn't speak, only breathed, and self-consciously that.

"I know another one," he said.

"Another what?"

"Another story. One you'd hate to hear."

I imagined it was going to be the sad tale of his life so far, and I dreaded hearing it, but it was for me and nobody else. "Go on and tell it."

He swallowed hard and held one hand with the other like he was a child or a woman. "Uncle Matius was the one that hit my mother. It wasn't you."

My breath was snatched right out of my chest, and it didn't come back. I couldn't speak. I couldn't move. I thought of my brother, his face like a full obsidian statue in my mind, and the ruin he'd let come of my life. I thought of Nell.

"I killed him," Duncan said quietly.

"What?" I didn't believe him.

"I buried him in the yard under some fence posts." Duncan stood and shouldered his pack. "I don't want you to come with me."

"Wait, you killed him? You killed Matius?"

"I did."

"My poor boy."

He was about to cry.

"There's somethin else."

"What?"

"She's not dead."

"Who?"

"My mother."

"Who told you that?"

"Don't matter. I was told she left us, that fat Haslett helped her."

"I don't believe it."

"Did you see her dead?"

I couldn't answer that. I went to sit down but fell over. Duncan was up and moving on.

"Wait. You don't even know where you're going."

"The coast." He stopped and opened his coat and tossed a packet of letters at me.

"What's this?"

He didn't answer me; he just walked away, and I followed him. I opened a letter as I walked, and her handwriting, her words, made me weep. I couldn't face it. I put the letter away and stopped and shoved them safely into my pack. My legs were soft beneath me.

When I had my office, I used to listen to him bang around in the apartment upstairs. I'd never imagined such a revelatory and adult piece of information could come to me by way of my son, but I'd always had a hard time believing it was me that did it. Had the thought: my son is a murderer, but I'm not. My brother is, or he wasn't either. Odd man out, and she's out there oddly alone. If my thoughts were the trees, Nell was the wind that moved them. It seemed I'd been angling for this all along, pushing against the rail of the current but unable to break through. The thing was, I hated Matius and wanted to be the one that killed him. I wanted to go dig him up and kill him again. I wanted my wife back, and since it hadn't been me that hit her, my wish didn't seem unreasonable, not to me it didn't.

I caught up to him and we walked through the day and covered ground I hadn't seen before. I forced myself not to think of Nell because I'd gotten fairly good at that. I could shut my mind down if I kept moving.

There was an abandoned homestead with a small overgrown apple orchard. The cedar shake house didn't have any windows, and the door was missing. I waited outside while Duncan went in and poked around. He came back with a bent and dirty spoon and what looked to be a couple of moldering fox pelts.

"How're they gonna eat or stay warm without these?"

"Left in a hurry, I guess."

"I think they died. There's a stain on the ground."

"We could stay here for the night and move on in the morning."

"You can. I'm goin."

Again, he walked off and I followed. Not much later I caught the glint of the spoon as he chucked it into a swamp pond. We climbed a series of low hills, crawled through tangles of brush in the troughs, and crossed into another drainage. The forest receded, and there was open ground. I don't think either of us wanted to cross the clearing. We waited in the trees for a half hour or so to be sure no one was around.

It was here that Duncan told me how Matius had cut his foot with the ax and gotten blood poisoning. I was hungry and sick to hear about it at the same time.

"He asked for me to kill him, and when I told him fuck you, I won't, he told me what he'd done."

"You believed him?"

"I put both barrels into his head."

"What if he told you that just to get his way?"

"Then fuck him for gettin it." He turned and faced me. "You should know. You should know what happened. You're just as bad because you let him."

He jumped to his feet and made his way across the field to the safety of the trees on the other side. Then he was gone. We'd gotten close to it. Right against the hot wall. I couldn't stand. I didn't feel like I could go on. Years play strangely on us. If Kozmin was there with his bottle I would've gotten drunk. Nothing could've stopped me. I sat there, and I don't think I'd ever felt so sorry for myself, and that's saying something. Then the dogs were loose again, barking, coming closer. I wasn't moving. I cocked my pistol and waited. Honestly, I'm afraid of dogs, but earlier I'd completely forgotten. They never saw me; they must've lost the trail for a moment because they were in the middle of the clearing, running in circles, when Chacartegui and the deputy came loping by. I watched them go. They were right on him, and they'd have him soon enough. The memory of walking out of Doc Haslett's house so many years ago wasn't so different. Duncan had thrown a rat at me. I could still feel the impact, the shame.

The two men were already to the other side of the clearing and into the trees, gone. I gave everything away. I should've buried my brother myself. I wasn't giving away my son.

Tartan

Tartan and Cherquel Sha poled a flat-bottomed canoe up the Johns River. The water was the color of rusted gunmetal, and the banks were dusted in snow. The smell of wet stone filled the air. Bellhouse and the McCandlisses had stayed in town to manage what Bellhouse called "the new union fervor." The call had been put in to San Francisco for more support, but Bellhouse's reputation as a thug and a murderer put even the toughs in the Sailor's Union off. They said he could go it alone until he showed progress. Didn't sit well. The labor unions didn't want anything to do with him. Bellhouse wanted Duncan on the spit to leverage against the remainders of the Boyerton clan. Martyrdom had not been ruled out. But hauling up a strike against a one-eyed teenager and his mother seemed in a general way to be a waste of time. Tartan cared less about the millworkers than he did about the sailors. Failure looked like a better option, let things continue as they were. It wasn't about dominance, no matter what Bellhouse thought. Who wanted the pig if you got chops for free and didn't have to sling the slop, either? Men like Bellhouse, as Tartan saw it, were successful right up to the point when they weren't, and then it was done. No second chances, no talking about it. He'd be on top one minute, dead the next. Best case, Tartan would find himself counting the reward money while he stood in a pool of Bellhouse's blood.

"How many days they been lookin now?" Sha asked. The boat glided along, and a viscid wake peeled off beside them.

"Seven or eight."

"If they ain't found him yet, he'd be slint to get caught."

"It's cold and lonesome out here. He'll be found."

"Cold and lonesome swinging from a rope, Dickerson."

"That ain't my name."

"Yer one Dickerson among a million. Yer all Dickersons. Like seeds from a dandelion blowing off in a cloud. Yer big round heads." He laughed.

"Fuck Dickerson."

"Dickerson killed Chenamus."

"You know, I looked into that, asked Lacroix who the fuck is Dickerson."

"He's a killer."

"Fifty fuckin years ago."

"Yer fifty fuckin years ago."

There was something on the shore moving among the blighted trees and stubby clusters of brush. "What's that?"

"I see him." Sha poled the canoe to the bank behind a water log, and they waited for him to show himself. They heard dogs barking in the distance. It was Duncan Ellstrom. He was trying to find a way across. They followed him upstream, riding the swirling pools of the eddies and eddy lines. Tartan had his rifle ready, and his right glove was in his lap so he could pull the trigger. Sha had his rifle too, but he hadn't bothered to unfold it from the blanket he kept it in.

"You aren't gonna shoot him, are you?" Sha said.

"No, I won't shoot him."

They banked on the western shore and mirrored Duncan's progress in his search for an adequate crossing. They rounded a bend, and there he was, halfway across the river, scurrying over a rockbar. Tartan was about to call out when the dogs came bursting from the trees at a dead run. A shot rang out on the eastern shore, and Duncan scrambled onto dry ground and ran, head turned to see his pursuers. It was Chacartegui and his deputy behind him, and they were both firing now. Tartan rose up and shot the deputy, and he fell. Chacartegui hadn't seen him yet, but he could see the smoke from his barrel. Tartan levered in another shell and fired again, and the sheriff dropped. Duncan spun and quickly put it all together. Tartan stood up, but Cherquel Sha stayed low.

"I won't harm you," Tartan yelled.

Duncan stood up and came carefully toward them, checking for movement from Chacartegui, from Tartan. He hadn't seen Cherquel Sha yet.

"Maybe you ain't a Dickerson," Sha said quietly.

"Maybe not." To Duncan: "I ain't takin you in. You go on and run."

"You might as well. They'll hang me for sure now. They'll think I killed those two."

"They weren't shootin to help you across. They were tryin to kill you. You'd be dead now."

"They'll be after me to California for Chacartegui."

Cherquel Sha stood up, and Duncan jumped back.

"Don't worry, I'm not shootin anybody," Sha said. "I got a canoe downstream a ways. You go on and take it."

"Take it where? They're all over in the South Bay. What else do I got but my feet?" He started to walk away, and then looked over his shoulder at Tartan. "Yer feelin bad about throwin me in the river, aren't you?"

Tartan nodded. "I told you I was sorry."

Duncan smiled, a defeated light in his eyes. He turned away and walked off. When he neared the tree line, Tartan lifted his rifle, then hesitated, then raised it again.

"Fuckin Dickerson," Sha said. "All of you, fuckin Dickersons."

"It's a kindness. He's dead anyway. Now at least he can do me some good."

Jacob

My first shot was wide, but the next hit home, and after the strange slapping sound against his gut registered, that big son of a bitch Tartan doubled over, and the man I recognized to be Cherquel Sha turned and held up his hands in a gesture of surrender. I didn't see Duncan anywhere. I waded in, pack and all, and swam the river with my pistol held high and climbed up the bank. I heard movement behind me and turned at the sound. Tartan was up and coming toward me. I emptied my gun at him, didn't aim, just fired. One round hit him in the shin and another in the face, and then he fell. The Indian came and stooped over him and touched his neck.

"Where is he?" I said.

He pointed to the trees.

I ran after him and found him squatted under a bush.

"He was gonna shoot me, wasn't he?"

"Yes."

"You saved me."

"We need to get as far away from this as we can."

Duncan nodded and followed me. Sha waved us over and led us to his canoe, and he helped me lay Duncan in the bottom and cover him up. We drifted downstream toward what I knew to be more manhunters, but we hadn't a choice. The sun dropped away and it started to rain, but we kept our course. The harbor was speckled with ship lights, but we hugged the bank and I believe we were part of the water and the rain and the trees and they could've been right on top of us and not seen us.

It was sometime after midnight when we made the coast. I set up shelter in the trees, and Sha started a fire. It wasn't the best idea but we hadn't a choice. Duncan was pale and drawn. He had a fever. I made him a bed and covered him up.

"Tartan's lucky he's dead," Duncan said.

"He ain't dead," said Sha.

"Yer sure?" I asked.

"He wasn't when we left."

The rain had stopped, but I hadn't noticed when. The sound of the ocean came up from the ground. Sha and Duncan and I shared a skin of water, and then Sha walked off into the dark, I assumed to refill the skin. I curled up next to my son and slept. I woke up in the night, and Sha was still gone.

Dawn found the three of us back in the canoe, sneaking the breakers, headed south. Duncan sat up for a while, but soon he was lying down and Sha and I were paddling. We went like a waterbug in the shallow, boiling sea, and it was exciting. Miles disappeared. I kept a watch on the bluffs for bounty hunters, but we didn't see anyone save for fishermen and three misguided otter hunters perched in a tripod of death thirty feet off the sand. Sha waved, and they waved back. Duncan was covered and looked like stowed gear.

"Otters are gone," Sha said to me.

"Seals around, though." We'd seen some earlier, bobbing and staring at us, dumb as bartenders and shopkeeps. "Might be shooting seals."

"I shoulda finished him off," Sha said.

"The walk out most likely did that."

"Somebody could find him."

"Could," I said.

I cherished the little jump we made over the broken waves. Sha and I leaned at just the right time and hit our strokes and flew down the back, where the water was only inches deep. Far offshore the waves stood and blackened thickly, and then slugged down and foamed, and that was the part for us; that was our ride. Our paddles, our haulage. How many times could you circle the globe like this? That was my question.

Oliver

In the morning I found my balls next to my pistol and gave them a scratch. I followed Chacartegui's trail west. Biltmore seemed in better spirits and the deadfall thinned and we made fair time, far as I could tell. Wet day with snow on and off. When I hit the river, I saw the birds. The sheriff and his deputy were tipped over, with their knees bent wrong and hands all a-gracey-grace with cold guns and blood. And where were their eyes? And where were mine? Searching for the killers with my pistol drawn, then I spotted someone. The other side of the river. A raised arm, swapping about in the limp grass.

Biltmore forded amiably, and only my feet got wet. The waver had a hole in his face and his coat and shirt were soaked black, and a pant leg too. I knew him by sight but had never dared to speak to him. He was Bellhouse's man.

"Get me outta here." Garbled in the broken teeth and black blood.

I was off Biltmore and helping Tartan into the saddle and in a flash he was off with me trotting behind him like a stableboy. We followed the river to the harbor, and then Tartan took my rifle and fired off all my shells. Half hour later he was on a steamer heading toward town. Three men from the ship came ashore and I led them to the bodies. They'd come from Oysterville with a cargo of by-god oysters. The eldest, Tully he said his name was, did all the talking.

"What happened?" he asked, not really directing the question at me, but who else?

"Ellstrom killed them," I said.

"You saw it?"

"No."

Tully produced a small lantern from inside his coat and lit it. "Don't go spreading rumors," he said.

"Tartan said that's what happened."

"And he's a pal of Chacartegui. Him and Hank both."

"I don't know about that. I thought you came from Oysterville. How do you know Tartan or anyone?"

"Who doesn't, ships in these waters?"

"There's a bounty," I informed him. "It's more than you'll make on ten boatloads of oysters."

"Not if we didn't score the bounty or sell oysters either."

"I guess you're right."

"You'd have to be a lazy pile to get in on a manhunt. Any salt, and you'd be too fuckin busy."

"He killed my father."

Tully lowered his head, dripping with shame. "I didn't know."

Soon we were all looking at the death mush that was Chacartegui's face. Tully handed off his lantern and pried the gun from the sheriff's hand and then did the same with the deputy.

"Your horse mind hauling corpses?"

"Probably not."

"Ever try?"

"Of course not."

"Not even a deer."

"No." We turned to Biltmore, and he turned away.

"Christ, he looks mean, but we'll give it a shot."

Biltmore didn't take to it, and we spent all of an hour getting the bodies lashed down and moving. My contribution was pother. I'd never seen dead men up close or handled them. Nothing simple about corpse hauling. The invention of the wheel came from it. No question. I think if Biltmore were given the option, he would've quit me and gone to work for someone else, and honestly, if I could've quit the manhunt and saved any kind of face, I would've gone home and had a bath and gone to bed.

When we hit the water, the oystermen took the bodies in their boat and left me with Biltmore to find my own way home, which I did, after a terror-filled night lost in the forest. By some miracle I found the Ellstrom camp again and slept there. I slept in the same dent in the ground that I slept in before, that was made by the man that killed my father. But I was going the other way now. I was going home, and he was on the run. I would live forever, and he would go to his grave. Death is a powder, and mine was wet. Duncan's, bone dry and ready to fire.

Jacob

_____

Sha and I carried the canoe into the trees and left Duncan to rest under a sheltering boulder. The Indian climbed up and fed a rope over a limb, and I tied it to the canoe, and with me pulling on the rope we raised it and Sha lashed it safely down. Standing back, you couldn't tell it was there. He hadn't wanted to round the point, said the currents were too strong and we'd sink. Sha knew a man in South Bend that would help us, but he'd go alone and talk to him. He might not be around, and if he wasn't we had to wait. There was nothing else but to trust him.

Two days later Sha returned with coffee and a venison roast and a pot of potatoes. We ate and then packed our things and went for the meager lights of town. I heard the bells clanging first, and then smelled sewage at the shore. No one saw us board, and by the next evening we'd cleared the point.

The captain's name was Doris. He was black haired and had deep lines going down the sides of his nose to the corners of his mouth that gave him the look of a sick-eyed cat. He advised me that Duncan and I shouldn't stop in Portland; he said we should continue inland to the Snake River. Land was cheap, and there were rumors of another gold rush. I had some money. Duncan and I could get outfitted and disappear. But I feared that it was only a matter of time until the cable would snap tight and yard Duncan back to the Harbor, to whatever justice might be waiting for him there.

The crew took turns shooting at seals with a Sharps rifle and hit a few but made no attempt to recover the carcasses. Crossing the bar, they all stood astern and pissed toward the setting sun, an act of unified affrontery that I saw as tempting the fates, particularly if you were a sailing man. Perhaps they perceived it opposite of me. We steamed up the Columbia while Duncan slept.

Next I checked, Duncan was tossing in his bunk, talking nonsense. His fever had spiked and his eyes were loose in their sockets and his lips were peeled back in a snarl. He said that Jesus was the first creator, and he was the second. He said he made me. The motion of the boat rolled him around in his bunk and made him appear even more mad. Sha said he stunk like a pickled turd.

When we tied up in Portland, Duncan and I stayed on the boat. Sha wandered off, I don't know where. For twenty dollars Doris walked the pier and found us a ride to Lewiston.

Sha returned, said he'd go with us as far as Lewiston and see how it went. I asked him again why he was helping us.

"The fish aren't runnin yet. Rain's gone cold. Nothin to do but sleep and try to outfart the dog."

Duncan appeared on deck and walked between us. He glanced back and hitched his jacket around his throat and crawled over the rail and dropped heavily onto the pier. I told him to stop and went after him, but he pushed me back. He fell going up the ramp toward the street, and I helped him up. We found a place to sit at the edge of the river. Sha stayed on board, leaning on the rail, watching the ships. Doris came out of the wheelhouse to speak to him. I didn't like the look of him, and judging by Sha's face, neither did he.

"This is Portland," Duncan said, craning his neck around to take in the scene behind him. It was a busy place, and much improved since I'd last seen it. Warehouses had been built up and down the river and ship-building was under way, the smack of hammers echoing across the water. The town proper had graded streets. Power and telegraph lines stitched the buildings together.

"I need some money."

"I'll give you what you need."

"I'm goin back."

"I was worried you'd say that, so I got us a ride upriver."

"Just give me some money so I can get out of here."

"What'll you do when you go back?"

"I don't know. I'll find her."

"Then what?"

"We'll leave together. We'll go to Alaska."

He went to stand, and I pulled him down by his shirt. He was pale as spruce dust and sweating. Men were walking by and staring at us. I didn't trust Doris, and wondered if he'd lied about finding us passage. He could've told the law, and they could be on their way.

"C'mon." I dragged him up to his feet.

"First you want me to sit, now you—"

I hooked an arm around his waist and led him into the street and we mingled with the crowd and I felt safer. I'd worked with a sniper years ago in California that'd told me about a place called the Time Shop and said he could be found there when he wasn't in the woods. I'd told this man, Taylor was his name, what I was running from and he told me that tragedy was the soul's version of gravity, called it the song of the goat. So I remember him.

The shop appeared to be more of a library than a mercantile. It was thick with cigar and cigarette smoke, and men sat at tables with coffee, reading the local periodicals. I found us some chairs and sat Duncan down. When I tried to get us some coffee, the man behind the counter scowled and hitched a thumb at a shoddily painted sign behind him informing patrons that this was not in fact a café: WE ARE PURVEYORS OF THE WRITTEN WORD AND IF LITERATURE BE PURCHASED COFFEE WILL FLOW, IF NOT, GET FUCKED. I tossed a newspaper on the counter and asked the angry little seedpod of a man if he knew someone named Taylor, a sniper.

"A what?"

"He cuts logs."

"So he's a logger. A faller."

"He shapes them," I explained.

"Nature does that, sun, water, and time. Sculptors."

"He shapes them once they've been fell so's they can be moved."

The seedpod grinned. "I fuckin know that." He held out his hand for my coins. I paid, and he tossed them into a jar on the counter, pointed at a large copper pot with a brass spigot. NOT FREE COFFEE, the sign said.

I took two cups and filled them and went back to the table, and then had to go back for my paper.

"Hey," the seedpod said. "If he's sitting here, he needs to be reading something."

"He isn't feeling well."

The man turned around and searched the bookshelf behind him until he found what he wanted, tossed it on the counter. "One fifty." It was a medical journal. I had the same book, or used to. I gave him a dime and picked out two more newspapers.

"Taylor won't be coming in today."

"Tomorrow?"

"Couldn't say. Maybe if you told me who's looking for him, I could get him a message."

"Tell him the doc from Camp Eight. He'll know who it is."

We stayed and read the papers and watched as a meeting of anti-public-utility advocates convened a few tables over. They were men mostly my age, missionary-eyed and stiff-necked. Their president used a policeman's billy for a gavel, left it on the table next to his hand while the secretary read over last week's minutes. A sad lot with a sad mission, thinking themselves a tough lot with a tough mission. I wondered if at the bottom of every argument against the rule of law is man's inability to accept kindness, the antithetical strains of loneliness and independence. An airy concept, sure, but looking across the table at Duncan reading his paper, I felt strength in a bond that I thought had been broken long ago. My heart was open to him, as a man stood against a wall and blindfolded is open to rifle fire.

Hours went by, and most everyone left but when the seedpod went to flip the sign and close up shop, Taylor pushed the door open, locked it behind him. He was a gray-haired man with a bushy mustache and a brown suit, wore spectacles.

"Good to see you, Taylor."

"Doc. Who's this?"

"My son. Duncan."

"He's a wanted man."

Duncan leaned back in his chair and looked toward the door.

"I won't turn you in," Taylor said. "None of my business what you did, but someone told the police chief that you're here. Rumor has it you came in on a fishing boat, and now you're headed upriver to the Snake. There's fifty coppers and who knows how many else looking for you now."

I told him about Doris and how I suspected he'd betrayed me. The seedpod came over and whispered something in Taylor's ear. He rose to his feet and told us to follow him out the back.

"I'm not going with him," Duncan said.

"They're coming for you," Taylor said. "They'll be coming through the door any minute."

I grabbed Duncan by the arm and dragged him after Taylor. The seedpod doffed his hat as we left the shop. The door shut behind us, and we followed Taylor through a series of dimly lit passageways until we came to a large steel door that opened into the alley.

We waited in the alley until a trash hauler came with his mulecart. Taylor talked to the man, and Duncan and I hid among the putrid garbage and were jostled away. Taylor said he'd meet us at the waterfront. The cobblestones made for a miserable ride.

"This is why I wanted to go back," Duncan said. "I can't hide. I might as well face what I've done."

"We'll make it out of the city at least. Taylor will get us to the coast. Every day at liberty is a day you weren't hung."

"I thought you were going east."

"Not anymore. They'll be looking for us."

"Nobody's looking for you," he said to me.

"I'm not leaving you to go it alone."

"I'd do it to you."

"And I'd deserve it."

Rotten apple slime was leaking out of a crate and onto my pants. I crabbed my way over to Duncan and leaned onto the low rail, peeked my head up while I kept my hand on my son's shoulder to keep him down.

"How far?" he asked.

"I can see the water."

"Good."

"First time I was in this city, your mother and I went dancing, stayed up until dawn, and had crab legs for breakfast." One memory triggered another. "I almost bought a hardware store."

"But you didn't."

"No, I'd committed to being a doctor already. The thing about lying is that you begin to need it more with every day."

At the waterfront the trash hauler had us help him throw his cargo into the Willamette.

"They frown on this generally," the man said. "There's a pit, but you have to pay. Don't see the point in paying for something you get better done for free."

Steamers went laboriously by, and their wakes sloshed against the trash and crates and scrap lumber and spread it onto the banks.

"Rain'll clear it out," the trash hauler said, taking a seat on the forerail of the cart. "Taylor said you should wait. I don't know what for or for who, but that's what he said."

I thanked him, and Duncan turned and held up a hand. We watched the cart wind its way up the low hill and back into the tangle of streets and alleys. Along the bank, sheltered from the wind in the tall grass, we found a dryish place to sit and listened to the mill and ships and the birds.

Taylor found us in the dark and led us to a muddy trail on the bank hidden in the tall grass, and we followed it by feel. We had to creep by several houses and warehouses with bright electric lights, and then we were into a bottomland of shanties, campfires, and derelict boats. Taylor walked faster here and more upright. We rested against the wrecked hull of a riverboat, and Taylor told us that his brother had agreed to take us to the coast with his mule train.

"What then?" Duncan asked.

"I don't know, son. Your father'll find a way to get you south, I guess. He's gotten you this far, hasn't he?"

"I'm not goin south," Duncan said.

"You go north, you'll have a short trip. There's no hiding. Everyone's looking for you."

I stood up so we'd keep going. I didn't want to let Duncan run himself down, worrying about what was next, because what was next was the rest of his life. He'd be living one move at a time for decades, or until he died.

Taylor took his hand and pulled him to his feet. We were back on the trail. The wind was blowing upriver, and I was glad we weren't rowing against it. I'd thought about stealing a boat earlier. This was better. Taylor wouldn't betray us. I hoped he wouldn't.

Eventually the trail ran into a plank road, and after a mile or so of walking we came to a stage stop that, judging by the shape of it, had fallen out of use. No one was around. Broken barrels were piled up in a jumble, ready to burn. The hoops were stacked neatly on the listing porch. Seeing the hoops for some reason made me think we could jump a train, maybe not in Portland, because they'd be watching, but somewhere else, maybe Salem or in between here and there.

We heard the lonely sound of the mules echoing down the road long before we could see them. Taylor's brother looked just like him except his hair hadn't gone gray yet. Before we were introduced, the two of them stepped away, and when they came back the man said his name was David, didn't care what we were called, and told us to mount up, Duncan on the penultimate mule, me on the last.

Taylor wasn't coming with us. He patted me on the leg and said safe travels and walked off the way we came. The trail disappeared into a wall of fern. The mules knew where they were going, and it wasn't long before I was nodding off. I'd never ridden a mule, but I found the ride preferable to horseback.

Jonas

He chucked the fence posts out of the way. The snow had melted, and the ground beneath was freshly turned. He paced out where he thought the body was and took up a shovel with a cracked handle and began to dig.

He had to hook a horse to the body, hug it to get the rope underneath, to get it out of the mud, and when it came, it made an awful sucking sound. He prayed that they would kill Duncan, but he took it back instantly and prayed for his salvation, for his freedom.

Hank Bellhouse and the McCandlisses arrived in the afternoon while Jonas was digging the new grave under the last tree on the high ground. Bellhouse passed over his father's shotgun.

"Where'd you get this?"

"The boy left it at my place, after he did that." Bellhouse nodded at the corpse. The blankets were stained black and muddy, and even through them it was obvious that Matius's head was crushed or gone altogether.

Jonas laid the gun across his father's body. "What'd you want?"

"You need help digging?" Bellhouse asked.

"No."

"Joseph, go find us some shovels in the barn."

"I said I don't want help."

"You'll get it anyway." Bellhouse took off his coat and carefully set a fine Jules Jurgensen pocketwatch on top of it, coiled the chain around it like a sleeping snake. Joseph caught his brother's attention when he saw the watch, and they both smiled.

With four of them digging, they made the hole deep and wide. Bellhouse kicked the McCandlisses out, and it was him and Jonas left.

"No idea where he is?" Bellhouse asked.

"I don't have a clue."

"Don't you want to hunt him for this? For what he did here."

Jonas climbed from the grave and perched there on his knees, catching his breath. "You can leave me to bury him now."

"I'll put you in that hole with him, you don't tell me where that little son of a bitch has gotten to."

"Chacartegui'll catch him first," Jonas said.

"Chacartegui's dead, and it was Duncan that did it. Shot my man Tartan full of holes too."

"Well, he's left the Harbor then—if he has any sense, he has."

"Where would he go?"

"I don't know. I don't care. Y'all can get the fuck outta here, won't bother me at all."

"Sorry for yer loss," Ben said.

Jonas didn't say anything as they mounted up and left, and when they were gone he held his palms flat to the mud. Had the thought: At least the ground hadn't froze. If Duncan did kill Chacartegui, he was gone. He was dead. Jonas had been dead once, and he'd come back. From one side to the other; he'd been in the open before. His father had taken him on a journey, now look at him.

Jonas and Matius: Alaska

Jonas stood on the dock and surveyed the western shore. The piledrivers and wharf carpenters were small and busy above the muddy and white-capped water of the Willamette. Buildings had sprouted in their wake like morels in a burn. *Puttin a skirt on her*, he'd heard said. This was February, when warmth and blue skies were mythical, like the Cyclops or Medusa, and Jonas had ceased to believe in a rain-free future. He'd resigned himself to the gray drizzle, and when it finally and suddenly subsided, it left him feeling a little abandoned. The gods had stopped warring and returned to the mountain. There was peace, but still; he'd been abandoned.

When he got home Mary was on the porch, surrounded by steaming raw lumber and mud. She lifted her hand to wave, and her face broke into a free and uneven smile. And with that the final tightness from the day's shift drained from Jonas's body, and he walked loosely. It was as if he'd been swimming a broad river and was tired and needed the shore and almost couldn't make it, couldn't go on, and then he let himself sink and tested the depth and unbelievably his feet touched. He was done. She set down her book and stood to hug him.

"Your father was here," she said.

"When?"

"A few hours ago. He's very skinny."

"He's always skinny."

"He's skinnier than I've ever seen him. And he's grown a beard. He left you something."

He followed her inside. Spread on the table was a map. Holding down each corner were small, smooth black stones.

"When did he say he'd be back?"

"He didn't. I told him you'd be home this evening, and he said he couldn't wait. Did you know he was coming?"

"Not so soon, I didn't."

The noise from the couplers slamming to in the train yard behind their house was enough to rattle the glass in the frames. Burnside was only quiet on Sunday mornings for an hour or so. Noise has different colors, and a person can grow accustomed to anything. What before had kept them up nights now lulled them into a deeper sleep. Mary had used a powdered soap to scrub the floor, and there was a picture of flowers on the box, but it smelled of ammonia. Years later he'd think of his young wife sitting like this almost daily, a small, beautiful girl waiting for him alone, and the ammonia would be thick in his mind and he'd go dizzy. He was nineteen and she was a year younger, added, mathematically prime. Pregnant but not showing, didn't show much even two months from when the child was born; she didn't look pregnant, only plump.

"Swallowed a crookneck," Matius had said, after he arrived unannounced and was told of the pregnancy. "Bodes poorly for both child and mother if she don't show."

"Doesn't mean that," Jonas said.

"Does."

"Not every time."

"I know a thing or two."

"So you have to say it."

Matius would be back, and there'd be more talking and lying and cajoling. Mary believed him. There was talk in the streets too, and stories in the paper. Who wasn't rich already? Who wasn't going? Jonas blamed his father. They couldn't leave yet. They'd spent their savings getting settled, and now that he'd found work in the mill and they had a house, he wasn't ready to leave it behind. And the quiet word at the mill was that Alaska wasn't so nice or golden as they said. True, the managers could've spread these rumors, but the mill was stable and could be counted on. Jonas didn't look out on great hillsides of gold, or even gold mines. It was trees, and if there was an end to them, he couldn't see it.

"I hate that we spend our days apart," Mary said.

"I have to work." He felt stupid for having to say it out loud.

"I'm so alone here. There's no one to talk to or visit, no women my age. I want an adventure, Jonas, not this dull place."

"It won't be any different up north. It'll be worse, I assure you."

"But we'll be together. We'll work together and build a place and make a fortune together. It'll just be us."

"That's all I want, Mary."

"So why don't we leave?"

"I told you."

"Your father agrees with me. We should make our way before the fall, or we'll be wintering here."

"I want it to be safe when we travel. I worry about the child."

"There's no more safety here than on the road."

"You don't know that."

"I know, Jonas. I know I don't. But I feel in my heart that we need to get on our way. If we stay here, it feels like we might not get another chance to leave."

He listened to her breathing while she slept and felt that he was destined to fail her. Portland wasn't so bad a place, if she could get used to it. He thought they could someday build a house on the other side of the river.

"Jonas, no."

"Purdy is selling lots. He told me. He said he'd let me make payments."

"I don't want to live here."

"Fine."

"Can we go?"

"I'll think about it."

"Talk to your father. He has it all planned out."

"Don't listen to him. He has nothing planned out. He'll lean until he's standing on us."

"Jonas."

"I'm serious."

"He's your father."

"That's why I said what I did. I know him. I know how he is."

"I hate it when you're not here."

"I know."

He thought: Maybe the old man and me, after the baby's born, we'll make a trip up there and get a place built, sink some holes and see what we can find. He imagined digging a hole, a deep, black hole, so deep he could stand up and see dirt ten maybe twenty feet above his head and a ragged piece of sky, a rent in the dirt fabric. Would there be gold there? One foot deeper? Two? Two hundred? How much gold? A fleck? A train load. Bags of it, enough to bar a flood. To be done, that's how much. He would be done working forever. Imagine that. Now, he thought, you're falling for his bullshit.

"We could go right now," Mary said. "I don't have to wait."

"It's not safe. We can't." It was easier to make the change in his mind and not tell her. In the end, it felt more up to him instead of what it was, a surrender.

He quit the mill, and their house went to another family. But by then he'd already rented Mary a room in a boarding house. She was on the third floor, with two windows that looked out over the river. The widow that ran the house had three young children and promised to keep an eye on Mary and help once the baby came. The corrals were nearby, but you couldn't smell them. Before he left they'd stood together at the window and watched the cattle mill in their pens. He promised to be back soon.

They'd only made it as far as Seattle when he got word about the child. At first he wanted to go back, but he couldn't make himself do it. He let his father's will drive him farther and farther north until he didn't want to go back, couldn't imagine facing her if he did.

They crossed the channel in a hired canoe. There was a small amount of water in the bottom and it sloshed around and rinsed the mud from their boots. Matius and the Indian that spoke some English were in the bow while Jonas and the other Indian, so far silent, rode in the stern. A quiet trip, but nervous. Three Tlingits had been killed, two hung, one shot, for the murder of a saloonkeeper at Gold Creek, and the Ellstroms were hesitant to get in the boat with the quiet men, perhaps father and son just like them. Not much of a choice, though, if they didn't want to wait for the scow to go over and have twenty men beside them asking for the same jobs.

When they first arrived, there'd been a gallows on the beach. They'd hung an Indian and left him there. It was an ugly sight, and the others on the steamer thought it barbaric. The Northwest Trading Company had a committee, and they passed the laws and judgment and hung Indians while keeping the majority, minus those necessary to maintain the ferry service, out of the town proper. The steamer only came once a month, so no one at the trading company cared what a bunch of tourists thought. The Indians were from Hoonah mostly, and they'd been getting fleeced and murdered by different brands of whites for a hundred years. If they wanted someone to hear their grievances, they wouldn't find him in Juneau. Formerly they'd been a warlike tribe, and the warriors among them were still amazed at the ferocity of the whites. A sense of humor was not something apparent in them, not without cruelty, without viciousness. They'd laugh at you bleeding, but not at you laughing.

Their light packs soaked up the water from the floor. The rest of their gear was stowed in a cabin rented from a blacksmith on the waterfront in Juneau proper. If the mill on the island hired them, they'd be going back for another trip to bring their outfits over. If not, men were dying in the Treadwell mine every day. Matius's back was humped against the rain, and he had a tick, shiny and crimson, buried in his neck, like it was the first pebble that would mark him turning into stone.

Like he knew Jonas was staring at him, his father turned, spoke: "You better at least act sober when we get there."

"I already told you I was sorry."

"I didn't say act sorry. I said act sober." His father spit a cottony dot onto the black water and turned to look into his son's face. "It's shameful."

"Then ignore it. Turn a blind fuckin eye."

"You don't even remember, do you?"

"I remember some."

"You'd be embarrassed if you could."

"I'm embarrassed, and I can't. I hardly see the difference." Jonas felt inside his jacket for his leather satchel, and it wasn't there. "You take something from my coat last night?"

"I did."

"Pass it over."

"I don't know what English these gentlemen understand, but I know that I don't want you talking about what we have in our pockets right now. You're lucky you weren't robbed."

"Apparently I fucking was."

The Indian in the bow smiled over his shoulder, and Jonas smiled back.

His father was silent. The Indians kept a steady rhythm with their paddles. Matius stared at the water defiantly.

The Indian in the bow said something.

"What'd you say?" Matius demanded.

"Nothing."

"I heard you say something."

"I said, he got out-white-manned."

The water was black and green. They were out in the middle of it now. They'd drown for sure if they went over. Bald eagles sat on trees on the shoreline and gulls turned effortlessly overhead. When the sound of the paddle behind him went quiet, Jonas looked back and the Indian nodded his head toward the shore. The mill was visible first by its rising steam and smoke and then by its black and shining shingle roof.

The canoe banked in the mud of low tide, and they stumbled out with their packs and slogged up the hill to ask for a job. Matius went first.

No drinking was allowed on the mill property, so Jonas was soon sober and alert, running an edger like he'd done in Portland.

The long hours allowed Jonas brief seconds of relief from a flood of memories. Green chain rolled off, and the dogs brought more and more. He didn't blame Mary, but he did.

At dusk he stood on the edge of the channel in the pouring rain, looking at the smattering of lights in Juneau. There was a canoe there, and he could take it. Nobody was awake to stop him. He went as far as to untie it from the stump, where it bobbed on the flood tide, but he didn't get in, and after a few minutes he clove-hitched it back to the stump, with two half hitches roughly put on to finish it. He wasn't a bad man, and he didn't see why he'd been cursed. Water cascaded down the cliff face across the channel. His father was suddenly beside him. He had a scab in the corner of his mouth, and it was oozing yellow pus.

"You can't keep dwelling on what's done," his father said.

"Let me be."

"She was weak-hipped."

"If you speak to me about her again, I'll beat your brains in."

"She wasn't built for it. It's the way—"

And Jonas struck him in the jaw as hard as he could, and it was lucky Matius was knocked unconscious and couldn't fight back, because Jonas hated him to his bones and would've killed him.

An Indian from Yakitat the mill workers called Sannup saw what had happened, and after Jonas went back to the bunkhouse, the Indian stayed with Matius until he woke up and then helped him to his bunk.

Jonas and his father didn't speak for days.

A month later the millwork suddenly ended when the owners decided to hire Chinese, and it got rough with the Indians and the strikers both. Jonas and his father left Douglas for Juneau and rented the same cabin over again and found work in the woods until the rain got too bad. It was just too much; it wouldn't stop. Treadwell still wanted men in the glory hole, but Jonas hadn't come this far to die, no matter what he told himself.

They watched as the Chinese were run out of town. The whole of the population, no less than fifty of the large Indian war boats, carried them away. The channel was calm, and they went without looking back. It was said that a schooner met them later and took them to Puget Sound. Some thought it was a benefit, but most missed them once they were gone.

They hired the same Indians to take them north. The tide was against them, so they made camp in a narrow cove and slept on the rocks, but it was summer so the sun only played at quitting. Jonas slept with his face buried in the crook of his arm and woke up cramped. As they set out the next day, the wind and tide were in their favor. Still, it took two more days to arrive at the Haines Mission, and they had to wait there for the tide to make their way up Dixon Straits. While they were in camp, a group of officers from a gunship paid them a visit and asked about their progress. Jonas said it was fine, but he needed a rifle. Go ask the captain, they said. The ship was moored two miles away, and Jonas went by himself and left his father playing cards with the crew. The captain was amicable and invited him aboard.

"You have a tough time ahead of you," he said.

"I know. My father's with me. We'll give it a go. Can you sell me a rifle?"

"I'll loan you one. Send it to Brady's Store in Juneau when you're finished, or head south yourself." He gave Jonas fifty rounds of ammunition. The rifle was a 45.90. The ship was called the *Pinto*. The captain's kindness made him uneasy, and several times on his walk back to camp he looked over his shoulder, thinking he'd been followed, but no one was there.

Recall, one golden evening. Mary set Jonas's plate in front of him on the table. "Should we wait for your father?" She rested an arm on her distended stomach.

"No. He can find his own dinner if he doesn't want to be on time."

"I'll keep his plate on the stove."

"Sit with me."

Mary sat down, and since she'd already eaten, she watched, smiling, while Jonas shoveled in his food. "The doctor was by."

"What'd he say?"

"All's fine. I told him about the pain I've been having, and he said it was normal and would pass."

"It's not so bad, then?"

"Not so bad."

He set down his fork and smiled at his wife. She remained optimistic, even with all the troubles they had. She trusted him, and he prayed he had the strength to keep her.

"Do you still think you could come with us?"

"Why do you ask? You said I'd wait here."

"I don't think I can stand to be apart from you that long."

She smiled. "We should go now and let the child be born in the Yukon. That's the way."

"No, it's not. I don't know what I was thinking." He picked up his fork.

"You're right. We'll stick to your plan. You and your father go first, and we'll follow. It's safer."

"I'll go mad without seeing you every day."

"You'll be fine."

They divided their provisions into four packs of one hundred pounds apiece and camped at the glacier crossing and waited for night so it would freeze. There was a rope across the river to hang on to, but it was rumored that men had died even with it; the water wasn't two feet deep, but it was swift. Jonas strung his boots around his neck. His father chose to wear his, and suffered for it later. At the summit they made a rough camp and hardly slept with the wind and the cold. The old man clutched at black toes. Jonas massaged them with bacon grease, and that seemed to help. There were other men around, but their isolation felt complete. In the morning they stumbled downhill, and Matius had to stop and rest and complain about his knees and his back and of course his poor fucking toes every quarter mile. Jonas took some of the weight from his pack, but he still complained. Indians were camped on Lake Bennett, and they said they were Stick Indians and that there was lots of big water four miles down the lake. They still had another trip back to the summit for the other two packs. Matius wandered off and found a flat rock in the sun and lay down, said he'd stay and see if he could get some of the Indians to help him cobble together a raft to make it across the lake. They'd brought the whipsaw and the crosscut saw with them on the first trip, but the ax was at the summit.

"I'll use my teeth," Matius said. The first smile to cross his face in two months.

Jonas set out feeling better without his father behind him, slowing him down.

Two weeks later they were camped with fifteen or twenty others at the mouth of the Forty Mile River. Two men had drowned in the canyon above. Jonas had a lean-to in the trees and had traded his extra gumboots for a bottle of whiskey.

Missionaries arrived by steamer and with them S. D. Staunton, the storekeeper, and they brought some mail. By chance Jonas and Matius each received a letter. The other men were envious. His father handed him the letter, and he opened it; it was from his wife. She was marrying a cranberry farmer from Seattle.

If you are still alive you need to send word and grant me a divorce so as not to be afoul of any law regarding polygamy.

Jonas thought that was fine; she could do as she liked; he didn't care, but he couldn't look away from the words.

"Good news?" His father said.

"Mary's taking a husband."

"She has one of those already."

"She thinks I'm dead."

"So she posted a letter to your corpse?"

"It has your name on it too." He held up the envelope.

"It does? I didn't notice Well, maybe you'll stop your moping now."

"Maybe I will." He motioned to the envelope in his father's hand.

"Your uncle Jacob, failure recounted."

"Is he coming here?"

"Hell, no, he's not coming here. He says he's become a logger, the little tart."

"Are we ready to go?"

"Nearly."

With Mr. Staunton returned, the store was opened, and soon everyone would be drunk. He had the miners unload his cargo into the tent, and within minutes he was open for business. The Indians on the bar weren't allowed to buy liquor and would have to wait for someone to bootleg it to them. The bonfire was stoked and loaded up, and smoke swirled around the bar and filled Staunton's tent until he shut the flap in disgust.

The missionaries that brought the mail said they'd recently been at the Pelly River and that there were men working the creeks there. Matius thought it to be as good a place as any to make a try with their new rocker. They made the rounds and said their good-byes and told the others where they were headed so they'd know where to look if they didn't return, or if they wanted to visit.

The birch bark canoe they'd traded for rode low but level with all the gear they'd piled into it. There was ice in the river, and a man came floating down in a listing craft, a boat that had been cut in half and boards nailed across the squared-off stern to seal it. He was using a coffee can to bail water.

"Me and my partner split everything down the middle," the man said when he came alongside.

"Seems like the balance leaked out your ears," Matius said. "Half a boat. Half a goddamn brain."

"This is no place for a compromise. You'll see."

"If I had a speck of dust for every time someone told me 'You'll see' in this country, I'd be set to go home and retire with my fucking tonnages."

The man paddled away, looked over his shoulder. "You'll see."

Jonas couldn't help but laugh.

"At least you had two paddles to divide, or you'd have to use half a blade," Matius yelled after him. "Half a board for half a boat. Half-wit."

The man bent down and searched among his effects and then held something in the air, and as the current turned the canoe, they could make out the shape of a perfectly bisected paddle. "I stole the spare when he wasn't looking," the man yelled. The ice slurried all around them, and they could feel it as it bumped gently against them.

They didn't make three miles before they camped. By noon the next day they'd hiked up a small, fast-falling creek and cleared eight ounces of dust and had a four-ounce nugget to marvel at over dinner. They spent the whole next day pacing out their future claim and cutting blazes.

Matius shotgunned a cow moose from ten yards, and they built a frame and cut it into strips and kept a fire underneath it to keep off the flies. When some Indians came by, they traded moose for fish and were told the story of a child killed by a bear, didn't know if it was true or myth. Sometimes it was hard to tell.

Jonas found a stranger up the creek, panning on their claim, and asked if he was in the habit of trespassing and stealing. The man threw a rock at him and they had a fight and Jonas was being beaten bloody with a stick when Matius got there and shot the stranger in the back with his shotgun. They buried the man under a downed tree they managed to roll uphill and then roll back once he was in the ground. They kept watchful, even stood guard, thinking that the man's friends must show up some-time, but he must've been a loner, because nobody ever came looking for him. A week after the man was buried, Jonas found his half-boat and his kit pulled up on the bank downstream and carefully covered with brush. Farther into the forest, they found the man's camp. They didn't know how they'd missed it when they hiked out the claim. They left the camp as it was and never found his gold, if he had any. Jonas found the dead man's blazes on the trees, and on one he'd peeled away the bark and writ-ten out the boundaries and size and angles of his claim in a carved long-hand. His name was Davis, and a man named Christianson had witnessed the carving in the tree. Not wanting to get hung for murder or shot by this Christianson while they were sleeping, they cleaned up. In the three weeks they'd been there, they'd cleared five hundred dollars in dust and had several nuggets too, maybe another one fifty or so.

A mob was gathered at Staunton's store. An Indian had killed a prospector, and a posse was being formed to hunt him down. Jonas asked if they'd seen the body and who he was and where it had happened, thinking it might be Davis and that somehow someone knew that he was dead. But it was some other man they'd never heard of. They decided to leave their kits with Staunton, like everyone else. The fat man sat on his chair in front of his tent and smoked. He told them he had no sympathy for a man that got himself killed up here; it was the way things went.

"God has business like I have business. I'll not get in the way a his," Staunton said.

"You'll watch our things?" Asked a man named Demetri, who owed Staunton a hundred dollars.

"Yes, for the agreed price."

"You'll charge us to watch em? Can you believe this bloodsucker? You got no backbone outside a that tent, Staunton."

Staunton smiled. "Get your hands bloody and get to work, Demetri. Pay me what you owe, or you'll see what kind of backbone I have."

"C'mon," Demetri said, but nobody listened, and he stood there like a fool until eventually the posse got under way.

"Safe travels," Staunton called after them.

They went to the Indian camp and found the man who had supposedly killed the miner.

"I killed him," the accused replied.

"You don't deny it?" said Demetri.

They had him stood up against a tree.

"If I could, I'd kill every last one of you."

"You heard him," Demetri said. "Get the rope."

They tested the knot, but it bound and wouldn't slip. They greased it with tallow, and it worked fine. They left the man swinging in the tree. Jonas was drinking whiskey, and Matius didn't try and stop him.

"That was a long bit of wretchedness," Matius said.

"We were part of it. Stood there. Partly our wretchedness."

"You know why we came, though, don't you?"

"So we don't get pinned for Davis."

"That's right. So we don't get pinned for Davis. I'm wondering if we shouldn't dig him up and blame that man hanging from the tree."

"We told everybody we were down there. They'll know something's wrong."

"Maybe not," Matius said.

"Leave him be."

"Nobody'll know when he was killed."

"I said leave him."

"Fine."

They fled south to Juneau for the winter but in the spring they returned to Forty Mile, and only one drainage over from where they'd buried Davis they filed two adjoining claims and built a cabin. They braved several winters, but never did as well as that first trip. Once or twice they went south vowing never to go back but they always did. Then, six months before Franklin struck it rich and flung open the door for the rush, they finally made up their minds and sold their claims and the cabin together for six hundred dollars. Jonas could think back on the time as he thought back on fevers he'd sweated, injuries endured. Maybe stronger for it, maybe not, just a breath away from greatness, or great wealth. If in fact they were different.

Jacob

A *t the fork the* mules went south to Hebo, and we went north. The next day we circled widely around a coastal village and stayed in the shadows until we saw the sea. The beach and the waves had the grand feel of industry. Work was being done, and we had wandered into it, at our peril. We tried to keep in the trees, but with the marsh and the brush, we couldn't. Gauging distance on the beach was no easy task. Duncan seemed nearly healed from his fever. I quit trying to change his mind. He was going back.

We had food from the younger Taylor, and for the time we ate well. There wasn't any hurry. We'd walk through the long day and then make camp. Ships were off the coast, but they wouldn't be able to see us with the breakers. I saw us doing it for a lifetime.

Problems started with the cliffs. Twice we were trapped by the tide. On the first occasion we were forced to wade into the frothing ocean and at times swim, which was a truly miserable experience with the icy water and waves slamming us against the rocks, but it was the second occasion that nearly killed us. The earth trembled, and pebbles rained down on our heads, punctuating the raindrops, and then a mudslide two hundred yards across slammed into the water directly behind us. We were covered in a yellow mud and soaked through. Nearly killed. So nearly killed we didn't speak afterward, just walked on, and for myself I can say I tasted the brined earth of mortality, and I didn't like it. We turned inland.

There were spatterings of townships, and we had to wait till night to move past them. Duncan stole a chicken from a house with no dog. His eyes were glassy and cold when he returned. He held up the chicken by the legs, and I put it in my pack. I told him I wanted to leave a silver dollar on the step of the coop, but Duncan wouldn't allow it. He was right. If I'd done it, I'd have sunk us; the law would be on us in no time.

Days passed, and we were still crawling through the weeds, found trails, lost them. Made a few miles on the beach and then back up the rocks. Twice we hid from people, father and son, side by side.

We made a good camp with watertight shelter under a cliff overhang, and Duncan slept for nearly two days. When he woke, he'd lost his fury and the madness in his eyes. He wanted to go home, for it to stop. Astoria could be a week away. I saw us getting nabbed there, or Oysterville. Big rivers to cross regardless.

"Let's move farther inland," I said.

"I can't see it being easier than what we've been doing."

"It'd be safer, is all."

"Crossing the rivers will be the end of us, won't it?"

"You've never been this far away from home."

"No. I can say I saw Portland now. Which might have to be enough."

"What of the girl?"

"I can't have her. It won't be allowed."

"It isn't likely. I wish it were."

"You could turn me in. For the money."

"I'd rather not." I wanted to urge him on, to give him the strength he needed. We'd come this far, but how much farther? Not for the first time, I thought of Tarakanov from Kozmin's story. "It's best to keep going."

"Not if I end up getting caught anyway. Shackled is bad enough, shackled and dead tired is, let's say, unfortunate."

"Maybe."

"Will they hang me?"

"Not if there's a trial."

"With the money on my head, nobody'll want the hassle."

"We should keep going."

"Lead the way."

The problem ceased to be the cliffs. Rivers, brush, and distance replaced them. I took a bearing whenever the sun came out from the clouds, which was rare. Seemed at least once a day we caught a break. Rain stopped, clouds parted, the angels sang or burped or screamed, and there was the sun, like a dream. Skirting the logging camps put us on a winding path, but it was easy to lift more food. Low-hanging fruit. Bull cooks generally sleep more than they work. When we used to roll back into camp at dusk, the bastards would be all aflutter, and haven't I been working all day, and isn't cooking just as much of a slog as chopping trees? And you couldn't tell them to suck it, or you'd starve. Power collects in the joints of the world and makes it arthritic.

They'd spiked shortline rail all over the woods, and we of course made the mistake of following it and had to double back to keep our course. We saw four black bears walking together through the trees, and not one of them was a cub. They swung their heads around when they scented us, and then they were gone. Duncan went after them for a way until I caught him. In the distance we could hear the chunking of the double bits like a galloping herd.

Pack trails came and went, some with fresh tracks, most without. Avoidance was our plan, and that kept us to the woods. High ridges were the best—not that we could see anything, but we didn't have to cross a creek every ten minutes.

Duncan told me how he and Teresa Boyerton had been close since they were small. I wondered who else knew this. I wondered if it mattered at this point who knew what about Duncan. He was quarry.

A sign was nailed to a cedar post, "Wolfskill" with an arrow pointing north. The trail we were on hadn't been traveled in a while, and we'd been crawling over blowdown and scrambling over mud and rock slides for miles.

"Sounds bad," Duncan said. "Wolfskill. Kinda name is that?"

"Normal somewhere, I'd guess. He was one of them that cut the Spanish Trail."

"How do you know?"

"I remember the name from when I was in California."

"He was successful in his exploring?"

"He died rich and fat in Los Angeles."

"We should follow his route, then. It can't be worse than any other."

"No, probably not."

Duncan touched the sign and tested the post, and we walked on. I
thought maybe Wolfskill came this way hunting otter. Maybe there were
other Wolfskills, as there are other Boyertons and Ellstroms. This track
of thinking led me to my brother, and I could see scattering his bones on
the black sand for the gulls to peck at and shit on. Understanding family
must be one of the most complicated acts a human can go through. And
it's because you know them that it is so hard. Because you think a thing
good. My thoughts were buoyed to a singular idea of faith, like a skiff at
the pier, and with the waves they bumped into religion and God and my
son walking in front of me. You think a thing good. You think a thing
real. I wanted to go back and stack stones around the base of Wolfskill's
sign so I'd know that it would be there, that we hadn't imagined it.

The salt was in the air. The day fell away finely without a fuss. I made
camp while Duncan hunted for firewood. We were on a grassy point
that looked down on a mired creek bottom. The deer sign indicated their
numbers to be in the thousands, or maybe only twenty that had been long
in residence. Lurkers in the hole. We could shoot one at dawn, I was sure
of it.

In the dark I stalked down to what I thought would be pistol range
and waited. The rain started as the sun lightened the tree line. A doe and
her fawn emerged from the brush. I stood uneasily on the pins and needles in my feet and leaned against a black alder for a brace and shot the
fawn. The doe ran off and didn't look back. The bark of the alder was
torn, and it had reddened my coat sleeve. I dug my thumb in it and spread
the color over the back of my hand that held the pistol. The young deer
wasn't moving. After a minute or so I climbed down to the creek bottom

and made short work of gutting it. Warm and limber, draped across my shoulders, nothing as loose and unmanageable as the freshly dead. Maybe once I would've felt bad about shooting the fawn instead of the doe, but I didn't now. We could eat the fawn before it spoiled. Both would've died if I'd shot the doe. Duncan helped me skin it, and we boned out the meat and spread it on the skin out of the rain. I stoked the fire, and Duncan speared the two loins on cut alder sticks and seared them in the yellow of the flame. We ate off the stick and with our hands, stuffed ourselves like a couple of ogres.

The day following we dropped from the ridges and wasted hours crossing creeks and rivers. Exhausted, we made camp early in the trees.

"I don't feel hunted anymore," he said.

"That's laziness."

"They can't always be after me. They have to stop sometime."

"Have some of this coffee. I can't drink it all." It was the last of our supply. We sipped coffee and watched the fire burn down.

"Why'd you let Matius be that way?" Duncan asked. "Didn't you get tired of it?"

"He was much older than me. I never thought to stop him. He could do anything, almost anything, and I'd forgive him."

"Do you forgive him now?" Duncan asked.

"No, I don't. I'll never forgive him."

"Me neither."

"Were you afraid of him?"

"Yes."

"I've been afraid my whole life."

I put my hand on his shoulder, and he reached up and patted it. I'd not felt so much love for anyone since the day he was born. I wanted to tell him, maybe a father always does, how he was once a waxy little being squirming in my hands, with only his mother and me to protect him. Things change, but not many, not often, not for long.

Three days later I paid a lone sturgeon fisherman to ferry us across the mighty Columbia. We both showed our weariness, but we had no choice but to keep walking.

Jonas

The excitement surrounding the manhunt kept Jonas from going into town. Bellhouse hadn't been back; nobody else had either. The Parkers had taken their goats and gone, Jonas didn't know where. They didn't say good-bye, and he didn't expect they gave him much thought, not after all that had happened with Duncan.

No matter how big a fire he built, the house still felt cold. Without knowing what else to do, he began straightening out years of his father's—and, he had to admit, his own—neglect. After they'd cleared the land around the house, Jonas took the job at the mill. He lived at the bunkhouse, ate at the chow hall, shopped for intimates at the store.

Sometimes he was angry with Duncan, sometimes murderous. Not often, but sometimes he was grateful. Grateful that it had all been sorted out. He'd known his father had lied that night, but not about what. He thought maybe he'd told Jacob to hit her, or maybe he'd hit her after Jacob had. The problem with being right was that he'd rather be wrong.

Kozmin showed up with the mail and the last few weeks' worth of newspapers. He'd been locked up, and they'd let him keep the papers when he left.

"What a show yer missin. They got U.S. marshals and regular law from all over, as far away as Montana. They say they might call in the army if they don't find him soon."

All three letters had already been torn open. One was from his mother; the other two had something to do with a sawmill his father had invested in. Reading the first and second letters, he discovered that his father's name had been at the top of the list of investors on a mill in Portland, and now that the owner had died, the equipment was to be liquidated and the profits, after fees, would come to him, or he could arrange to have the equipment hauled away. So long ago, he'd told his father what a fool he'd been for investing in that fraudulent mill. But it hadn't been fraudulent. Maybe he was the only one that hadn't gone back to get his money. Maybe the cheat with the phony mill just needed that first bit of cash to make it come together. Regardless, his father had left him something useful.

"You hear me?" Kozmin said.

"The army. Yeah, I heard you." Jonas took the bottle when the old man offered it. Kozmin had a broken blood vessel in his left eye and a cut on his lip. "They beat you up in there?"

"No, I did it to myself last night. Bellhouse came and got me out and gave me some money, he said, for my trouble. I went rabid, musta fell down."

"He send you here? Bellhouse?"

"No. Well, I guess. He gave me yer mail to give you."

"The hell is he doin with my mail?"

"I don't know. Said he tapped the postman for it."

"You read this, didn't you?" Jonas held up the letter.

"I looked at it." Winter wind through the trees like flat chalk over the board. "Bellhouse says if we can get Duncan a message, he'd appreciate it."

"And what's that?"

"Teresa Boyerton's with him."

"What's that mean?"

"Think just what he says. It means she's with him, if Duncan wants to find her."

"I don't see it."

"Doesn't matter if we can't tell Duncan."

"No, it doesn't."

"What will you do about that letter?"

"I'm gonna go down there and load the whole show into a boat and bring it back here. I've been handed a bit of a blessing with this mill. I plan to take advantage."

"I could help."

"You can come if you want to. I won't stop you."

"I know how to set up a mill. I done it before."

"It's just a little fucker."

"Even when they're small, it's a lot."

"Small enough to move, though. They've hauled bigger."

"People see you leavin town, they're gonna say yer goin to help him."

"Fuckin Bellhouse already read my mail. Let him figure it out. He can tell everybody what I'm up to."

"When're we leavin?"

"I don't have a thing keepin me here. I say we go now."

"I don't have any money for my passage."

"I'll cover you. Take it out of yer wages once we get to work."

"I didn't say anything about wages."

Jonas stood and went into the bedroom and packed a bag. It'd be good to be moving, to get out of the Harbor.

Tartan

He *hung on to* his crutch and squatted over the bedpan and stared at the open door, pants around his ankles. Bruises leaked from under his stained bandages. The hole in his face and the shattered teeth were hard to understand. His tongue didn't believe it and wouldn't rest. Dr. Haslett had brought him a milky concoction of cocaine and vinegar, but it had made him restless and tasted horrible so he'd gone with whiskey. A fire had been lit in the stove downstairs and the door left open to let in the warmth.

He didn't bother to read the newsprint before he wiped with it. A sketch of the boy was enough for him to know what it was about. Finished, he one-handed his braces and, with the crutch in his armpit, two-handed his buttons. He gave the pan a boot, and it slid across the floor into the hallway.

Hank would be by soon. I'm on the dark side of it now. Moss growing, mushrooms sprouting. My usefulness was my guts and my fists. My usefulness is done. Nitz's mom came for the bedpan but didn't bother looking in on him. It was early still, and the stink and fuck noise had finally shut off.

Boots on the stairs, and then Hank was in the doorway.

"Dressed for your funeral?" Bellhouse said.

"Had to get out of bed, didn't I?"

"I ask you: What's the point?"

"Clothes make me feel less spinsterish."

"Oh, you're still plenty young to take a husband."

"What's the news?"

"Manhunt continues," Bellhouse boomed.

"Yer fight?"

"We settled it."

"How much?"

"Not any of your concern, my little henny huhn. But I brought you a gift." He passed over the Jurgensen pocketwatch.

"What's this for?"

"Services rendered. A retirement present."

Tartan opened the watch and squinted at the inscription. "Who the fuck is CSB?"

"Coast Sailors Boys. You'll always be one of us."

"I'm healin."

"Fucking broken. Take the watch. I'm done with you."

"Bounty's up on the boy."

"I got marshals and straight badges by the dozen crawling all over my docks, all over the goddamn coast. This is your fault."

"I made the choice."

"She admits the error of her ways but can do nothing to heal the damage."

"What peace is there? Leave me to rest, Hank. I'm lackin the necessary bluster for an argument."

The gold teeth flashed, and Tartan caught the scent of what was coming. "The elder McCandliss said something to me made me think you might be trying to set a springboard against my position. Any truth to that?"

"There's no ax comin for you, not from me there's not."

"That's good to hear."

On his way out, Bellhouse bent at the waist and inspected the trail of urine and shit that had leaked from the kicked bedpan. "Filthy cow," he said, and then he was out the door and down the stairs, two at a time. Tartan looked down at his hands, and they were shaking.

Jonas and Kozmin

Jonas at the rail. Kozmin sleeping on the engine hatch. They could've never known that Duncan and Jacob were standing on the other side of the breakers, watching as the ship lights glided by. Jonas felt something, though. He lifted his eyes from the frothers and curling black and studied the blotted coast. A cut hole in the bluish evening. White stumps like cut rope. There'd be someone out there. There'd be ax-swinging maniacs hacking at the world, working in the shadow of a bear. Work was on his mind. Like climbing stairs, and someone had given him the first tread, but he had to build the rest as he went. Mill. Lease. Labor. The foundations of the Boyerton show were crumbling. He made it in time, he could get a lease or two when they went on the block. Didn't matter how much he had to borrow or steal. Get skin in the fight.

He had to hire a lawyer to get the deed to the mill. The machinery had been gone through, but Kozmin said it'd still work. They hired mule teams to get it to the water and then walked it on board in two dozen pieces. The old cruster knew his business and worked like a young man. Jonas suspected that he might not be as old as he said. Sometimes thoughts of Duncan rose up in his mind, his father, too. The hours and time generally, without the regimentation of the mill, went by recklessly. He'd forgotten how quickly a day could pass. Time was no drudge. If a person were to stand back and wait, they might learn something. They might starve or be trampled. The throat of the mill was big enough to cut six-footers. Small miracles.

Back up the coast like a couple of thieves. Resilience is the ability to get on the boat and be gone. Jonas imagined no welcome home, no notice at all, and that's what they got. Tied up at the wharf, watching the gulls shit and the water blacken and deeper than blacken the pilings. Now fuckin what? More money out of the wallet. More hauling, more freighting. But it's terminal now. Cut all spring, summer, and fall, let em soak. Winter mill. Kozmin called the amount of work biblical in scope.

"How much you have saved?" the hermit asked.

"Like I'd tell you."

"Better hire some fools."

"Lots of fools to be hired."

"This'd be classed under gyppo, I believe. Junk show."

"Nah, pure fancy. Pure through to the heart."

Jacob

We *traveled at night.* During the day we watched the road. Men walked by with rifles and dogs but didn't venture into the forest. A contingent of soldiers clattered by in a wagon with a broken spoke. They couldn't all be hunting Duncan, but they were. Sitting still was the hardest part. I led us through the forest to a trail that I'd only seen once and was surprised to find it again. It was dawn when we reached the Soke. I told Duncan to stay hidden and knocked on Salem's door.

"Doc, the hell you want?"

"Invite me in. I could use a rest."

The door closed behind me, and the room was dark. A cot was in the corner, a table and two chairs in front of a cookstove of stacked brick and rock with a redwood stovepipe.

"Have a seat. Want coffee?"

"I'd appreciate it." I lifted the lid on the pan on the table, but it was only the chicken bones.

"I could get us some eggs."

"I'm fine with the coffee. The manhunters find this place yet?"

"There was one back when it all started, worked for Bellhouse. That big fucker with a fancy coat that got himself shot along with slint dick Chacartegui and his deputy."

"Tartan."

"That was it."

"No one else? None a the soldiers or lawmen?"

"Nah. Fearful of the dark, they stick to the roads."

"I'm gonna tell you somethin, and you need to keep it quiet, get me?"

"Sure, Doc."

"The one they're huntin—"

"Yeah?"

"He's my son."

"You ain't got a son."

"I do. I left him a long time ago. He's lived in the Harbor this whole time, raised by my brother."

"You got a brother that lives around here? I've known you for years, didn't know that. I thought your people were all out east."

"Most of em are. Can you help us?"

"Us? He's with you? The one who killed Boyerton and Chacartegui? Fuck me, he's worth five thousand dead. Did you know that?"

"He didn't do nothin to Chacartegui. That was Tartan."

"He shouldn't be here." He studied my face for a few seconds. "I don't know your name. I only know you as Doc. What's your name proper?"

"Jacob Ellstrom."

"I feel the cobwebs sliding from my eyeballs."

"You could take us to the cave."

"What for?"

"He wants to get to town."

"Take the fuckin road."

"Do me this favor."

"I don't know where it is."

"You told me you knew."

"I coulda lied." Salem grinned. "You better get yer boy in here before someone sees him."

Salem fed us eggs and potatoes. The rain beat down on the roof, and the walls were black from leaking. Duncan looked caged and held his fork like a weapon.

"I seen you before," Salem said.

"Maybe."

"I seen you with all those tough pricks gaggled up in front of the post office. Look where bein a tough prick got you."

Duncan blinked, and then tilted his head and smiled. "Bet it'd be nice livin out here with all these scurvious whores if you weren't related to em."

"Yer welcome for the food."

"Tell us how to get to the cave, and we'll be gone." I was worried Salem would go for the reward. I didn't think he would at first, but now I couldn't see trusting him.

"You should show us," Duncan said.

"I don't wanna do shit out in that weather. And I'm not gonna do a friendly turn for you anyhow."

Duncan slid his plate away, licked a mottle of egg from his thumb.

"Then do it for me," I said.

"Why're you puttin me on? I ain't done anything against you. Not once."

"I'll pay you fifty dollars if you come with us and show us the way in."

"You'll get lost. There's more than one cave."

"We'll need lanterns."

"And food," Duncan said.

"Don't have but one lantern, and you just ate my fuckin food."

"One will be enough. Let's get. I don't wanna wait for folks to get stirring around outside."

"Fifty dollars?"

I dug out my billfold from my coat and handed him his wet pay. Dogs were barking outside. Salem smiled and folded the bill three times and slid it into his pocket.

We were soaked through by the time he led us into the shelter of the cave mouth. Water dripped from the brims of our hats, dripped from our earlobes and noses. The cave was dry and smelled earthen, like a grave. Legend said the path through the cave was marked by quartzite rocks that sparked blue when you chipped them together. I saw no quartzite.

"Hundred feet in, it drops and you gotta climb down. There's a river below." Salem was trying to get the lantern lit, but it wasn't taking. Animal turds, maybe wolf, against the wall at the mouth. Looking out at the storm gave me the feeling that I'd conquered something.

Duncan wandered into the darkness and threw off his pack and sat on it. There were broken pieces of cratewood and glass shards mixed in with the sand on the floor. The lantern sputtered to life, and Salem went wordlessly into the cave. Duncan stood and followed him. The way was steep at first, and we had to climb ass first down and down, and it got colder as we went. Salem led and handed up the lantern when he needed both hands; then Duncan would hand it to me. It was a clean place below, no dirt or sign of animals. The sound of running water got louder and louder.

"If we run into anyone down here, I believe I'll fuckin combust from fear." Duncan laughed, and Salem joined him. He was doing his best to be brave by saying how scared he was. There were unnameable threats filling the darkness, all the space of the cavern.

The river was freshwater and clean tasting. I was sure we were below the level of the harbor and also of the sea. I'd expected brackish at best.

"How deep you think it is?" I asked.

"Don't know," Salem said. "I always stopped above. Never made it this far."

"How do you know where we're goin, then?" Duncan asked.

"Heard people talk. My woman's dead husband had been down here. He told me."

"How'd he die?" I said.

In the flickering light Salem smiled. "My God is a vengeful and wrathful God. He doesn't deal in mercy and kindness."

"Your God is everybody's God," Duncan said. "Sure as shit he's mine."

I was about to tell Salem he could go back when I realized he couldn't. One lantern. We were going together to the end. Duncan sat down against the wall, his feet splayed before him. He took off his hat, and his face glistened with sweat. We'd been going down for maybe an hour, seemed like. I couldn't tell. I played my hand in the water before having another drink.

"Let's follow it down," Salem said. "That's the way."

Duncan had a boot off and was picking at his toes. "You ever gone downhill for that long and not run into the harbor? Shit, we started in a swamp. So it pours out where, the fuckin Orient?"

"I don't know," Salem said. "Don't seem like it can pour out anywhere cept if it runs uphill."

"Well, maybe that's how it goes."

Duncan stood up, pulling on his boot. "A boat is what we need."

"Can't get a fuckin boat down here," Salem said.

"I know that. Said we needed one, didn't say we could have one."

I snatched up the lantern and headed out with the current. We had to stay together. The water disappeared a few times, but we could always hear it. We entered chambers of different sizes and shapes, and none of it was flat going. I made an effort to remember each one because the farther we went, the greater our chances of getting lost. And I hadn't thought that until I thought it, and after I couldn't much think of anything else. There'd be other ways to go down, so there'd be other ways to go up. Maybe we weren't as low as we thought. Maybe the river poured out as a spring somewhere, and we'd have to dig our way to daylight.

"There's a door out?" I said to Salem.

"I don't think there's a door of any kind. I've been told there is a way out, but this was by a man whose wife I was givin the prod when he wasn't around. He could've been tryin to get me killed."

"But I've heard others speak of the cave. Indians used it."

"I never heard nothin," Duncan said. "It look like Indians been down here?"

I had to admit that it didn't. We seemed to be the first. Our scuffs were the only scuffs.

"Think we should go back?" Salem asked.

"Might be a little late. I think we'll be in the dark either way when that lantern runs out of fuel."

"So we try to find the mouth of this river? If it can be called a mouth, when it don't have headwaters, as far as anyone knows."

"I think we should."

"Keep goin? This lantern goes, and you might want to change yer mind."

"I already want to change my mind. Hurry up. We can move faster than this."

We went quickly, in a bit of a panic. Twice we had to go in the water and float beneath the low ceiling. The water was ice cold and deep; I had the sense that it wasn't living water, water before life, water before danger. Blue blood in the veins before it goes red on the ground. If we died down here, I thought we'd never go to heaven or anywhere. We'd become the loneliest ghosts in the world.

Out on the rocks, three men staring at a lantern mantle like it was the face of God. No time. Back in the water, there was a chance that the river could siphon away and pin us down in some hole.

The lantern banged against the cave roof as we floated along. We could bounce with our feet on the cave wall, and it wasn't like swimming; it was like I imagine flying to be. Salem bounced too high and lost his hat. The water was going faster, and there was no shore to climb onto. Duncan went under first, then Salem, and the lantern went out. I worried that Salem had let go of the lantern because I could feel he was hanging on to me with both hands. Duncan was lost. It was absolute and total darkness, and I'd never felt so held and terrified in all my life. It's like my very skin had turned into living fear. I had to hold Salem away from me so he wouldn't keep me under. Then we were in the air and he was moaning, whimpering. Someone had me by the shirt, and was hauling me and Salem out of the water onto a slick stone ledge.

"Did you lose it?" It was Duncan. "Salem? Do you have the lantern?"

"I kept it." The tinny sounds of it being handed over above me. Duncan had matches in an oilskin pouch in his hat, and he struck one and the lantern hissed and sputtered to life. We crouched, panting like run-out dogs. Duncan held the lantern up.

"Look. There's an opening." A small crack in the floor widened in the wall and was man-size in the roof. We fit ourselves into the crack and shimmied up. We were in the bottom of a fishtrap. Duncan climbed up, and he was nimble with one hand and kept the lantern safe with the other. This was good. This was the way. It opened wider, and we entered a chamber that was as big as any we'd passed through.

"Which way?" Duncan said.

"You choose," Salem said.

"Some guide. You hear him crying back there?"

"I'm doin the best I can."

"Leave him be, Duncan. He's scared."

"I don't want to be blamed for killing us," Salem said.

"We'll be too dead to blame anyone. Which way?" Duncan said.

I took the lantern and circled the chamber and chose the way that gained the most elevation. I couldn't tell if it was me climbing and getting warm, or the air itself. Duncan was on my heels, and Salem on his. The lantern flickered once, and we stopped and watched it like it might say something, good-bye, explain itself on human terms, apologize for dying and leaving us in the dark. We needed it, and I prayed for it and hurried on. I was running where I could see. The path began to descend, and my heart fell with it. We'd have to go back.

"We can't go back down," Duncan said.

"Let's try it for a while and see," I said. We rounded a few corners and climbed over a rockpile and found a new chamber and climbed nearly straight up from there. The first thing that stopped me was a cut piece of lumber, gray and splintered, but saw cut. Then there was dirt, powdery and dry, with mouse tracks in it. We'd found a way out, or so it seemed. At the top of the chimney there was a deep, flat shelf, and at the end of it was a boulder wall dripping black water. There were chambers to the left of the wall, but they both died in solid rock.

We dug like animals and rolled rocks away and under us and pushed them to the edge and heard them crash all the way down. The lantern flickered again, but this time it died and we were digging in the dark. Water drained in and made a muddy pool. Duncan climbed up and pushed against the boulders and they rolled outward. The air was fresh, but it was still dark. It was more cave, wet and muddy. We felt for the edges with our open hands. I speared my hand against a spiny stalk of devil's club and finally realized we were outside, and it was night.

"We made it," Salem said.

My son's shape rose from the lesser darkness. The night was moonless, and the clouds covered the stars. I wanted it to rain so we would know for sure we were back in the world.

With two matches to spare, we had a fire going. I thought we were south of where we started, but Salem wasn't so sure. We'd been turned around down there. It seemed we were near the coast, but that would mean not only that we passed under two rivers and who knows how many creeks but that we'd slipped beneath a mile or so of open harbor. We put our backs to the trees and watched the fire. Dawn came a few hours later, and with the light came our bearings.

"I know where we are," Duncan said.

Salem touched my shoulder and walked away.

"Where's he goin?"

"Salem, come back here."

He held up a hand. "I'm goin to spend yer money, Doc. Whores with teeth and beautiful smiles and turpentine-free whiskey." He'd already gained the road, and in another hour he'd be over the bridge and into town.

"He's gonna turn me in."

"No, he won't."

"How do you know?"

"Oh, he might turn you in, but nobody'll believe him. Nobody'll even listen."

Tartan

Out the second-story *window,* into the rain, garbled howler. "I'm not waiting, Haslett. You'll hurry the fuck up, or I'll kill you. Hear me?"

Dr. Haslett, squinting against the drops. "Fine. I'll be back in an hour."

"Half an hour." Tartan slammed the window frame down, and the impact, the very sound, hurt his teeth and his guts. *Haven't shit in six days. Last time I pissed, I thought I'd goddamn die. Just hurry with the painkiller, Doc, cuz the whiskey does nothing.*

"Woman," he yelled. "You old cow, get up here and fetch my crutch." He had his pistol out, and his knife was stuck in the window sash. Footsteps on the stairs, and then there was a girl, sixteen or near it; he didn't know her, hadn't seen her before. He pointed to the crutch and mouthbreathed at her. She wasn't afraid. She picked it up and tried to hand it over, but he had to stow his pistol before he could take it.

"One or the other." She had a sweet voice, and lips like she only fed on beets.

He shoved the pistol in his belt. The grip went against his shot gut, and he didn't know it till he bent to steady himself on the crutch. The pain pulled the rug.

"Blacked out," the girl said.

He was looking at the ceiling, and then he was looking at the tit that had slipped out of her dress. "You'll need help to stand me."

Then she was squirming under his neck, under his back, burrowing. She had her legs under her now, and she was squatting. "Hook my arm."

He did as she said. She was brutally strong. He thought she might be the strongest woman that ever lived. A marvel.

Doc in the doorway.

"About time, fatass."

He put the bottle and package of powder on the bedside table. "Sit."

"Just got up."

"Help him to the bed, dear."

The girl was under his good arm, a hand under his ass cheek, hauling him on. Set him down like a sack of eggs. Doc opened the package and mixed the white powder with a little of the liquid from the bottle in a small ceramic bowl from his bag and made a paste. "Dip your finger in it and slime it around your mouth."

The taste was awful, but the relief was instant. The girl licked her pinkie and dipped it in and sucked it clean. "Yell if you fall again."

"Yes." All he could say through the joy of the pain disappearing. Doc folded the paper and slid the rest of the powder into the bottle, and then shook it up and passed it over. "Drink it sparingly. And don't think you can move around, even though you don't feel pain."

He drained half the bottle and then sucked the bitter from his teeth. Haslett shook his head and went to leave.

"Know what I told him?" Tartan said.

"Who?"

"Ellstrom, the outlaw Ellstrom. Said his mother left and wasn't dead. That was cruel of me."

"He came to see me," Dr. Haslett said. "I know what you told him. It doesn't matter why. I pity that boy. We've all failed him. Probably me most of all." Haslett took a pull from one of the bottles of whiskey on the table. "They haven't caught him yet. Two hundred men on the roads. I heard another hundred are out on the water. They got every bridge, every crossroad, and every rail station. It's a national obsession, as far as that goes."

"If he lives, he'll be comin here," Tartan said.

"No, he wouldn't."

"He'll want to kill me. And he'll want the girl."

"Why would he want to kill you?"

Tartan took the bottle and swirled the liquor. "Because I deserve it."

"We all do. Don't drink all this, and don't think you got the strength to get your prick up for that girl that was in here."

"I'll know when I know."

"Your heart might stop, and then you wouldn't know anything."

"I have a heart?"

"Made of rotten leaves and fish guts."

He listened as the fat man descended the stairs. Without hope, he licked the powder remaining on the paper and decided the best would be to camp out at the Boyerton house and wait for Duncan to return. He could get Mason to haul him up there in a covered wagon, park him up the street. Get some more a this powder and wait. That's a plan, a timber to cling to. Happy with himself, he called out for the girl. He waited on the bed with his prick out and blood seeping from the bandage on his stomach into the dark hairs.

She entered the room and dead-eyed him, with a thumbnail scraping the crusted lipstick from the corner of her mouth.

"Might be harder to do this than liftin me from the ground."

"I doubt that." Her dress came off like a shadow.

Bellhouse

He'd called the marshals to the union hall, and they all sat drinking coffee, waiting for Bellhouse or whoever else to say something. The McCandlisses had been told to hitch a team to Tartan's wagon and bring him here. It was time to get these lawmen out of town, Bellhouse didn't care how. They were ruining business. Teresa Boyerton was there with Oliver, and she looked scared. He'd had a talk with her last week and made her cry. She understood now. Delilah took care of the one-eyed brother.

When Tartan came through the door, leaning on his crutch, Bellhouse got up from his desk and helped him into a chair.

"The hell is this?" Tartan said.

"Check his pockets," Bellhouse said. "He carries the dead man's timepiece with him at all times." A marshal approached, searched Tartan's coat, and came up with Boyerton's watch.

"What's your father's full name?" the marshal asked Oliver.

"Charles Samuel Boyerton. That's his watch. I can tell from here."

"Hank, you gave that to me not five days ago," Tartan said.

"Now, don't start lying. You told me you stole it from Boyerton the night you killed him." Bellhouse shook his head, held up his hands in surrender. "Time to confess, my old friend."

"We need your real name," the marshal said. "And we need to know what happened out there when the sheriff was killed."

"What the hell we doin here?" Tartan said to Bellhouse. "You spinnin the wheel on me? I didn't do nothin, and you know it. You gave me the fuckin watch. Coast Sailors Boys. That's what he told me. Coast Sailors Boys. Christ." Tartan laughed and kept laughing until he saw Cherquel Sha come up the stairs.

"You come here to lie too?" Tartan asked.

"I don't lie."

"Who shot Chacartegui and the deputy?" the marshal asked.

"This Dickerson here."

"Who shot me, then?" Tartan asked.

"Who cares," said the marshal. "Who fuckin cares."

"I'll take the bounty now," Bellhouse said.

"You'll be paid, sir, soon as he's convicted of the murders."

Bellhouse and Teresa glanced at each other. Delilah brought Oliver a glass of beer. The room was far from jubilant. Oliver slid his hand up her leg, whispered, "Mabel."

She smiled at him and went back to the bar.

The marshals worked quickly, and in moments Tartan was gone, hauled down the stairs and out the back door of the hall. His crutch had been left behind.

"I'm buyin," Bellhouse said, looking at Oliver and Teresa.

"We have to go," Teresa said.

"I don't," Oliver said. "I'm stayin with Mabel and and Mr. Bellhouse."

"Whatever suits him," Bellhouse said.

"I'll see you at home." Teresa grabbed an umbrella going out the door, and it wasn't until she was in the street that she realized it wasn't hers. She considered taking it back, but what did it matter. There was a mudslide on the hill, and everyone was looking at it. Someone had her hand, and it was him, and it couldn't be. It couldn't be him. It was. He was smiling when she heard the shot and closed her eyes.

Jacob

***

K_ozmin came in the_ house for dinner. We'd sold our first batch of slabs the day before, and the crew had finally been paid. Jonas had gone to town with them to make sure they were treated as well as they could be. They'd stuck with us when they didn't have to, and that's worth something more than a payday.

The old man and I sat at the table and ate in silence. Nell's diary was there between us, but he never asked what it was or even glanced at it. The person I was in her words was a shameful man. But she'd abandoned Duncan. I was one thing, her son another. She shouldn't have done that. If we spoke again, I'd tell her. Maybe that's all I'd tell her.

After dinner Kozmin and I sat by the fire with a bottle.

"Should I finish the story about Tarakanov?"

"I'd like that. I'd nearly forgot. He was on the move last time you stopped, wasn't he? Going to save Anna Petrovna."

"That's right. He snuck into one of the Indians' lodges in the middle of the night and took two Indian women captive. He believed he could trade them to get Anna Petrovna back and that he was one smart promyshlennik, and everyone was happy for the first time in a long time. Bulygin promised him everything but the crown.

"Understandably they were more than surprised when they went to make the trade and Anna Petrovna didn't want to go with them. She wanted to stay with the Hoh people because they treated her well. She didn't want to starve alongside her husband, trying to get rescued by a ship that'd already sailed. Bulygin didn't know what to say, but Tarakanov did."

"What'd he say?"

"He said: I surrender." Kozmin was smiling. "His comrades couldn't believe it, but they knew that Tarakanov was the smartest of them all, and if he thought it a good idea, then it most likely was."

"They all just surrender to the savages?"

"If they were savages, would Anna Petrovna want to stay with them?"

"I'd suppose not."

"Half the group surrenders, the others drown trying to cross the bar in their canoe."

"Bulygin?"

"Surrendered, and by the grace of his captors he was even permitted to live with his wife."

"Grace? They were slaves."

"Better to be slaves than dead and drowned."

"I've heard arguments to the contrary. In fact, most arguments are to the contrary."

"From those who haven't spent a winter coast-bound with no food or decent shelter or hope of rescue. Thirty days of servitude is shorter than thirty days of starvation."

"So they treated them well."

"Those that earned good treatment. Bulygin died, and so did Anna Petrovna eventually, but Tarakanov lived, and years later he was ransomed and returned to New Arkhangel."

"All that, and he just went back?"

Kozmin filled his cup and my own, and then set the empty bottle on the floor. "Above all else, survival."

I drank and felt my regrets swell in my guts. "When I was young," I said, "I was afraid I would be hurt or that I would be a failure. Now I'm afraid I'll be alone. Makes me think the only true coward is him that fears love."

"Well, that's a cold dead one, isn't it?"

I nodded that it was and closed my eyes, felt the heat of the fire on my face and hands. "Yer a good friend, Kozmin."

"Yep, couldn't do much better than me."

I *was on the balcony* of the Eagle, waiting for Salem to come back with our drinks. I'd had two already and was ripe for more. The crowd below was facing toward the scar on the hill left from the mudslide; it looked a little like a man's face in profile with the fallen trees and ripped stumps cluttered around his throat.

Then I saw her, the girl, and I knew who it was. She came from the Sailor's Union, alone. In the street she stopped and looked at her umbrella, confused.

Duncan stepped from the alley. I'd left him at Macklin's church. He promised me he'd stay until I came back. He had to run to catch her, and in the crowd it seemed he was safe. When she turned, Teresa Boyerton realized who it was and smiled and lifted his hat from his head and kissed him.

The crowd parted when the rifle came up. It was Zeb Parker, our old neighbor. He'd grown tall, his clothes hardly fit him, he had a scar on his face, and his eyes were wide and scared and locked on Duncan. He fired and the shot hit home and Duncan fell on his side on the muddied planks. Then the soldiers on the walk saw him and there was another volley, but they shot high and Zeb stumbled backward from the splintering boards and fell. Teresa was the last one standing. It was a miracle she hadn't been wounded. She held her arms out, screaming, and went toward the soldiers with her hands raised, begging them to stop. Behind her, Duncan was suddenly on his feet and running away, ran right by Zeb, gave him a look that said: I knew that it would be you, but I'm not angry. My boy had blood on his hand, and his shoulder was wet with it. Zeb rolled to his feet and gathered himself and ran after him, but slipped and fell headlong, and the barrel of his rifle augered in between two planks and stuck there. A soldier shoved Teresa to the ground and took aim at Duncan's back; he had a clear line, but Ben McCandliss came through the Sailor's Union doors with a knife in his hand, and the blade flashed across the back of the soldier's neck and his shot went into the boards. The other soldiers turned on Ben, but his brother was there, swinging, and finally the marshals got in the middle and broke it up. Teresa stood in the street, looking after Duncan, but he was gone. Zeb left his rifle where it was and walked away with his head down and his hands out, like he wanted to shake some foulness from himself. I knew that gait, that full measure of sorrow.

When I looked up, Bellhouse was alone on the balcony of the Sailor's Union, looking back at me. We were two men above the fray. I imagined myself to be the tired, lost face of the Harbor, while Bellhouse, with his unapologetic symmetries and fearlessness, was the face of time itself. I wasn't scared of him, and he looked away first.

Last anyone saw Duncan, he was heading east toward the Wynooche. There were rumors and sightings; people called him the Wild Man, and he joined the skookum and the other ghosts that had dwelled and would forever dwell in the forest. If he lived, he had to know that he was no longer wanted. He had to have heard that much. We searched for him up and down the river and into the gorge. Salem and I even went back to the cave to see if he was there. He was gone.

Boyerton's sold the mill to a California outfit that was snug with Bellhouse, so the floating fleet went thin. Ben McCandliss was convicted of attempted murder on the soldier he slashed and put in the same prison as his father. His brother Joseph vowed publicly to break him out.

Tartan died of his wounds before he went to trial. No one was sure of his real name, so Cherquel Sha carved a marker that read DICKERSON. He's buried on the hill, not fifty feet from Nell's empty casket. I dug it up. I saw the box. Looked like someone had filled it with rutabagas; they were all webby and shrunken to nothing, but still there. Go with God. I put her letters inside and covered it up.

We still pretend that there will be a great city here someday, but the big trees are getting farther and farther out. We work harder for less, which is the way of the world. As the honing oil dries and the stone crumbles, the blade goes dull and rusts. There're more hills and trees upon them, and it's an insult to our very souls to look out at the wasted fortunes. I fear that what we crave is destruction, the barren world, a final and permanent bottom. For us, and this is most unfortunate, not even the end is enough.

People say Teresa split with her family and went east by herself. Maybe Duncan's with her. I like to think that he is, and that they have a child, but unlike me, and unlike Nell, they've left their selfishness behind. If I could give him any advice, it would be that one thing matters, and it isn't you; it isn't you at all. Protect your family.

Epilogue

R everend Macklin stood outside the post office and studied the letter. It had no return address, and the handwriting was poor. The streets were noisier than usual, clogged with people getting supplies for the holiday. The excitement of tomorrow was a stain on every child's face. There was to be a boxing match after the logger's contest. The new baldheaded governor would be giving a speech on the steps of City Hall and doing a ribbon cutting at the new high school. The pews would be empty come Sunday, or maybe not. It was hard to judge. Sinning swelled the ranks, but so did prosperity.

The reverend flipped the envelope over a few times, and then produced a pocketknife and slit it open. Inside was a single handwritten page folded in thirds; he opened it, and a feather fell at his feet. He stooped to pick it up and studied it for a moment, same color as his coffee when he used the goat's milk, white tufted base, an eagle's feather. Without thinking, he brought it to his nose and smelled it, smiled. The envelope had been addressed to him, but the letter wasn't. He stopped reading after the first line, slipped the paper back in the envelope, folded it, and put it in his coat pocket. He looked at the feather, and a broad grin spread over his face. The ferry whistle was blowing. He had to hurry if he wanted to make it upriver to the Ellstroms' before it got dark. He had to run for the dock. He felt the eyes of the townspeople on him as he went, and he smiled for them and waved the feather above his head, ridiculously.

The triple whistle tells us it's payday, and no work tomorrow either. Meaning we got two consecutives to drink ourselves stupid and watch the fireworks and the fights, like we're short on noise or smoke or even marvelous brawls.

At the locked gates of the mill we wait in a long and boisterous line and stamp our feet on the planks like stalled cattle.

"You must be thankful she's safe."

"I am. Never been more fearful than that. Made my guts bleed, waiting for the doc or the sound of the child, either one."

"It was a fever that followed?"

"Worry caused it, but she's safe now. The child will survive. My wife, she can't help but worry. We've lost one already."

"Do you think they'll have yer pay, since you went missin?"

"Been wonderin that very thing."

The last ship at the docks is hitched to the tug and hauled under the open bridge. When it drops it won't come up until the dawn of the fifth.

The man door swings wide at the mill yard, and we get right and begin to file in.

"What if they don't have it? What if they stiff you and tell you yer done?"

"I'll gut the fucker that steals from me."

A few heads turn and bob yes to the prospect of violence. We want it now. The ox has horns for a reason. We step forward once every half minute like we're all in a dullard's wedding.

A ferry boat steams by in the channel and blows its whistle and we wave and whistle back. She's been freshly painted and the rails and stacks are all done up with streamers and gold ribbons.

"Ain't she a sight."

"Beauty is a vessel that ain't crushed by lumber."

"But also one that is."

"Look at her go."

Acknowledgments

The author would like to thank Bill Clegg and Terry Karten for their support, understanding, and advice; Van Syckle and Weinstein for the spark; Dustin Schumaker, because nothing beats experience; John Dominguez and the HRL, one man's trash, another man's reference material; Greg Koehler, Marla Akin, and Adam Gardner; my parents and sister; and most of all, Rachel and Madeleine, one little white house to the next.

About the Author

Brian Hart was born in central Idaho in 1976. In 2005 he won the Keene Prize for Literature, one of the largest student literary prizes in the country. He received an MFA from the Michener Center for Writers in 2008 and is the author of the novel *Then Came the Evening* (Bloomsbury, 2009). He lives in Texas with his wife and daughter.